P9-DKF-936

# WENCH

# MAXINE KAPLAN

# WENCH

AMULET BOOKS • NEW YORK

Library of Congress Cataloging-in-Publication Data:
Names: Kaplan, Maxine, author.
Title: Wench / by Maxine Kaplan.
Description: New York : Amulet Books, [2021] | Audience: Ages 12 and Up. | Summary: When Tanya's guardian dies, having lost her home and the tavern where she has spent most of her life, she sets out on a perilous quest to petition the queen for help.
Identifiers: LCCN 2020011335 (print) | LCCN 2020011336 (ebook) | ISBN 9781419738517 (hardcover) | ISBN 9781419738524 (paperback) | ISBN 9781683359869 (ebook)
Subjects: CYAC: Voyages and travels—Fiction. | Taverns (Inns)—Fiction. | Fantasy.
Classification: LCC PZ7.1.K345 Wen 2021 (print) | LCC PZ7.1.K345 (ebook) | DDC [Fic]—dc23
LC record available at https://lccn.loc.gov/2020011335
LC ebook record available at https://lccn.loc.gov/2020011336

Text copyright © 2021 Maxine Kaplan
Book design by Hana Anouk Nakamura

Printed and bound in U.S.A.
10 9 8 7 6 5 4 3 2 1

Amulet Books are available at special discounts when purchased in quantity for premiums and promotions as well as fundraising or educational use. Special editions can also be created to specification. For details, contact specialsales@abramsbooks.com or the address below.

Amulet Books® is a registered trademark of Harry N. Abrams, Inc.

**ABRAMS** The Art of Books
195 Broadway, New York, NY 10007
abramsbooks.com

For my parents

Part One

# Chapter

anya was good at many things, but her most useful gift was breaking up bar fights.

The skill was one she had honed from her earliest days at the Smiling Snake, the biggest tavern in Griffin's Port. When she was very small, all it had taken was stamping her foot and scowling. This stern-little-girl routine so amused the brawlers that they'd stop fighting to laugh, at least long enough for Froud to swoop in with a warm back-clap and a free round. No one ever clocked that it was, in fact, a *routine*, devised by a girl with a job to perform at the most inconvenient height of four-feet-nothing.

But, tonight, she wasn't in the mood.

Tanya was, of course, the first to hear the raised voices by the hearth. She sighed and looked over at Froud; he was snoring away in a rocking chair next to the bourbon barrels. He wheezed through a particularly loud snore, knocking his head against the wall. She pulled her cloak off its hook and bundled it into a pillow, slipping it behind his head.

"Tanya! Tanya! *Tanya!*"

Froud slipped off his chair a little and Tanya caught him. "I've got my hands full, not my ears, Kit Brightblood," she snapped. "What can I help you with?"

"Oooh. Feeling a little cheeky tonight, are we?"

Just tired. Like she always was, but who could complain about too much work? "Don't you worry about my cheeks," she said. "What is it?"

"My table wouldn't say no to another bottle of wine."

"In five minutes, Kit. I just have to settle Froud and then take care of whatever nonsense is happening by the fire first."

By the time she was eleven, breaking up these fights was second nature. Froud had gotten so deaf and sleepy that he rarely even *noticed* when two drunken brawlers were on the brink of destroying the furniture. As with so many things at the Smiling Snake, it had fallen to Tanya to throw down her rag, turn the key in the cashbox, and vault her tiny, round body into the middle of any given fray.

Though tonight, looking down at the decaying old man she didn't know how to help or fix, she thought that the next time two idiots decided to fight in her bar, she might just let them break each other's heads open.

Tanya caught herself and shook the thought out of her head—doing nothing was never useful.

She settled her guardian's head back on the makeshift pillow. He made a noise that almost sounded like a whimper.

Tanya frowned. He should really be in bed.

A glass shattered. The fighters' voices got louder, the spectators going quiet. That was never a good sign—she had let it go on too long.

She grabbed two bottles of her strongest honey wine and a tray laden with tumblers. Bumping the side door of the bar open with one hip, and balancing the tray on the other, she went to work.

Tanya put her age at about seventeen. She hadn't gotten much taller since she first arrived at the Snake, but she had gotten ever stronger, and she maintained perfect, constant control over herself and her domain. She was everything a tavern wench should be.

It was a typical night at the Snake. A local crew was about to embark on two weeks at sea—a young batch of fishermen, several on their first overnight expedition. Tanya mussed the younger boys' hair, made eye contact with the mothers—*good, no one is getting too drunk*—and nodded with satisfaction that the blueberry syllabub she had brought over had been properly demolished. She could hear new arrivals coming through the door, a boiling wind in their wake.

The boiling wind transformed midair into hail, sending chips of ice skittering across the floor.

By now an expert at managing the environmental irritations of the Aetheric Revolution, Tanya neatly skipped out of the way and booted them into the ash pile.

No one offered to help her, but Tanya found it easier to do things her way anyway. She put grabbing a mop on her list, right under putting Froud to bed, serving Kit his wine, and breaking up the fight by the hearth.

Something crashed and Tanya sighed—*All right*, she thought. *Let's break up this damn fight.*

She knew the moment she turned around that it had not been a moment too soon. Gregor Brightblood, the huge and hotheaded older brother of Kit, had two men in a headlock.

That was neither unusual nor something that Tanya couldn't easily dispatch. The wrinkle here was that the two young men were dressed in the pale blue coats of the Queen's Corps. And more corpsmen, more than Tanya had realized were on the premises, all twinkling with dangerous hardware and even more dangerous legal authority, were surrounding them.

Tanya might not have particularly liked Gregor, but it wouldn't do to have him escorted from the Snake in chains.

She moved.

Tanya rapped an elbow with the wine bottle and bounced through the subsequently vacated space. "Now that's a sight I like to see," she said, tidily breaking through Gregor's left-hand headlock with the sharp end of the tray, sending the smaller corpsman plummeting to the floor. "One of the strongest specimens the Port Cities has to offer in an exhibition with the esteemed soldiers of the Queen's Corps—easily the finest men in Lode." She put her hand on Gregor's right hand, which was wrapped around a skinny corpsman's collarbone, and pried his fingers away.

She shoved Gregor in the back with her second wine bottle, pushing him toward his brother. The Snake regulars, knowing Gregor's intractability when drunk, closed up behind them, and Tanya turned her attention to the corpsmen.

"Gentlemen," she said, with as much honey in her voice as she could conjure. "Allow me to show my deep appreciation for your patience with our rowdier townsfolk—he's just a crabber and is not equipped with the manners and discipline we of course expect of the Queen's Corps." She pulled out a chair for the first corpsman, still struggling to his feet, and dropped to her knees to retrieve something that had gotten knocked out of the skinnier one's hands in his fall.

It was a box. A glossy, wooden box carved with a single flame. Tanya thought she heard something humming inside and moved to put it to her ear—only to have it snatched away by Skinny.

Still on her knees, Tanya recovered quickly and grinned. "Trinket for a sweetheart, sir? Lucky girl to have a handsome corpsman guarding her treasures so valiantly."

The skinny corpsman was part of the way toward a smile when there was a scream from the bar and Tanya's life as she knew it ended.

After the scream, no one moved fast enough except for Tanya. She knocked over the table, splashing beer all over her clean floor, and pushed past the crowd that had drawn up slowly around the bar—too slowly for Tanya to push past it. No one thought to make her a path and, of course, no one hopped the bar themselves to tend to the old man.

No, no one had moved *fast* enough, either toward Froud or out of her damn way, and by the time Tanya got to him, he was already dead.

# Chapter

The wagon carrying Froud's coffin stumbled to a stop outside the Shrine of Herold. Tanya hopped down and surveyed the red-dyed stones of the temple and the badly kept grass of the graveyard beyond. For the first time since Froud's death, she felt tears behind her eyes. She hated to think of gentle Froud in Herold's wild and neglected burial ground. But Froud had loved the boisterous god of revels and squalls, wind and rage.

There was a temple. She could see it, mottled black and red, nestled under a burnt-out nut tree. There were priests, but she knew not to expect a reception—especially as a girl. The priests conducted their burial rites in secret and no women were ever allowed.

Tanya surveyed the scene and, finding nothing useful for her to do, turned to walk back to the Smiling Snake.

She walked briskly down the sandy road, smelling the fish and salt of Griffin's Port more with every step. It was rare that she even noticed the smell. But then, she hadn't left the small, shabby city she called home much in the last ten years. When she was young and first came to live with him, Froud had often wanted to take her down the path that led to the woods—to go to a fair or a market or a festival even—but she had been too frightened. Frightened that she would get lost, that she'd never find her way back. Frightened that Froud would simply leave her under a tree.

The fears didn't last more than a year, but then they no longer mattered. She was too busy to leave. The place wouldn't function without her—she had made sure of that. Fear of being left under a tree was for other, less important, girls.

Tanya passed through the Talon Gate, a monstrous stone arch half formed by the leaping figure of a griffin, leonine hind legs so old they were rooted under centuries' worth of packed salt and silt, the eagle head and claws thrusting thirty feet in the air to clutch at its prey, the perishing mermaid that made up the gate's west side. Tanya scowled at the ossifying mermaid diving into the earth. *The griffin can fly and he's already got your fin,* she always wanted to scream at her. *There's no escape down. Find another way. Move faster.*

The Smiling Snake was located just inside the horrific gate. Tanya felt warmer as she approached her inn. It was salt-whitened clapboard, sturdy, fortified at the joints with oxidizing copper, green and sinewy. Tanya looked up at the wide, four stories of her home, presided over by its sign, a diamond-cut block of polished oak, painted green and brown with the carved image of a grinning serpent. She straightened her back, pulled her key ring from the pouch around her waist, and stuck it in the rusting lock.

The lock gave right away and the door swung open. Tanya stumbled backward, surprised. She thought she had locked the door before leaving for the temple. Then Tanya heard voices and was *sure* she had.

She drew a deep breath and walked calmly into the inn, slamming the door behind her.

"Can I help you, sirs?"

When none of the assembled men—damned corpsmen all—answered, Tanya walked behind the bar and retrieved the tinderbox.

"We're closed, I'm afraid," she said, striking a match and lighting the lamp. She moved to the front of the bar. "If you need rooms, we're always happy to accommodate the men of the Queen's Corps, but you'll have to fend for yourself for dinner."

Someone cleared his throat and the crowd shifted to reveal a man seated at the best table, the one in front of the fire. The fire was lit, and the table was set with a cold roast turkey leg and a whole cask of Tanya's best wine, the rich, sweet red that one of Froud's trader friends had brought from across the Swept Sea as a gift.

The man reached for the cask and Tanya's attention moved from the meal he had simply taken from her kitchen to the man himself. He was clearly the commander, she could see that from his well-pressed coat, brushed shiny and free of all debris—she had cleaned enough of those coats to know that the wool picked up lint like anything.

He was also the most physically imposing man she'd ever seen, his head nearly clearing the mantelpiece while he was sitting down.

"I apologize for startling you, madam, but I believe there's been a mistake." He stood slightly and inclined his head toward the chair opposite him. Tanya sat down carefully, not liking the look in the giant's eyes. "It *was* my understanding that Froud Loomis employed a serving wench. That was you?"

Tanya's eyes narrowed, but she nodded.

He took a large gulp of the wine. She noted that he was using the wrong sort of glass—that narrow tumbler was for cider—and inwardly shook her head.

He put his incorrect selection of glassware down and rubbed his finger along its edge. "You are not the man's daughter?"

"No."

"Were you his mistress?"

Tanya felt sick to her stomach. "To whom am I speaking?"

He smiled and pulled a parchment out of his breast pocket. "I am Kiernan Rees, commander of this corps. And, in my authority as a representative of the Queen and Council, I have requisitioned this inn and all its contents."

"What?"

He handed her the parchment. "Read it for yourself."

Tanya snatched it out of his hand. She read, "'Writ of Requisition. By the order of the Queen and Council, all accommodations, provisions, livestock, and sundries deemed necessary by the commander of this corps, Sir Kiernan Rees, are to be surrendered upon request. The Queen and Council thank their citizens.'" It was signed by Councilman Hewitt, known even to Tanya as the Queen's closest advisor.

Tanya found her voice. "This is fake. I don't believe it."

Rees leaned over and drew her attention to the second signature. "It was certified three days ago by a Sir Clark. I believe he is the tax collector in these parts."

Tanya knew that signature well. It was the same one she saw on the tithe documents every other month.

Suddenly she found that she was standing up. "The Smiling Snake is mine."

Rees held out his hand. "Show me a writ of leaving signed by Loomis and certified by Sir Clark, or another appropriate official, and we might have something to talk about."

Tanya started trembling. She couldn't quite tell if it was with rage or with the beginnings of fear. "I'll find it," she said loudly. "But it doesn't matter. Ask anyone in Griffin's Port. Froud meant me to run this inn. He always said so."

"Are you sure he meant that?" Rees leaned forward, a sharp glint in his eyes. "Are you sure he wasn't just trying to keep his unpaid help happy? Anyway, even if you do find it, *this* writ is signed by both the Queen and Councilman Hewitt himself. It can't be reversed by just a tavern wench with a scrap of paper."

Tanya, defiantly, met his eyes. "That is unacceptable. *Sir*."

"I don't make the rules, tavern wench. You'll have to take it up with the Queen and Council."

Tanya didn't answer, but she did snatch the cask of wine off his table before shoving her way through his men and climbing the stairs to her room in the attic.

The attic still acted as storage for the Smiling Snake, but Tanya had made a nest for herself among the chests of linen and piles of silver waiting to get polished.

Two overstuffed, oversize canvas sacks of goose down piled on top of each other was all she had for a bed, but they were made up in immaculately clean sheets of rather fine white linen. Her blanket she had made herself out of scraps of bed coverings and curtains from the inn, again overstuffing it with goose down. It might have been catch as catch can, but for all that, it was probably the most comfortable bed in the house. Tanya sat down on it heavily and took a drink directly out of the cask.

She unlaced her boots and kicked them off, then took another drink. She would wait until the men had put themselves to bed, or more likely fell asleep in tavern chairs, since she was damned if she was going to light fires and change sheets in the rooms for them. Then she would creep downstairs to the little room off the kitchen where Froud kept his books. That's where the writ of leaving would be. Tanya knew it was there. It had to be.

The Smiling Serpent was the key to Griffin's Port. It was the biggest room in the city where everyone was welcome and equal.

The pirates that everyone pretended weren't pirates could carouse at the stalls by the docks, but it got cold there at night. The rich mineral merchants could host lavish dinners in their homes, but they couldn't get any news there. The fishermen had their own cozy homes with their cozy families, but sometimes even respectable fishermen needed to drink. Everyone needed something that only the Smiling Serpent could give them, and Tanya knew, without a glimmer of a doubt, that *she* was the one who made it happen.

Tanya was the cook, the brewer, the distiller, the laundress, the housekeeper, the waitress, the hostess, the landlady, the muscle, the drunk-wrangler, the comforter of the brokenhearted, etc., etc. Tanya passed messages. She stored up information. She flirted with the boys who were just starting to be men and a little too nervous to be in the big tavern room with the grown folk. The nice boys anyway. The bad ones she scowled at, though they seemed to like that just as much.

She mattered here. After ten years, this was *her* inn.

Tanya repeated that fact in her head over and over again until she was finally soothed into a fitful sleep.

She jerked awake at dawn the way she always did. The inn was still. She tucked her hair into a black knit net and crept down the stairs in her stocking feet.

The clutter in Froud's office was of that annoying variety that makes perfect sense to its owner and absolutely no one else. One wall was completely taken up with a huge scarred wooden desk, covered in towers of parchments, neatly stacked, but poised to collapse the second they were disturbed.

She sighed and opened the first letter her hand touched.

By the time the sun was fully up, Tanya had cleaned half the desk and found nothing. No mentions of her in any letters to friends, no deeds, no ownership slips, no loans, nothing with her name on it at all. If a stranger read these papers, they would have no idea that Tanya even existed, let alone that she was practically the man's daughter and had essentially run his inn for him for the past five years.

She heard the soldiers in the next room start to stir, checked that the office door was locked, and kept working.

By noon, Tanya was hungry, thirsty, covered in paper cuts, sore in the legs, and angry as hell. The writ wasn't there.

Froud had never made the arrangements. She had no rights to the Smiling Snake.

Tanya let that thought sink in for a few minutes before she stood, rejected the notion of exposing herself to the sneers of that smug commander, and climbed out the window instead.

She paced the yard, the stables, moving faster and faster and faster until she was running, she hardly knew where. She found herself panting in front of the doom-seeking mermaid and screamed.

A few people stopped to look, but none of them were locals. The locals had already gotten their fill of Tanya as spectacle when she had turned up on the beach at age seven, shivering, pathetic—and alone—until, nearly a whole month later, Froud turned up and led her by the hand to the Snake.

*Everything will be safe now, little bit*, he had said. *What do you like to eat?*

Tanya wandered back to the Snake slowly, taking the long route along the docks. She stopped to watch a trading ship from across the Geode load its hold with great barrels of selenium, beryl, and tin.

Tanya leaned against the salt-whitened wooden railing of one of the few empty slips and marveled at the size of the ship, the unfamiliar symbols on its sails, the mottos wrought in foreign letters she couldn't even begin to read. When Tanya first came to Griffin's Port, the rise of magical engineering had only just begun, and the traders were far more uniform and far less grand. They came in narrow ships with plain sails and sold wine, lace, spices. It had been quieter, somehow—easier to hide. These days, the docks were changing constantly and smelled of strange powders and dust from the miners. Magic users needed raw natural materials to manipulate the aether, and apparently the caves around Griffin's Port were rich in what they called "minerals."

Tanya wondered whether she would even have survived if she had been dumped as a small child in the Griffin's Port of today. She thought of the random fires, floods, and quakes of the last decade, and doubted it. One could plan for ordinary evils—people. But one couldn't plan for what one didn't know, and no one—not even the magicians themselves—ever knew what was going to happen when they manipulated matter. *Not matter*, she reminded herself: *aetheric strands*. That's what she had been superciliously informed was the proper name for the energy the magic users tapped.

A crack sounded from the sky and Tanya looked up. Magic users made a rock bigger somewhere and somewhere else, a waterfall flowed upward. No one could figure out what magic made what change, and yet amateurs persisted in practicing with whatever they could find. Tanya supposed she couldn't blame them; they were just making a living. But it was hell on someone trying to decide whether to wear a hat. A bolt of lightning could portend a rainstorm or sandstorm for all she knew. "Junkoff," they called it—junk and runoff combined. As far as Tanya was concerned, it was the perfect name for such a waste of both time and normal, neutral reality.

By the time she reached the inn, the wind was whipping the spindly trees back and forth. She yanked open the door as the first fat raindrops fell. Just a natural rainstorm, then. She struggled to slam the door against the wind and leaned her head against the door for a moment, savoring the peace.

She lifted her head. Why was it so peaceful? Soldiers caroused—it was what they were known for.

Tanya whirled around, but the fine men of the Queen's Corps were already hiding whatever had silenced them. All Tanya saw was a glimpse of a rather plain-looking box made of some polished wood.

Tanya caught her breath as a swift current of rage ran through her blood. *That. Damned. Box.* She recognized it immediately. It was the one that had distracted her as Froud died.

One of the corpsmen, a short, tanned one with gray-blue eyes, moved in front of it, blocking her view.

Tanya *wanted* to bring beer mugs down on every single one of their heads. But they were corpsmen and she was a tavern wench and thus had no outlet for revenge, except to make them extremely uncomfortable.

She put a hand on her hip. "Am I interrupting something, gentlemen? I'd hate to be in the way."

The corpsman smiled, a sunny, crooked specimen that didn't quite reach his eyes. "No, miss! We were just packing."

"Well, I'm certainly happy to hear that." She took a step closer, peering around his square shoulders. "Is that box yours?"

"Yes," he said too quickly, moving again to position his body between her and the table. "Just mine."

Tanya was faster. She darted behind him and was sitting on the table, box in hand, before he even thought to stop her.

"Yours, huh?" Tanya smiled and tossed it from one hand to the other. "Doesn't really look like it, does it?" She tossed it lightly in the air and the corpsmen gasped.

Tanya laughed. "It's just a box, boys. I may not have the athleticism of a member of the Queen's Corps, but I can catch a *box*, especially one as light as this. What's in this thing, anyway?"

The men shifted uncomfortably, but none ventured an answer. Tanya gave an elaborate shrug and threw it underhand as high as she could—

—and for a second, it was as if time slowed. Tanya looked up at the box, arcing back down to her in a perfect, uncanny spiral. She thought she could hear bells chime and feel warmth gathering in her toes, spreading to her knees, to her thighs—

—and then a broad hand shot out, snagging it from midair and pulling it out of sight. A voice behind her answered, "Nothing for a tavern wench to worry about, that's for sure."

Tanya whipped around to see Rees. She folded her arms. "When are you leaving?" she asked.

"Tomorrow," he said, pocketing the box. "We are eagerly awaited."

That's when Tanya noticed yet more corpsmen carrying barrels out of her kitchen and forgot the box. "Where are your men taking my food?"

"To the barn. My men are taking *my* provisions to be bundled into cargo for the horses."

Tanya ran across the room into the kitchen. It was almost completely bare.

"All of it?" she called from the kitchen. "You're taking all my food stores?"

"Pickles and all, my lady," he called back cheerfully. "We're also taking your cashbox, all the beer, the wine, any medicinals you have lying around, blankets, extra boots, there's a very nice hammer in that little room—"

"Thank you, I understand," Tanya cut him off. She surveyed the empty shelves and walked out of the kitchen to face Rees. "What direction will you be traveling?"

He cocked his head. "Through the Marsh Woods. South. Southeast, actually. Why?"

Tanya visualized the map in Froud's study. "You're heading to the Capital?"

"Yes. Why so curious?"

Tanya eyed the man, frowning. "Why are your men so poorly

provisioned?" she asked. "It doesn't make sense for a corps assigned to the Capital to be so in need of supplies."

"We have a long journey to the Capital," he said flatly. "I don't need to explain the workings of the corps to you. Anyway, I'm locking the door when I leave, so you should pack up your belongings, too, such as they may be."

Tanya was only half listening, trying to work out the math in her head: How much beer could she buy on credit? And would enough people patronize a technically broken-into tavern—one that had recently seen a death, no less—in time to pay back the debts?

"All right, then," Tanya sighed, heading toward the stairs. "I'll be ready to leave with you the day after tomorrow."

"With us?" Rees whipped his head toward her. "Meaning what exactly?"

Tanya turned. "You're going to take me to the Capital with you."

He folded his arms. "Am I? Why should I do that?"

The rest of the room had gone quiet, the bustle of the men slowing as they strained to hear. Tanya looked around at the corps. Most of them were skinny and unshaven, their cloaks ragged and poorly patched.

She stepped off the staircase to face Rees. "I have a proposition for you."

He smiled. "Let's hear it."

She crossed her arms over her bodice. "It's not that kind of proposition. It's very simple. I need to get to the Capital and it's easier for me to get there traveling with a party of Queen's corpsmen than it is by myself."

Rees snorted. "You wouldn't make it a day alone."

She ignored the barb, as it was probably true. "So, I'll trade with you."

"What could you have to trade?"

She looked him in the eye. "To speak frankly, you make a very poor showing. You're obviously an important corps, or else why would you have a writ from the Queen and Councilman Hewitt himself? And yet you had to ransack a tavern just to feed yourselves. Your men have been barely eating, whether because they didn't have food or any notion of how to prepare it, I don't know. Their uniforms are in terrible condition. I haven't been in the stables, but I'm betting the horses look as shabby as the men. I can fix all that. If allowed to join your party, I will cook, do the laundry, mend any rips, and curry the horses. I promise you, by the time you reach the Capital, you'll be shining."

Rees narrowed his eyes. "You'll come along as a skivvy? Do all the maid work? And you'll follow my orders?"

"Within reason, yes. I will," Tanya answered, hoping that she wouldn't regret it. "I believe that if you think about it, you'll realize that you're getting the much better deal: a first-class cook and seamstress for no additional expense. All I'm getting is the, let's say, *pleasure* of your company through the Marsh Woods."

Rees pursed his lips and nodded. "Deal," he said, brushing past her to the kitchen.

Tanya followed, meaning to dig out her secret cache of chocolate, but a burly, wide-eyed corpsman stopped her.

"Excuse me, miss," he said, his voice halting and gentle. "If there's something you need doing in the Capital, I'd be happy to do it for you."

Tanya looked at him suspiciously. "And you are?"

"I'm Rafi Darrow, miss, from Grimstock Village in the Glassland Meadows."

"And why should I trust you to do *anything* for me, let alone something so important that I've decided to leave my home—yes, *my* home—in order to accomplish it?"

Darrow knit his eyebrows together. "I don't wish to pry . . ."

"Then why are you?"

"Why are *you*, Miss Tanya?" he blurted out. "Why do you need to go to the Capital?"

Tanya turned and walked up the stairs to pack. "You heard your commander," she said, her back to Darrow. "If I want my inn back, I have to take it up with the Queen and Council.

"And that's exactly what I intend to do."

# Chapter

About three quarters of the men had horses, and there were several more donkeys dragging wagons laden with supplies. Tanya had expected to be riding on one of those wagons, but when she started to clamber on top of the sacks in one of the stronger-looking specimens, someone slipped hands around her hips and pulled her back to the ground.

She shook the hands off and turned around. "What do you think you're doing?" she asked Rees.

He looked down at her. "Funnily enough, I was just going to ask you the same thing."

"I'm riding on the wagon. I checked. This one doesn't have anything that heavy on it."

Rees leered. He reached out and brushed the rolled flesh of her waist. "I don't know. I don't think the wagon can take the weight."

Tanya wasn't impressed. She had done her filling out in the hips, chest, and rear over three years ago, and she was quite used to this sort of nonsense. "It can take it."

"I don't think so, my lady," answered Rees, making "my lady" sound more like an insult than Tanya would have thought possible. "It would be irresponsible for me to tire the donkeys."

"And it's more responsible to compel me, who has never spent any time traveling and has no knowledge of woodcraft, to match the pace of trained corpsmen? You call that commanding?"

Rees shrugged. "I need the donkeys."

Tanya narrowed her eyes and shouldered her belongings, neatly rolled up in a tight bundle secured with rope. She turned her back on Rees and started walking.

Seven hours later they were still walking, despite the fact that the light was sneaking behind the trees and the moon was almost up. Tanya's ankles were swollen and her stockings caked with mud up to her knees, but she regretted nothing. Rees hadn't bothered her since they began walking. She should have realized she could do whatever needed doing *without* the courtesy or assistance of corpsmen.

Then Tanya slipped and slid up to her hips into a thick and viscous gravelly swamp.

She shook off her pack and threw it to the side, sighing with relief when she heard it land on solid ground. She heard the men swear loudly, the horses whine, and the squelch of the swamp as her traveling companions also found themselves stuck.

It was darker now and there was a mist rising over the swamp, along with a sick smell, like rotten eggs. Tanya squinted and made out the figure of Darrow, also on foot, thrashing around as well as one could thrash whilst glued to a . . . whatever it was.

"What is this?" she asked him.

He shrugged helplessly, apparently too anxious to answer.

She heard Rees call out through the darkness. "Everyone stay where they are. We've hit some junkoff."

The men all groaned and Tanya opened her mouth, appalled. "You didn't consult a scout?" she shouted angrily. Everyone knew that travelers had to plan around potential junkoff now; what was there one week might not necessarily be there the next. Off-season fishermen had developed a sideline of selling weekly updates to annotated maps—overpriced, Tanya was sure, since the work could be done by children, but an essential public service nonetheless.

She heard mirthless laughter through the mist. "It's clear you've never left Griffin's Port. Nobody has time to map this shit. Crap, half-bit magicians are multiplying like rats—junkoff is everywhere."

"Well, if you don't have *time*, then by all means get your entire regiment drowned," spat out Tanya, struggling until her arm was clear. "Apologies for expecting professionalism from a commander of the Queen's Corps." She hit the mud angrily. Corpsmen had always been among her most favored guests: courteous, tidy, and with a discretionary budget simply perfect for tipping. Standards must have really fallen.

Tanya struggled to move her legs through the sludge, one part sand, one part salt, one part sulfur, and one part mud. Junkoff: natural phenomena spontaneously bursting into existence due to sheer disorganization and incompetence.

The overlay of aetheric strands spanning the known world had been discovered before Tanya could remember—a web of invisible, interconnected threads of energy emanating from every raw material found in nature, vibrating at different frequencies. The problems came more recently, when it was discovered that anyone with just a smattering of training, a little bit of psychic ability, and something that passed for a wand could begin manipulating those strands.

Tanya liked it when "magic" just meant knowing what plants and rocks did what, how to read the information readily available in the stars, poems that helped you focus on specific problems, etc. Or, as Tanya preferred to call it, "common sense."

Tanya kicked hard, groaning with the effort, but the movement plunged her shoulder into the swamp. "Damn it," she yelled, even more stuck than before. She regained her footing and twisted around. Two or three of the corpsmen had halted the horses in the back of the baggage train before they could fall into the swamp with the rest, so at least most of the supplies were safe.

One of the humans who had been spared by their quick thinking was a rangy kid who was currently laughing, leaning against a tree, still clean as anything. She screwed up her mouth to scold him when an arrow whistled over her head and bolted his shoulder to the tree.

He stopped laughing and started screaming.

A hooting sound traveled from tree to tree. Tanya followed the sound with her eyes, twisting in a circle. There were shadows in the trees, hidden by leaves and swamp-smog. One of the shadows jumped down.

His face was hooded, but she could tell that the figure striding through the sticks and leaves toward the boy was confident in his ability to hurt. The man put his hand against the boy's chest and he cried out even harder.

"Where is it?" The hooded man's growl was enough to make Tanya's legs twitch uneasily. She was almost glad she was in the swamp.

Tanya watched the boy gulp manically, screeching as the hooded man pressed his shoulder against the tree, exposing more of the bloodied arrow shaft. Eventually the kid ran out of oxygen and just gasped.

Another arrow whistled through the air and, to Tanya's surprise, struck the hooded man right through the back of his hood. He shuddered and emitted a gargling sound before he hit the dirt, falling with his head against the boy's legs.

There was a moment of silence while Tanya whipped her head around, looking for who had shot the hooded man, but she saw no one with a bow in their hand. The silence was broken with a shout of "Yes!" from one of the dry men on the bank—a sleazy specimen, the kind of customer Tanya secretly watered down the beer for—and then Rees shouted, "Nice shot, Hart!"

A cheer rose up among the rest of the corps, but Tanya narrowed her eyes. She was certainly no expert at archery, but she *could* hear, rather well, too, and that was *not* the direction from which she had heard the snap and the whistle. But Rees seemed not to care as he called out to one of the other men still on dry land and not nailed to a tree. "Liir, check the cargo—the you-know-what—and then work on getting us out of here. Greer, get the kid out of the tree."

Tanya started struggling through the muck again, wondering what the hell had just happened. She noticed Liir by the baggage and called out to him, "That's the wrong bag. The ropes and hooks are in the green burlap."

He waved her off. Tanya scowled and started to protest, but then stopped when she noticed what he was doing. He was deliberately fishing out a small bundle wrapped in fine red velvet. He cradled it to him and Tanya saw a flash of gleaming wood.

*It's that box*, Tanya realized. The corpsman shouted to Rees and held it up. Rees nodded approvingly, and the corpsman took great care in wrapping it back up tight.

She narrowed her eyes. What was in that box?

Eventually, the few dry members of the party managed to drag the rest out of the swamp. Tanya stamped her sleeping feet and shook out her legs, made heavy with sandy mud. She was filthier than she had ever been—stiff with filth. And she wasn't the only one. The men were stripping off their clothes and running back down the path they had come from, splashing into the clear-water lake they had passed right before the junkoff.

Tanya didn't even have a moment to be shocked by the nudity before she noticed that they were throwing their sodden clothes at her.

"Oh no," Darrow sighed. "Most of the horses lost their shoes."

Rees laughed bitterly, pulling off his own shirt. "That follows. There's a village about three miles to the west, right?"

Darrow looked like he was thinking hard and then smiled. "Yes. It's a little out of our way, but Ironhearth will definitely have a smithy. Or fifteen."

He nodded. "Take the horses who threw shoes. Go slow, we need them to last. Bring Hart with you. We need one presentable corpsman anyway. Speaking of presentable . . ." He turned to Tanya.

"Don't even bother," she grumbled, gathering up the sandy, soaking clothes. "Although I will say that this is a little beyond what would reasonably be expected of the average corps skivvy. You're very lucky to have me."

Tanya scooped up the last of the discarded clothes and marched over to the riverbank. The younger corpsmen were splashing and laughing, relieved at having escaped first the hooded rogue and then the swamp.

"Ahem," Tanya said loudly, and they turned toward her. "Those of you who didn't already throw your filthy rags at me may bring them for me to wash."

"And who's going to wash the washer?" called out one of the bolder boys, who was relaxing on a rock. "Come take a bath with us, tavern maid." The others laughed.

Tanya met his eyes. Greer. The boy she had snatched the box from back in the Snake. Since then he hadn't given her a reason to notice him. He wasn't what you would necessarily call handsome. He was muscular, but short and ropy, not tall and broad the way the pretty boys are in tales. His nose was also too broad and long and his mouth strikingly large. But looking at him on the rock, with his sly, crooked smile and direct, sharp gaze, Tanya somehow felt that if she was going to have to look somewhere, it might as well be at Greer.

"You think you're shocking me, don't you?" she asked, dropping the clothes on the light, proper sand of the bank. She started unsnapping her bodice, formerly green, but now a muddy gray. "Do you know how long I've been, as you say, a tavern maid?"

Greer was closely observing her progress with the snaps. "Haven't wondered really."

"I see," she said, throwing the bodice on the pile at her feet. "I've been a tavern maid for almost ten years. I'd bet that's quite a bit longer than you've been a member of the Queen's Corps. What are you, nineteen? And you fancy yourself a man of the world. You've taken a punch? Seen some bloodshed? I bet you've even tumbled a serving wench here and there, haven't you?" He inclined his head and laughed. Tanya laughed right back, stepping out of the plain-spun dress of red cotton. Standing in just her shift, she started to wade into the river.

"The thing boys like you tend to forget when you're working on a wench is how much more we know than you do." Some of the other boys, all of whom were now listening, started to protest and laugh, but Tanya waved them silent, carefully stepping into deeper water. "I'm not saying I know more about woodcraft or swordplay or what have you. But you've met, what, ten of me? I've met hundreds of you. Every tavern wench you've met knows precisely what you're about. You haven't fooled or surprised a single one."

And now Greer wasn't among the laughers. *Odd, that*, thought Tanya. What little notice she had taken of Greer had been of a boy almost always laughing, either with his eyes or his mouth, though not often both. But he was just watching her curiously, listening.

Tanya felt herself growing both warm and shivery. She shuddered. Such a sensation was wholly impractical.

It would be much better for *him* to feel under scrutiny, rather than she.

Now up to her neck in the water, she shimmied out of her shift and tossed it onto the rock next to Greer. She dunked her head under the water, swimming in place for a moment, feeling the sand drift away from her hair, strand by strand. She shot out of the river and threw her hair back, feeling the muddied water drip down her neck. When she opened her eyes, Greer was still on the rock, but she had successfully reset the energy: His legs were crossed more tightly than before and he was flushed, looking away.

"You seem dry to me," she told him, savoring her triumph. "Why don't you put on something clean and bring a barrel and a box of soap, so I can wash all the dirty clothes?"

She dived back into the water. She was a much stronger swimmer than most of the corpsmen and soon had left them far behind.

By the time she swam back to the rock, the riverbank had mostly emptied and a box of soap flakes was indeed waiting for her, on top of a washboard from the Smiling Snake that she hadn't even realized had been packed. There was also, she was surprised to see, one of her clean dresses.

"Thank you, Greer," she murmured.

The silt from the junkoff had caked itself firmly onto the uniforms. It was nearly full night by the time Tanya finished scrubbing them all out.

She rose and stretched. Walking barefoot back to the main camp, she smiled ruefully as her feet moved instinctively toward the dried meat and barley. She should be exhausted, but found that this felt familiar. Hadn't she been on her feet from sunup to sundown, going from chore to chore, since she was a girl? The sun had gone down. To Tanya, that meant it was time to prepare dinner for whoever was in her care.

Generally, though, people paid her for that.

She made a note to charge any member of the Queen's Corps double when she got her inn back.

By the time Darrow and Hart rode the horses back into camp, it was truly night. Tanya was dishing up stew by the light of a miniature bonfire when she heard new horseshoes clopping down the packed earth of the road from Ironhearth. She turned like everyone else, but had to catch her breath and didn't see the riders dismount.

Tanya had glimpsed the sky.

There was natural beauty to be had in Griffin's Port. But it was the beauty of silvery, wet shadows floating through fog and bright orange leaves falling on the white salt beaches. She had never been near skies clear enough to see the stars. At least not like this.

Tanya tore her eyes away from the sky only when she heard the last sound she had expected to hear.

A girl was laughing.

Hart was playfully bowing to a girl perched behind the saddle of his horse. She smiled down at him and slid neatly off the horse into his arms.

"Thank you, sir," said the girl, and the fire flashed light onto her upturned face.

She was small and narrow, with shining dark hair flowing like a waterfall over her brown shoulders. Tanya tried to get a closer look, but when she finally caught the girl's eye, her mouth bent in an odd angle and she glanced away as if Tanya weren't even there.

Normally, Tanya would have rolled her eyes and left the girl to serve herself, but instead, frowning, she gathered up three bowls, one for Darrow, one for Hart, and one for the strange girl.

There was something odd about the way the girl had looked at her.

By the time she got to the newcomers, they had already gathered a small crowd. Rees turned to her with a smirk. "Meet our guest, wench." Addressing the girl, he said, "Jana, this is Tanya, camp skivvy. If you need anything during your stay, please let her know and she will do whatever she can to accommodate you."

Jana didn't respond, because she was nuzzling Hart's ear in a way Tanya assumed she thought was subtle.

It passed that Jana was a cousin of the smith and had come back to camp in order to collect the rest of the payment for the horses.

Hart would take the fastest horse and drop her off the next morning as the rest of the party continued down the road to the Capital, meeting up with them at a corps way station outside the city.

Tanya chose not to join the circle by the fire, preferring to claim a tent to herself and sit in it, alone.

She had picked one of the smallest tents. But she had also appropriated a sheepskin to line it with, as well as her pillows from her own bed at home. Propped up against them, with a lantern on one side and a plate of cookies—previously hidden away from greedy hands deep in her pack—on the other, she felt really rather comfortable. A little bored, perhaps, with nothing worthwhile to do. She was unused to leisure and it hadn't even occurred to her to pack a book.

She shut her eyes for a moment and dredged up a memory of a small, threadbare book, turning it around in her hands, running her fingers over the gray-green cloth. It was the first present Froud had ever given her, the first thing she remembered ever being told was hers and hers alone.

*"I don't know how to read it,"* she had whispered.

*Froud inclined his head toward her until their foreheads were touching. Then he tweaked her nose. "I'll teach you."*

"Tanya?"

She opened her eyes and sat upright, startled. "What?" she asked irritably.

Greer was looking at her curiously. "What were you doing?"

"Thinking! Ever try it?"

Greer chuckled a little grimly, and shook his head. "Wish I could stop," he told her. "Might get in less trouble that way."

She crossed her arms. "Was there something you wanted?"

"That girl Hart brought back wondered if she might borrow a nightdress."

Tanya leaned back against her pillows and lifted her eyebrows. "Did she? That seems unnecessary."

Greer snorted, but muffled his laughter as the tent rustled open behind him to reveal Jana. She was even prettier up close. Her nose was crooked, almost as if she had broken it, but it suited her, with her bright mouth and brighter eyes.

Jana pushed past Greer and bent down to Tanya's level. "I'm so sorry to interrupt you. Truly. But I do need something to wear tonight other than this dress."

Tanya felt herself soften. That dress did seem to fit her very badly; it couldn't be comfortable. She handed Jana the nightdress she had unpacked for herself.

"Is this the only one you have?" the girl asked, alarmed.

Tanya waved her off. "I have more than one shift with me. I'll sleep in the extra."

The girl slowly took the nightdress from Tanya. "Well, all right. If you're sure you won't miss it."

Tanya laughed. "I think I can do without a nightdress for one night."

Jana dimpled prettily and scampered out of the tent.

"Are those chocolate cookies?" asked Greer, reaching for the plate.

Tanya, who had forgotten he was there, smacked his hand away.

"Out!" she ordered. He grinned, snatching a cookie before he obeyed.

$\infty$

Tanya awoke in darkness to the smell of smoke.

At first, she yawned and snuggled back into the pillows, wondering idly why no one was tending the bonfire—it was the middle of the night, someone should be on guard. But she kept sniffing the air, somehow aware, even more asleep than not, that something wasn't right.

Then she heard the whistling. It was expert; melodic and jolly. Then came the crashing of metal, a low moan, a spark of flame—and still the whistling, tunefully singing in the background.

Tanya crawled forward and untied the strings holding her tent together, carefully, so as not to make any noise. She poked her head outside.

About a third of the corps, including Rees, were tied to trees around the clearing. They were gagged and gagging, their heads rolling back on their shoulders. The bonfire itself was now smoking and spitting an evil-smelling vapor. Tanya grabbed her dress and pressed it against her nose, and then crawled a little farther out of the tent.

A sound of a rough blade on wood drew her gaze and there she discovered the source of the endless whistling. Jana, dressed only in Tanya's nightdress and a kerchief around her nose, was dancing around the supply wagons, whistling that happy tune, and smashing them to kindling with a sword.

# Chapter

**T**anya's mouth fell open and she nearly dropped the dress as she watched the girl step back and forth daintily, twirling and slashing a bundle here and overturning a barrel there. She might have been at a square dance, except for the destruction she was happily wreaking.

Jana did a wild dip-and-spin move and then swaggered rhythmically toward the final, untouched wagon, stopping every few seconds on the way to sidestep, first to the right, then the left, then the right again.

She vaulted into the wagon and pawed through it, casually glancing at each item before tossing it over her shoulder.

Tanya looked around her nervously. Those of her traveling companions that she could see were either nodding off or closing their eyes in pain, quite aside from being firmly knotted to trees with good, strong rope from Griffin's Port. She peeked into the nearest tent and found a small clump of sticks and leaves tied together with string, smoking quietly, but potently, in the corner. Experimentally, Tanya lifted up the cloth covering her mouth and smelled the same sour odor from the bonfire. She quickly put the cloth back up and backed away from the tent.

Jana's whistling got louder as she tossed out boxes and bundles more rapidly.

Tanya stood next to the bonfire, utterly unsure. Nothing in Tanya's life had prepared her for this scenario. What did one do when a little smithy tart takes out an entire corps and destroys their camp before your eyes?

There was only one thing she knew how to do.

Tanya walked swiftly over to the wagon and cleared her throat loudly. Jana stopped whistling and turned to face her. The smile died a little on her lips when she saw Tanya's stern expression—what the delivery boys in Griffin's Port called her "shark face."

Tanya put her hand on her hip. "What do you think you're doing?"

Jana's eye crinkled in a way that made Tanya think she was smiling. "I'm looking for something," she explained, and then turned back to the wagon.

"And why have you incapacitated the corps?"

Jana snorted, tossing her hair back. "Because if they were awake it would be harder to get away with the—ah, here it is!" She hopped off the wagon and unwrapped the red velvet triumphantly.

Tanya stepped forward, eyeing the item in the other girl's hand. "I know that box," she said, more resigned than curious.

"It's not about the box," said Jana excitedly, moving so that she was standing next to Tanya. "It's what's inside the box."

"Lady of Cups," Tanya muttered. "*What* in Lode is in that damned box?"

"No idea," Jana answered cheerfully. "I'm not even supposed to look." She looked at Tanya and smiled broadly. "Gonna anyway. Wanna see?"

Tanya sniffed. "It couldn't possibly concern me."

Jana shrugged. "Your choice," she said, and started backing up into a patch of moonlight, far enough away from the fumes of the bonfire that she loosened the kerchief around her mouth and nose and let it fall to her neck. Still facing Tanya, she opened the box.

A white light briefly exploded around the box's edges. Tanya felt the light on her skin and met the other girl's eyes, bright and black in the moonlight, before they were hungrily drawn back to the contents of the box.

Tanya frowned. Did what was in the box concern her? No, it did not. But was it fair that Jana got to see it, and she, Tanya, who had been holding that box at the moment of Froud's death, didn't? No, by all the gods and demons there were, it was not!

Tanya charged, snatching the box away from Jana's hands—which were as wide and rough as Tanya's, now that she was looking.

"Hey!" cried Jana.

"Oh, hush up, you'll get it back," snapped Tanya. She looked down and felt her heart unaccountably skip a beat.

The box held a feather. A feather quill, to be exact.

It was a paragon of a feather: long, pure white, with a smoothly curving shaft and a wide swath of plumage, tapering to the left exquisitely.

And it was glowing.

Tanya looked closer. Jana's hair brushed against hers as they peered inside the box. The feather wasn't just glowing—although it was certainly doing that, shining out a bright, white light, stronger than anything Tanya had ever seen come off a lantern, strong as the two moons themselves. It was also glittering. The feather sparkled like it had been sprinkled with a thousand tiny, twinkling diamonds.

Jana reached out to stroke it, but Tanya grabbed her hand before she could. "Stop that," she said sharply. "What is it?"

"I have no idea."

Tanya gave her a look. "Take it from a port city tavern wench: Don't touch things you can't identify. Especially if they sparkle for no reason."

Jana nodded, frowning, and sighed. "It's a good rule." She drew a small black pouch and a white handkerchief out of a garter. Carefully, she picked the feather up with a hanky-covered hand and slipped it into the pouch.

Tanya blinked as Jana slipped the pouch into the front of the borrowed nightdress, the box tumbling out of her hands to lie forgotten on the ground. While the feather had been visible, she had felt transported. As the pouch disappeared into the strange girl's cleavage, Tanya suddenly remembered where she was and then, quickly, so did Jana and the tip of her blade was thrust against the top of Tanya's throat.

Tanya craned her head backward, trying to avoid the sharp, steel point. "What now?"

Jana smiled a quite friendly smile. She shrugged, keeping her blade level against Tanya's flesh. "Not much really," she said. "I steal a horse and get away."

"And me?" Tanya swallowed. "Are you going to kill me?"

"No!" Jana looked offended. "Why would I kill you? I'm a *brigand*, I'm not *evil*."

"Well, that's comforting."

Jana grinned and pressed the blade a touch harder. "Turn around and walk toward the bonfire."

Tanya obeyed, walking with the blade just barely pressing into her back until Jana told her to stop.

"Sit down." Tanya knelt in the dirt. "Not like that," Jana said impatiently. "Make yourself comfortable."

"Give me the sword, then."

Jana sighed again. "I'm making this so easy for you. What do you care about the corps' stuff? You're not their, like, *follower*, are you?"

"Certainly not! I'm trading domestic work for safe passage to the Capital."

She snorted. "Not that safe."

Reluctantly, Tanya had to agree. This particular regimen of corps had been a thorough disappointment. She settled herself comfortably on the ground.

Jana knelt in front of her and uncoiled some rope from around her thigh. For the first time, Tanya started to panic. Jana caught her eye and shook her head. "I'm not going to hurt you," she told her. "I'm just going to tie you up a little."

The girl grabbed Tanya's wrists together in one hand and started wrapping them together with the rope.

Tanya found that she did not at all like how it felt to lose the use of her hands.

"Listen," she said, breathing hard. "Do you really have to tie me up? I have no idea how to fight. I don't even know how to hold a sword. You don't have to tie my hands or"—as Jana moved to her ankles—"my feet, for the Lady's sake. I'm *barefoot*."

"So am I and *I'm* going to run. Look, I'm really sorry, but I do have to tie you up. I have a reputation and it's just too sloppy not to."

"Oh," Tanya whimpered as Jana pulled the knots tight. She winced, partly in pain, partly from embarrassment at whining. She regained her composure and looked at Jana with the sharpest daggers her eyes could conjure. "You're a real piece of work, aren't you?"

Jana shrugged, seemingly unconcerned. "Hey, at least I didn't drug you, right?" She looked at the sky. "The potency should be wearing off by now, so you're fine to breathe. I think."

Tanya frowned. "Why didn't you drug me? And, come to think of it, how did you even know we had the . . . feather thing? Do you have a spy in the corps?"

Jana stood up and pointed at something behind Tanya's head. Tanya twisted awkwardly, hampered by the ropes.

"That," said Jana, "is a very good climbing tree."

Tanya followed her glance and saw a tree on the other side of the magical swamp. She remembered twisting in the junkoff slop, feeling as if something was moving around among the leaves. She *knew* Hart couldn't have made that kill shot.

"You were waiting for us," she said softly. "You wanted to see how the corps reacted when they were threatened. The first thing they did was check a parcel." She turned and looked back at Jana, who was already leading one of the newly shod horses away from the herd.

"Here girl," she cooed. "Who's my good girl?"

"Wait, you shot your own man?"

Jana chuckled, vaulting neatly onto the horse's back. "He was hardly mine." At Tanya's appalled face, she urged the horse over to her. "Don't be shocked, Tanya. I promise you, he was awful." When Tanya primly screwed up her mouth and didn't answer, Jana sighed and reined in the horse. "Well, anyway, it was nice meeting you. I hope you get to the Capital."

She turned and had already started to ride down the path when Tanya remembered something. "Why didn't you drug me?" she called.

Jana called something back. Tanya couldn't be sure, but she thought she heard something about a nightgown.

꧁

By dawn, Tanya's knees were sore from being bent in one position for so many hours, her sinuses were blocked from being out in the cool autumn air, and her nerves were jangled from having to endure the muffled curses and groans from the men on the trees.

"I can't help you," she had eventually shouted, annoyed. "I'm tied up. Instead of whining, you'd be much better served shutting up and trying to rest." But they didn't listen.

"Idiots," Tanya grumbled. She scooted on her bottom across the forest floor until she found an unoccupied tree to lean against, and endeavored to take her own advice.

Greer was the first of the drugged to stumble out of his tent, bleary-eyed and yawning. He made for the almost-banked fire, seemingly blind to all the havoc around him, until he came face-to-face with Tanya and stopped short.

His mouth fell a little open. "What are you doing there?" he asked, groggily.

"Ropes, Greer!" Tanya shook her bound feet and hands at him. "Would you wake up and untie me already? *Now*, please."

But Greer wasn't paying attention to her anymore. He had noticed his fellow corpsmen on the trees and was running from trunk to trunk, slicing them free with his sword—starting with Rees.

As soon as Rees had spat out his gag, he shouted, "Check the baggage! Now! What did she take?"

"She?" asked Greer, sawing through the ropes around a particularly tightly bound Hart. "Tanya took something?"

"Not her, moron!" yelled Rees at the same time that Tanya yelled, "Not me, idiot!"

The men released from the trees were scrambling through their belongings, bellowing. The men who had been drugged in their tents started crawling out, dumbfounded and screeching questions, the smoke from the smoldering bundles still stinging everyone's eyes. And, through all the chaos, Tanya remained tied up, unheeded, by her tree.

Only when the whole corps had been brought up to speed on the theft and subsequent desertion of "that smithy tart" did their attention turn to Tanya.

No one made a move to untie her.

"What was she even doing out here?" asked Hart sulkily, dabbing at a mysteriously split lip. "She had supposedly gone to bed, but instead she was out here talking to *her*?"

"It's a good question," answered Rees, turning toward her with his arms folded. The corps fell silent behind him, all eyeing her with suspicion.

Finally, Darrow broke the silence. "Well, we need breakfast anyway, right sir?" He stepped toward Tanya and turned his head to his commander. "Sir?"

At Rees's nod, Darrow bent to one knee and started gently unraveling the knots around Tanya's wrists. "Are you hurt anywhere?" he asked in a low tone.

"Just my sense of honor," she huffed. "Last to be untied, indeed. I at least have an excuse for being defeated—you all were armed!"

He smiled and moved on to her ankles. "You've got some vinegar in you, miss. There," he said, pulling out the last loop of the knot binding her feet together. He frowned and rubbed her toes together between his fingers. "Your feet are freezing."

Tanya looked behind his big, round shoulders to the hard eyes of his companions and said, "Never mind that. Better help me up."

As Tanya scrambled to her feet, she cast an eye toward the back of the camp where the rangy kid was furiously rooting through a ransacked wagon. He spotted the polished wood box on the ground and yelped, tripping over himself to run it over to Rees.

"It's here, sir," he said breathlessly.

Rees visibly relaxed, followed quickly by the rest of the corps. "Well that's that, no harm done. We'll teach her a lesson if we run across the trollop again, but for the moment, I believe it's high time our other tart"—with a nod toward Tanya—"started brewing us some coffee."

Amid the tension-relieving laughter, Tanya, annoyed and rubbing her sore wrists, said sharply, "Yes, yes, the box is here. But your sparkly feather is quite thoroughly stolen." Abruptly, the laughter stopped.

Rees stepped toward her. "The girl from the smith stole the contents of that box?" he asked quietly, pointing at the now dim-seeming container.

Tanya stood up straight. "Don't look at me like that," she said sternly. "I'm not the one who brought her to camp. I didn't help her steal it, she held me at sword-point! She just happened to show me the feather first." It didn't seem necessary to include that the feather had actually been in Tanya's possession at the precise moment of its abduction.

Rees seemed to think for a moment. Finally, he said, "You're right. You didn't bring her to camp." He turned around, walked three paces, and punched Hart in the face. He punched him again and again, until he fell to the ground.

Tanya looked around curiously. Was this normal? No, judging by the expressions on the rest of the boys' faces, it wasn't, although most looked as though they would like to get in a few licks themselves. They were all surveying the tableau with varying mixtures of fear, dread, and rage. It was dead silent.

When Rees felt he had made his point, or his arm had simply gotten too tired to go on, he turned and barked, "We ride to Iron-hearth. Now."

Tanya hurried through the throng to her own tent, as even she could sense that there was no wiggle room in that order. But as she started bundling her belongings together, letting her well-honed efficiency take over, her mind cleared enough for her to remember that Ironhearth was not on the way to the Capital. It was, in fact, several miles out of the way.

She stormed out of her tent, collapsed it, and threw it on the nearest wagon. Greer was the first person to pass her, so she grabbed him by the shirt collar.

"It's a feather," she said flatly. "A very pretty feather, I'll give you that. But it's a feather. Why are we going out of our way to retrieve a feather?"

Greer shook free of her grasp. "It's not a feather, it's a . . ." He scowled and shook his head. "Doesn't matter. Rees says we need it and I believe him."

As he took off across camp, Tanya stamped her foot in irritation. She picked her way across the chaos of wagons and parcels toward Rees, noticing again just how much of the supplies were her own from the Snake.

"Freeloaders," she murmured. "Thieves."

Rees spared her a glance. "You get on a wagon," he ordered.

"Really?" she asked, surprised. "I get to ride?"

"We don't have time for anyone to walk, least of all you," he snapped. "Don't make it a festival. Darrow!" The corpsman looked up from where he was stacking crates. "Put her on a wagon." Rees stalked off.

Darrow took Tanya by the wrist and marched her over to the wagons.

"Darrow! Slow down," Tanya fruitlessly ordered as he put his hands on her waist. "What do you think you're doing? Take your hands off me."

He grunted and deposited her heavily on top of a folded canvas tent. "Sorry miss," he said. "Following orders." And he, too, rushed off.

Tanya knew that if Darrow wouldn't make time to be polite, then no one in the company would. Biting her lip with frustration, straining against every instinct toward action, Tanya literally sat on her hands in an effort to keep still and be patient.

Finally, the men were packed and on horses and, in a great stroke of luck, Greer hopped on the horse hitched to her wagon. She'd be able to get something more out of him.

Rees got onto a horse in front and yelled, "Forward." Greer snapped the reins from side to side and the still-sleepy horse pulled their carriage through the clearing into the forest proper.

Tanya clambered from the back of the wagon to the front, until she was directly behind Greer's left ear.

"Are you really a corps?" she asked.

Greer jerked the reins back on the horse, who whinnied in protest. He twisted his neck to stare at Tanya, his eyes wide and wild.

"You sneaky wench," he exclaimed, tense, but, Tanya thought, not displeased. "How did you get back there?"

"I was deposited back here. As baggage. Are you really a corps?"

Greer scowled. "Of course we are. What a ridiculous question."

"Is it?" she asked, leaning in, suddenly sure she was onto something. "You were very poorly provisioned for a corps. Especially for one claiming to be from the Capital. Are you on probation or something?"

Tanya watched as the red stain blossoming under the skin of his cheeks spread to his ears, and his fingers fidgeted around the reins. "It's none of your affair," he sniffed.

Tanya smiled. "You don't know what your corps is supposed to be doing, do you? You think this is strange, too, but you have as little information as I do."

"Listen: Shut up."

"You're right," she said. Satisfied that she was at least correct and that no one here knew what they were doing, she lay down on the wagon and stretched her arms over her head. She yawned. "I might take a little nap. I didn't sleep."

Greer only grunted.

In Ironhearth, the air was thick and heady. Charcoal dust floated lazily from forge to forge like smoke, and the smell of burning hay tickled Tanya's nose. She rubbed her eyes and clambered to the edge of the wagon, looking at the town with bright eyes. She hadn't left the Port Cities in over a decade.

Ironhearth was a town known for its foundries and ironwork. It was gray and cacophonous with the sounds of metal striking metal and sizzling pokers. Tanya peered over the wagon and saw roads crisscrossed by narrow brick pathways leading from building to building—nothing like the sandy streets and limestone curbs of Griffin's Port. Enormous apple trees, ancient and gnarled, hung over the main road like gargoyles.

The corps' caravan stopped and Rees jumped out of his saddle. After a quick word with Darrow, he moved toward a low, rounded building tucked near a stream a few paces off the main row. He pounded on the door, taking a surprised step back when the door opened quickly and a young boy in a dusty red cap, obviously the blacksmith's apprentice, politely bowed him in.

Tanya rolled her eyes and turned back to the main road, where sparse groups of people, uniformly dressed in gray, hurried to various tasks. "Is there a festival or a fair nearby?" she called up to Greer.

"No." He turned to face her. "Why do you ask?"

"There's just . . . not a lot of people out," Tanya said, swinging her legs over the edge of the wagon. "There should be more street life in a town this size. Don't you think so?"

"These single-industry towns can be a little prim, I guess. What do you think you're doing? Stay in the wagon—damn it, girl!"

Tanya had already jumped off. She tumbled a little on the dismount and tipped forward, landing hard on her hands and knees.

"Ugh." Tanya lifted one hand and inspected her red, dirty flesh. "Ouch."

Suddenly Greer was at her side and picking her up by the elbow. "Well, what were you expecting?" he asked crossly. "You're too little a wench to have made that drop without help."

Tanya wrenched her elbow away. "I made the drop fine," she said icily, ignoring the sharp pain in her kneecap. She opened her mouth to deliver the second half of her retort, but was interrupted by a thin young man, almost as short as she was, slamming into her shoulder as he ran down the thoroughfare

"Sorry miss," the young man called. He did sound sorry, but not sorry enough to stop running, still tripping on what looked to Tanya like a very inconveniently long scholar's robe.

"I hope you have somewhere very important to be," she yelled after him as she rubbed her freshly injured shoulder.

"Are you all right?" asked Greer. "Did he hurt you?"

Tanya shook off his hand. "Don't be absurd. I outweigh that boy by at least fifty pounds. Don't say a word," she added, noticing Greer's quick look down her body.

A roar came from the blacksmith's forge. Tanya and Greer whipped around just in time to see Rees throw the door open and storm out, his face red and contorted with rage.

"That bitch," he growled, and kicked a tree. Tanya and the corps watched him in silence as he stood, mumbling, his brows low over his eyes. Finally, he looked up and, stone faced, walked purposefully over to one of the wagons and started rooting around the supplies, throwing provisions into a canvas sack.

Darrow approached his commander carefully. "Sir," he asked, in his slow, placid way, "may I ask what you found out about the girl thief?"

Rees laughed, but didn't stop packing. "Well, Darrow, since you ask, she is certainly no blacksmith's cousin. The blacksmith has no family at all aside from that apprentice of his—his nephew."

Darrow frowned. "Then who was the blacksmith I met at that forge?"

"Damned if I know. As far as the boy knew, it had been standing empty for some twenty days. The smith and his apprentice were taking the waters at the hot geysers in Juniper Hill, three towns over. They just came back yesterday and found the smithy quite thoroughly ransacked. The girl must have had an accomplice." Rees tied the canvas sack shut and hurried toward his horse.

"Wait, where are we going?" asked Greer, moving toward the wagon. "Aren't we supposed to report to the Capital?"

"I am going to find somewhere far away from this contingent of pimple-ridden little boys to get drunk," answered Rees, bridling up his horse. "Then I plan to find the thief and claim my reward from the Queen and Council. You are going to do whatever is in your heart."

"Sir," cried Greer in protest, but Rees was already barreling down the road into the forest.

When Rees had disappeared from sight, Tanya turned to Greer, stunned. "What just happened?" she asked.

Greer was staring woodenly after his former commander. "I just lost a future," he said in a monotone, and walked back to the wagon.

It took Tanya a moment to gather her wits. She wasn't the only one. The main road leading from Ironhearth to the woods was clogged with stunned soldiers—half-trained boys, really—scratching their heads. In that moment, Tanya and the men of the Queen's Corps had something in common. But there was a key difference between her and the corpsmen:

They had horses.

One of the boys knocked into her and she fell against a horse. She grabbed desperately at the reins, but he already had a rider—Hart.

"Don't get trampled, wench," he said distractedly.

She scowled up at him. "Don't get seduced and robbed, dunce," she spat.

A hand fell on Tanya's shoulder and she startled and spun, knocking Darrow back a couple steps.

He was holding a scrap of paper with some crude lines and chicken-scratch names scrawled on it. "Here, miss," he said, holding it out. "I drew you a map."

Tanya took it. "This will take me to the Capital?"

Darrow drew his brows together, confused. "No, ma'am. That map will get you back to Griffin's Port."

"But I don't want to go back to Griffin's Port. I want to go to the Capital. And *then* go back to Griffin's Port."

Darrow frowned. "Miss, I'm not sure the journey to the Capital is still happening. Our commander means to find the thief first, you see."

"Yes, I did see, Darrow," she said impatiently. "I was there when he said so and then ran off to get drunk."

"Well, you can't go by yourself." Darrow moved as if to put a hand on Tanya's shoulder, then seemed to think better of it.

"No, that doesn't seem practical," agreed Tanya. She looked curiously at the solid, deferential young man before her. "What are your plans now that you're no longer a member of the Queen's Corps?"

He bowed his head. "Forgive me, but that's not accurate. I am sure Commander Rees will be back. But, even if he isn't, I swore my vows to the Queen and Council, not to Commander Rees."

In spite of herself, Tanya was impressed. She nodded, encouraging him to continue.

Darrow straightened his back. "I promised to visit my mother as soon as I could. If the commander does not return, I'm off to her herd on the Glassland Meadows and then to the Capital, to join another regimen of corps." He looked at Tanya. "If you wanted to join me at my mother's and then onward to the Capital, you'd be welcome, miss."

Tanya met his eyes, surprised. "I would be? Why on Lode should I be?"

He took a step back. "It's not my intention to be forward, miss."

"Yes, I gathered that from how you call me 'miss' instead of 'wench,' or 'tavern maid,'" answered Tanya, crossing her arms. "I wasn't suggesting any such thing, Darrow. I must admit, you at least are a gentleman."

He blushed and looked pleased. Smiling shyly, he bowed a little. "My mother would like to believe so. Miss Tanya, I believe that your claim to the Smiling Snake is as valid as anyone's and I would be more than happy to serve as escort to the Capital."

Tanya smiled back at him. "But only after the Glassland Meadows?"

"I made a promise to my mother."

That was undeniably nice, if inconvenient. "Thank you, Darrow."

He bowed again and turned toward his horse, leaving Tanya once again alone in the dusty road. She wandered into town to think.

Everything was rooted to the earth in Ironhearth. After a lifetime of needing to pay attention to the patterns made by wind and waves, Tanya found herself stumbling a little at the muddy ruts in the road and listening too closely to the men calling to each other over low stone fences, all—*all*—in the same flattened growl of a Marsh accent. Her ears strained to locate other accents, snatches of Lumen or Gobi mixed in with her native Lodeiann. That familiar hint of the foreign, the new, the faraway wasn't present in Ironhearth.

Tanya paused under an ancient copper-willow tree and blocked the sun with her hand, scanning the nearly identical coal-coated buildings until, at length, she spotted hanging from the arched doorway of a building a small scrap of a red flag bearing sketchy gold stitching in the shape of a salamander. She sighed with relief and made for Ironhearth's tavern.

She hadn't gotten halfway there when a shrill whistling caused her to pause and turn her head. Her eyes widened and she tripped backward, falling and sitting hard on the packed dirt. An eye-stinging rush of wind blew her hair back.

"It's a funnel," someone yelled. "Take cover!"

# Chapter

5

anya didn't even have the time ask what a funnel was before she saw it herself: A dusky column spun toward her, spitting out hard particles that cracked windows and made horses squeal. It was moving fast.

Tanya scrambled to her feet and ran. The funnel picked up speed, but Tanya had no more speed to acquire. "Oh, come on," she moaned as it gained on her. She reached the inn, collapsed on its stoop, and yanked off her apron, throwing it over her head. "So, this is happening," she grumbled, and the funnel hit her.

Tanya had angled her body away from the wind, so it wasn't quite as bad as it could have been. But it was bad enough.

An endless swirl of sharp pebbles, thickened by dust, pummeled her, each one hitting her skin like a needle prick and a punch at the same time. It seemed to go on forever and the sting of each tiny assault intensified exponentially, so much so that the funnel had passed all the way through the village for several minutes before Tanya realized it was over.

She pulled the apron away from her face and dragged in an uneven breath. Eyes still closed, she turned and leaned against the wall of the inn. She opened her eyes and gasped.

The whole of formerly drab, brown Ironhearth was blanketed in a fine, sparkling powder of the palest pink.

Tanya sat up, wincing at the pain. She drew one finger across her arm and came away with a layer of gritty pink. She moved the tiny rocks between her forefinger and thumb, bringing it to her eye.

"Rose diamonds," she breathed. She had never even touched a

rose diamond. Now she was covered in the dust of an endless sea of the stuff.

A scraping sound next to her made her look up. A small, lithe figure in a black-hooded cape was kicking the diamonds into a pile like a child building a sand castle. They were whistling. The tune sounded familiar, but it wasn't until the figure stuck a slender hand into the pile and deposited a careless handful or two into a hip pouch that Tanya recognized Jana.

Tanya was torn. On the one hand, it was smarter to ignore the thief, continue into the inn, and barter for a respectable night's lodging. Tanya had raised herself to value order. Complications were to be avoided wherever possible. An organized plan of action was to always be preferred and pursued.

On the other hand, Tanya was *really* angry.

She felt the rage starting to boil in her veins and was gathering her skirts together to stomp toward Jana when the other girl threw her hood back and lifted her face to the sun. Jana, as content as a cat on a windowsill, spread out her arms and inflated her chest with air and sunlight.

The white, sparkling tip of a feather poked through the top of her shirt.

Tanya zeroed in on the quill. Rees had been taking it to the Capital. And he bore a letter from the Queen and Council, granting him incredible power to complete his mission.

Tanya felt a sudden clarity of purpose: That quill, whatever it was, was somehow a ticket to the only people in the kingdom who could give her back her inn.

Jana suddenly became still. Tanya ducked behind the doorway, pressing her back to the wall. She tried not to breathe too loudly.

Tanya heard Jana take two slow, crunching steps toward her. She desperately scanned the yard for escape.

The door to the inn opened, letting out a rush of noise and hot air. The people of Ironhearth began streaming out into the street and Tanya heard the light, crunching footsteps quickly recede. Tanya dared to look over her shoulder and watched as Jana slipped into a stable.

Tanya found a tree to sink behind and waited for the sun to go down. If Jana had waited until darkness to steal the quill, then Tanya would, too. Tanya firmly forced herself to forget that she had no idea how she would get the feather off Jana, no idea how she was going to get to the Capital—no idea even whether to turn right or left off the main road. She had learned how to make soufflé in an oven where the temperature was always one hundred degrees off. She could learn this.

She didn't need Darrow's help—or anyone's.

When the moon was up, she made her way back into the inn's yard. The stable was dark and silent. She began to push the door open, but started back at the scraping whine of the boards. A girlish mutter sounded briefly and then fell silent. Someone was in there, breathing the deep breath of sleep.

There was a gap between the sliding door and the wall, but it was narrow. Tanya inspected it and instinctively put her hand over her belly, which jutted softly away from her hips. She would never make it through.

Frustrated, she bit her lip so she wouldn't curse and stepped away. She peered around the building, lit only by dim moonlight. There was no other door.

But there *was* a window.

It was high on the left side of the stable, near the back of the building. It probably led to the loft, Tanya thought, walking underneath it. She put her hand to the wall. Smooth boards. No slats she could climb.

A light, raspy snore floated out the window. Tanya stood on her toes, futilely trying to see through to the barn. More murmurs, a snorting, and then a honking snore.

Jana was well and truly asleep. *As well she might be*, thought Tanya, casting about until she found a ladder lying on its side by a chicken coop. She went to fetch it. "How nice for her that she gets to sleep," she grumbled, dragging the ladder through the mud and diamond dust. "What a lovely luxury after being up all night."

The ladder was dirty and full of splinters, but it was sturdy and held Tanya's weight as she climbed the wall to the window. Once at the top, Tanya planted one hand around the sill and gathered up her skirts with the other. Moving as quietly as she was able, she thrust one leg through the window, reaching until her foot found the loft.

The snoring was coming from the far corner. She was buried under a cloak and a horse blanket, but Jana's silky black locks poked through, reflecting the shadowy moonlight in the otherwise dim and dusty stable.

Tanya leaned forward until she was on her hands and knees. She inched across the wooden slats. Her boot tip caught on a nail and Jana mumbled. Tanya held her breath, but Jana only mumbled again and flopped over onto her side.

Jana was now facing Tanya. Her lips puffed out and air whistled through her nose with each breath. Her arm was flung out and across her chest. *As if she were hugging herself to sleep*, thought Tanya.

Tanya crawled forward until her face was directly over the other girl's. Jana's hair was fanned out across her chest. Not sure what else to do, Tanya blew softly on the hair, floating it back toward Jana's shoulders. The thief smiled faintly in her sleep and angled herself to be more directly in the path of Tanya's pursed lips. It *was* stuffy in the stable. Tanya lifted a wrist to wipe the sweat off her upper lip.

Tanya blew softly one more time and Jana's hair parted like a curtain. Tanya saw the pouch holding the quill, pressed between Jana's brown, sunburnt neck and her own nightdress.

Tanya hesitated. The pouch was hanging from a cord around Jana's neck. There was no way she could get it off without Jana waking. But she had been serious when she had warned the thief not to touch something she didn't understand.

Tanya grasped the hem of her skirt and wrapped it around her fingers, lowering them to Jana's neck.

The cloth dragged across Jana's neck and the girl shot upright, her eyes still closed.

Tanya threw herself flat, fear coursing through her veins. But Jana merely sat upright for a few seconds before collapsing back onto the pillow.

Tanya slowly pulled herself up onto her knees, searching her pockets for a handkerchief, but finding none. She bit her lip. She was going to have to risk touching the feather.

Crawling toward Jana, she pushed her thumb and forefinger together, and, wielding them like tweezers, lowered them to Jana's chest. She grasped a tiny scrap of the satiny filaments making up the quill's feathers and pulled.

She had expected resistance—friction from the pouch, stickiness from sweat—but instead the quill slid out of Jana's pouch into Tanya's hand like water over a cliff.

Tanya gasped, her fingers suddenly burning, then cold, then burning again. She lifted the quill and stared as it seemed to ignite, throwing a dancing, golden light across the walls.

Jana mumbled again and Tanya quickly tucked the quill into the pocket she had sewn into the inside of her sleeve.

Something snorted.

Tanya looked up, but Jana was still. The snorting sounded again, closer this time. Tanya inched to the edge of the loft and peered underneath.

A horse was tied up underneath the loft.

It was the most beautiful horse Tanya had ever seen. It was pure, shimmering gold with a flowing creamy mane. It was long legged and muscled like a war horse, but lithe. It moved, and Tanya realized with a surprised start that it was a mare.

Adrenaline thrumming through her veins, Tanya changed direction, crawling past Jana to the ladder leading to the ground level.

The golden mare was asleep.

Tanya could count on both hands the number of times she had actually ridden a horse. She approached the mare carefully.

"Ush, shush, shush," she whispered in the mare's ear, not touching her. The mare opened her eyes, blinked a few times, and turned calmly toward Tanya.

"Ush, shush, shush," she whispered, smiling triumphantly. She might not have had enough leisure to ride a horse, but she knew more than enough about calming strange ones. There had been no stable boy at the Smiling Snake—just her.

Tanya glanced around the mare's stall, looking for evidence of her owner. All she found was what looked like a new saddle and bridle, stiff and shining with fresh oil. No livery, no banners, no insignia that she recognized on the tack. She turned to look up at Jana—the mare couldn't be hers?—and her foot caught on something soft buried in the hay.

It was a gray velvet cap. She picked it up, turning it around in her fingers. She recognized it; the boy who had almost mowed her down this morning had been wearing it. Someone had entrusted *him* with this glorious horse?

Tanya studied the insignia on his hat: a triangle and a circle. She didn't recognize it. It wasn't from any noble family she'd ever heard of nor any guild. He wasn't representing anyone important.

It would be a lot faster getting to the Capital if she had a horse.

Tanya tried hard to dismiss the thought as soon as it popped into her head. "You are not a thief," she whispered.

But, as she had recently learned, thieves were everywhere. And her inn was standing empty and unprotected—ransacked, but still valuable. Every minute she was away from the Snake, she was risking someone else claiming it for themselves. Every delay in gaining an audience with the Queen and Council meant that some miscreant was that much closer to simply burning down a vacant building and constructing their own inn in its place.

She walked determinedly to the saddle, yanking it from the hook on the wall. She had left Griffin's Port to get her inn back. She was getting. Her. Inn. Back.

The mare sleepily turned her head, calmly surveying Tanya as she strapped the saddle around her midsection. The harness slipped over the mare's golden head just as easily.

The mare yawned through Tanya's preparations, placidly allowing all handling. The moment Tanya pulled on the lead though, something changed.

The mare went stiff and lifted her head toward Tanya. Tanya made eye contact with the mare and felt something shrivel up in her chest. The mare's expression was human in its disdain. She snorted and shuffled her feet, never taking her eyes off Tanya.

The two stared at each other for a long moment, weighing the other's movements, matching the other's position in front of the door. A snore sounded from the sleeping loft and the mare looked up.

Seizing the chance, Tanya grabbed at the mare's harness and swung herself into the saddle with a yelp of exertion. The mare reared and whinnied furiously, bucking Tanya sideways, her feet swinging wildly, far wide of the stirrups. Only adrenaline kept Tanya hanging on.

"That's not fair," sighed a girlish voice.

Both Tanya and the mare looked toward the loft, where Jana was flushed with sleep, but awake and pointing an arrow right at them.

When Tanya didn't respond, Jana shrugged and pulled back her bow. "You haven't given me the impression that you deserve to die, but I can't let you get away with that feather-thingy. So . . . hmmm." Jana frowned and then her face lit up. "Got it," she said, and pointed the arrow almost to the floor—aiming right for the mare's left flank.

Tanya and the mare exchanged a quick glance. Tanya was tangled in the mare's stirrups and there was no time to shake her loose. The mare neighed sulkily and then tore through the barn door with Tanya on her back, sending planks and splinters flying.

An arrow whizzed past Tanya's ear. The tavern's door opened and out spilled the townsfolk, looking wide eyed at the careening golden warhorse carrying a scrubby girl barely hanging on to her saddle. The mare looked around wildly, shaking wood shavings out of her ears. Tanya watched as the boy in the oversize scholar's robe pushed his way to the front of the crowd and dropped his jaw. She only had time to shrug at him before the mare crashed into overgrown brush to the east.

They rode hard for an hour, but eventually, after the noise of pursuit had long died away, the mare stopped in the middle of the clearing and shook her head so violently that Tanya hopped off in sheer self-preservation.

"Fine, yes, I hear you," she snapped, landing shakily on her feet. She bent over, massaging her aching thighs. "Trust me, I don't want to be on your back any more than you want me to be there."

Tanya eased herself down onto the forest floor, wincing as muscles she didn't even know she had shot through with pain on impact. Inching her legs out and leaning backward so the small of her back was on a rock, Tanya finally inhaled, exhaled, and looked around.

She had absolutely no idea where she was.

It was dark except for moonlight and lightning bugs floating around a nearby creek. The only noise came from crickets and the mare's snorts as she wriggled against a tree, trying to shake off her harness.

Eventually the mare gave up. She stopped, huffed, and looked to Tanya with an accusing stare.

"So now you want me," she grumbled, painfully pulling herself back to her feet. "But you did get me away from Jana, so I guess I owe you this much." She unstrapped the saddle and lifted it away, but hesitated at the harness. "Are you going to just run away if I take this off?"

The mare looked away. "You are, aren't you?" Tanya sighed and began to wind the lead around a nearby tree. The mare reared up in protest. "What do you want me to do?" Tanya asked, aware that she was whining, but too tired to care. "I can't let you run away. I'm in the middle of the woods with no supplies and no idea of where I am. I at least need a horse."

The mare put her nose in the air.

"I'll make you a deal," said Tanya, loosening her grasp. "If I undo the harness and let you go free, will you stay with me at least until I hitch another ride?"

The mare eyed the rope in Tanya's hand and briefly made eye contact with her. Her head went up and down.

"Thank you," breathed Tanya.

Tanya liked to think of herself as a reasonable, no-nonsense sort of person, and so it was with trepidation that she released her hold on the mare. "I have just made a verbal agreement with a horse," she murmured to herself. But the horse stayed, only wandering off a few feet, nudging the forest floor with her nose, in search of something to graze.

Tanya sat back down. Her stomach grumbled. And her mind was uneasy: She needed to feel like she was doing something. She thought she would prefer that thing to be eating, but, as that wasn't an option, she pulled the quill out of her shirt and studied it instead.

It wasn't glowing the way it had before. It looked just like an ordinary white quill feather, albeit a rather large and overly symmetrical one. Tanya turned it around in her fingers and noticed a dark smudge on the quill point. She moistened her finger and touched it to the edge. Her fingertip came away stained blue.

A sketch formed in her mind. The map that Darrow had given her—she had lost it in her flight from town . . .

Eager for a task, Tanya pulled off her apron and laid it out in front of her. She leaned over the grimy white cloth and gripped the quill hard—and then snarled out loud in frustration.

The map had been from Ironhearth to *Griffin's Port*. Even if she could trace her steps back to Darrow's hastily sketched road, it wouldn't lead her to where she need to go, to the Capital.

"*Useless*," spat Tanya. Impatiently, she licked the quill—briefly tasting something burning and sweet and utterly unlike ink—and angrily scratched a message on her apron:

*Just get me from here to the Capital, you stupid shiny feather!*

The wind hushed. The creek ceased its gurgle. The stars blinked out.

The quill exploded with white light. Sparks vaulted upward and around Tanya like a shower of diamond raindrops, until they floated up, up, up, settling into the places the stars used to be. A great blast of air blew back Tanya's hair, rippling from the stem of the quill itself, only barely ruffling the feather's strands before dissipating into the cool night air. A pool of muddy water formed around Tanya's sitting form before it trickled across the forest floor, propelled by some invisible force, and dissolved back in the creek bed.

The quill's glow illuminated the apron on the ground. Tanya

stared as the faint ink from her angrily scratched message *moved*, the lines wriggling across the fabric like live worms until they coalesced into one inky blob and grew, separating into disparate shapes made up of words: *oak, packed sand, fertile soil, granite, water, gold*—Tanya's eyes widened.

The quill's light pulsed, vibrating with each flicker. Swallowing her fear of strange magic, Tanya licked it again and put the edge to the still-blank half of her apron. She drew a circle. She drew an X with her name underneath.

As soon as she lifted the quill, the ink started coalescing and dissipating, forming words, lines, symbols.

When it was done, her apron was a map. An X marked where Tanya was sitting, and arrows marked a path to a main road. Several turns later, another X marked the Capital.

Along the way were towns, lakes, mountains, a cavern. But all of it, every mark, was made up not of plain blue lines, but of little words: *gravel, granite, salt.*

*Gold.*

Tanya put her finger cautiously on *gold*, and felt a shiver pass through that finger. She stroked the word and then jumped back with a yelp. When she stroked the word *gold* again, the *gold* moved in the direction her finger was moving in. She did it a third time and felt the ground underneath her rumble.

Tanya looked up and around, desperately wishing for a way to verify what had just happened. With no other option, she reluctantly turned to the mare.

"What was that?" she asked. The mare, her eyes wary, shrugged.

Tanya's eyes fell on the creek. She looked back at the map and saw *fresh water* idling very close to her X. She put her finger on *fresh water* and closed her eyes. She took a breath and dragged.

The mare felt it first and yelped, jumping away. Tanya opened her eyes and started laughing.

The creek was moving.

It was churning up the earth and bedrock, flinging dirt and tiny rocks in every direction, but the path of the river was visibly moving, angling itself toward Tanya. She felt the tip of her boots get wet and lifted her finger. The creek rumbled to a halt.

Tanya was too stunned to move until a blueberry bush to her left burst into flames.

Tanya scrambled to her feet, kicking away her apron. "Junkoff," she sneered. "Great." Turning her back on it, she dipped the empty leather saddlebags into the newly repositioned creek and put out the small fire.

She moved back to the center of the clearing and primly arranged herself on a nearby boulder. With distaste and suspicion, she eyed the quill, abandoned in the dirt, but still glittering.

"No, thank you," she said firmly. The mare ambled up next to her, chewing on some greenery, and snorted her agreement.

Tanya smelled the rosemary and chicory coming from the mare's mouth. She hadn't eaten in a very long time.

She could pick the chicory, but it was a tough root, and it wouldn't do much good to her without a fire—which she had just extinguished. Tanya sighed and went over to the singed blueberry bush, scanning for uncharred fruit. There was none.

She turned and her eyes fell back on the quill.

Tanya screwed up her face in concentration. She didn't like amateurs. And everyone who was using this magic was an amateur, so it naturally followed that she had developed a distaste for magic.

But one thing Tanya did respect was a tool. This quill was a *kind* of tool.

And she was really hungry.

She picked up the quill.

Less than an hour later, Tanya was roasting chestnuts over a roaring fire, several sweet potatoes buried in the embers. A small pile of salt sat on her left and a patch of sweetgrass to her right, the mare happily—if begrudgingly—grazing.

"Well, that wasn't so hard," said Tanya, sprinkling a few grains of salt over a chestnut and popping it in her mouth. Yes, at some point cotton had started falling from the sky and she had noticed a sinkhole opening a few leagues away on her apron map, but who cared? The cotton was hardly dangerous and the sinkhole was easily fixed with a few strokes of the quill, all without moving from her comfortable spot by the fire. All that was required was a little organization.

Tanya dug out the sweet potatoes and offered one to the mare. The mare flared her nostrils and turned away.

"Fine. Be snobbish." Tanya shrugged, carefully peeling the skin away from the potato. "But, I'm the one who brought you your dinner and, as far as I can tell, I caused no harm along the way. From where I'm sitting, that makes me the best magic user in the kingdom."

The mare snorted. Tanya threw a chestnut shell at her.

Tanya yawned. Now that she had filled her stomach, it dawned on her that she had gone without sleep for even longer than she had without food.

She eyed the clearing. It was rocky and dusty. She turned to the map and made a few quick movements.

The ground groaned and sprouted a thick bed of moss. A creek spurted into existence a few miles away. Tanya smiled and directed it so that it irrigated a nearby wheat field. Then she drew the apron around her shoulders and snuggled down under it.

Tanya slept.

She slept peacefully, lulled by crickets, and no longer hungry. She probably could have slept for twelve hours.

She could have slept for twelve hours, that is, if she had gotten the chance.

Something was kicking her. Tanya shifted away. "Leave me alone, horse," she mumbled. She flinched as a drop of sweat splattered down her cheek.

"I'm trying to sleep, horse!" Tanya groaned and threw out her arm.

Someone caught it at the wrist.

# Chapter

**T**anya's eyes flew open.

She wrenched her arm back and tumbled across the moss, landing in a particularly rough patch of upturned dirt, courtesy of the root-diving mare.

"Augh," groaned Tanya, rubbing her smarting thigh. "*Bad* horse."

A whinny drew Tanya's attention. She turned and saw the golden mare held—barely—by a nasty-looking piece of black leather tack and three nastier-looking men.

"What are you doing?" asked Tanya, creaking to her feet. "You can't honestly be trying to rob *me*. Not unless you're very bad at your business."

"Why's that?"

Tanya turned around. A young man had made himself comfortable on the moss and was twisting her apron idly around in his hands.

Tanya made a move to grab her apron, but the youth shifted enough that she could see the very sharp blade at his hip. She snuck a glance at the men holding the mare and saw that they were similarly armed.

He spoke again. "Why can't we be robbing you, girl? What disqualifies you?"

Tanya spoke carefully. "It was my understanding, sir, that the highwaymen gangs tend to attack carefully chosen targets: caravans, transports, couriers."

He smiled and stood up. "And you don't consider yourself an attractive target?"

Now that he was standing in the moonlight, Tanya got her first good look at the man. He was younger than she would have expected. The men holding back the mare seemed older, but there was no doubting the confidence radiating from the thief in front of her. Tanya thought back to the first time she saw Rees, his leadership clear from his enormous size and even more enormous ego.

It wasn't the same with this boy, for that's what he was. His eyes were shining with warmth and amusement; his smile was easy and open. Tanya felt that he was someone who would be very easy to say yes to.

Tanya was very glad that she was practiced at saying no.

"Frankly, no," she told him, eyeing the mare, mind racing, trying to plot an escape. "I don't have any gold, any weapons, any valuables at all, unless you count my horse and, well, to be honest, she's not a very good horse."

"She's very pretty."

"That doesn't count for much with a horse, does it?"

The youth shrugged, still eyeing the mare admiringly, and unrolled his fist. The map-marked apron unfurled from his fingers. He held it up.

Tanya forced herself not to blink. "May I have that back?"

"I don't think so. Sorry."

She crossed her arms, shivering. "It's just an old apron. You're going to steal a girl's apron? You really are terrible highwaymen."

"Did you draw this map?"

Haughtily, Tanya laughed. "A map? I was just doodling. A girl gets bored traveling alone."

"So, you *did* draw this."

She felt prickles run up her neck. She had made a mistake.

He cocked his head. "No answer? OK. Since we agree, then, that you drew this map—for that's what this is, a map—can I ask what you drew it with?"

Where had she put that quill? She had been so tired by the time she had finished playing with it. A tingle flickered over her ankles and she remembered: She had stuck it in her left boot.

Her legs began to shake. She couldn't give up that quill. She needed it to get her inn back.

Tanya was still working out a plan when the boy apparently lost his patience, sighed, and signaled to one of the other men.

A finger lightly touched Tanya where her throat met her head, and then everything was dark.

It was still dark when Tanya woke up.

Her legs were tied at the ankles and her hands were tied behind her back. The knots were much tighter than the ones Jana had used. Tanya thrashed around blindly, but she couldn't even wriggle to a sitting position.

A burlap sack had been thrown over her head and tied down around her chest. She would have been suffocating except someone had thought to cut three holes, one for each nostril and one over her mouth.

They were small, but Tanya knew how to scream loud.

"Help!" she screamed. "Help! Help, I'm being kidnapped by road thieves! Help, someone, help—"

"Don't bother," said the smooth voice of the youth. "We're nowhere near the type of villagers that would be inclined to leave their houses at dawn—not to attend random screams for help."

Tanya ignored him and continued to scream her head off until, eventually, her voice gave out.

She had no choice but to calm down.

Once she had access to what her ears and body were telling her, it quickly became clear that she was traveling, tossed like a sack of potatoes in the back of a wagon or—gauging the soft rolling motion flinging her tied-up limbs against the hay—a cart, the large kind used to transport heavy cargo, like livestock, or gangs of highwaymen.

A horse whined and Tanya stiffened. They had captured the mare, too.

She really wished they would take the sack off her head. Tanya knew how to read a room. She knew that if she could just see her captors, she would know the right way to handle this. But, as it was, all she could do was lie there, prone and helpless.

Tanya hated being helpless.

The cart pulled up short. Strong arms—male, with the sleeves rolled up—slid underneath the small of her back and scooped her up, lifting her up and then down, until she was nestled, helpless, against a bony collarbone draped in a, thankfully clean, linen shirt.

"Apologies for this." It was the youth again. "No impertinence meant," he continued, and started walking.

Tanya automatically opened her mouth to deliver a tart retort, but found that part of herself frozen.

She was scared.

Tanya had not felt fear in years. But every muscle in her body seemed to cramp. Every breath hurt. She was cold and sweating.

That was all uncomfortable. That didn't help. But what really grabbed her heart in a vise and squeezed was this: She was under someone else's control.

*They're going to take the horse and the quill,* Tanya thought, her breathing accelerating rapidly. *I'm going to be left in a patch of dirt, shivering, alone, with nothing.*

*I'm going to be nothing again.*

The youth deposited her in a chair.

"This is the girl, sir."

"I can see that, Riley." This voice was softer, higher, but with a low rasp in it, like a wagon wheel rolling over fine gravel.

There was a sigh. "I'm not in the mood," said the voice. "Riley, could you?"

Tanya felt Riley's arms go around her. He fiddled with the ties around her waist until the burlap fell away and then lifted the sack off her in one swift movement.

She blinked. She was in a large tent, dimly lit with one lantern, which was sitting on the corner of a lightweight but capacious and paper-loaded desk.

"What's your name, little one?"

Tanya turned her head. There was a smaller, lower table directly to her right, laden with an ornate silver tea service. The scent of jasmine and something green and spicy that she couldn't identify floated up with the steam. Tanya swallowed as her practiced nose wrinkled and sniffed the air: Somewhere nearby were freshly baked biscuits and bacon just about to burn.

"Would you like some breakfast?"

Tanya put aside her empty stomach and focused on the man sitting behind the teapot. He seemed to be rather a little man, although maybe that was just because he was sitting on the floor, propped up only by a broad, thick cushion encrusted with dense embroidery in some dark, lustrous thread. He was round in body and face, with a rather prominent chin and a shiny scalp underneath a thin rim of flyaway white hair. He was older. Not as old as Froud had been, but he was just starting to tip out of middle age into grandfatherly.

The man grasped the handle of his teapot with thick, soft fingers and poured its contents into a dainty silver mug.

He looked up and she met his eyes. He smiled. "Do you like tea?"

Tanya found her voice, hoarse as it was from her earlier fruitless screaming. "I do," she said gruffly. "But I need my hands to drink it."

The man smiled, dimpling. "Riley, untie the girl. She's not going anywhere."

Tanya shivered, but nodded at the little man. "Thank you. I would like breakfast."

"Of course." He signaled to a shadowy lackey, who pulled up his hood and went out into the rain. "And with whom do I have the pleasure of breakfasting?"

"You first," she answered as Riley untied her. As soon as she was free, Tanya immediately bent over to untie her feet. She stretched out her aching calves and sighed.

That reminded her. "What happened to my horse?" she asked.

"She'll be very well taken care of," spoke up Riley. Tanya turned to look at him. He had pulled up a sturdy little chair and was straddling it backward. He smiled. "I treat my horses well."

The tent parted and an attendant entered with the biscuits and bacon Tanya had smelled, along with a covered dish. The lackey pulled another table over to the little man and spread out the food. The dish turned out to hold eggs, scrambled with cream and salmon roe.

Tanya's mouth watered. She never got to eat salmon roe. Froud had caviar in stock, but only for the highest-ranking guests.

The little man began filling a plate. Unable—and disinclined—to ignore her training, Tanya noted how fine the dishware was: opalescent china with beautiful gold leaf scrollwork along the edges.

She noticed the man watching her noticing and quickly looked away. The man looked at her thoughtfully and then started spreading butter on a biscuit. "I'm not really anybody," he said, his voice warm. "If I told you my name, you wouldn't know it."

"Well, I have to call you something."

"Why don't you call me Uncle Tommy?"

Tanya stared. "Uncle Tommy?"

He smiled. "That will work." Riley choked out a laugh behind Tanya, and Uncle Tommy grinned. "What? She reminds me of my niece."

Tanya briefly closed her eyes. "Fine," she said. "Why was I snatched in the night by your errand boy?"

Uncle Tommy offered her the biscuit. It was yeasty, but the butter was of the highest quality.

"Riley just did what he was told. You're here because of this." Uncle Tommy picked up a bundled piece of cloth. He held it high and let it tumble open.

It was her apron. It was the map.

Tanya chewed on a piece of bacon. Finally, she asked, "My apron? Do you need a kitchen maid? Your ingredients are good, but whoever your cook is doesn't have a firm grip on proportions, I agree."

He folded it up neatly and placed it on the table. "This is a very unusual map, what with the . . . *annotations*. Who drew it for you?"

Tanya opened her mouth and then shut it. She felt the quill poke her from deep inside her boot.

"A girl I met on the road," she said carefully. "Some tavern maid traveling to the Capital."

Uncle Tommy's eyes narrowed behind his smile. "A tavern maid on her way to the Capital."

Tanya didn't like the way that wasn't a question. "That's right," she said, crossing her legs, as if that could conceal the lie.

The little man in front of her frowned. "That is disappointing," he said. He sighed and looked her in the eye. "I was enjoying this."

He signaled behind her with two fingers and the lackey wrapped his arms around her. He yanked her hands behind her and held them around the back of her chair.

"Hey!" Tanya kicked the air, trying to buck him, but she couldn't get enough momentum or leverage to even bounce her way off the chair. "I'm not the girl. I didn't draw the map! Leave me alone! Wait—" Two more men surrounded her, both of them big, both of them looming over her, reaching for her. "No—"

"Tanya!" a girl's voice cried.

Everyone froze. Uncle Tommy paused midsip. "So that's it. Good for you, Tanya," he said, raising his cup at her. "Smart not to give anything away for free."

The lackey relaxed his hold on Tanya and she ripped out of his grasp, turning to see the newcomer who apparently knew her.

"Jana," she breathed, her heart lurching into her stomach.

This was a very different Jana from the one Tanya had seen at the camp, simpering up at Hart in a frilly dress. This Jana was dressed in tight leather pants and a loosely fitted blouse made of some cheap but shiny gray fabric. This Jana wasn't in tiny slippers, but heavy black boots laced up to her knees and a complicated garment combining a vest and a belt made of brown suede and brass buckles. Tanya counted two knives, three throwing stars, and a crossbow all strapped to that vest, and she somehow knew that those were just the weapons she could see.

Jana was dirty and breathing hard. There were scratches on her arms and a twig in her hair.

She looked unlike anyone Tanya had ever seen.

Jana crossed her arms and glared. "That was mean, Tanya," she said. "Do you have any idea how hard it was for me to get here this fast from Ironhearth? *I* was going to steal that horse! I had to travel on foot!"

"So, you know our tavern wench, Jana?" asked Uncle Tommy. Tanya shot him a glance and he answered her next question without her having to voice it. "Tavern maids can never not criticize other people's cooking."

Tanya slumped over in her chair, putting her head in her hands. Jana knew that she was the one who had stolen the quill. She had lost—she was never going to get to the Capital, never going to get to the Queen, never going to get the Smiling Snake back. The only thing she could possibly salvage was herself. She could maybe, just maybe, get out of this camp alive and intact.

"OK," she said, aware that she was handing over the one piece of leverage she had left in the world. "You win. I put the quill in my boot."

Uncle Tommy looked pointedly at Tanya's feet. She sighed and bent over to unlace the left boot, feeling the quill heat up and quiver against her skin.

When she had loosened it enough, she slipped in her thumb and index finger and drew out the quill.

A hush fell over the tent. The white fibers seemed to vibrate in Tanya's hand and the quill's tip glowed, throwing out tiny, blindingly bright sparks. She looked at it regretfully. It was really a very pretty thing, and a useful one, after all. She wouldn't have wanted to give it up to anyone less than the Queen and Council. But here she was.

She held it out. "Here you are, *Uncle.*"

He took it from her, an oily glint in his eye. He looked at the quill like it was a chocolate cake and he'd been fasting.

The quill dimmed a little in his hands, but he didn't seem concerned. "Excellent," he said, almost to himself.

Tanya started to stand up. "I'm free to leave now?"

Uncle Tommy was still looking reverently at the quill. Riley cleared his throat. "Sir?"

He looked up. "Yes?"

Riley motioned to Tanya. "What should we do with the girl?"

Uncle Tommy seemed surprised to see Tanya standing in front of him, as if he had forgotten she existed the moment she had handed him the quill. "Oh, take her to Lukas," he said. "Have him set her up in the kitchens. She's right about his cooking, he burnt the bacon."

"Wait—" protested Tanya as Riley took her arm. "You can't just *commandeer* me! I'm a citizen!"

Uncle Tommy sighed and finally put down the quill. "No, my dear, what you are is a girl, alone and unarmed, apparently without any money or valuables, and, now," he added, holding up her apron, "without a map. Believe it or not, I'm actually doing you a favor by not turning you loose on the road in this particular part of the country. We're packing up soon. When we get to Bloodstone, you'll be free to go, if you want. It's not the loveliest of towns, but there will be ways for you to earn an honest wage. In the meantime, nobody in my camp gets a free ride. Everybody works."

"Bloodstone," breathed Tanya. That city, buried in the shallow, rocky mouth of a burnt-out volcano, had haunted Tanya's nightmares as a child. Regulars gave travelers from Bloodstone a wide berth, but Tanya had had to serve everybody at the Snake. One particularly scorch-eyed woman, with a high, pointed forehead and thick, lustrous hair the improbable color of summer grass, had taken a liking to the literal-minded little girl who listened so wide eyed to her stories.

What she had told Tanya about Bloodstone had made her shake.

She opened her mouth to lodge a protest, but was yanked out of the tent before she had the chance to formulate one.

The camp was a hodgepodge of colorful multilayered tents and different factions of men wearing elaborate matching patches or vests, indicating varying allegiances. Riley wheeled her past the spectacle to a temporary but sturdy-looking structure that had been set up next to the creek.

A harried-looking boy, younger than Tanya, was struggling with a pot of porridge. He was scraping the bottom with a frantic fork.

"Your flame's too high," said Tanya automatically. The boy looked up at her with wide eyes.

"This is the second pot I've tried to make," he said emphatically, not even bothering to ask who she was. "I have no idea how to do this."

She sighed. That was a big pot of good oats and long-grain rice. She couldn't let a second batch just get thrown out. It would be too irritating.

"Move," she said, shoving the boy out of the way and turning off the burner. "Get me some heavy cream."

While he ran to the creek to fetch a bottle out of a makeshift icebox, Tanya tasted the concoction, wrinkled her nose, and started rooting around the free-standing aluminum shelves for cinnamon and brown sugar.

"Well, it looks like there's nothing more for me to do," said Riley cheerfully. "You're right at home here."

That brought Tanya back to her senses and she dropped the fork on the counter with a thud.

"I am not at home," she told him sternly. "I demand to be allowed to leave so that I can go home." *To a home that is no longer yours and now will never be since you've lost that quill and have no other way to gain audience with the Council let alone the Queen.* Tanya firmly told the voice in her head to shut up. She would find another way.

Riley scratched his head and yawned. He'd probably been up all night, Tanya realized. Her fingers started to move automatically toward the coffeepot, but she forced them down at her side.

"Sorry, tavern maid," said Riley, blurring the words through his yawn. "If the Tomcat says you're coming with us to Bloodstone, you're coming with us to Bloodstone."

Tanya scowled. "In that case, get out of my kitchen." Riley grabbed a biscuit, winked, and obliged.

Tanya watched him saunter away, swinging his hips, and felt an insistent twinge of approval. She liked seeing someone with energy.

There was a slam of metal against wood and both Tanya and the boy jumped.

"I'm very thirsty, very hungry, and very annoyed," said Jana petulantly, pushing her recently deposited sword belt to the side of the picnic table and straddling the bench. "Is that ready?" she asked, pointing at the porridge. "Can I have pancakes instead?"

Tanya looked from the incompetent boy to the hungry girl. This was not the Snake. This was not her inn. She needed to remember that. But just because she didn't have the Snake back—yet—that didn't mean she would choose to be useless. Being helpful kept other people at bay, kept her safe.

"Pancakes, you said?" she asked, putting effort into making her voice as pleasant as possible. She even flashed her best fake smile, the one she used to convince well-dressed ladies to spring for dessert.

But Jana was yawning and didn't even notice it. Tanya narrowed her eyes. The girl, however unusual she looked, was a common liar and a thief, neither characteristics that recommended themselves to Tanya. But she no longer had an inn, or a quill, and lacking other resources to get by, she might have to settle for—Tanya stifled an impatient sigh—a *friend*.

Tanya threw a pat of butter in the pan and began making batter for pancakes. "Jana," she said, "what is this place?"

Jana sniffed. "What do you mean? Like where are we?"

"That would be a start."

Tanya looked at Jana and saw that she was grimacing. "It's a nasty piece of miner country," said Jana. "Dull, dirty, and mean."

"What kind of mining?"

Jana began unlacing her boots, a long process considering the length. "When I was little it was chalk. Got all over everything. Then the chalk started running out and it was coal, which *really* got all over everything, but there wasn't much of it. Ah, that's better," she said, wriggling her toes, filthy and nail-broken, in the sun. "Then, a couple years ago, a gigantic salt deposit just showed up."

"We're near the ocean?" Tanya asked excitedly. She knew the Port Cities. If she could escape the camp, she'd be able to find her way.

"We're nowhere near the ocean," said Jana, and Tanya's heart sank. "That's what made the salt so valuable. Food got better. People got worse."

"And this camp? What is it?"

Jana seemed puzzled by the question. "It's the Tomcat's compound."

Tanya flipped a pancake onto a plate and handed it to her. "I don't know what that means," said Tanya.

Jana motioned for Tanya to hand her the syrup. Tanya complied and the other girl poured a glob of it directly into her mouth before cramming the pancake in whole.

After swallowing, she said, "The Tomcat's a criminal. I guess you know that."

"Yes," answered Tanya dryly.

"But the thing is, he's a *master* criminal. He's no pickpocket; he comes up with the really big scams. Other gangs contract with him for a piece of the pie. The gangs come and go, but there's always a stable."

Tanya wrinkled her forehead. "This is a *guild*? A guild of criminals?"

Jana smiled and nodded.

Tanya stared at the enigma in front of her. Who was this girl who smiled at a guild of blackguards? "You said 'when you were little,'" said Tanya suddenly. "You're from here?"

Jana came up next to her and snatched the half-cooked bacon, still dripping with fat, off the stove. "Depends on what you mean by 'here,'" she said, juggling the sizzling meat from fingertip to fingertip. "This isn't really a place. This is just Chalk Deposit 36. Nobody ever bothered to name it. Until the salt."

"What's it called now?" asked Tanya, putting herself between Jana and the open flames.

"People call it 'the White.'"

Tanya poured herself a cup of coffee. "Your parents were miners, then?"

Jana perched on the table. "My mom was. I don't remember her. My dad wasn't. I was born in Chalk Deposit 36. But we went back and forth a lot."

"From here and where?"

"Bloodstone."

Tanya spat out her coffee. "You went back and forth from the chalk mines to *Bloodstone*? As a child?"

Jana shrugged nonchalantly and licked the bacon grease off her palms.

Tanya was shocked. "What does your dad do?"

Jana pulled a knife and whetstone from her belt and started sharpening. "A little of this, a little of that." She noticed Tanya staring and stopped sharpening for a moment. "He had to take me with him. What was he supposed to do? Just leave me in the woods?"

An image of a woman's back, tall and straight as an oak in Tanya's memory, as she strode away from her into the woods washed over her. "I suppose not," she said stiffly, turning away.

"'Course, there would have been more convenient cities than Bloodstone for him to just up and die in."

"I'm sorry for your loss."

"Nah, he never cared much about life and death. I tried not to let it bother me and it's been a good four or five years now anyway."

Tanya snuck a look behind her shoulders. "How old are you?"

Jana furrowed her brow. "Not sure. Seventeen, maybe?"

Tanya turned all the way and really studied the girl kicking her feet off the table. She was lithe, but her shoulders were broad and muscled. Her hands were callused and filthy, but the fingers were dexterous, delicate. Her clothes were a hodgepodge and clearly designed for a boy, but they all fit well and were clean and well made.

This was someone who knew how to take care of herself—who knew how to make herself useful to survive. Tanya felt a flicker of recognition.

She was still thinking of the right thing to say when Riley came around the corner and hollered, "Jaybird! Tomcat wants you."

Jana jumped off the table. "Gotta go."

"Oh. Sure."

Jana hesitated. "I'm sorry, by the way. That you got stuck here. But, hey, it's not so bad. Tomcat will let you go once we get to Bloodstone. He does what he says he'll do. Mostly. And Riley was right to take you out of those woods. You don't know how to fight, do you?"

Tanya folded her arms. "I can take care of myself."

The other girl sighed. "Do you know how to throw a punch? How to use a knife?"

Tanya stayed silent. Jana shook her head. "You wouldn't be that safe around the White these days. Not by yourself."

Tanya turned back to the dishes. "I might surprise you," she muttered. She knew how well she could manage by herself.

# Chapter

**A**ll day Tanya worked hard, scrubbing old barrels and filling them with portioned provisions, handing out sandwiches, drilling Lukas on egg cookery (the boy might as well get passable at the trade), setting a stew to slow cook for the camp's dinner—but, most importantly, she worked on crafting the most decadent and beautifully plated dinner she could manage.

When a towheaded man, broad shouldered and silent, showed up and Lukas started to dole out the stew, Tanya yanked him away. Then she flashed a smile and presented the silent man with a tray. "This is the one you want," she told him. He took it from her without meeting her eyes. She followed him for a few steps, making sure that she hadn't mistaken him. When he turned toward Uncle Tommy's tent, she relaxed.

Even under duress, Tanya never ignored the help.

When it started to get dark and nothing had happened, she began to worry. What if she had misjudged the Tomcat? What if the lackey had waited to serve it until it was too cold? What if one of the dishes was underseasoned?

But then Riley came jogging around the corner and cupped his hands around his mouth to shout at her. "Hey, tavern maid. Boss wants you."

She breathed a sigh of relief.

Tanya entered the boss's tent to a slow clapping of hands. Uncle Tommy sat at the same low table as that morning, in front of him the remains of the dinner Tanya had prepared for him. She was pleased to see that those remains were very scant indeed.

"Well, you have my attention, Tanya," said Uncle Tommy, beaming. "That was an excellent meal. I haven't eaten so well on the road, ever."

She stood up straight. "I know."

Uncle Tommy sat back and put his hands on his stomach. "Duck confit with a red wine sauce. Potatoes gratin with what I have to assume was a cheese you made yourself, because I don't remember buying mascarpone. Garlic-roasted asparagus tips. A cream of mushroom soup. Fresh bread with garlic butter. And a crème brûlée with caramel sauce for dessert. I don't know *how* you managed a brûlée in that kitchen."

Tanya bent her head in a curtsy. "I'm glad my lord was pleased."

He smiled. "I'm not a 'my lord.' Tell me, Tanya: Why did you bother?"

She looked down in a way she hoped seemed demure. "Only to show my gratitude for your protection in my passage through the White."

"It's our pleasure. It seems as though you're more than going to earn your keep."

Tanya looked up through her lashes. That's what she was waiting for. "I'm glad you've found me valuable," she said. "I hope to prove I'm worth more than my keep."

There was a silence. Then Uncle Tommy laughed. "So, the tavern wench wants a tip, huh?"

She shrugged. "I need to get to the Capital. Getting dumped in Bloodstone isn't going to help me get there. I have no idea how long it takes to get from here to Bloodstone, and I wanted to make sure you knew what I could do if properly motivated."

"And what made you think I would even entertain this request?"

Tanya smiled. "I watched you this morning. A man with your fine taste doesn't ignore a good meal in the middle of a chalky brush with just camp provisions."

"And you were determined not to fly under my radar. You wanted to be a part of my comforts."

"I'm a waitress, sir. I know we're invisible to most powerful men. But I can't afford to be. I have to get to the Capital."

He nodded approvingly. "Well thought out."

"So . . . do we have a deal? Do I get payment at Bloodstone? Real payment?"

He chortled. "Oh, absolutely not."

"But . . ."

Uncle Tommy waved his hand, brushing away her protest. "My girl, you've forgotten a very important variable. I have numerous fighting men with very good weapons at my disposal. You are utterly defenseless—you don't even have proper boots! I could simply *force* you to continue working in that kitchen. For the rest of your life, if I wanted to. Now, don't look so disappointed, Tanya. You are an excellent cook and you've been very bold. I respect skill, and I respect initiative. I will most certainly recommend you to the inn at Bloodstone; or, if you choose to stay on with us, at the tavern in the first town you like. In the meantime, I give you my word that no one in this camp will harm you. Fair enough?"

Tanya was deflated. But she had no choice. She nodded, watching the Smiling Snake dissolve into sand in her mind's eye.

Uncle Tommy nodded, satisfied. "Good, now go to bed. That boy, the incompetent one—"

"Lukas," she said dully.

"Yes! Lukas. He'll show you where you can sleep. Get some rest. I eat breakfast early, as you know, and after tonight my expectations are high."

Tanya turned to go, but stopped when she saw a familiar glimmer on the desk. She asked, wistfully, "Are you enjoying your new toy?"

"Pardon?"

She turned to him. "The quill. I hope it's all you wanted it to be. It's cost me enough."

His face got very still. "It's a work in progress."

Tanya inched closer to the desk. The quill was lying askew across an ink-blotted parchment. She craned her neck around to study it further.

It was a mess.

Someone—Uncle Tommy, she surmised—had started, very modestly, by writing "GOLD" in an elegant, looping script, large and confident across the paper. Clearly that hadn't worked the way he wanted it to, because he had followed it by "SILVER" in slightly hastier handwriting, down and down the list of valuable substances until there were nothing but angry scribbles.

Tanya looked over at the quill. It appeared tired. It was pulsing with a faint, white light. She felt a strange urge to stroke it, as if it could be soothed.

"What do you think you're doing?"

Uncle Tommy was standing up. She had never seen him standing before. She dropped her hand.

"Nothing," she said, stepping away. "Just . . . saying hi."

"Good night, Tanya. Riley, escort her back to the kitchens. *Now.*"

A firm hand gripped her by the elbow and steered her toward the exit. She shook it off. "It's not my fault he hasn't figured out a system yet," she grumbled as Riley pushed her forward. "No need to get rough."

"Stop!" Tanya and Riley both stopped in their tracks. The Tomcat strode toward the desk and looked at the paper. Then he looked back at Tanya. He held out his hand. "Bring me her apron."

Riley's hands immediately went to her waist. "I beg your pardon," exclaimed Tanya. "I'll remove my own clothing, thank you."

But the apron was already in the Tomcat's hands. He waved a hand at Tanya. "Take her away."

❧

The next morning, Tanya was begrudgingly mixing strawberries into a brown-sugar-infused whipped cream for biscuits, when the serving lackey turned up at her table.

"I'm not done with his breakfast yet," she told him, frowning. "I can get you some porridge."

The lackey shook his head and held out his arm. She stared at it. "Biscuits take a certain amount of time to bake," she explained. "I can't magically make them appear."

The silent lackey shook his head and again thrust his arm out at her. He inclined his head behind him. She followed the gesture. "He wants me now? With or without his breakfast?" The lackey nodded.

She found Uncle Tommy sitting up at his desk. Yesterday he had been scrupulously groomed and nattily attired, but not this morning. His hair was disheveled and greasy, as if he'd spent the night riling it up, and he was wearing the same vest and shirt as he had been wearing the night before, and both were hanging open and wrinkled. He was scowling and his eyes were bloodshot.

"Are you not feeling well?" asked Tanya bluntly. "I have many talents, but I'm not an all-purpose domestic machine. I have no skill at healing."

Uncle Tommy pointed at the chair sitting opposite him. "Sit," he ordered.

She sat. The chair was considerably lower than Uncle Tommy's.

He pointed. "Pick that up."

She followed his finger. He was pointing at the quill, which was lying quiet and dormant, an ordinary white feather.

Tanya looked at the feather and saw her ticket to the Capital. To the Queen and Council. To the Smiling Snake. Her ticket back to the only thing she wanted. Her fingers trembled.

"Now!"

Tanya grabbed at the quill and held it tightly. The quill shivered in her grasp, the spines tickling her palm.

"What now?" she asked.

He reached under the table and retrieved a wadded-up piece of cloth. He threw it at her. "Tell me what I'm looking at," he demanded.

Tanya smoothed out the cloth to find her apron. It was wrinkled and dirty, but the map shone out dark and clear, without a single smudge. Her eyes drifted across the desk and saw that the scratched-out, misbegotten demands had multiplied overnight. Discarded paper cascaded onto the floor like driftwood after a shipwreck.

She looked at Uncle Tommy. "You couldn't get the quill to work?"

His fists tightened into an even thicker coil and Tanya heard a gasp from behind her. She had made a mistake.

Uncle Tommy stared at her and then drew a very sharp dagger from his belt. He pointed it at her. "Tanya," he began. He seemed to reconsider his positioning and moved forward in his chair, leaning over his desk so that the knife's point was less than a centimeter away from Tanya's wrist.

"Tanya, are you listening?" She nodded, her eyes on the knife. "I'm betting that you're a girl who hates to waste time. Riley gave me a full report of your campsite. I know it matches where he found you on that map. I know that on your way to my camp, he passed an irrigated wheat field that wasn't there when he left, but *was* very clearly marked on your map. You made the quill work and you're going to show me how. Or you're going to be very sorry."

Tanya didn't move. She couldn't stop staring at that knife. She had thought she could control this situation, as she had controlled every situation since she was seven years old, but this was very clearly not the Smiling Snake.

The thought occurred to her: Maybe the Snake was the only thing she was *capable* of controlling.

"Tanya." She ripped her eyes away from the knife and forced them to refocus on Uncle Tommy's stormy face. "Do we have an understanding?"

She nodded.

He thrust a fresh piece of parchment at her. She felt the quill tingle in her fingers. They hovered above the paper.

She hesitated. "What exactly do you want me to do?"

"At this point, I don't really care. Conjure anything. Conjure gold if you want to make me really happy with your job performance."

She frowned. "I can't just conjure gold out of thin air. That's not how this works. At least, I don't think it is." Tanya thought for a moment and bit her lip. "Can I see what you were working on?"

"Why would you want to see that?"

She sighed. "I've used this quill exactly once. I want to see what didn't work. No offense," she added quickly.

He studied her through narrow eyes and then pushed a stack of scribble-covered papers at her.

"Thank you." Tanya bent over the desk to examine the failed attempts.

He had gone wrong from the very beginning.

Tanya perused the list of demands to the universe listed on that paper. *Give me fifty gold pieces. Give me a diamond the size of my head. Give me a bucket of the finest wine in Lode.*

"Give me, give me, give me," she muttered under her breath. Where did he think it was all going to come from?

She grasped the quill more firmly and brought it to her mouth so that she could lick the tip, this time a slight shock rippling through her tongue at the touch.

The feather sparked, throwing out rainbow specks of light so bright they cast shadows on the dim tent walls. She put the fresh piece of parchment on top of the rejects and wrote: *Draw me a map thirty miles wide. Put me in the center.*

The ink soaked into the paper, disappearing. Then it exploded, energetically spreading itself across the paper, forming lines and landmarks, as if it had been waiting for just that request.

*It was waiting for me.* Tanya quickly dismissed the thought as fanciful. Jobs get done. The job doesn't wait for the right person.

She got to work. She surveyed the landscape. She saw a lot of chalk and a lot of salt, just as Jana had said. But remembering how dangerous the salt deposit had made the White, she decided it was best not to mess with it and moved farther out.

*There*. Just over the river near the kitchens was a small ravine. In the ravine was a tiny thread of copper. It was too small for anyone to bother mining. She took the quill and marked an X at the copper ore. Then she drew it to her, marking the parchment with an arrow when it got to the center.

There was a *pop* and *whoosh*, and then the ground rumbled beneath them. With a crack, the earth underneath them was thrust up and out, knocking several men off their feet, nearly overturning the table. A ripple of something solid materialized under one of the carpets.

Uncle Tommy stood up. Tanya kept working. She pored over the map, looking for junkoff. She found it in a nearby town called Loomstead: A snowstorm had broken out. Tanya carefully redirected it into the river next to the camp's kitchens.

There was a splash in the distance. Tanya nodded and put the quill down. She pushed the piece of paper across the table. "Here you go."

Uncle Tommy didn't answer. He was staring at the carpets. He made a gesture. Riley leapt forward and began peeling back the carpets, pushing back furniture, piling up pillows. Eventually, they cleared the way to reveal a dirty green column of what looked like moldy rock.

Tanya frowned and bent over to examine it. "That's copper, right?" she asked. "I'm no miner."

"It's copper ore," said Riley, looking stunned. "You have to extract the copper, but . . . it's in there."

Uncle Tommy stepped around the desk and crouched to examine the ore. He looked up.

"Explain how you did this."

Tanya shifted nervously at his tone. She didn't want to insult the armed and powerful man who had spent the night attempting to do what she had accomplished in a matter of minutes. But it was really so simple.

"It's just a matter of organization, I think," she said finally. "The quill doesn't create things, or at least, I haven't gotten it to do that. But it can sort of . . . rearrange raw materials. The thing is that if you move one thing, something else goes weird—it's like the junkoff!" Tanya got excited, suddenly realizing the implication. "That's why those brainless magicians cause junkoff! They don't know how to fill in the blanks they make, or make the junkoff useful. They can't even know where it is. None of them are organized enough." The quill shivered, rolling over on its own. Tanya put her fingers on it. "This is an excellent tool."

"You're probably right," Uncle Tommy said mildly.

Tanya looked up. She hadn't even noticed him moving, but he was settling comfortably into his breakfast nook, looking perfectly calm and amiable again.

Tanya picked up the map. "Did you want to keep this? It's a fairly simple system. I just stumbled into it."

Uncle Tommy turned to the serving lackey. "Go get some porridge from the boy. I'm ready for breakfast."

"The biscuits should be ready by now," Tanya interjected automatically. Then she shook her head. "I'm sorry, you don't even want to look at this? Isn't that why I'm here and not in the kitchen?"

Uncle Tommy poured a cup of coffee. "Oh, you don't work in the kitchen anymore."

"Excuse me? You're firing me from the kitchen? *Me?*"

He sighed. "Unfortunately, I am. It's a shame, really. You're an excellent cook and a very funny waitress. That tavern you ran away from must have been a first-rate place."

"I didn't run away from it. I'm going to the Capital so I can get *back* to my tavern."

"Well. Whatever. *That,*" he said, pointing at the quill, "is your new job."

Tanya was quickly installed in a small tent adjacent to Uncle Tommy's. This one was just a small circle of canvas, tall enough for Tanya to stand up straight, but just barely, and just wide enough to fit a bedroll, a desk, and a chair.

It was only when she was left alone with a lantern, a stack of parchment, and the quill that Tanya realized how much trouble she was in.

She had been conscripted into being a thief. And she had never met a queen, but she was pretty sure that queens and their councils weren't enthusiastic about granting the requests of thieves.

There was a guard outside the front of her tent, so Tanya got on her hands and knees and crawled out the back.

She got about five feet before she was caught by three men with clubs, all about twice her height, three times her weight in solid muscle, and bearing the red-and-black patch that marked them as sworn to Uncle Tommy. Before she knew it, she was back in the little tent at the little desk. Except this time, both her ankles were tied together with a thick rope staked into the ground with an iron bolt.

"Tanya, I really don't see why all this fuss is necessary," said Uncle Tommy in a weary voice, while Tanya struggled and kicked.

"Oh, you don't, do you?" Tanya gave so ferocious a kick that she threw herself off the chair and landed bottom-first in the dirt. Riley unsuccessfully stifled a giggle and Tanya shot him her most dangerous glare.

Uncle Tommy also sent a *tsk* in Riley's direction. He stepped forward and offered his arm to Tanya, but she shook him off, struggling to her feet by herself.

"I am not a thief," she said hotly. She sat down with as much dignity as she could muster.

Uncle Tommy sighed. "Fine. So, I've done you a *favor* by tying you to a stake in the ground. You're not a thief, you're my hostage." He smiled, and Tanya looked away, sniffing primly. "Chin up, my girl," he continued. "And find me some gemstones." He nodded to Riley and left the tent. Riley gave her an apologetic shrug and followed his boss.

Tanya was left alone. "I am a tavern maid," she whispered. "I am not a thief." *Except for that one time when you stole a horse*, she thought. *And a quill.*

The quill was lying dormant again, as if it had decided that with all the commotion, it might as well take a nap. Tanya sighed and picked it up. At her touch, it immediately sparkled to life, twitching and throwing off sparks.

Tanya sighed again. The damn thing seemed to like her.

Great.

# Chapter

**W**ithin minutes Tanya got a paper cut. It was a deep slice, and in the shock of the moment, she fumbled with the quill, getting blood all over it as it dripped down her arm.

"Oh, come on," Tanya moaned out load. Not only did it hurt, now she was covered in a disgusting mess she couldn't clean up, chained down as she was.

Tanya hated not being able to clean a mess.

There was a sucking sound from the desk. Tanya looked down and saw that her blood was absorbing—disappearing—*into* the quill.

"That's a thought," she said, staring at the tidy little operation. She picked up the quill and a fresh piece of paper. She drew the outline of her bloody arm and then drew a little starburst labeled "Me." The drawing was rough, but it was undeniably of an arm. She drew a quick dash to signify the cut. She drew a crude feather.

She wrote *Blood spilled* next to the paper cut and an arrow connecting it to the quill.

Tanya watched as the blood lifted off her skin and sleeve in a sheer, red vapor and settled into the quill like mist into the sea.

Soon, the quill felt fused to her fingers, feeding the cells there with energy and heat, so that even when Tanya was so tired that her brain was ready to turn off, her fingers urged her to keep going, to keep scratching out questions and lists, to keep flipping over new sheets of parchment.

To keep learning.

Under Tanya's directions, the quill could not only make maps, it could also lay out interactive charts of the resources available in any given piece of the landscape. Very soon, Tanya had found, cut, and extracted a specimen the size of her fist from the ruby deposits in the caverns of Mount Beryl, a fog-enshrouded, rolling mass of rock near the north shore of the Smelt Sea.

She could have stopped there. Perhaps she should have stopped there. But that wasn't all the quill did.

It started when Tanya came across a phrase she didn't understand: "diatomaceous earth." She searched her brain, but she was starting to realize that the stores of information she kept up there were limited at best.

Tanya had never truly been to school. Froud had taught her to read and write. She knew how to measure and how to make the accounts come out even. But she had never been taught anything that prepared her for life outside the Smiling Snake. She had never learned anything that wasn't secondhand, picked up from a barfly.

Confronted by her own ignorance, Tanya thought about how she had discovered the quill's mapmaking abilities in the first place. Licking the quill as she had done before, she wrote: *What is diatomaceous earth?*

The ink absorbed into the paper and then spat itself back out in the form of words:

*A white- to light-colored powder that is produced by crushing the sedimentary rock known as diatomite. It can be used as a filler in building materials, as a filter, as a drying agent, an absorbent, and as a mild abrasive.*

After that it was off to the races. Anytime Tanya encountered something new, she could ask a question: *Is it safe for people to swim in the river around the Mount Lia Volcano? Does jasmine have medicinal properties? How many girls sailed on merchant ships out of the Western Ports last year?*

Tanya didn't like being a thief, but she did like learning. Which, come to think of it, was something of a surprise. Tanya hadn't ever felt the need to learn anything the Snake couldn't teach her. She never thought she would be able to use it.

Two days later, Riley entered the tent with a blanket and a clay jug, but stopped short and wrinkled his nose.

Tanya wrinkled hers right back. "I'm aware of the smell," she said archly. "It happens when a girl is chained to a chair for several days and wears the same muddy dress for a week."

Riley looked at the jug. "I was going to give you this beer," he said, stepping closer to the desk. "But I don't think I want to add that to the . . . um . . . bouquet."

"Give me that." Tanya grabbed it. She was thirsty. After taking a long gulp, she wiped her mouth and ordered him, "Tell the Tomcat that I require soap and a change of clothes."

Riley gave her a warning look. "He doesn't really like it when people make demands."

Tanya smiled. She picked up the ruby and held it out. Riley's eyes went wide. "Bring him this. We'll see."

Ninety seconds after Riley left her, the ruby in hand, the silent lackey was untying her legs and Tanya was free to stand, to stretch, to walk.

She stepped out of the tent and took a long, deep breath, letting the breeze brush the little hairs on her arms, feeling the skin around her chest and neck prickle. Then her nature asserted itself and she practically ran to the kitchen.

She found Lukas cleaning up a mass of broken china and Jana perched on the picnic table, munching an apple and laughing.

"I need soap," Tanya announced. The two looked up at her in surprise. "What?" she asked. "Does soap not exist in this camp?"

Jana hopped off the table with wide eyes. "Where were they stashing you?" she asked.

"I was in the little tent near the Tomcat's," said Tanya. "Did you think I just disappeared into thin air?"

Jana kicked the ground. "I worried the Tomcat had sold your contract. Or that you had tried to escape. That would have . . . annoyed him."

"You thought he had me *killed?*"

Jana looked up at her, quickly meeting her eyes, before shrugging and looking away. "I hoped not," she said, tossing her hair in poorly feigned nonchalance. "But you never know." Her eyes narrowed and she nodded at something behind Tanya. "What did you do to deserve them?"

Tanya whirled around. There were two men lurking several feet behind her, both covered in knives.

Tanya turned back to her. "I have to wash," she said, ignoring the question. "If I have to have an armed guard, can't it be you?"

Jana pulled her own blade from a sheath strapped around her hips. "Let me see what I can do," she said, and walked toward the other guards.

One arm-wrestling victory later, Tanya stood neck deep in the river, enjoying the quiet. Just to the east of the camp, the river dipped into the woods, forming a roundish bowl of clear, still water. Tanya dipped her head back and squished her toes farther into the damp sand, letting the water flow over her closed eyes.

"You know that if you try to escape, I have to catch you, right?"

Tanya lifted her head. "What?"

Jana was sitting on a boulder, sharpening a knife on a flat red rock. "I wanted to warn you." Jana smiled cheerfully. "Just because we're friends doesn't mean I won't knock your head against a tree trunk if I have to."

Tanya knew Jana to be perfectly serious. And yet, unaccountably charmed, she found herself smiling back.

Tanya kicked out her legs. She needed to move.

"Hey, Jana?" she said, looking around the bend in the river, where she saw a lily patch.

"What's up?"

"Understanding that I'm both naked *and* fully cognizant of your threat of bodily harm—"

"Just stay in sight."

Tanya blinked. "How did you know what I was going to ask?"

Jana shrugged. "You've been in a tent so small I didn't notice it for five days. It's tough for a strong person when they're not allowed to move. I've been there."

Tanya shivered at the implications, visions of the firepits of Bloodstone dancing in her head. She plunged her head into the water and stretched out her arms, propelling herself through the river with one sharp kick. By the time she emerged into the sunshine, she was deep in the center of the lily patch.

If she turned around, she could just see Jana through the trees, still perched on her boulder. She waved and, squinting, saw the other girl give a slight nod.

"Shhhhhhh."

Tanya turned her head. There was no one there. There were just the lilies and a few scrubby trees stubbornly clinging to life in the sandy soil.

"Shhhhh. Shhhhh."

Tanya kicked around, whipping to look at the other, equally empty side of the riverbed. A robin poking at a lavender plant was the only sign of animation. "I'm sorry, did a bird just shush me?" she asked.

The robin exploded into a cloud of feathers. Tanya screamed and ducked back underwater.

When she came back up for air, the bird was gone. In its place was a hawk-nosed boy about her own age, still waiting for his last growth spurt. His gray scholar's robe drowned him, puddling around his wrists and ankles.

"Who are you?" she asked, just as he asked, "Where's my quill?"

"*Your* quill? Wait a minute," said Tanya, studying his face, his beautifully woven but plain gray robe, the delicate points of his shoulder blades poking through the cloth. "I've seen you before. You're that little scholar who nearly ran me off the road in Ironhearth."

The boy sniffed. "I'm older than you are, madam."

She snorted. "Maybe, but for your all your education, clearly no one's ever taught you how to hem." She treaded water until she was a little closer. "Did you follow me from Ironhearth?"

"No. I followed her." He nodded in Jana's direction.

"Because you thought *she* had the quill." Tanya started moving the pieces around in her head. "And she didn't catch you because you were disguised as a bird. Hey, what kind of scholar are you, anyway?" she asked, suddenly suspicious. "I didn't recognize the sigil on your hat."

Still looking away from her, the boy drew himself up to his full height. "I am a senior apprentice of the Royal College of Aetherical Manipulation."

"Oh wonderful," she sighed. "You're one of *those* amateurs."

"Excuse me, I am not," he said hotly. "I am diametrically opposed to those amateurs mucking up the aetherical field. That quill is ours."

"Oh, I see. Just because you imagine yourself particularly *fancy* magic users, you think you get to have it!"

"No, we get to have it because one of our scholars made it!"

Tanya still had her mouth open, the better to spit out a quick retort, but shut it when her tongue stalled out.

The boy scholar seemed pleased by this outcome, because he allowed himself a grim smile. "That quill has the power to change the world and that power belongs with me—I mean, *us*. The scholars. The Royal College of Aetherical Manipulation."

Tanya raised an eyebrow. Something wasn't adding up. "The *Royal* College. So aren't you owned by the Queen and Council?"

"We were commissioned by the Queen and her Council as a public good, but our work is independent and without jurisdiction."

"Tanya, I'm hungry!" Jana called out. "Let's go!"

She turned toward Jana. "Be right there," she called back.

The boy scrambled toward her on the riverbank, reaching out for her, grappling for the prize. "Give me the quill," he urged.

She gave him a withering glance. "I don't have it on me. I'm *taking a bath.*"

The boy furrowed his eyes in concentration and feathers started to poke through his robe, jumping into existence like popcorn on a stovetop.

"Tonight then. Behind your tent," he said, his voice weak and reedy. He coughed out a scrap of birdsong and when he lifted his hand to his mouth, three of his fingers had been replaced by thin, scaly talons.

"Tanya, now!" ordered Jana.

"Fine!" yelled Tanya, and ducked underwater, swimming hard, leaving the boy/bird squawking behind her. She eventually resurfaced on the other side of the riverbend. Jana was stretching on her rock and a bird was flying overhead.

Tanya looked at the boulder where she had laid her dress to dry, but it was empty.

"I cut it up into scraps." Jana held up a tidy ribbon made up of Tanya's dress—her only dress, since she'd lost her luggage in the flight from Ironhearth.

"No good for traveling," said Jana nonchalantly, pocketing the rags. "Might work for bandages though, now that it's clean. I brought you something of mine to wear."

Tanya eyed the other girl, who was clad in tight leather. She doubted that she would be able to cram herself into such an outfit.

Luckily, it seemed that Jana had taken that into account. The pants were a wide-legged and loose gray muslin, cinched at the waist with a drawstring. The blouse, brown and made of canvas, was a little bit tighter, but after Tanya had donned the plain white shift it was folded with, she found that she could loosen the laces on top without sacrificing any modesty.

She put her hands on her waist, where it was tightest.

"It's good to be snug there." Jana had come up behind her. "It keeps you upright and alert. I got you this belt, too." She held out a wide swath of black leather, bookended by tarnished brass buckles. "Here, let me help. The snaps can be a bit tricky."

Jana wrapped the leather around her waist. Tanya felt her fingers through the blouse as a soft, insistent tickle. It pinged a strange answering pang in her abdomen. She had never so much as had someone button her cuff or braid her hair before. There had never been anyone to do it. And now this strange girl, who the first time they had met had held her at sword-point, was carefully fastening her belt.

Tanya turned around and met the other girl's eyes. "Now you look like a proper road thief," said Jana, smiling. Tanya felt herself smile back without having to remind herself to.

"Look at you!" exclaimed a male voice behind them. "Jana, what have you done?"

Tanya turned to face Riley and Jana's hands fell away. His arms were crossed and his smile sweet, and that ping in her stomach kept humming.

Tanya put her hand on her hip and posed. "Don't like my new look, horse thief?" she asked, unfamiliarly good feelings suffusing her body.

He laughed. "Jana! She was respectable before. Now you've made her look like one of us!" He stepped forward and slung an arm around Jana's shoulders. "Dinner's ready. Hungry, ruffians?"

Jana, her cheeks rosy, punched him in the shoulder and ducked out from under his arm. "Always," she said, throwing a backward glance at Tanya. "Don't listen to him. You look natural as fleas," she said before running off to the kitchen.

Tanya furrowed her brow. "Was that a compliment, do you think?" she asked Riley.

He looked her up and down, still smiling. "I'd imagine so," he said, grabbing her hand and pulling her after Jana. "I particularly like the belt."

Tanya let him hold her hand all the way to the kitchen. It was the longest anyone had ever touched her. Ever.

# Chapter

**A**fter dinner, she made her way back to her tent.

It was a clear night, which, considering she was going to a clandestine meeting with a wizard, was bad luck. And the firepit in the center of camp was still blazing, throwing light everywhere. Anyone could see her creeping about.

She stepped into the tent and peered through the back flap, but something was blocking her vision. She frowned and pushed the flap back—

—and squealed as a fury of feathers and tiny, sharp claws careened into her face.

"Owww!" cried Tanya, batting away the increasingly frantic robin. The bird trilled back, equal parts indignant and panicked, as it flapped around her head, getting its claws tangled in her hair.

Tanya grabbed at the bird, in a futile attempt to extricate it. "What are you doing?" she hissed. "Don't you know how to use that body?"

The robin trilled in a manner that Tanya believed herself equal to interpreting. She sniffed primly and yanked her hair back once and for all. "Well, you don't have to be rude about it," she said.

The bird flapped its way to the ground and exploded in a burst of blue down, revealing a panting boy sprawled across the bedroll.

He glared at her and opened his mouth, but Tanya swiftly clasped her hand over it.

"Don't yell," she said seriously. "There are armed thugs outside this tent and somehow I don't think they would respect the rank of trainee magician, Royal College or no."

The boy's eyes flickered to the tent flap. He nodded and Tanya removed her hand.

When she did and stepped away, she revealed the quill lying on the desk: dormant but still eye-devouringly, glowingly white.

The boy and Tanya locked eyes and, for a moment, the world stood still. Then they both leapt forward, grabbing for the quill.

Tanya was nearer. She threw herself across the desk and scooped it up before the boy even hit his palms against the wood.

He snatched at the quill in her hand, but he wasn't fast enough. Tanya had already tucked it between her breasts and he grabbed air.

"No one's ever fast enough," Tanya muttered.

The boy looked ready to cry with frustration. "What do you want with it, anyway?" he asked.

"I'm not keeping it to hurt you, boy." Tanya picked through her pockets and found a currycomb, the kind meant to brush a horse. Well, it would at least help. "What's your name, lad?" she asked in her kindest, firmest voice. The kind that made it a moot point that she was addressing a boy roughly her own age as "lad."

He folded his arms. "Rollo," he told her.

"Rollo." She smiled at him. "You are covered in dust and feathers." She tossed him the comb.

He caught it awkwardly against his chest and his lips curled in horror when he saw the state of his robe. This was clearly not a boy who liked to roll around in the dirt. How had he managed to turn himself into a bird, such a wild creature?

"You're a little more presentable now," she said as Rollo finished brushing himself off. "But that only solves one problem. We can't leave this tent unobserved, so unless you can turn me into a squirrel or something"—she paused, remembering his skin bursting with feathers—"no, never mind, even if you believe yourself capable of doing it, I think I'll take my chances with the Tomcat's men."

Rollo tossed her back the comb. "I wasn't planning on performing an animal glamour on you, no. You wouldn't know how to maintain it anyway."

Tanya rolled her eyes. "So, what was your plan?"

Rollo smiled. "Get behind me," he told her.

Taken aback by the confidence in his voice, she obeyed. He reached into his sleeve and pulled out a long, thin, cylindrical instrument. It was a bleached white color, like coral or bone.

Rollo twitched the wand between his thumb and his forefinger and a low hum filled Tanya's ears. She looked closer at the wand and blinked.

It was vibrating.

Rollo stepped toward the back of the tent and Tanya followed. He pointed the wand at the gap in the canvas and moved it in a tight, counterclockwise circle. He did it again, faster and tighter, then drew his elbow back, muttering words that Tanya couldn't quite make out.

The sliver of the night she could see from inside the tent unfurled itself from reality and, twisting into a spiral, retracted into Rollo's wand, leaving an exact replica in its place—or rather, she realized, Rollo had somehow *made* a replica of the image of the night and sucked it into his wand.

Tanya held her breath. Rollo twisted the copy of the world he had extracted around his wand like a ribbon and then, with a quick flick of the wrist and a bended knee, he shot it all back out again, throwing it around himself and Tanya as if it were a blanket, or a cape.

Tanya dropped her jaw. Rollo, the whiny harassment of a boy she had dismissed as a consummate amateur and sycophant to fools, had somehow made a copy of the world and thrown it over them. She could see through it, but it was like looking through fishing net.

"Can they . . ." She swallowed and tried again. "Are we . . . invisible?"

She had heard a story about people who could cover themselves in a cloak of the world. A young pirate with puppy-dog eyes and deliciously pouting lips had spent an evening at her bar in the Snake, telling her tales from his travels. He also told her about water dragons that made themselves look like beautiful human women to lure men to their dooms; about a forest of sentient trees and their midnight Council meetings; about a village of giants where there was no money, government was shared, and they mostly liked to read.

Tanya had enjoyed those stories. She had enjoyed the way he looked telling them, getting drunker every minute, his cheeks growing warm and rosy. She had bought him the drinks. But she hadn't *believed* any of the stories. She wasn't a fool.

Rollo looked at her over his shoulder and smiled. He put his finger in front of his lips and motioned for her to stay close. Keeping his wand arm slightly outstretched, Rollo nudged a wider opening in the tent and led them out into the smoky twilight.

Tanya twisted her head around her, daring someone to spot them. But no one even looked in her direction.

It was cooler in the woods behind the camp. And it was damp— Tanya was grateful for Jana's tall boots. "What are we doing out here?" she asked.

"You need to meet my professors. They'll explain everything."

"What?" Tanya stopped short, not having anticipated an ambush. "How many wizard-y people will there be?"

"Actually, we prefer to be referred to as 'masters,'" came a voice behind her.

She spun around just in time to see a rangy man with a flowing silver mane part the moon-shadowed forest like a curtain. He flung it to the side and the illusion shattered to the dirt, revealing ten dusty and rather fractious men of a certain age.

*No women,* Tanya noted, nodding to herself. She had gotten that feeling.

Still, if Rollo was to be believed, this company of so-called masters was authorized and bestowed with certain liberties by the Queen and Council. Tanya knew how to behave.

Tanya had been drilled in etiquette by a visiting duchess, an elderly woman with a bouffant of soft white curls and a tongue that stung like a wasp, who had stayed at the Smiling Snake for a week when Tanya was twelve. She had been alarmed at the rough manners of the girl—raised by drunks and Froud—and had taken it upon herself to teach her how to address her "betters." Tanya had loathed her at the time, but she had developed a retroactive gratitude to the old duchess. Her tutelage had come in handy.

Therefore, Tanya knew that she curtsied very well and was duly offended when she lifted her eyes and found the company of masters surveying her with distaste, except for the inevitable two who were leering.

She turned to Rollo, but he was no help. He was as deferential to the masters as she had been—even more so! His head was still bent.

Tanya turned back and saw that the silver-haired master had stepped forward. She folded her arms and tried to look as if she had every idea of what she was doing there.

"How may I help you gentlemen?" she asked.

The rangy man flinched at her voice, as if it were a mosquito flitting around his face. He took a step closer and held out his hand.

"You have something of ours," he said. It was not a question.

He was not what Tanya pictured when she thought of wizards. His skin was weather-beaten and, despite his age, his muscles were ropy and visible through his—beautifully fitted and elaborately embroidered—robe. In a different outfit, he could have passed for one of the longshoremen from Griffin's Port.

The thought gave Tanya the confidence to drop the pretense that this man was among her "betters." No, he was just another grabby, rude codger, wanting what Tanya could give him, but without acknowledging her existence.

She put one hand on her hip and used the other to flick the air in the direction of his outstretched hand. "Holding out your hand without even saying 'hello,' let alone 'please,' isn't going to get you anywhere with me," she told him, sneering. "I expected better manners of such 'exalted gentlemen' as the masters of the Royal College of Aetherical Manipulation."

Darkness flashed through the man's eyes and he tightened his hand into a fist at his side.

A different master—tall, with beautiful brown skin—stepped forward.

"Forgive us, young lady," he said, in a gentle voice that was like having butterscotch poured in your ears. He moved into a patch of moonlight and Tanya stifled a gasp at the finely chiseled bones of his face—he was as old as Froud, but that didn't stop him from being among the most gorgeous men she had ever laid eyes on.

He smiled at her and held out a palm, offering it to her. "My esteemed colleague Master Jape is simply eager. We hope to be allies in this cause, and friends, too."

Tanya, dazed by the soothing tones of his voice, put her hand on top of his. He put his other hand on top of hers and she felt nourishing warmth spread through her bones.

"I am Shan Polis, Master of the Royal College," he introduced himself, still grasping her hand between his. "Whom do I have the greatest of pleasure in addressing?"

"Tanya." She heard her name come floating out of her mouth as if drawn out by a tide. "Tanya . . . of Griffin's Port."

His eyes glittered at her, seeming to suck her into a whirlpool of black pearl. "Tanya of Griffin's Port," he said. "Wonderful. And you do have our quill?"

"Yes. It's in my shirt." Again, Tanya wasn't aware of speaking until she heard the words in her own voice. She shook her head a little, trying to clear the cobwebs.

"Would you give it to me?" Master Polis's voice floated into her consciousness like perfume. Her hand started to move toward her chest, where the quill was tucked neatly underneath Jana's blouse.

One of the other masters coughed and poked a hole in the fog clouding Tanya's brain. Gritting her teeth at the pain of leaving such comfort, she ripped her hand away from Polis's grasp and stepped back.

"No!" she barked. "Unless you can offer me safe passage to the Capital and an audience with the Queen and Council, this quill stays with me!" *It's not like they had been making good use of it*, Tanya thought angrily, thinking of all the junkoff they could have fixed and didn't.

The conclusion came to her then, the one that had been lurking at the corner of her mind since the moment she had licked the quill's tip:

*I'm better at this than they are.*

A wave of angry whispers rippled through the masters, and Polis, dropping the gentle expression, frowned. He was still a better-than-average-looking man, especially for his age, but the hypnosis was gone; he seemed tired and peevish.

"Enough of this," growled Master Jape, pulling a wand out of his sleeve, and muttering under his breath, violently thrust it at her.

A breeze turned into wind turned into a hurricane, blowing leaves and twigs every which way, and headed straight toward Tanya.

It hit her square in the chest.

She cried out in pain and fell to her knees. She felt the quill begin to tremble against her skin. There was a crackle and she smelled singeing cotton as the quill threw off sparks, burning through her shirt.

The wizard pulled back his wrist and the quill flew away from Tanya with a whistling shriek.

"NO."

The quill stopped midair.

The woods were silent. The masters were frozen in place, staring at the quill. It was gently rotating, sparkling pink then blue then green.

Tanya had commanded "NO." And the quill had obeyed.

She beckoned it with her forefinger. It flew through the air, landing neatly between her thumb and forefinger.

Still on her knees, Tanya eyed the quill—twinkling merrily between her fingers—with extreme suspicion and not a little bit of pride. How in all the heavens and hells had she done that?

An arrow zipped through the air, piercing the bell-shaped sleeve dangling from Jape's arm, nailing the torn scrap of gray satin to a tree.

The masters' silence broke into alarmed arguing. They twisted and turned in the night, peering through the trees for the source of the arrow.

Only Tanya knew to look up.

Sure enough, Jana was perched in a tall oak tree. She was straddling a wide branch, bracing her shooting arm against the trunk.

Jana caught Tanya's eye and shrugged a little, with a small, confused smile, as if she was as surprised to be there, shooting at a bunch of wizards, as Tanya was to see her there. Then she reached back to pull another arrow from her quiver.

She hooked it to her bow, aimed, and called out, "Up here, masters."

They looked up at her. She drew her bow and shut one eye. "Not for nothing, gents, but I have a full quiver up here," she said conversationally. "And even if I had missed in my last shot—which I didn't—I have the advantage of height, of being a small target, and years and years of killing people. I might not get all of you, but I'd get enough." Rollo gave a little yelp and Jana nodded at him. "The little cutie over there's got the right idea. What was your name, sweetie?"

He swallowed hard, but, to his credit, stood up straight. "Rollo," he told her. "Apprentice to the Royal College of Aetherical Manipulation."

"That's a real fancy title, Roly Poly. Now . . ." She let an arrow fly, which promptly landed in Rollo's boot. He howled in pain, jumping on one foot, trying to cradle the other. Jana raised her voice over the noise. "Tell your masters to get a poultice on your big toe and to get the hell away from my prisoner."

Two of the other masters, a kindly looking one with more wrinkles than Tanya would have thought possible and a tall one with a long, dark braid, swooped forward and gathered the whimpering Rollo into their arms.

"Now, Jape," said the kindly one, fixing a stare at the rangy master. "We'll live to fight another day."

He swept out his wand arm and, muttering something under his breath, began to coil a copy of the world around it, like noodles twirling on a fork. He spun it around his head and let it fall on his companions, who were clustering behind him.

They disappeared behind the curtain of night—and were gone.

Jana jumped down from the tree, landing behind Tanya with a tidy thump.

"I . . . ," began Tanya, before she was sure what she was going to say. "Thanks," she tried again, but Jana put her hand up, stopping Tanya's half-formed thought in her tracks.

"I don't know what I just saw," she said, her voice grim and low. "But I do know that it's not the kind of thing you should tell anyone. Frankly, you should be nervous that I saw it. Oh, I'm not going to tell." Tanya felt herself exhale. "Not now, anyway. But I can't promise that the day won't come when I need some leverage with the Tomcat. And there's no reason to look at me like that."

Tanya put the quill back in her cleavage, hiding it from view. "How am I looking at you, Jana?" Tanya suddenly felt—really felt— how tired she was. How long had it been since she had been running this unfamiliar race all alone? Not that she wanted someone with her, but sometimes it might have been helpful to have *anyone else* do something useful.

As Jana, she realized, just had.

The girl thief seemed to struggle to find the words. "Like I'm a . . . a slug. Or something," she finished lamely. "A girl's gotta survive. Every which way, but going belly up, a girl's gotta keep her weapons."

"Well, then." Tanya held out her hand. "Got an extra knife?"

Jana laughed, a short, choked-sounding laugh. "I do not," she said. "My knives are mine. You just hang on to that feather for as long as you can, though, and I think a knife will be the least of your enemies' problems."

The two girls stared at each other for a minute. Then Tanya looked away and straightened her hair. Out of the corner of the eye, she thought she saw Jana doing the same.

"How did you happen to be up in that tree, anyway?" she asked.

Jana laughed. "Hasn't anyone told you I'm best tracker in camp?" she said. "I recognized the bird that flew into your tent. And then when I checked inside, it was empty, so I tracked the footsteps."

Tanya stopped fidgeting with herself, unavoidably impressed. "You're kidding." She'd heard of skilled trackers, but this was beyond the scope of what Tanya had thought *anyone* could do.

But Jana was nonchalant, already moving back to camp. "The Tomcat sent me to get you, anyway," she said. "He wants you in his tent and to bring that feather."

"Why?" asked Tanya, hustling to catch up.

Jana broke into a run as they neared his tent. "Time for your first heist," she called behind her shoulder.

The quill burnt merrily against the skin of Tanya's chest.

The atmosphere in the Tomcat's tent was one that Tanya recognized. There was a great deal of conversation, but the tones were low and focused, centered around the desk where the Tomcat sat hunched over a wrinkled piece of parchment.

It reminded Tanya of the Snake, just before a voyage that no one was totally sure was a good idea.

Riley was at the Tomcat's left side. "There," he said, pointing to a spot on the parchment. "I need a way through that and we're golden."

Tanya moved closer and saw a schematic drawing, rather like a map, but of a building rather than terrain.

"Is that a *palace?*" she asked, seeing the vast array of labeled chambers under Riley's index finger.

"Yes," answered the Tomcat mildly. "You're going to rob it."

"Excuse me?"

Riley answered, "It's a targeted burglary, nothing too risky. We're after one thing: a tiara. And, this"—he pointed again—"is our only obstacle."

"You want me to remove a floor?" Tanya asked.

"Yes, of course," said the Tomcat, his voice cross. "We've been over this. If you two girls weren't late, you'd know already. Instead, you took so long, I started to worry."

That was a question and it was shot to Jana like a dagger. Tanya held her breath, but the other girl couldn't have looked more careless. She simply shrugged and plopped to the floor to unlace her boots.

"I stopped for a snack," she said, stretching out her calves with a little, satisfied groan. "The kitchen kid's biscuits have gotten a lot better in the last couple days. Oof," she exclaimed, wriggling her toes. "That's better."

The Tomcat had stopped listening at "biscuits." He turned his attention back to Tanya.

"The foundations of the castle are a mishmash of materials," he told her. "It's an old place and what with sieges, fires, bad taste, good taste correcting bad taste, etc., etc., the palace has been rebuilt over the decades in a dozen or more places. However"—he put his finger on the cellar—"I happen to know that the foundations of the cellar are pure alabaster marble. And only alabaster marble."

"Why?"

The Tomcat put on a dainty pair of spectacles and peered up at her. "Why pure alabaster marble or why do I know that?"

"Both?"

He smiled. "I know, because the duchess is a lush. She bragged to a colleague about her new wine cellar. And pure alabaster marble is currently believed to be the best environment for preserving wine."

Tanya thought back to her wine cellar at the Snake. It was a pit dug out of the earth and lined with ocean rock. It worked fine.

She shook her head. "Rich people," she muttered.

"Now, now," said Uncle Tommy, pulling his glasses down to the bottom of his nose and peering back at the map. "Mustn't envy our betters, Tanya."

She and Riley snorted at the same time, briefly catching each other's eyes. Tanya thought she recognized the expression on his face as he circled points on the parchment, the way his mouth turned up in something that wasn't quite a smile. She had seen it in the mirror often enough.

Riley stopped scribbling and tapped the map. "The tiara is here," he said, indicating a small space off the master bedroom.

Tanya leaned in. "What is that? A closet?"

Uncle Tommy answered. "It's a safe," he said. "I thought of asking you to extract the tiara itself, but I'm worried we'd get the silver, the diamonds, and the pearls in three separate piles and that wouldn't suit my purposes at all."

Riley gathered up the map and rounded Uncle Tommy's chair, landing at Tanya's other side. He rolled it out in front of her and bent over it, pointing out the various locations.

"There's an old chalk mine here," he said, pointing out a wavering line to the east of the main building. "These are underground tunnels that no one's used for years. The duchess's wine cellar is a new addition and was built right on top of this tunnel."

"OK," Tanya said, leaning in, getting interested in spite of herself. "So if I move this alabaster marble, you can just climb up. But then how do you get from here"—this time she put her finger on the cellar—"to the duchess's bedroom all the way up here?" She moved her finger to the north tower. "How do you do that without anyone seeing you?"

Riley grinned lasciviously. "Don't worry about the duchess. She'll be occupied."

"Ugh." Tanya shuddered. "Fine. But, what about servants? Guards?"

Riley looked in front of him and nodded. Tanya followed his gaze to where Jana was methodically pulling the sharp edges off of her toenails, one by one.

"I can be quiet," Riley said. "And if worse comes to worst, I have *her*."

Tanya didn't ask any more questions.

Uncle Tommy raised his head from his desk and, removing his glasses to polish them on the flannel of his blazer, peered at her through squinted eyes. "Have fun, children," he told them. "Bring me back something pretty."

# Chapter

anya was frog-marched to the stables. "Why do I have to actually *be* there when you steal the thing?" she asked, looking over her shoulder at Jana. "What am I supposed to do that I couldn't do from the relative comfort of my tent?"

Jana yawned. But Riley stopped so short that Tanya crashed into his back.

"What do you know about breaking and entering?" he asked.

"Um, nothing, thank you very much."

Riley turned around and fold his arms across his chest.

"Well, I know everything," he told her. "I know how to pick locks, I know how to drug guards, I know how to scale walls. I've been doing it over half my life. I learned to burgle before I learned to read. But what I don't know is this aetherical magic-y stuff, except for the fact that nobody really knows it. In thieving, something always manages to jam up the works. If that something in this job is your quill, I'm going to know it's happening. And that means I need the quill with me. And that means I need you with me."

The silence was only broken by Jana's burp.

"You all right, Jaybird?" asked Riley, not breaking the eye contact that he had established with Tanya. Tanya forced her eyelids to go wide, refusing to look away first—if she was being honest, not wanting to. She respected what she saw.

"I'm still starving," Jana groaned, striding past them and bumping into Tanya's shoulder, finally startling her into looking away. "I want to stop by the kitchen, even if all I do is shove a handful of sugar in my mouth."

"I swear Jana, if this job gets screwed up because you've upset your precious stomach—"

"Stretch your abilities and relax, Riley," she snapped, swinging onto the back of a black charger with the grace of an acrobat. "I'll just grab a snack from one of the guys, then." She angled the horse out of its stall and rode toward the nearest campfire, the one tended by jolly, bearded men—brothers or cousins or something. All Jana had to do was hold out her hand and scowl; they laughed and filled it with some kind of preserved donut that had been reheated by the flames and smelled of chili and pomegranate.

Riley focused on the tack shelf on the right, so for the first time Tanya had a clear glimpse of the golden mare.

She was in bad shape.

She hadn't been mistreated. That much was clear from the shining fleece of her coat and the full bag of hot mash within easy reach. There was adequate hay and a warm-looking blanket on the floor of her stall.

Tanya took a step toward the mare. She startled at the noise and turned from side to side, dazed.

"What's happened to her?" Tanya whispered, reaching out.

Riley stood next to her, frowning. "She hasn't stopped trying to escape for one second since I put her here. *And* I had to give her three times the normal dose of tranquilizers just to get her calm enough to get to camp. She hasn't slept, hasn't eaten; she's barely drunk any water. She's exhausted herself. I don't know what to do with her."

The mare was tied around the neck to a bolt in the ground, much the way Tanya had been restrained in her tent. Her hooves and calves were scratched and bruised, with little rivulets of dried blood tangling the rough hairs. Her chest was covered in bruises and her eyes were bloodshot.

Tanya took another step. "You could let her go," she said angrily. "You just needed the quill, you weren't under orders to steal a horse, too!"

Riley shook his head. "I'm *always* under orders to steal valuable horses."

Tanya put her hand on the mare's neck. The mare threw it off with a snort, not even looking at her.

"So, you do know it's me," Tanya muttered. Raising her voice, she asked, "Can I ride her to the castle? I think she could use some exercise."

"I'm sure she could. But I can't trust either one of you not to run away, so you're not getting your own horse."

She turned and saw that Riley had kitted out his chestnut horse and was all the way on the back of the saddle.

"Thanks," she said, folding her arms. "But I didn't particularly like the last ride you took me on. I'll ride with Jana."

Already on horseback, Jana charged past them and raced into the woods. "Hurry up, slowpokes," she called over her shoulder.

Tanya sighed and accepted Riley's outstretched hand. He pulled the horse around and, with a click of his tongue, they hurtled after Jana.

Tanya briefly locked eyes with the miserable golden mare. The mare blinked her liquid black eyes at Tanya and looked away, as if to say, *You're useless, I'm done with you.* Then they plunged into the woods and the mare disappeared from view.

The ground was slick with chunky, day-old mud, and the horse's hooves squelched with each footfall. An acrid, wormy smell of fallen, decaying flowers tickled her nose.

They shot through that heady muck without conversation, and Tanya was almost on the verge of falling asleep when Riley pulled up the horse and jumped off.

"We'll leave the horses here," said Riley, keeping his voice low, pulling a sheaf of blank parchment out of his pocket. "The mine shaft is a quarter mile that way into the White."

"Are we in the White now?" Tanya asked, lifting her head and curiously peering in the direction of Riley's outstretched finger.

The thick greenery of the woods stopped abruptly at the edge of the White. One minute, the world was lush, fertile, and energized with the buzz of insects and birds. But the next, all signs of life stopped in their tracks.

The White was a vast expanse of cracked, pale clay, perfectly flat except for the occasional looming accumulations of salt or chalk, dirty glittering pyramids of raw material considered too low grade to sell, and the skeletons of rickety steel and wood machines crumbling into ruins.

The terrain was bleached beyond the suggestion of color, but, in the very center, in an oasis of dense shadow, was a castle surrounded by a circular stone wall.

Jana, holding a pair of bronze binoculars up to her eyes, stepped in front of Tanya. She frowned.

"Well," she said. "I've got good news and bad news."

Riley nodded casually, as if that was only to be expected. "Dealer's choice," he told her, handing the parchment over to Tanya, who stuck it in her belt.

"The duchess's little two-seater carriage is gone, so we don't have to worry about her. But . . . do we know who the Tomcat arranged to seduce her?"

Tanya snorted. The nobility could be so common.

Riley grimaced. "It was either going to be the Baron of Carrabon's dopey second or some corps commander that he started a con on this week."

"Yeah. He chose the corps commander. And the corps commander brought his corps. And the corpsmen seem like they're looking for something to do."

"What?" Riley grabbed at the binoculars, but Jana held them out of his reach. He sighed. "Fine. I'll take your word for it. It doesn't change anything. We just. Stay. Quiet."

Jana clapped him on the back. "We know. We can do quiet." She looked at Tanya.

Tanya frowned. "I've never actually tried to be quiet," she said truthfully. "I'm usually as loud as I can be, to make sure nobody forgets to tip or that I don't walk in on someone naked." Jana giggled and Riley glared. "But yeah," she went on. "I can be quiet. How hard can it be?"

Riley just shook his head, did a final check on the horses' restraints, and headed out into the White.

Jana was about to follow when Tanya stopped her. "Can I borrow your binoculars?" Remembering her reaction to Riley's grab, Tanya used her politest voice.

Jana tossed them at her with no hesitation. Tanya just barely caught them and looked at Jana, surprised.

The thief just smiled. "They're not special," she said. "I stole them on my way out of the Tomcat's tent. I'll return them later. I just like to teach Riley manners. You know, be a civilizing agent." Laughing again, she followed Riley, slipping silently onto the tightly packed powder of the White.

Tanya put the binoculars to her eyes. She had never had the opportunity to examine a castle.

The castle's marble terraces and towers glowed faintly in the moonlight. Warm golden light, steady and even, poured out of every window, illuminating lush gardens, dotted with improbably large lilies and wild, cascading trees. The mica-spackled wall that surrounded it extended to a private pathway in the back, leading out of the White altogether.

The duchess might live smack dab in the middle of the White, but she was doing everything in her power to forget it. Frowning, Tanya moved the binoculars to the right of her castle, toward the makeshift city the actual people of the White occupied: ramshackle wooden structures, iron walkways over mine shafts, and a few feeble attempts at what looked like potato plantings. She looked to the left and saw *that* village's ugly twin. Then she looked back at the castle.

It shouldn't have even been possible to have so much life blossoming in that wasteland—at least, it shouldn't have been possible without the magic of the quill. But the quill was still safely tucked in the folds of Tanya's shirt.

It should have taken magic, but instead it only took money.

Suddenly Tanya felt a lot less guilty about stealing a tiara.

A short, ferociously windy walk later, Riley stopped. "This is it," he said, crouching down and jimmying open a circular ironbound slab of wood inset in the ground. With a grunt and a wince, he lifted the top edge with his fingertips and shoved it to the side, revealing about a foot of empty space.

The three of them looked into the hole.

"It's dark in there," commented Tanya.

"I have a lantern," answered Riley, searching the hole's perimeter with his hand.

"Do you also have a perfumed handkerchief?" asked Tanya, leaning in after him and sniffing. "It smells like rot."

Riley's hand stopped. He smiled and pulled up a ladder that must have once been wood, but now seemed more like barely solid mulch. "You're not wrong," he said with grim amusement. "That would be this." He hooked it to the edge of the hole and looked at his companions, who both appeared skeptical. "What? I had to pick an entry point that would have absolutely no miners hanging around. This was it."

Jana put her hand around the ladder's edge and squeezed. She squealed and pulled back.

"What?" asked Tanya sharply, examining the ladder. "Bugs?"

Jana held up her hand and wiggled her fingers. "Sticky," she explained.

Riley pulled a small lantern out of the leather bag strapped to his back and, carefully shielding it from the wind, lit the wick. "OK," he said with a grin, clearly in his element. "Let's go."

Precariously, step by step, he disappeared down the hole.

Tanya looked at Jana. "After you." Jana shook her head, her nose still wrinkled.

Tanya gulped and kneeled on the ground next to the ladder. Gripping the top rung—which was indeed sticky, in a dried-out extra-disgusting way, like some small beastie of the night had died on it—as tightly as she could, she stepped down into the black.

With great relief, her feet found the lower rungs of the ladder easily enough, although they were unreassuringly soft under her boots. But after a few moments of exploratory pressing, they seemed willing enough to hold her weight, and so Tanya climbed down steadily until she stepped on solid ground, let go of the ladder, and looked around the abandoned mine shaft.

Riley was about a yard into the tunnel, but the light from his lantern was enough for Tanya to make out her surroundings. A second later, Jana slid down the ladder with a whoosh, lit a match, and illuminated the rest.

In an odd way, the mine made Tanya feel as if she were home. The rough-cut, angular rock walls could have been one of the caves down by the islands to the south of Griffin's Port. The dust she kicked up as she moved forward had the same look of what she inevitably tracked into the kitchen after every trip to the fish docks in the summer. But mostly it was the smell that did it. The briny, musty air of the salt mine was the claustrophobic cousin of the air she had breathed every day of her life.

But, still, salt air or not, it was a dark, low tunnel and an abandoned worksite at that. The uneven footing was lumpy and littered with dented eating utensils and shattered glass. Tanya made sure to pick her steps very carefully.

Riley led them through the shaft at a swift and steady pace, angling himself through a spot where the wall had collapsed under its own weight and partially blocked the path. Both Riley and Jana easily slipped through the narrow opening; it took Tanya a minute to maneuver after them. She tried to simply walk through as the other two had, but she eventually had to accept the inevitable, flattening her back against the wall and inhaling to raise her rib cage, attempting to get her stomach to recede.

"As if I haven't already been subjected to enough indignity," grumbled Tanya. With a final push, she tumbled out of the crevice, scraping her arm on the jagged edge.

"Ahhh." Tanya sucked in her breath at the sting. She squinted down at her arm and was dismayed to see blood already blooming in a thick line. She quickly stopped to order the blood away with the quill, but found she didn't have to write the order. The second the quill touched her skin, the blood zipped straight up her arm and into it.

Still looking down at her now-clean arm, she walked forward and again slammed straight into Riley.

"We're here." He pointed to the ceiling above them, smooth and white, with clean, orderly angles. "Do your thing, tavern maid."

Tanya focused on the ceiling of marble and, as if answering a call, the quill woke up, sending little sparks of light skittering across the dim stone.

Tanya suddenly felt better. She might not be able to fit through a keyhole, but she seemed to know how to do *this*, and this was infinitely more useful—even if the use was burglary.

She sat down on the floor and pulled out the parchment Riley had given her. Licking the edge of the quill, she put it to the paper and started writing, the lines and words populating rapidly across the parchment.

Suddenly she frowned. "Wait. That can't be right."

"What's wrong?" Riley was by her side immediately.

Tanya started to laugh. "Your duchess either got cheated or she cheaped out. Look," she said, pointing at the diagram of the ceiling, the lines formed out of tiny bits of information. "It's mostly marble, but not completely. The middle is filler—it's a mishmash. There's concrete, brick dust, compressed driftwood." She stood up, still holding the quill and parchment, and examined the ceiling. "I can't just *remove* the ceiling. At least not quickly."

Jana kicked the wall and Riley turned green. "I'm sorry," she said hesitantly. "You couldn't have known. The Tomcat will understand."

Riley's throat bobbed up and down, like he was swallowing bile. "You've never disappointed him before," he said, his voice quiet and gravelly. "It's . . . unpleasant."

Tanya looked at Jana, who was searching the walls, her knife clutched hard in her fist. Looking for a way out.

Jana, of all people, was scared. Tanya didn't like seeing that.

So she'd have to make it work.

The ceiling was shot through with impurities, more filler than marble. She could remove each element one at the time, of course, but that would not only take forever, it would inevitably cause a wide array of junkoff. It was deeply inefficient.

That left the other option.

"Riley," she said, touching the edge of her tongue to the quill. "I'm going to stick to the plan. I'm going to remove the marble. You might want to step back a little bit."

She looked at the map. Moving with as light a hand as possible, so as to disturb as few elements as possible, she circled each instance of *marble*.

The mine shaft rumbled. Riley and Jana exchanged a glance and moved to the back of the alcove.

Tanya barely noticed because she suddenly realized that no one had told her where to *put* the marble. She scoured the landscape, trying to find a good spot, but they were in flatlands. There was no convenient cavern or mountain range in which to insert it. It would wreak havoc in the forest.

She sighed, cursing her inexperience in thievery—she really should have thought of this. But there was only one obvious answer. She braced herself and drew arrows from the circle directly into the walls of the mine shaft themselves.

It started slowly—just a slight vibration in the stone underneath her knees. But it spread outward and outward until her vision blurred and a faint but distinct and steady buzz, like a gathering swarm of bees, filled the air.

"Tanya . . . ?" asked Riley, bracing himself against the wall.

Tanya looked at the ceiling and held out a hand. "Wait," she said softly. Out of the corner of her eye, she spied Jana holding out her arms and balancing on the balls of her feet, swaying to the deep, rocky hum as if it were music.

A cracking sound echoed through the chamber and Tanya refocused on the ceiling as deep grooves in the surface formed, widened, and, finally, exploded.

A white, sandy slurry that defied gravity poured out of the ceiling in controlled but unstoppably heavy streams, wriggling like snakes, winding their way out of the ceiling, into the walls, and pooling briefly around their feet, soaking their boots before being absorbed into the floor with the sucking sound of a whirlpool.

The mine shaft stopped shaking.

Tanya stood.

Haphazard bars of clay and tubes of red dust, somehow still suspended in the air, partially blocked her view into the wine cellar. But she could see it. She had done it. They could climb up.

She laughed in amazement and, after a moment, Riley joined her, bending over at the waist as he exhaled what must have been a very long-held breath. Jana cupped her hands around her mouth and whooped.

Tanya looked down. The marble had settled into the bottom of the shaft as if it had always been there, inlaid in an attractive swirling pattern. She lifted her boots, now inundated with damp, pale grit, and grimaced at the heaviness before breaking out in another smile.

She had dissolved marble.

Looking up again at the dust she had suspended in thin air, she was filled with awe. She lifted a finger and touched a strand of pulverized red brick.

It collapsed at her touch.

"Huh," she said, frowning at her reddened fingertip. "That's a worrying—"

Before she could finish that sentence, the remainder of the ceiling rained down on her head, coating her head to toe in soot and brown powder.

Tanya barely had time to spit the grime out of her mouth when the mine shaft began rumbling again.

"What did you do?" yelled Riley, bracing himself again.

"Nothing," she yelled back, equal parts panicked and furious at how clean he still was. She hesitated. "Or maybe—hang on." She dipped to the floor and snatched her most recent map. "Oh no."

"Oh no? What is 'oh no'?"

She looked up. "We should climb up into the castle now. The mine shaft's going to cave in."

# Chapter

Jana didn't hesitate. She vaulted into the air and, with a grunt, she caught the jagged edge of what used to be the cellar floor.

The whole shaft shuddered again, like a giant about to be sick, and Jana's left arm slipped from the edge. Tanya cried out and Riley stumbled to her side.

But Jana appeared unconcerned. She hung by one flexed wrist and angled her head backward, calmly surveying the wine cellar, its gold-leaf-edged shelves supporting an endless variety of bottles.

Jana said, "Got it," and hurled the dangling left side of her body upward, catching one of the shelves. The muscles in her arms visibly rippling, she pulled the rest of her body up so that it was level.

She repeated this pattern three more times, until—before Tanya could begin to figure out how she was making her limbs move the way they were—she had clambered across the shelves to the door, which she casually opened and hopped through.

Jana looked down at them from the hallway. "You better hurry," she warned, pointing behind them.

Tanya and Riley turned. A brown, humid tidal wave of liquefied rock and mulched earth was heading straight for them.

Riley stood under the cellar and raised his arms. "Boost me," he ordered Tanya. "I'll pull you up after."

Tanya crammed the quill and map into her belt. She bent beneath Riley's waist and hoisted him up, her arms falling squarely between his knees and his behind. She thought a prayer to the Lady of Cups, patron goddess of tavern maids, and lifted.

He was bonier than she had expected and lighter, too; *underfed,* thought Tanya. He shot up through her arms and grabbed at the second-lowest shelf. He swung his legs up to land on the shelf underneath that.

The mine shaft shook and muck started to pool around Tanya's feet. She could hear him knocking over bottles and muttering something under his breath. Taking a deep breath and biting his lip, he let go with one hand.

He arched backward, swaying in the shuddering, dusty air. He gulped and stretched his hand out to Tanya.

The groundswell was already up to her knees, sticking to her clothes and sucking her in. She jumped.

She caught his hand and swung like a pendulum in a grandfather clock, heavy and horizontal.

"Careful," gasped Riley as she finally managed to jam her feet into the shelves.

Together, they scrambled across the shelves until they found the door and tumbled through, rejoining Jana. The mulch was still rising, sealing off their exit.

Riley sighed. "That's a shame," he said, and Jana shut the door.

They made their way down the corridor, following Riley as he hugged the wall. "Behind this door is a small staircase leading to the serving gallery behind the banquet hall," he told them in a low, urgent voice. "From there, our route to the duchess's bedroom is"— he began ticking it off on his fingers—"from the gallery, to the dumbwaiter, which leads to the dressing room directly off the bedchamber. The tiara is under her vanity in a safe. I crack the safe—"

"Or I smash it," broke in Jana.

"No, you don't." Riley threw her a freezing glance. "We don't want her to know the tiara's missing until it, we, and the whole camp are long gone. I'll crack it. Don't you worry about that. You're just here for insurance." Riley opened the door.

The sight of the serving gallery hit Tanya with a wave of home-sickness so strong that in that moment she would have given both her companions food poisoning and snapped the quill in half in order to be back at the Snake.

Tanya forced her eyes away from the tidy sideboard of bitters and liquors to focus on the dumbwaiter. Jana hopped in first, followed quickly by Riley.

Tanya moved to squeeze in after them, but frowned when she couldn't maneuver even one thigh into the box. "Can one of you scooch back?" she asked, giving Riley's knobby shoulder a shove. "I can't fit in there if you're going to sprawl around like that."

Riley shoved right back. "That's fine," he said, starting to pull down the door. "You're staying in the pantry."

Tanya gaped at him. "What if someone catches me?"

"Look, someone's got to pull us up. And you're the tavern wench, aren't you? You're going to look much more at home with all the cutlery and whatever than we are."

"Not in pants and covered in brick dust!"

"You can't track that filth into the duchess's bedroom. They'd be onto us in a second. Make yourself useful and find us another way out of here."

"And if an armed, drunken, likely violent corpsman finds me first?"

Riley shrugged and gestured at her chest. She scowled and Jana giggled.

"Not that," he said, smothering a grin. "The *quill*—bring the ceiling down on 'em." He pulled the dumbwaiter shut and then opened it a crack. "Or I guess you could try taking off your shirt. What do I know about corpsmen?" He slammed it down again, muffling, but not hiding, Jana's bubbling laughter.

Tanya kicked the door after him before using the rope at the side to pull them upward.

She knew they were right. Any muck she had tracked in from the mine shaft would be much better explained in the serving gallery than in any of the upper floors. She couldn't fight and she couldn't pick locks. She wasn't good for anything that needed to go on up there. In the end, she'd be a liability, not an asset.

She hadn't wanted to be a burglar, but having entered into the field, it galled her to be incompetent at any part of it.

Tanya sighed and unfolded the map. She settled onto the floor, her back against the dumbwaiter, and licked the quill. If this was her job, she would do it, unglamorous though it might be compared to slinking around a duchess's bedchamber with a knife at her hip.

But before she had a chance to begin her work, the door banged open and a disheveled corpsman staggered in.

The corpsman didn't notice her, scrunched as she was against the dumbwaiter. He lurched toward the sideboard opposite her and threw open the liquor cabinet, peering inside with such slow, dense intensity that she lost all concern that he would discover her or be a threat if he did.

He was narrow-hipped and ropy. His hair needed a good pulling through with a wet comb, but his uniform was in fine repair: quite clean and impeccably tailored to his form. She could spot a place by the knee where a seam had split, but whoever had patched it up knew what she was about.

The corpsman reached for a bottle of gin infused with violets, but missed and sent it crashing to the floor in a wet catastrophe of glass and flowers.

The gin flowed onto Tanya's already mostly destroyed boots, sending her to her tidiness-loving feet on pure instinct.

"Useless corps," she spat out. "Don't you ever do anything but drink and steal other people's provisions?"

The corpsman straightened up—not without some effort, but he made it. "That can't be you," he said, in an incredulous voice.

Tanya recognized that voice.

Steps approached the serving gallery, slower and more sure-footed.

"Is everything all right, Greer?" Another corpsman, this one shaped like a barrel and stone-cold sober, stuck his head in the room. "I heard a crash."

Greer started laughing.

The second corpsman sighed and walked in, saying, "Pass me that broom. I'll clean this up."

Greer collapsed further into giggles, leaning against the sidebar with the effort.

"Come on, man," implored the second corpsman wearily, stepping forward and retrieving the broom leaning up against the cupboard himself. Turning around, he said, "At least pretend to be a . . ."

The second corpsman stopped talking when he caught sight of Tanya.

She cleared her throat. "I guess you didn't make it to the Glasslands, huh, Darrow?"

Greer finally turned around and Tanya was rather gratified to see that he looked awful: greasy and sunburnt, with deep circles under his eyes.

"We haven't made it anywhere, have we?" he slurred. "We got stuck in the shithole that is the Queen's Corps."

Darrow paid his companion no attention. He was studying Tanya with confused, knitted brows, looking as if he were trying to solve a math problem that was too hard for him.

"You stole a horse," he said slowly. "That's what they said."

"I . . . actually did," Tanya admitted. "I did steal a horse."

"People . . . these scholars." He was struggling. "The scholars said you were going to be imprisoned by the Queen."

Tanya tossed her muddy hair back. "They haven't caught me yet," she told him, folding her arms.

Darrow blinked once. He blinked again. Then he dropped the broom and pulled his sword from its sheath.

"Tanya of Griffin's Port," he said solemnly. "In the name of the Queen and Council, I place you under arrest."

"Wait, really?" asked Greer, sobering up. "You're going to arrest her? We thought she could be dead. You . . . you said a prayer to whatever the hell wind god the Glassies pray to! She turns up, out of nowhere, at this weirdo duchess's palace, and you're going to hold her up at sword-point?"

"Yeah, really Darrow," Tanya said crossly. "I hate to agree with Greer, but you can't be serious."

"I have to, Tanya," he said, his face grave. "It's not only the lawful thing to do, which is my sworn duty, it's also the only way to keep you safe."

"I don't need you to keep me safe."

"You're unarmed. This is a dangerous part of the country once you get out of the duchess's compound."

"I'm aware of that, thanks," she told him, her voice rising, the quill starting to heat up in her hand. "You have no idea what I've had to do since your Commander Rees dissolved his corps like so much butter in a hot pan. Lady of Cups, why can't either of you find a *normal* commander to enlist with? Do you have any idea what's going on in this castle tonight?"

They weren't listening to her anymore. They were staring at her fist, because her fist, wrapped tightly around the quill, was glowing red.

"Tavern maid," asked Greer, still looking at the quill. "I've actually been wondering just that. What *is* happening in this castle tonight?"

Tanya stared back at him, furious. It did not escape her calculations that the sudden appearance of members of the Queen's Corps
who could vouch for her character was exactly what she needed. She
need only give up the Tomcat, give up Riley, give up Jana, and produce the quill. She would be instantly escorted directly to the Queen
and Council to make her request. She could come out of this looking
like a brave and loyal subject, one who had suffered for Lode and
safeguarded what was likely to be the most valuable magical artifact
in the country.

But that would mean trusting whoever this corrupt commander
turned out to be—and she knew that he had at least been bribed to
seduce a duchess by a notorious crime lord.

It might mean surrendering the quill to a personage less than the
Queen herself.

In short, it would mean trusting her person and the power of the
quill to someone not *Tanya* herself.

And that, well . . .

That was unacceptable.

A sharp knocking echoed down the wall at her back. Ignoring
the corpsmen's probing eyes, Tanya turned her back on them and
opened the dumbwaiter door. She yanked the rope, pulling the
chamber down.

Riley and Jana slid into view and tumbled out into the serving
gallery. Riley was slightly flushed and Jana was wearing an amethyst
around her neck, but they were otherwise unruffled.

Riley shifted the bulging sack strapped over both shoulders so it
sat more in the center of his back. "There was a lantern signal across
the White while we were in the duchess's dressing room," he said
hurriedly. "She and the Tomcat's dupe are on their way back early.
Did you find us a way out?"

"Um . . ."

Riley followed her gaze to the corpsmen, his eyes widening when they met Darrow's.

Darrow was gaping, too. "You're . . . you're the blacksmith," he said slowly. "The one I met at Ironhearth." Riley's face hardened and he pulled a knife out from his belt.

Jana stretched out her back as she stood. "You two!" she said brightly, pointing at them "You were in Tanya's corps! I remember you. You came to Ironhearth with the idiot"—she pointed to Darrow— "and you"—pointing to Greer—"you gave me whiskey and wasted no time at all in barging into Tanya's tent yourself when I asked where she slept so I could borrow a nightdress! How've you been?"

The two boys were too slack-jawed to answer, so after a moment of pleasant, smiling silence, Jana pulled out her sword and, with one swift, horizontal movement, smacked them both across the temple with the hilt.

With a crashing of glass and spilled wine, they collapsed onto each other in a heap. Greer's arm knocked the storage closet at the bottom of the sideboard open, revealing neatly folded linen with a simply embroidered hem.

Tanya stepped over Greer, pushing him to the side. She pulled out the fabric. "I think I've got a way out," she said.

Five minutes later, Greer and Darrow were stripped to their underwear and tied up together like two husks of corn. Jana and Riley were pulling on the collars of their uniforms, both far too big for them. Tanya was wearing a clean white kitchen smock and had her hair tied up in a maid's kerchief.

She frowned down at Darrow and Greer. "They'll be OK, right?"

Jana came to stand next to Tanya and nudged Darrow with her boot. "Yeah, see, he's groaning a little. Listen."

Jana kicked Greer, too, and a thin, creaking sound escaped out of his mouth.

Jana shrugged. "They might be a little . . . what's the word? Concussed? But as long as they don't go swimming or get drunk or something in the next couple days, they'll be fine." She paused. "There will be some bruising."

Riley stepped over the corpsmen, looking like a twelve-year-old shrugging around in Darrow's gray coat. Jana, tucking her hair under Greer's cap, looked more convincing.

Tanya saw Riley sneak an appraising look at Darrow's body. She thought she could imagine his feelings: It's never fun to feel like your body doesn't fit. Tanya had gotten over that feeling years ago, rejecting it full stop, but then, she was likely more self-possessed than Riley.

"How are we getting out of here?" Riley asked Tanya. "I'd like to stop wearing this outfit as soon as possible."

Tanya pulled out the crumpled map. "Our horses"—she pointed—"are all the way over here, on the other side of the castle, across the White. We could walk it, but we can't do it now. There's nowhere to hide on that walk and that's the direction Tomcat's dupe and the duchess will be coming from. I'd say let's steal a horse and just make a break for it"—*Who I am?* wondered Tanya wearily—"but everyone else has horses, too, and I think they'd probably come after us."

Riley frowned. "So . . . what then? Why am I dressed like an idiot?"

"Because we're going to wait it out. We're going to wait until the majority of the corps is passed out from the free food and booze—trust me, it will happen—and then we're going to walk right out of here like it's the most natural thing in Lode. In the meantime, to answer your question, you're dressed like that because . . ." She took a deep breath and grabbed a surviving jug of ale. She put on her best waitress smile. "Because we're going to join the party."

A door from the serving gallery led out into the kitchen garden.

Tanya left first, balancing the jug and four pewter mugs on a silver tray.

It was pleasant in the garden. Wind ripped across the empty expanse of the White, but the tall stone of the castle blocked its progress, leaving the climate merely on the autumnal side of balmy. Roses of all colors—purple, blue, red, yellow, white, and pink—grew in a twisty, winding thicket all along the south side of the castle.

When Tanya turned the corner, she was greeted with hollers, whistles, and whoops.

Apparently, the corpsmen had been serving themselves until her arrival. Greer and Darrow seemed to have joined an even rowdier crew for their second stab at soldiering. She couldn't blame the duchess's genuine housemaids for wanting nothing to do with the two dozen or so men and boys currently littering the grass with pork bones, chicken wings, ash, singed paper, peanut shells, corks, and empty jugs.

She was surrounded in a matter of seconds. Tanya moved through the throng, refilling mugs and holding out her tray for soiled napkins, at least to those who had deigned to employ them. Tanya felt herself smiling, heard herself asking, "More, sir?" saw out of the corner of her eyes whenever another supplicant tried to catch her eye, mindlessly shuffled them into a queue, and, for the first time, wondered what it was about her that made her so good at this. It wasn't something she had ever questioned. If anything, she had *prided* herself on her efficiency, her adaptability, her practicality. She had never thought about how that meant she was always serving. She had never wondered what in her face made people instinctively give her their dirty dishes.

Eventually, she had placated the men and found herself standing next to Riley. He was looking at the corpsmen with as much disdain as Tanya felt. Jana had already pounded a beer and challenged a baby-faced giant to an arm-wrestling contest.

The light from the duchess's carriage grew brighter and brighter as it traveled across the White. A black stallion came into view and it was soon apparent that it was the largest horse Tanya had ever seen—not just the tallest, but the thickest, too, its flanks bursting with muscle. When the stallion detoured away from the carriage, turning the corner into the yard, and its rider dismounted, Tanya could understand why. The man was enormous! He was easily closer to seven feet than six, with a chest like the prow of a ship.

These observations skittered across her brain and then froze, sinking to her rib cage and hanging there, suspended like ice in whiskey.

A giant of a man, riding the biggest horse in the corps, wearing the gold stripe of a corps commander. A man who had taken a bribe, the type of libertine who had been sent to distract a flighty duchess. A man, his face still in shadow, who seemed not at all displeased to find that his men had ransacked a host's wine cellar, and in fact who was filling a cup full of liquor before his horse's pants had even slowed.

Tanya grabbed Riley's shoulder. "We have to go," she whispered. "We have to go now."

Riley raised an eyebrow. "Now? The commander *just* showed up. We won't be able to get away undetected for hours!"

"We can't risk him recognizing me or Jana."

"Who are you talking about? *I* barely recognize Jana in that getup. And who would *you* know in this part of the world?"

"Kitchen maid!" His voice carried. Tanya froze.

The commander stepped forward, raising his voice. "I'm calling you, wench! I need a little service."

Laughter rippled through the men. The commander took a few

steps closer, moving into the lamplight—Tanya was sure it was him now.

"Wench—*now*."

*Rees.*

Tanya swallowed and looked at Riley. "You see?" she asked quietly.

He looked at her, understanding in his face. He nodded briefly and walked away. She waited until she saw him lean into Jana's ear before pulling her kerchief low over her brow and heading toward the commander.

She picked up various items for her tray on her way to him—a half-eaten meat pie, a flask of cider, a packet of tobacco—and kept her eyes down.

He had found himself a seat, an elegant wicker lawn chair. She offered him the tray. "Anything else I can get for you, sir?" she asked, her voice as demure as she could manage.

"I wouldn't mind a pretty little thing to sit on my lap," he said lazily, snaking an arm around her waist. She deftly spun out of his grasp.

Rees chortled. "Although this one's got such a plump backside, I don't know if I could take the weight. Oh, don't be embarrassed, wench, no need to turn your face! Just a little joke—a real man likes a girl with curves. Here"—he twisted his hand around her apron strings and yanked—"give us a smile, and I'll give you a silk—"

His voice cut off as he saw Tanya's face. Her kerchief had loosened in the brief struggle.

"You," he said wonderingly. "The wench from Griffin's Port. I would have thought you'd run along home to the Port Cities by now. What are you doing . . . ?"

The question faded on his lips. He was looking at her chest, and not because of her personal attributes. Tanya didn't even have to look down to know what he was looking at. By now, somehow, she could feel it.

There was a warm, golden glow emanating over her heart, articulated into the shape of a perfect feather quill.

She took advantage of his moment of surprise, pulled her apron back, and, in a moment of inspiration, reached behind her to grab an empty wine bottle and smashed it over his head. Out of the corner of her eye, she saw him go down, but by then she was running.

# Chapter 12

She didn't look back, not even to see if Riley and Jana were behind her. She heard footsteps at her sides, took it on faith that it was them, and the trio ran headlong into the White, with only the light of the quill illuminating their path.

Tanya didn't know how far they had run before she ran out of breath, only that it wasn't far enough. She stopped and bent over her cramping stomach, wheezing.

Jana and Riley ran ahead, until they realized that they had left their only light source behind them. There was as much chalk in front of her as there was behind and she could hear men shouting and warhorses neighing behind her.

Jana leapt at Tanya and shook her. "Move, damn it," she said sternly. "Rees is coming—I can see him. He's saddling that monster of his and—yep, now he's on the White. Move!"

"I can't," Tanya said helplessly, hiccupping with the effort of breathing and talking. "You have the tiara, just go. He's a commander of the Queen's Corps. He's a thug, but he won't hurt me."

"He will to get that thing," said Riley, pointing at her chest. "Anyone would."

"Oh?" Tanya straightened up. "Go ahead, then. Take it." She pulled out her map and thrust out her chest. "Take it!" she furiously dared him.

Jana looked at Riley, who seemed to shake his head slightly. The girl thief shrugged and took a step toward Tanya with her arm out, but the quill suddenly went dark.

It was still glittering, but the glitter was the pitchiest of pitch blacks.

"Why'd it do that?" asked Jana, sounding calmer than seemed entirely warranted to Tanya with the hoofbeats drawing nearer.

"Because it likes me, and it doesn't like you," she said tartly, stamping her foot a little. Her boot kicked up a cloud of chalk.

*Mostly chalk here,* she thought. Tanya kicked again and pulled out her map. She quickly licked the edge of the quill and scrawled, *I am X—detail the ground.*

All packed chalk in a ten-foot radius. No salt. No dirt.

Riley and Jana stared as Tanya bent to a crouch and laid the map on the ground. She, very carefully, began tracing a circle.

"Tanya . . ."

She didn't answer, just waved a hand at Riley and started working on a second circle, on a different section of the map.

The horses were nearly on them, Rees out in front. Jana threw off the stolen corpsman's cap and pulled her sword out of her belt. She changed her stance, turning to the side and bending her back leg. Riley drew a breath and pulled out his own knife.

Tanya ignored it all. Eyes squarely on her work, she drew an arrow going one way from the first circle to the second, then an arrow going the other way from the second to the first.

The arrows lit up like embers—the quill seemed to understand. But nothing happened. Tanya bit her lip. How did this thing work?

"You might want to stand up," Riley told her in a strained whisper as his fist clenched around his dagger.

The arrows were pulsing now, the light fading and strengthening in what Tanya suddenly realized was the exact rhythm of her breathing.

She held her next breath in. The pulsing stopped. She exhaled. The pulsing resumed.

Tanya smiled. Her blood, her breath: her rules.

The horses were on them now. Rees held up a hand. "I'll grab the tavern wench, then you deal with the rest," he ordered, and jumped off his horse.

Jana stepped closer to Tanya, defending her flank. Riley was already behind her. Tanya put her thumb and forefinger on the arrows' bases on the map.

The moment she turned her hand over the map, Tanya felt the glow from the arrows seep into her skin, sending prickles of heat and cold all the way up to her hair follicles and down to her toenails.

Rees pulled his own sword, sneering. "You think I don't remember you, smithy tart," he spat at Jana. "You don't have any of your foul herbs now. I should have known this other one helped you steal my quill. Never trust a wench!"

"Actually," said Tanya, "it's the Queen's quill." She looked up and smiled again. "But nope. Never trust a wench."

She waved and, with a flick of her wrist on the parchment, reversed the arrows.

There was a ferocious gust of wind, narrow but stronger than anything that came off the sea from the docks at Griffin's Port. She felt herself, Jana, and Riley revolve on the spot as a blur of color raced past her eyes, too fast to make out any shapes.

And then the revolving stopped. The wind dissipated, and they were no longer in the White.

Well, that wasn't quite accurate. They were standing (in Tanya's case, crouching) on the same patch of chalk they had been. But they were back in the woods where they had started, a circle of dusty white in the verdant trees. Their horses, still tied up, blinked at them, startled and sleepy.

Tanya exhaled and slowly got to her feet.

Jana was still frozen in her battle position, sword out and ready.

"What the . . . ?" she whispered, and then swore so filthily that Tanya didn't even understand it—and she had grown up around sailors.

One of the horses whinnied and Tanya turned to see Riley already tying the pack carrying the tiara to its saddle.

"We should move," he said, his voice shaking a little; he cleared his throat before speaking again. "I want to get back to camp before dawn."

Jana laughed like she was gargling knives. "Why bother riding?" she asked, a note of hysteria in her voice. "Let's just have Tanya draw us there!"

Riley silently gestured for Tanya to stand in front of him. He boosted her up into the saddle, and then vaulted up behind her.

"You didn't seem very surprised that I could do that," remarked Tanya. She was a little miffed at his nonreaction to the miraculous escape she had single-handedly wrought.

"I was," he said slowly. "It was well done, Tanya."

He was warm behind her, his heart beating fast.

She had *flown*. Tanya felt her blood sing through her veins, through the quill, her own heart beating as fast as Riley's, thrumming harmonically together.

They had done this. Jana, Riley, and her.

Her and Riley.

Her breath coming rapidly, their shirts sticking together with proximity and each other's sweat, Tanya gulped and reached behind her, her fingers finding Riley's.

He ripped his hand away and pulled the horse up short.

"Both hands on the saddle horn, please," he told her, his voice short. "Wouldn't want to lose the damn quill."

Tanya, mortified, obeyed. When Riley spurred the horse back into action, he was stiff and held himself far away from her.

They rode fast through the forest, with no more conversation. Jana rode still faster and was soon out of sight.

The message to Tanya was clear:

Riley, and Jana, too, were obligated to protect the quill. They didn't have to like it—and, now that they knew what she could do, they didn't like the girl who wielded it, either.

In the dark and the wind and the silence, Tanya remembered that she was alone. And she was furious that she had forgotten. There was a reason, after all, that she had kept to herself. She was much safer that way—life was more reliable alone.

Tanya missed Froud. That relationship had been uncomplicated. Froud got help and Tanya got a home. Easy.

By the time Tanya and Riley's horse slowed to a panting stop in the clearing, there was barely a camp to speak of. Trunks were being loaded into wagons, bundles tied onto yawning horses, and all but a few of the more elaborate tents were gone, dismantled into unprepossessing piles of sticks and fabric.

Even the Tomcat was in action, pacing impatiently in front of the brushed dirt where his tent had been.

Riley jumped off the horse and met the Tomcat where he was clearly waiting for him, alerted by the faster Jana. Tanya was left to scramble off the horse's back herself, her short legs swinging perilously around the animal's knees as the creature, tired and unhappy at being so unceremoniously abandoned by its rider, tossed her still-hanging torso down and then off, sending her to the ground with a thump.

"Never mind," Tanya muttered to no one. "No one panic. I don't need any help getting up out of this mud. I'm fine alone."

Dirtying her hands still further, she pulled herself to her feet and found herself face-to-face with the Tomcat.

He was holding a silver tiara. In spite of herself, Tanya felt her eyes go wide.

The silver was dull, but there was supernatural magnetism in the dullness—it pulled her gaze insistently, almost violently. The Tomcat stepped closer to her with it and the scent of roses filled her nostrils.

"Jana said you used the quill to fly," said the Tomcat softly.

Tanya yanked her eyes away from the tiara. "Not exactly," she said.

The Tomcat did something unexpected. He smiled, stretching out his hand to tousle Tanya's hair before putting his arm around her shoulder and steering her toward the last active firepit. "Very well done, niece," he said. "Uncle Tommy is quite proud of you."

The smell of strong tea hit her nostrils, waking her up a little, building her confidence through sheer familiarity. "I'm glad you're pleased, sir," she said politely.

He sighed, his arm slipping through hers. "Enough of 'sir,' Tanya. Haven't I told you to call me Uncle Tommy?"

Tanya locked eyes with Lukas, the unfortunate kitchen boy, who was managing a rudimentary cook stove. His eyes were wide as he watched them.

"Apologies," she said quickly. "It won't happen again, Uncle Tommy."

"Excellent! See that it doesn't. Now," he said, "I'm famished. Let's have breakfast before we begin our journey." She moved to the cook stove, but he stopped her.

"Allow me," he said.

He busied his hands with something, his back to her. When he turned around, he was carrying a neatly arranged little wooden tray laden with a small carafe of tea, a pot of honey, a tiny pitcher of milk, and a plate piled high with cornbread biscuits.

Tanya had to admit that she couldn't have done better, certainly not as quickly as the crime lord had.

"Thank you," she said. "I'm not used to being served." She couldn't quite keep the question mark out of her voice.

The Tomcat twisted his mouth into something that was almost, but not quite, a smile. "I imagine not."

"I would have thought that you had as little experience serving as I had being served," said Tanya, picking her words carefully. She wasn't sure she liked being pampered. It meant somebody wanted something from her. The thought of what the Tomcat might want from her this morning of all mornings—the morning after plans weeks in gestation had finally been put into motion—frightened her.

"Well, you'd be wrong there," said the Tomcat, surprising her. "I spent my youth as a page in the Glacier, serving the Queen and Council."

Tanya dropped her jaw. The Glacier was the Queen's home and the seat of ultimate power in Lode. To serve there was a mark of the highest distinction for the help class. A port city tavern wench like her wouldn't be considered refined enough, no matter how well she could cook.

The Tomcat's silent lackey came to stand next to his chair. The crime lord sighed and stood up.

"Apologies, my dear, but we will have to cut this breakfast short," he said, removing her tray with—yes, she saw it now—a well-trained flick of his wrist. "Your unfortunate familiarity with Commander Rees has made it necessary to rush."

Tanya imagined she looked pale, because he quickly added, "I don't blame you for that, my girl! I do have the tiara and, after all, it's no great inconvenience to reach Bloodstone earlier than planned."

Tanya collected her wits, standing and smoothing her hair. "Right," she breathed. "Bloodstone."

The Tomcat's face didn't alter from the pleasant indulgence he had had plastered on all morning. "Don't fear, Tanya. You won't be there long, I suspect," he said. "I'm still considering all your options. Talents like yours shouldn't go to waste."

He bowed at Tanya's frozen face and strode off with the silent man.

Jana appeared about twenty feet away, hauling a messily wrapped bundle over the back of her horse.

The girls locked eyes. Jana had ratted her out for using the quill to "fly." Tanya's eyes narrowed and she crossed her arms. This usually conveyed her contempt clearly, but Jana didn't react the way Tanya would have expected.

Jana smiled.

It wasn't a knowing smile or a canny smile or a wicked smile, or even a tense smile. It was a friendly, comradely smile, the kind she had been sending Tanya's way since they met in the corps' camp by the junkoff. Jana waved a little and went back to securing her measly luggage, whistling away.

Jana might very well have *had* to give the Tomcat valuable information in order to maintain her position. But that meant Tanya should never, ever trust her again.

It came as a shock that she had started to trust Jana at all.

She was in for another sort of shock at the stables, where Riley was fitting a saddle to the golden mare.

"Who gets to ride her?" asked Tanya, trying to catch the mare's eyes, avoiding looking at Riley. Tanya hoped that Riley would be the lucky one, if only because he was among the lighter of the men.

Riley cleared his throat and stood up straight. "Actually, *you* get to ride her." He bowed ironically. "My lady."

Tanya looked up at Riley and then back at the mare. The mare had stopped shuffling and shaking her head. For the first time, she was still. She wasn't looking at Tanya, she was looking at the ground, but her ear cocked in Tanya's direction. It twitched once, twice, three times, in a slow, purposeful rhythm.

Tanya reached out and stroked the mare on the ear, and the mare let her. Riley snorted.

"What's so funny?" she asked, pulling her hand away from the mare.

"Nothing really," he said, shrugging. "Just . . . he serves you breakfast, you get to ride *her*—this is some recruiting pitch. I guess he treats you a little differently when you're a great big girl with something he wants and not a skinny brat who can't steal enough to eat on his own. That goes a little differently, let me tell you."

"You got a different 'pitch'?"

"I got a bowl of stew, a cookie, and bedroll," Riley told her, smiling ruefully. "But that was a long time ago."

The mare's ear had felt like velvet. Tanya reached out to stroke it again. She asked, "Do you like being a thief?"

Riley frowned and crossed his arms. "I don't really think about it like that," he said thoughtfully. "I've always been a thief. I've never been anything else. I'm good at being a thief. I like that I'm good at it. Is that close enough?"

Tanya shrugged, not quite sure why she was asking.

"Why? Do you like being a tavern wench?"

Tanya winced. "Must you call it that?"

"What? That's what you are, isn't it?"

She thought of her life at the Smiling Snake. She thought of the cleaning and the cooking, the serving and the washing, the flirting and the scolding and the bargaining. Did she truly like any of that?

Tanya looked up and parroted his words back to him:

"I like that I'm good at it."

Riley hesitated. "In that case, you might want to consider being a thief," he said. There was laughter in his voice still, but it was careful laughter, tinged with a bit of respect.

"Why should I?" she asked, irritated. "So I can be even less respectable than a port city serving wench?"

"Because, you're not bad at it."

"Really?" Tanya asked, surprised.

"I mean, you have no foundation in the basics," he said quickly. "Your inexperience would be a liability in almost any heist and you have no respect for the small movements—and keeping your movements small absolutely keeps you alive and free. But you think fast and you're a good liar. And I don't know for sure that anyone else could make that feather do what you can make it do. The Tomcat couldn't get it to work and he's the best thief I've ever seen."

*Then the greatest of thieves lacks basic organizational skills*, thought Tanya. But she declined to criticize Riley's boss and instead said, "You seem like you hate the quill."

Riley stretched again, feigning a nonchalance that Tanya knew he didn't feel. "Relying on that thing was what got us into that mess in the first place," he said. "Because none of us knew anything about it, we forgot about finding a place for marble, and that cut off our escape route. But . . . it—or rather, you and it—did get us out clean. I'm willing to keep an open mind. I just don't like magic." He shivered. "Never have."

"I agree. Magic seems very unreliable."

Riley still looked uneasy. "It's not that it's unreliable, exactly," he said. "It's that it's . . . not fair, maybe?"

Tanya snorted. "The thief complains about fairness."

Riley smiled, cheering up a little. "Hey, the way I see it, if you haven't adequately protected your property, that's your fault."

"Maybe magic just scares you." The words slipped out of Tanya's mouth before she even knew they were on her tongue.

Riley stiffened for a moment and then shrugged. "Maybe. I've never seen anyone I trust use magic and I've never seen it used for good. You'll see when we get to Bloodstone. Things get twisted."

Tanya swallowed—was he saying he trusted her? She reached for his shoulder. "I don't want to twist you," she said quietly.

Riley looked down at her hand in surprise. Someone called

his name and he shook her off, hurrying away with a mumbled, "Excuse me."

When Riley had gone, the mare lifted her head and, her eyes wide, took a step toward Tanya. She nudged her on the shoulder—not the affectionate nuzzling Tanya had witnessed from lesser horses, but a hard, sharp push—and tossed her mane in the direction of the forest.

The meaning was clear: *See? There is nothing and no one here for you. Let's get the hell out of here*, she was saying. *Untie me and let's go!*

Tanya put her hand on the mare's temple, feeling the vein pulse there. "If we run now, we *will* get caught," she whispered. "Jana is fast and when he wants to be, I'd bet Riley matches her." The mare snorted. "Even if he doesn't, Jana would be quite enough: She tracked your little magician friend when he was disguised as a *bird*."

The mare looked up sharply at the mention of the boy wizard and kicked her hooves. "He's fine," Tanya said quickly, understanding. "The Tomcat and Riley don't even know he exists. He's not here anymore, anyway. He's safe with the other wizards."

The mare snarled at their mention and Tanya nodded in agreement. "Useless, I agree," she said. "Listen to me. We will find our moment. But if you run with me on your back, they will bring you down to secure me. They won't care if they kill you."

The mare seemed to think about this for a moment. Then she tossed her head downward, shaking the rope around her neck.

"What? Look, I'm not fluent in horse!"

The mare did it again and then nudged Tanya again, a true nuzzle this time, rubbing the rope against the exposed skin on the girl's neck.

"Oh," said Tanya softly.

If she untied the mare now, while everyone was still packing up and distracted, she just might get away—Tanya would still be stuck there, but the mare would be free.

Tanya looked to the side, and then to the other side. They were nowhere near alone. But then again, no one was looking at them, either. As nonchalantly as she could manage, she bent to her knees and put her hand experimentally on the knot tying the mare to the steel stake piercing the earth.

The knot was tight and elaborate, made of thick, rough rope. It was too tough and made of too strong a material for the mare to break away on her own, Tanya could see that. It was too tight to dismantle at all without a knife to jimmy the weak spots loose.

Well, for most people, it would have been too tight. But Tanya had grown up with sailors. She had learned to tie a knot before she learned to read, and even now, her fingers could undo a jumble of twisted rope quicker and more neatly than they could write.

Tanya slipped a fingernail into a seam and began to tug.

"What are you doing?"

Tanya whirled. "Riley said I get to ride her," she said. "I'm just going to get her ready."

Jana was munching on an apple. She came to stand next to Tanya and patted the horse on the head. To her surprise, the mare flared her nostrils, but allowed the touch.

Using small movements, Tanya continued working the knot. "Excited to go home?" she asked.

Jana laughed, but didn't sound amused. "Oh yeah," she said. "It will do wonders for my skin."

"What? Why?"

"The steam."

Tanya turned and looked carefully at Jana. The other girl's face was confusing. There was a curious flattening of her features, as if she had purposefully squeezed any and all emotion into a rubber ball and she was trying to keep from bouncing away.

"Steam?" Tanya asked, still watching the other girl's face. "Is there a hot spring nearby?"

Jana looked at her. "Technically, yes. But you don't want to go swimming in it." She turned and pitched her apple core into the clear blue lake. "The steam comes from Bloodstone itself. It rises off the brimstone canals. They boil, you see."

"Bloodstone . . . *steams?*"

Jana nodded. "And smells like hell's kitchens. The air is so thick, you're going to sweat off five pounds, if that's the sort of thing that worries you."

Tanya shuddered, her skin suddenly prickling, thrown backward into the fear from her childhood, the nightmare of Bloodstone etched into her heart.

Jana stepped toward her own horse. "The thing you have to know about Bloodstone," she said slowly, petting her horse on the nose, looking anywhere but at Tanya, "is that whatever you have, people will want it. Whatever you don't have . . . that will cost you." Jana looked up abruptly. "Do you know what I mean?" she asked, looking Tanya straight in the eye.

Tanya returned her gaze and nodded. And she did know.

Jana was warning her.

Jana nodded and hopped on her horse's back. She looked behind her shoulder at Tanya, just once, before riding away.

Tanya stared after her, one thing crystal clear in her head. There was absolutely no way that she was going to voluntarily go anywhere *near* Bloodstone.

She redoubled her effort on the knot, speaking in a low tone. "Listen to me carefully," she said to the mare. "We are getting out of here"—the mare looked up quickly—"yes, *both* of us are getting out of here."

The mare inclined her head down, looking pointedly at all the thieves around them.

"Yeah, I know," said Tanya impatiently, finally finishing the knot. "Don't move. Let me think."

The mare froze, her eyes wide.

Tanya shut her eyes against the mare's glare and began to organize her thoughts. She was good at organization; she *could* figure this out.

Her assets were the dubious loyalty of a moderately supernatural horse and an exhausted quill.

She pulled the quill out of her shirt. It was quiet. It had been hours since she had displaced a circle of the White and it still hadn't woken up. But with no time to worry about that, Tanya licked the quill, and, still not entirely in possession of a plan, started scrawling on the fabric of her shirt.

Nothing came out.

"What?" whispered Tanya. "No. No!" She sucked the edge and tried again, but *nothing*.

"What am I going to do?" she whispered. She had never even had to use *ink* before with the quill, and there was no way she could surreptitiously search the rapidly packing camp for a bottle.

She whirled wildly around the stable, looking for something, *anything* that might work as pigment, but there was only water—no other liquids at all.

Except . . .

Tanya held her arm up to her eyes and examined the nearly totally healed gash from the mine shaft. She looked around. No one was watching her. She looked at the quill.

Maybe . . . it was hungry?

"This better work," she sternly told the quill and rolled up her sleeve.

The world seemed to hold its breath as Tanya whispered a prayer, bit her lip, and stabbed her forearm with the moistened quill.

She felt her blood bubble out of her veins and into the quill. The spine engorged and spat pink-and-red pigment onto its feathers.

It didn't hurt. But it cost her something she couldn't put her finger on. The energy flowed out of her faster than blood and, for the sake of efficiency, Tanya decided not to twist herself in knots getting purchase on her shirt and instead just scrawled into her arm, the quill slipping past the barrier of her skin with only the slightest pressure.

As she finished, she felt her knees buckle. She grabbed the mare's bridle, gritted her teeth, and kept drawing until she heard the word "Now!" torn from her own throat, ragged and deep and entirely unlike her own voice. She repeated it: "Now!!"

A breeze whipped through the camp, lifting stray bits of nature and tossing them into the air.

A whistling noise grew into a roar, and suddenly the whole camp was staring, Jana and Riley were charging, and the Tomcat was shouting, but it was too late.

A gust of tightly packed wind blew through the clearing, flattening the entire company and covering them in dust and pebbles.

Except for Tanya. The wind created a vortex around her, one hand on the quill, the point still stuck in her arm, the other on the mare's harness.

The wind picked up speed until Tanya felt herself lifted into the air.

A scream rang out and a remote corner of her brain identified it as both too low and too high to be anyone in the Tomcat's crew before the cry was crowded out by a piteous whinny, and she lost her grip on the mare. She looked down at her feet, now hovering some eight or ten feet above the ground, and caught sight of blue feathers, a gray robe . . .

. . . and all the while, the wind spiraled tighter and faster and faster and faster . . .

Cushioned by a narrow pocket of soft air, Tanya felt herself pulled forward by the rib cage until she was horizontal. Acting on some previously unknown instinct, she put her arms out behind her, slightly spread, and shot forward.

She was moving too fast to see anything clearly, but there was a flash of red, interrupted by a jagged edge, and then the swirling color changed to brown to blue to white again, this time intertwined with gold.

Tanya spiraled through this whirlwind *impossibly* fast. The tips of her ears, nose, and fingers went numb with cold, but her hair flew behind her and the sun beat on her face, and Tanya was flying.

She flew over rivers, over the huts on stilts in shrimping basins, over the razor-sharp grass of the Glassland Meadows, over miners' settlements, over farming villages, over castles—over everyone and everything on Lode. She was the highest person in the world.

For a time anyway. Eventually, the wind slowed and, like a spool emptying itself of the last of its thread, spun one last, lazy time and deposited a girl who had moments before been the most powerful person in the kingdom onto a dusty road underneath a walnut tree.

Tanya blinked, propped herself up on her elbows, and, finding that too difficult a position to maintain, fell onto her back.

She was dirty, hungry, exhausted—a fugitive from the Queen's Corps and the target of a crime lord. Her right elbow was caked in blood an inch thick and so was her hem.

But she was alive. Tanya, moving slowly, her bones creaking, painstakingly rolled onto her knees, wincing as the joint popped, and, finally, pushed herself to her feet.

The sun was setting and Tanya had to put her hand up against the glare. But, there, a quarter mile down the brick road past a corridor of weeping willow trees, was the famous marble wall of the Capital, the pure white stone streaked with red and orange from the sinking sunlight. And right in the middle of the wall were the gates, made of pure gold and topped with razor-sharp spikes, as beautiful and terrible as could be.

Tanya was nothing but a tavern wench, that was undeniable, but she was a tavern wench that had made it. On her own, thwarted at every turn, she had made it to the Capital's gates *and* she had something the Queen and Council wanted.

"What did you do???"

The wizard boy rode out of the forest on the golden mare, his face red and furious, hers smug and content, apparently unbothered by the strange mode of travel.

Tanya didn't blink. Instead she looked at the mare. "So, after everything, you really just *belong* to this *kid*, huh?"

The wizard blushed even redder and the mare neighed in indignation.

"I am Magus Rollo, senior apprentice of the College of Aetherical Manipulation and second son of the Earl of Vermillon's Pass," he said, hopping off the mare. "You will address me as such and cease referring to me as 'boy' or 'kid' or any other diminutive."

Tanya snorted. "Yeah? Well, I'm Tanya, the tavern wench who just flew you across the country with the stroke of a quill, so you might want to reconsider your tone."

"Look at what you did!" he screeched, pointing at her arm. "It's an abomination. Look at yourself!"

Tanya took the opportunity to do just that and caught her breath.

In the stable, she had hastily drawn a funnel—*fast, strong wind*—a tornado, really, with herself as a stick figure in the center. She had drawn an arrow with the words *safely flying me to* scrawled alongside and the point ending in the words *the Capital*.

She had drawn this, using her own blood as ink to make shallow scratches in her skin. The sketch had been just that—"chicken scratch," as Froud had used to call it, constructed of rickety, overlapping lines.

That was not what was on her arm now.

Spitting on her apron, she scrubbed away the dried blood to reveal a tattoo in a brilliant red, the lines thick and sure.

The raw ideas of the original sketch were the same. There was a tornado, an even, tightly wound spiral with a starburst in the middle that Tanya realized with a jolt was meant to represent her. A leisurely looping line traveled across the length of her forearm, from her elbow to her wrist, landing with a splash like an exploded starburst right on her pulse in front of a perfect, tiny representation of the Capital wall, complete with the gate in the middle.

But that wasn't all the quill had done. There was a map of Lode covering every spare inch of flesh on her arm—every river, every hill, every field she had passed was represented, to scale and in topographical detail.

Tanya lifted her arm to her eyes and revolved it, marveling. The quill was still lodged in a vein, but she didn't even feel a sting when she pulled it out. It slid out as easily as a knife through butter, and her skin closed around the puncture with a tidy popping sound.

She rubbed the spot where the quill had been, now marked by a tiny red diamond. "Is this going to be permanent?" she asked the wizard.

He scowled and held out his hand. "I have no idea," he said hotly. "We don't perform such reckless experiments on ourselves at the college. Now give me back my quill."

Tanya let her arm drop, pulling the quill away from him. "I don't think so," she informed him. "No, I think I'm going to take it to the Queen."

Rollo stamped his foot. "It's not your place!" he cried, his voice cracking. "It's not fair! The quill was my idea in the first place and I had to fight the whole college for the right to present it to the Queen and Council. Then," he said, ticking off the offenses on his fingers, "I get robbed, my horse gets kidnapped, I have to be a bird for *days*—which is *really hard*, by the way—a girl shoots me with an arrow, humiliating me in front of the senior faculty, and then a rank amateur, a *tavern maid*, uses *my* work to fly me across the kingdom, just so that *she* can present it."

There was a silence. Tanya decided to break it, patting Rollo on the shoulder. "If it helps, I'm sorry Jana shot you," she told him. "It wasn't personal."

Rollo stiffened. "It doesn't help," he told her. "But it also doesn't matter. Gillian!" The mare trotted up to him.

"*Gillian?*" said Tanya, crossing her arms. "You're telling me her name is Gillian."

Rollo climbed onto her back. "Yes, her name is Gillian. She found me drowning in the lagoon by Vermillon's Pass as a boy. She saved me and I named her Gillian. Do you have a problem with that?"

"And where exactly do you think you're going?" she asked as Gillian walked past her. "What do you mean, it doesn't matter?"

Rollo turned. "I am Lord Magus Rollo of Vermillon's Pass. I have *my* name and you have none. Want to bet who the Queen and Council sees first? Let's go, Gillian."

They started trotting down the road. The magician didn't look back, but Gillian did. Tanya glared at her.

The mare blinked and looked up at Rollo with soft eyes. She looked back at Tanya, and her eyes were hard again.

*But* . . . the mare slowed down. Almost imperceptibly, she slowed to a walk. And Tanya realized: She was giving her time.

Time to do what, Tanya wasn't exactly sure. But she had to think of something—*anything.*

Rollo was right. She wasn't even going to get through the door to the palace *kitchens* in the time it would take him to reach the council room and make sure that they issued an order for her immediate arrest, assuming Rees hadn't already beaten him to it.

She had no title to be stripped of, but she would be stripped of the quill and her freedom in short order. The Snake? She'd never see it again, let alone regain its ownership.

She would be useless. She would be no one.

Tanya shut her eyes. Why should she allow *that*? So that people far less competent than she could achieve even greater power than they already had? She didn't think so. Setting her jaw, she stuck the point of the quill into the center of the little red diamond on her wrist.

"Tanya!"

She ignored Rollo's wary cry and moved the quill, which again slid through her flesh like a reed in the shallows, smoothly and almost imperceptible. And then, in the sky above her starburst self, she wrote: *Fire.*

A fire bolt cracked across the sky, a stark flash of bright color against the darkening blue of the newly starlit sky, a great gust of smoke and ash in its wake.

The fire bloomed on her skin, too. She caught the tail end with the quill point and dragged it down and in a circle, tracing it several times, so that the line was thick and dark.

A circle of flames, red and burning blue, burst into existence around Tanya. Gillian stumbled backward with a shocked whinny, nearly throwing her charge.

"What have you done?" cried Rollo, shouting to be heard over the sizzle.

Tanya turned on the spot and smiled at him through the flames.

"Do you think they'll see me now?" she asked.

The blaze rose higher and higher, coating the woods outside the Capital gates with a rosy haze of smoke. Rollo answered, but Tanya couldn't hear him over the blaring of the military horns ringing through the trees.

# Chapter

As the horns and hooves grew louder, Tanya turned and bowed as low as she could, her front knee brushing the undergrowth.

Her eyes down, she said, "My deepest apologies for the disruption to your evening, gentlemen. My name is Tanya. I'm a maid of Griffin's Port and did not know to whom I should apply—but I have something the Queen and Council have been looking for."

After a moment of hesitation, the corpsman at the head of the party chose to sheathe his sword.

Tanya nodded at him and moved her fingers over the quill, catching the edge of the wind tornado still tattooed on her arm and stealing a bit of it to blow out the fire.

The commander hopped off his horse and took a couple careful steps her way. He looked at her closely, his eyes lingering on the blood.

"Young woman," he said, a sliver of razor blade in his voice, "are you injured?"

"Far from it." With the fire gone, Rollo had regained his seat on Gillian, and the two cantered in between Tanya and the commander. "Commander, I am Magus Rollo of Vermillon's Pass and this young woman is a thief."

The commander's eyes flickered over Rollo. He found the insignia of the Royal College of Aetherical Manipulation on his cuff and his brow furrowed. He directed his next question to Tanya.

"Are you, madam, *connected* with the Royal College? I was not aware that they had admitted any women . . . ?"

She started to answer, but before she could, the quill point started to vibrate wildly in her vein, and both Gillian and the commander took a cautious step backward.

Tanya clamped her hand down on her wrist, closing her fingers around the feather's spine, but the vibrations continued to travel up her body until they reached her head and the ends of her hair lifted with its power.

The commander observed their progress with widening eyes. He turned to Rollo. "Sir, I appreciate your concern and civic duty. Moreover, I am acquainted with your elder brother and have the utmost respect for your family and your scholarship. But, to be honest, her thievery seems to be rather beside the point at this particular moment and you may debrief me later." He turned back to Tanya. "I believe it would be more prudent for you to remove the quill now, before we enter the city gates," he said.

It was, all things considered, the best result she could hope for. Before she could change her mind, Tanya grabbed the top feathers and pulled.

The first time she had disentangled the quill from her flesh, it had slid out like quicksilver, weightlessly.

Not this time. It stuck and stuttered, as if it were pulling through a swamp rather than Tanya's own insides. At the same time, a sharp pain pierced Tanya's skull, starting at the nape of her neck and radiating to her cheekbones.

She fell to her knees, but the commander made no moves to either help or hinder her, and so still she pulled.

"This is my arm," she hissed through gritted teeth, "and you, quill, will listen to me!"

The quill popped out and Tanya fell on her back. Red steam floated above her. Warm flecks landed on her cheek and she realized it was her own vaporized blood.

A gurgling noise drew her gaze to her side. She watched as the tattoos writhed on her arm, twisting in on themselves, and a black substance, like ink, but shinier and more viscous, drizzled out of the wound on her wrist.

The drizzle slowed to a single drop and her flesh closed up again with a pop. The diamond, Tanya noted, had transformed into a sunburst. Or was that supposed to be a star?

Thunder rocked the clearing and the sky opened up.

The corps commander removed his glove and held open his palm, capturing a few drops of the deluge.

It was raining gold.

More than raining; it was pouring gold. Fat drops of it got stuck in her hair and when Tanya wiped her hands across her eyes, shining grit got under her fingernails.

Tanya sat up and stared at the junkoff. The gold in the hollow of her apron could *buy* her a new inn and provision it, too. That is, it could if she wasn't under arrest.

Wordlessly, the commander cleaned his glove with a tidy handkerchief.

"My name is Sir Artur Lurch," he told her as she accepted his hand and pulled herself to her feet. "I am the captain of city guard and I have an advisory seat on the Queen's Council. I will take things from here." Sir Lurch placed his hands securely on Tanya's hip bones and, as impersonally as if he were lifting a pot off the stove, deposited her onto his horse's back, at the very front of its saddle. "Captain Tristan."

"Yes, sir!" One of his entourage saluted sharply, his face hidden behind a helmet of patterned steel. This was a very different standard of corpsmen than Tanya was used to turning up in the Port Cities.

Sir Lurch didn't even look behind him. "Select however many of the corps you need to remain behind and secure this grove," said the commander while mounting the horse behind Tanya. "I want no gossip in the Capital of what transpired here tonight."

"Hang on—" interrupted Rollo, but was cut off with a brisk, soldierly, "Understood, sir."

"Carry on then." Sir Lurch reached around Tanya to take control of the reins, sending the stallion charging down the lane, leaving Rollo shouting in their wake.

She turned her head and saw the clearing as a shining column of gold—the untold wealth literally pouring from the sky was limited in scope to that one undergrown patch of forest.

The famous gates were upon them, but Sir Lurch reined the horse into a sharp left, plunging them into the spiky thicket that lined the southeastern wall instead.

"Are you crazy?" screamed Tanya, throwing her arms up over her face, tensed against thorns. But after a moment during which she realized nothing was pricking her, Tanya lowered her hands.

"Oh," she said, putting down her arms entirely.

They were underground. The sharp and thorny bramble had hidden a smooth pathway in a moldy red brick tunnel, musty with the smell of earthworms and dust. "Where are we?" she asked.

Sir Lurch didn't answer. He was busy awkwardly pulling something out of a hard-to-reach inside-breast pocket.

"Finally," he muttered, pulling out a small bundle of wadded-up scrap of parchment. He placed it in the palm of his right hand and began to slowly pull back each of its four corners.

"Regalia," he whispered, tracing a pattern with his index finger in the space above the paper. "Solar minimum." He placed his free hand over his open palm and shut his eyes.

After a long moment of silence, Tanya found herself incapable of keeping her mouth shut. "What on Lode are you doing?" she asked. "Are you praying? It doesn't seem the best time for it."

"May I risk rudeness by asking you a personal question, Miss Tanya?"

She shrugged. It was the least suggestive time a strange man had requested to ask her a personal question in the dark. "I suppose so."

"Have you ever found yourself in a situation in which refraining from offering an opinion and simply observing carefully—and silently—was the best course of action?"

Tanya took a moment to review his query. "Are you telling me that I talk too much? Because, honestly, no. No one's ever told me that I talk too much. They're too busy being made comfortable to their exact specifications in a flawlessly run tavern."

She saw the commander's mouth twitch in the darkness. "That actually wasn't precisely what I was driving at, miss," he told her. "But, for the time being, you are indeed talking too much. Now be quiet or I'll put cuffs on you and bring you to the deepest dungeon in the Capital, as I would have every right and reason to do, rather than where I'm actually taking you, which is . . . not that. So, hush."

Tanya chose to obey.

"Regalia," he whispered, and again traced a pattern with his index finger in the space above the paper. "Solar minimum." He placed his free hand over his open palm and shut his eyes.

Tanya watched as a kernel of light materialized from within the wadded-up paper. The kernel multiplied and swirled in expanding ellipticals until it shot up to the curved ceiling, illuminating the tunnel with a cold, white light, entirely unlike fire.

Sir Lurch clicked and his horse resumed moving through the tunnel. Tanya blinked, her eyes adjusting to the light.

The horse had stopped in front of a blank brick wall—a dead end.

Sir Lurch dismounted in one fluid step and reached up to help Tanya down to the ground. He then stood in front of the solid wall, the grout between the brick laid so finely that Tanya reckoned she could chisel for a century and not pick her way out.

But Sir Lurch did not produce a chisel, or tools of any kind. He merely removed his other glove and, transferring the witch-light from hand to hand, raised his fingers to the wall, then carefully placed them, fingertip by fingertip, on five separate bricks. With his fingers splayed out wide, he pressed hard and rotated his wrist to the right.

It was as if a whole swath of the wall became liquid—a swirling eddy of color and light, stretching thinner and thinner until Tanya could see something just past it.

Sir Lurch grabbed Tanya by the wrist and pushed her forward into the eddy.

For a moment she was on fire . . . and then she was freezing . . . and then she was standing in a dim cellar filled with bright swords hanging neatly in racks. A sleepy boy slumped over a desk in the corner, his red velvet cap slipping over his eyes.

The boy sat straight up and stared. "What are you doing there?" he asked.

Tanya blinked. "I honestly have no idea."

Sir Lurch came through the eddy next, his hand on his horse's bridle.

"You, boy," he said. "Have you had this watch long?"

"No—no, sir," stuttered the page, straightening his cap. "I'm the ward of the Seneschal, I've only been at court for—"

"Never mind," broke in Sir Lurch. "You know your way to the stables from this part of the palace?"

"Yes sir," said the boy, still staring at Tanya, who realized anew that she was still covered in blood and gold and dirt and Lady of Cups knew what else. "But, my patron, sir, he said to remain at—"

"I know Lord Horado very well and I will vouch for you," Sir Lurch told the boy, radiating command. "Now be sure to take extra special care of Jubilee, here. He dislikes this mode of transport."

The boy obeyed, taking the reins, and, with a last glance over his shoulder at Tanya, opened a plain door built seamlessly into the wood-paneled wall and led the horse out.

Sir Lurch watched him leave, waiting until the door shut behind him before turning to the boy's recently vacated chair. He pushed it out of the way and slid open a panel on the floor. Tanya crept forward to look.

The false floor hid an array of brass bells and cords. Sir Lurch bit his lip and pulled a lever on a bell near the top of the panel.

"Yes, I think we had better," he muttered to himself and pulled another lever, this one connected to a dusty-looking bell at the bottom of the array.

Something the boy had said suddenly floated to the surface of Tanya's brain.

"Sir Lurch, are we in the palace?" she asked, desperately smoothing down her impossibly soiled clothes.

"Yes," answered the commander, distractedly, still contemplating the mechanisms below him. "I think that should be sufficient for now." He slid the false floor back over the mysterious contraption and moved the chair back into position.

He stood straight and looked at Tanya, who was breathing hard.

"Are you sure you're all right?" he asked, frowning. "It might be important for you to make a good impression on the person I've called down here. Oh, good, Violet." Yet another door, a grander one with an iron handle, opened to reveal a woman of middle years, dressed plainly but expensively, her iron-shot hair piled on her head in elaborate braids. "I need you to find me as long a cloak with as large a hood as you can, please. Very quickly."

"A cloak?" cried Tanya. "I'm in the *Glacier* and you want to cover all . . . this . . . with a cloak?"

"Only temporarily. Violet will have to rustle up something appropriate for you to wear, especially if we're to present you at Council, but that can wait until we get you to a bath. Ah, Count Hewitt. Thank you for coming so quickly."

Tanya turned. A sleek man stood in the doorway, surveying her with narrowed eyes. Acting on reflex, Tanya narrowed her eyes right back.

"Of course, Sir Lurch," said the sleek man, his voice smooth and high pitched. "What is the bell system for if not to quickly—and discreetly—contact one's colleagues?" He stepped into the room and shut the door behind him. "And, without knowing the facts, I'd say you were right to employ discretion. Who is this young woman? Does she have something to do with the disturbance at the city walls?"

Sir Lurch smiled wryly. "Should have known you'd have heard about that already, my lord. Yes, I'd say she does."

The count circled Tanya. "Does she speak?" he asked mildly.

"Yes," answered the corps commander quickly, forestalling Tanya's automatic retort. She caught his eye and perceived a slight shake of his head.

"I came across her about a league down the path from the gates," explained Sir Lurch. "She claimed to be in possession of some information important to the Queen and Council."

"Did she also claim to have been attacked by wild dogs? The state of her! Why not simply arrest her, Sir Lurch? She certainly looks disreputable enough to be a criminal." Tanya winced. Normally, she would have been affronted at such insult, but in this case the insult happened to be true.

"I had plans to do just that, but then . . ."

The count turned to look at the corpsman, who was struggling to explain. "Well, Sir Lurch?"

"It started raining. But only in the grove; there was no rain on the path. It might still be raining in that grove. I left a few deputies to guard it."

"And?"

Sir Lurch hesitated. "It was raining gold, my lord. Fat drops of liquefied gold."

This caught the count's attention. "Really? Well, that is interesting," he said, looking back to Tanya. "My network has reported unusually productive junkoff throughout the kingdom, but gold falling from the sky . . . that is very interesting. What does that have to do with the girl?"

"The rain started after she pulled a quill from her arm. Immediately after, that is. It was difficult not to connect her to it, although I'm at a loss to explain the connection."

The count had gone very still. "A quill, Sir Lurch? You're absolutely certain?"

Sir Lurch's forehead crinkled with confusion. "Yes, sir."

The count's eyes did not move from Tanya's face as he asked, "Have you confiscated the quill, Sir Lurch?"

"Well . . . no, sir. It was just a quill."

"I see," said the count icily. "Look at me, girl."

Tanya forced herself to meet his glare. She could not remember ever feeling more cowed in her life. Not by the Tomcat, not by the lord overseer of Griffin's Port, not by any rough-hewed pirate in the Snake, not by any imperious duke who wanted a little something extra with his wine, not even by the stall keepers who'd shooed her away when she was left alone and hungry on the docks, tiny and nameless.

"Your name," he demanded.

She took a breath. "Tanya of Griffin's Port, proprietress of the Smiling Snake inn and tavern," she said.

He raised his eyebrow at her lack of family name. She could read his unspoken thought: *an orphan or a foundling; no one of consequence—expendable.* She felt anger inject some steel into her spine, and she stood up straighter.

"Show me," he commanded.

Tanya, seeing no advantage in resisting, extracted the quill from her sleeve. She held it out to him and he snatched the quill away from her grasp.

"Hey!" cried Tanya, but Sir Lurch's hand on her arm held her back.

"My lord?" asked Sir Lurch, his voice curious. "Is the quill important?"

The count's eyes glowed as he examined his prize. No longer interested in the tableau in front of him, he waved away the corpsman's question with a flick of a ruby-ringed hand.

"Thank you very much for alerting me to this, Sir Lurch," he said, his eyes never leaving the quill as he turned toward the exit. "Please be assured that you did precisely the right thing and the Queen will be informed of your sense and service. I'll send my own men to the grove you mentioned."

"What shall I do about the girl, my lord?"

"The what? Oh, the girl. Clean her up, I suppose. Assure yourself that she's committed no crimes and, if she's honest, send her on her way with some appropriate token of the Queen's gratitude."

Tanya cleared her throat. "My lord, if the Queen wishes to reward me, I do have a specific request. . . ."

The count had turned away, one foot out the door, the bedraggled girl who had brought the quill already forgotten.

"Pardon me," he muttered perfunctorily as he collided with Violet, who had returned with a hooded cloak of rich green cloth.

"My *lord*," called out Tanya, but the count didn't stop.

Violet hurried forward and began arranging the cloak around her shoulders. Tanya frowned and shook her off, stepping into the door-way. The count was hurrying down a long hallway.

Tanya threw off the cloak entirely and flexed her fingers. She felt the quill thrumming in the count's grasp—and *pulled*.

"Ayeee!" The count yelped as the quill scraped his palm in its arc back down the hallway. Tanya, her tattoos pulsing, caught it neatly between her thumb and forefinger.

The count turned around, cradling his injured palm, and looked at Tanya as if he hadn't actually seen her before.

With the quill firmly back in her possession, happily spitting golden sparks into the air, Tanya dipped into a deep curtsy, dripping with sarcastic respect.

"If the Council would make the time for one so *common* as I," Tanya spat, "I have left my home and traveled far expressly to peti-tion it. In doing so, I trusted my person to one of my Queen and Council's corpsmen, and instead of receiving protection, was set upon by thieves, imprisoned, and escaped all on my own, with no help from the corps. But here I am and somehow I have managed to safeguard this quill. I will continue to do so until I have seen the Queen and Council, and have said what I came to say."

# Chapter

14

The count walked forward. As he came down the dim hall, Tanya saw that he was smiling—a not entirely pleasant expression.

He pulled a handkerchief out of his breast pocket and began to wrap it around the cut on his palm. To Tanya's eyes, he was a little too practiced at making impromptu bandages for one so well dressed.

"What did you say your name was, girl?" asked the count.

Tanya repeated her curtsy. "Tanya, my lord," she said. "From Griffin's Port."

"And you say you were traveling with a corps?"

"Yes sir. Commander Rees's Corps."

"Yes, of course it would have to be Rees," the count muttered, apparently to himself.

Sir Lurch cleared his throat. "When I found her, she was with the second son of Vermillon's Path. The little one who got sent to the Royal College of Aetherical Manipulation."

"Really?" The count looked both curious and amused. "And *she* had the quill? Interesting. What have you done with him?"

"My men will escort him to the Corps Complex. He'll be made comfortable until I can debrief him."

"Please oblige me and make sure he does not leave the complex, at least not before little miss Tanya here presents her petition to the Council."

"I am to see the Council, then?" blurted out Tanya.

The count approached her and Tanya bit her lip.

"Yes girl, you will, and the Queen, too," said the count quietly. "Whoever bears that quill is bound to be very important in this court. That might have been Commander Rees; it suits me that that is no longer the case. Are you ready to be important, Tanya of Griffin's Port? Because, if you are, for the moment, that will work for me. But are you sure your petition is worth you being an object in this court? If I'm not much mistaken, this is not an environment in which you have much experience, and, if you have any at all, it's as a serving girl. Are you ready to be more than a . . . what? Not a *proprietress*, truly. Tavern wench?" Tanya started a little and he smiled a little wider. "Are you willing, tavern wench?"

Tanya looked the count in the eye. She felt a little thrill of fear as she did so—she would never have imagined herself looking a count in the eye.

To return to her tavern, the tavern maid had to stop being a tavern maid.

"I'll do what I have to, sir, in order to get what I came for," she said steadily, her mouth feeling odd and empty around the missing deferential of "my lord."

The count looked over her shoulder at Violet. "You may take her to the blue room in the eastern turret," he said. "My sister's room at court, but she'll never know, not gallivanting with husband number three in the Cotton Trees. And for the Sky's sake, woman, *cover* her in that cloak. Use whatever of my sister's gowns will fit her and make her look as presentable as possible. I'll come for her when I'm ready." And with that, he turned heel and disappeared up a spiral staircase.

Tanya was left standing, still as a scarecrow, in the corridor. A corridor that, with its ebony-and-pearl sconces and gold-leafed ceiling, was probably the grandest room she had ever been in, for all that it was adjacent to a supply closet.

She was still standing there, gold and blood dripping from her wrists onto the imported red tiles, when Sir Lurch muttered a few words to Violet and disappeared out the side door. Violet draped the green cloak around her shoulders and lifted the hood, but still Tanya couldn't move.

The older woman began to do up the buttons, as if Tanya were the pampered daughter of some lord.

"I can do that," Tanya said, breaking out of her shock, raising her hands to the next button. "No need to wait on me, my lady."

"I'm not a 'my lady,'" said Violet, stepping back and allowing Tanya to finish fastening the cloak. "I believe 'ma'am' will do."

The words came swiftly and dispassionately, but her tone was not unkind. And, as Tanya knew from many interactions with ladies' maids delighted to find someone beneath them in the hierarchy, an upper servant of the Glacier would be well within her rights to accept a "my lady" from Tanya.

"There," said Tanya. She spread out her hands. "Will I do, ma'am?"

Violet looked at her critically. "Hide your hands in your sleeves," she said. "They're filthy and I haven't even examined your fingernails yet. I have a feeling I shall not approve." Tanya obeyed. "Now, where I can, I'll keep to the servants' passages, but sadly the councilman's tower is on other side of the Queen's Hall and at this hour"—she checked a brass watch hanging from her belt on a plain chain—"I can't guarantee that we'll be able to keep you entirely out of sight. Keep your hood up and your chin down. Don't speak to anyone and move as quickly as you can. Do exactly as I say."

"Yes, ma'am." *The Queen's Hall, the Queen's Hall, the Queen's Hall.* Tanya pulled the hood farther down over her eyes. She breathed deep. "I'm ready when you are, ma'am."

Violet nodded and briskly turned heel, leading Tanya up the same spiral staircase the count had taken. Tanya, careful to keep her eyes on her feet, followed as best she could.

But first she stopped. Violet had called the count "councilman."

Count Hewitt was *Councilman* Hewitt, the Queen's closest advisor. The very man who had signed away the Snake.

*And he didn't even know your name before you told him.* Tanya gritted her teeth and followed Violet up the stairs.

All she saw was floor—polished mahogany planks, opalescent marble, thick-piled velvet rugs with impossibly intricate patterns, and more of the red tile. She eventually walked straight into Violet's back. The older woman had stopped.

"Quiet," she ordered.

Tanya obeyed, still hidden within the cloak. A buzz of masculine voices filtered through the hood, but her vision was blocked in every direction other than down.

Tanya obeyed the order to remain silent, but as seconds turned into a full minute, she decided it couldn't hurt to lift her eyes just a *little*, just to see where they were, and what they were waiting for.

They had stopped behind double doors of highly polished rosewood carved with a design of a rose trellis, each thorn so lifelike, and so sharp, Tanya felt sure they would actually draw blood.

She cautiously lifted her chin higher, peering through her lashes, and gasped.

Through the gap in the double doors was an immense hall, the brightest lit that Tanya had ever seen, heavy with the scent of roses and vanilla. And in the center of that hall were the seven most beautiful young men Tanya had ever seen.

They were moving so rhythmically, with such acrobatic and convoluted grace, that it took Tanya a moment to realize that they were not, in fact, dancing.

They were fighting.

Not a one of the seven looked alike. They had dark skin, light skin, freckled, tanned. One had golden curls, another had coal-black locks sticking up in pieces, and another had nothing but reddish fuzz covering his head.

Their weapons were distinct, too. Tanya spotted a long sword, a set of double-pronged daggers, some sort of whip, a staff, and three other armaments that she couldn't begin to identify, but all were wielded with deadly, controlled force.

The fighting men were moving across the floor, a many-tiled masterpiece in blue glass, green gems, terra-cotta, ebony, and mother-of-pearl, swiftly, but mostly silently.

The buzz came from the ring of richly dressed men—and a few women, although not as many—who stood in a loose ring around the hall, sipping something pink and bubbling out of elegant crystal glasses shaped like tulips and eating tiny tarts.

And all the way on the far side of the hall, on a dais that appeared to be made entirely of roses, was the Queen.

The Queen was a flower in human form, her flesh as luscious as the peach-colored blossoms on cherry trees. She was clad only in a silvery-white lace gown, an empire waist and cap sleeves flowing seamlessly into a silken train that concealed her feet.

The Queen wore no cosmetics that Tanya could see. Her hair, the same silver-white of her dress, fell loose and shining to her waist.

The Queen wore no jewelry except for, of course, the crown. The crown . . . it was as tall as a small child and blindingly bright—too blinding to discern anything but three glittering spikes, two shorter on the outside, and one taller, tapered one in the center.

The Queen's face was unnervingly still—not stern, not withering, not unpleasant. Not anything. Not *human*.

Tanya shuffled closer to the door, staring over Violet's shoulder. She realized that she had no idea how old the Queen was, and this, her first glimpse of her, did nothing to change that. Her skin was as smooth as a girl three years younger than Tanya herself, but there was something ancient in those eyes . . .

With a shock, Tanya realized something else: She didn't know the Queen's name. She had always simply been . . . the Queen.

A quintet of musicians—a harpist, a lute player, a recorder, a drummer, and a singer—gathered in front of the Queen's dais. The singer began, trilling out pleasing nonsense syllables. The nobles circled around, turning their backs to the fighters—and the doors.

Violet opened the door enough for them to slip through unnoticed, hustling Tanya through the hall.

Finally, they reached the top of a twisting staircase where there was a carved door of pale wood. Violet brought out an enormous iron ring from inside her sleeve and placed a key in the lock.

Violet grunted and the door gave with a sticky thud.

"Of course, his lordship's household ignores the rooms not immediately in use by himself," she said caustically. "You, girl, go in there and remove your . . . let's call them clothes, although they hardly merit the name anymore. I trust you can run yourself a bath?"

"Yes ma'am. Is there a stove or shall I heat a pot in the fireplace . . . ?"

"Heat a pot? No, girl, simply lower the bucket down the water shaft by the hearth."

"Water . . . shaft? Like, a well?"

"What? Where did you say you were from? Never mind," said Violet, interrupting Tanya's half-whispered answer. "I'll run across the hall to the councilman's chambers and send over one of his girls to help you. And I'll see what has been done with the Lady Louisa's wardrobe, although I doubt we'll find it kept in good condition. Well?"

Tanya's head snapped up. "Ma'am."

Violet had already left the room and was standing in front of a different, larger, and grander door. She pointed past Tanya into Lady Louisa's room.

"In you go," she ordered her. The grander door opened and revealed a startled-looking girl in a spotless kerchief.

"I don't know you," said Violet, pushing past her. "Are you new? What's your name?"

"Jasmine, ma'am," whispered the startled girl, shutting the door behind her.

Tanya stepped into the tower room and stood very still for a moment. She moved to the window and threw open the heavy velvet curtains, flooding the chamber with starlight, illuminating her path to the center of the room.

And there she stayed, spinning slowly on her heels, until a sudden flicker of light drew her eye.

"I'm so sorry you had to stand in the dark, my lady," said the little maid from across the hall as she traveled the entire circle of the tower room, lighting each lamp in its individual golden sconce. All the sconces were gold, but one was in the shape of a roaring tiger, another was a strange creature Tanya had never seen with a long hose coming out of its face where its nose should be, and yet a third a roaring cobra with glittering diamond fangs, and another . . . Tanya couldn't keep track.

Once the tower was illuminated, Tanya found herself sinking to her knees.

"There now," said the maid, sounding relieved and much more confident now that she had successfully completed a task. "I'll get that bath ready for you, my lady, and perhaps some hot cocoa before bed . . . my lady?" She rushed to the center of the room and knelt discreetly at the carpet's edge. "Are you ill, my lady? Shall I fetch a healer?" When Tanya didn't answer, the maid crept an infinitesimal bit closer. "My lady?" she asked again. "My lady, are you all—"

"I'm not a 'my lady,'" snapped Tanya. The maid blinked and fell back. "Sorry," said Tanya. "But, I'm not a 'my lady,' really. I'm not even a 'miss.'"

The maid, who Tanya now remembered had called herself Jasmine, smiled gently. "I don't know," she said quietly. "Whoever you are, you're staying here, aren't you? You're going to sleep in that bed tonight."

Tanya looked toward where Jasmine was nodding and shook her head. *I'd rather sleep right here, on the carpet,* she thought to herself, feeling the plush threads cushion her knees, at least six inches deep. *It's nicer than any bed I ever had.*

This room, the room in which she was expected to bathe, sleep, and dress, was unlike anything Tanya had ever imagined.

She had caught glimpses of grandeur over her years serving at the Snake. Traveling chests made of the iridescent scales of sea serpents and bound by gold; ruby-stoppered bottles of scent; jade combs, studded with pearls; a matchbox, small and made of plain enamel, left behind by some lord's careless daughter as a useless and easily forgotten trinket, but so beautiful that Tanya had kept it among the bottles of liquor behind the bar, ostensibly so that she could quickly return it if the lady came looking for it, but really so she could admire the rainbow, shimmering and sun bright, painted on its top.

Tanya had seen all this and thought she was sophisticated enough, or at least sensible enough, to keep her composure in the face of all the beauty she was never to possess. But then Jasmine had lit the lamps and the full impact of this room had hit her.

The stone, inlaid with some glittering mineral, arched all the way to the pointed top of the tower, some fifty feet high, sending sparkles of light dancing across every reflective service, and fully half the left-hand curve of the wall was covered in a vast array of ornate mirrors. The armoire was made of rose quartz and studded by rose diamonds. There was a large vanity, which at first seemed simple, just a plain white table and chair, padded in pink velvet, until you noticed that they were both made of mother-of-pearl.

But it wasn't the luxury, in the end, that felled Tanya. She had known hardship and she had known, if not "plenty," then certainly "more than sufficient," and she was satisfied with the latter. She knew her place.

A pair of silk stockings, sweat stains soiling the heel and the toe, had been thrown across the back of the vanity chair.

That's what shocked her: not the opulence, but the disarray; not the unfamiliar grandeur, but the all-too-familiar, unavoidable squalor of human life. That stocking hinted at the existence of a person who was no different than Tanya.

Tanya had seen men (they were almost always men) who identified as "revolutionaries." They muttered over tall mugs of beer and shouted about the oppressive nobility. She never paid them much attention. She didn't have the time, thank you very much. She was a useful person with a job to do. She worked hard and earned her keep. She was proud of that.

But standing there, she found no evidence of any functional difference between her and the count's sister. Yet Louisa lived in a soaring tower and Tanya had to fight for the right to live in her cramped attic.

Dazed, she walked toward the marble arches, pulled in by the steam, thick and fragrant with the smell of lemongrass and lavender. Jasmine pulled a rope in what looked like a large, metal-bound dumbwaiter, and it eventually hoisted a giant kettle up and over the tub.

The moment Tanya slid into the steaming water and tipped her head back to rest on a convenient pillow, she immediately fell asleep. Jasmine woke her, dried her off, and wrapped her in a nightdress as if she *were* a helpless noblewoman, sending her off to sleep in the now-made bed of the perfectly tidied room.

# Chapter

When Tanya awoke, her eyes immediately flinched away from the sun's glare. She was not accustomed to waking up when the sun was so high.

Tanya pulled open the gossamer curtains around the bed and saw enough food for an entire corps: fluffy yellow eggs scrambled with onions and smoked fish, toasted bread drenched in herbed butter, and piles of spiced ham.

Acting on pure instinct, she fell upon the food, turning an ankle on her way; she had severely misjudged the height of the bed.

"The lady awakens," said a dry voice behind her.

Her mouth stuffed full of ham and sweet potatoes, Tanya turned and saw both Violet and Jasmine buried in the shimmering contents of the armoire.

"Is it very late?" asked Tanya, suddenly feeling a panic that she couldn't quite account for until she realized that she had usually knocked out at least twenty-five items on her daily to-do list by the time the sun had even fully risen.

"You should have woken me up," she said reproachfully. "I don't feel well when I sleep late."

"That's too bad," said Violet, pulling out and rejecting a capelet stitched with silver thread. "Because I have been put in charge of making you look as though you belong in the council room, and an exhausted urchin with circles under her eyes and stress eruptions across her nose wasn't going to cut it. When I say sleep, you sleep." She turned to face Tanya. "In short, my girl, I don't care how well you *feel*, only how well you *look*. Now eat your breakfast, drink your tea, and then sit at that vanity and don't speak unless spoken to."

Tanya obeyed, thoroughly enjoying her breakfast, although she quite disagreed with Violet about the benefits of sleeping late. Something in her shoulders and back felt off, and she had a strange floating, *relaxed* sensation behind her eyes. It didn't feel safe.

"We need to see which of these we'll have to alter the least." Violet took a gown from Jasmine, holding it up critically. "The councilman will be here to inspect you in four hours, so we don't have an abundance of time."

Tanya eyed the dress. Too narrow in the hips and too long, but just a matter of a quick hem and letting out stitches in the bodice. *Nothing that would take four hours to accomplish*, she thought a little scornfully.

"I'd be happy to do any alterations myself," offered Tanya, not quite hiding a smirk. "If you're too busy, ma'am, that is. You shouldn't be bothering yourself about me."

"I agree," answered Violet, not looking up from the fabric. "But I answer to the Council and I'm bothering myself on its business, not yours. And, more importantly, you're out of your salt-baked port city mind if you think I'm letting *you* take a needle to this gown. Don't you see what it's made of, girl?"

Tanya lifted her eyebrows. "It's silk, isn't it? Rather fine, I daresay, but I do know how to safely hem a silk dress, ma'am."

Violet's mouth quirked up at one side. "Not quite," she said, sounding amused, but again not unkind. "Come here, child. See for yourself."

Tanya stood and crossed the room.

"Stand right there," said Violet, indicating a spot in front of the open wardrobe door, its inside lined with yet another mirror.

Tanya obeyed and Violet stepped behind her, the silver gown in her arms. She shook it out behind Tanya. Tanya frowned at the unexpected sound, like the faraway wind chimes of some tiny, fairy picnic. Violet swung her arms in front of her, holding the dress in front of Tanya.

"Now look at yourself in the mirror," Violet instructed.

Tanya rolled her eyes. It all seemed rather a to-do for a silk dress. "Like I thought, ma'am," she said confidently, looking at the line of the fabric against her body. "I'll need to let out the bodice some and lift the hem, but nothing very complicated. The count's sister and I are rather of a size, although how she's thinner than I am with a breakfast like that every morning, I don't . . . wait." Tanya frowned and leaned forward. "Wait . . ."

"There it is," said Violet, sounding smug.

"But that's . . . that's . . ." sputtered Tanya. "Is this dress actually made of *silver?*"

"Silver and moonstone actually," answered Violet. "The best dressmakers in the Capital have developed a way to hammer precious metals into narrow rods so fine that they can be weaved like thread into fabric. Unbelievably expensive of course, but you can't beat the effect. Jasmine, get the tape measure."

"But . . . but it's absurd," stammered Tanya. "That's the most ridiculous thing I've ever heard in my entire life."

"Arms up," instructed Violet, pulling the gown away. Still dumbfounded, Tanya obeyed and Violet pulled off her nightdress. "Tape measure, please Jas—thank you."

"No, I'm serious," said Tanya, feeling the heat rising in her cheeks. "That's *crazy*. What could possibly be the point? It looks just like silk. What is the point of weaving it out of precious metals worth more than thirty people's wages for thirty years of work, except to make it incredibly expensive and impossible to wash? What is the *point?*"

Violet was moving up and down her body with the tape measure, murmuring numbers to Jasmine, who was industriously writing it all down in a little notebook. "All right, arms can go down now," said Violet mildly. "If I take care of the tailoring, can you sort out her undergarments? You know the sort we need? They can see the curves, but only just barely, and Lady of Cups, don't let any of it *move*, if you know what I mean."

"Yes ma'am," answered Jasmine with a curtsy. She moved to the back half of the closet and started pulling open drawers.

"Now then," said Violet, looking at Tanya. "We should do something with that hair. You certainly aren't modest, are you, girl? Most port city maids would have been desperately clutching back the nighty by now, or so I'd imagine."

"I . . . I . . . I . . ."

Violet looked closer. "Lady of Cups, girl, are you shaking? Are you quite well?"

Tanya shook her head and whispered, "The waste. The stupidity. I'm . . ."

Violet nodded, a little approvingly. "I understand," she said. "The opulence of court can be somewhat overwhelming when one is new to it. Trust me, the ideas behind it begin to make sense once you're accustomed to them."

But Tanya wasn't overwhelmed. She was enraged.

*No, not enraged*, she corrected herself—*outraged*.

Fine workmanship was one thing and luxurious materials another. Tanya understood the aesthetic and even practical uses of such things. But an insistence on luxury to the point of farce, to the point where the actual function of the object is called into question *because* of that luxury—Tanya couldn't respect that. That was folly. That was nonsense.

That was *useless*.

And just like that, Tanya ceased to be cowed by the Glacier. All the awe, all the fear melted away.

She looked up and around the grand tower room, this time with a certain disdain. Yes, the bed was comfortable. The bath had been lovely and the system with the hot water was no doubt very clever. The breakfast cooks knew what they were about.

But it wasn't magic. It wasn't special. It was just rich.

There was nothing, *nothing*, that was forcing her to respect these people. Her mind was her own and these people were simply ludicrous.

She spent the next several hours in a state of mildly appalled indifference as she was painted and polished and finally squeezed into the ridiculous silver gown.

Violet stepped backward and put her chin in her hand. "Jasmine, pull that loose curl out from behind her ear." Jasmine complied and Violet shook her head. "No, that doesn't work either. Can we find something to clip it back with? One of the pearl-tipped pins, I think."

Tanya shifted a little, shaking out her feet, already squeezed numb by diamond-encrusted high heels that were far too tight. Then Jasmine pulled a perfect corkscrew curl that Tanya didn't recognize up and around the intricate plait wreathing her head.

Tanya wondered how much of the shining brown masses was her own hair. She put it at about 30 percent, but she couldn't be sure—she wasn't accustomed to staring at her own reflection for that long and had lost track.

The magic tattoos were gone, covered by a thick layer of cosmetic powder.

Violet sighed. "Well, I think that's the best we can do for the moment." As if on cue, a sharp staccato rapping on the door announced the arrival of Councilman Hewitt.

He entered without waiting to be invited in. He joined Violet, putting his own chin in his hand, pursing his lips. "Well, I'd say you did your best, Violet," he said. "It's certainly an improvement."

Jasmine stepped away and Tanya took a halting step forward. Her ankle wobbled in the heel and the councilman's eyebrow went up.

Tanya arranged her hands so they were gripping the edge of the trailing silver skirt, something she had seen ladies in similarly shaped gowns do, and was relieved to find that the movement helped her maintain balance.

She took another step and this time her ankle didn't wobble. Still carefully keeping her hands on her skirts, she swung one ankle behind the other and bent her knees, her eyes on the floor.

Councilman Hewitt lifted her chin with one kid-gloved finger. He turned her face to the left and to the right. He nodded and let her go.

"You'll do," he said crisply. "It's only for an hour. You can curtsy, anyway, so that's something. You have the quill? Good, I'll escort you down."

He led her at a fast clip, faster even than Violet had, the shimmering surfaces barely registering as they flew by until they were suddenly in a hallway of singular stillness—and emptiness.

Tanya shivered suddenly. "Is it cold in here?" she asked, the hair on her arms prickling.

Councilman Hewitt smiled and nodded at something behind her, so she turned, hugging herself.

"Why did you think it was called the Glacier?" he asked.

They were in front of two gigantic oval doors, their shimmering white and blue fractals dazzling the eye and reaching higher than they could see.

"Is it diamond?" she asked, in wonder.

The councilman stepped forward and pulled off his glove. He put his hand on the door for a moment and then placed it on Tanya's wrist. She gasped.

"Ice," he said. "It never chips and it never melts. These doors were carved from the foundations of the Glacier itself and predate the monarchy."

Tanya stepped forward, reaching for the ice herself, the sheer cold of the doors making the air seem to buzz, dance, tickle her skin. "Where did it come from?" she asked. "The ice that makes up the Glacier?"

"I don't know," said the councilman. "That's a mystery for another day. Now, in there: Don't speak unless asked. Don't interrupt. Don't contradict me. Understood?" She nodded and he stepped forward. He cleared his throat. "Councilman Hewitt," he said softly, "escorting a maid of Griffin's Port."

Tanya thought she felt a breeze float lazily over her, frigid and unfriendly. But the doors opened with a musical sound, like the tinkling of chimes hung in a window.

Once the ice doors opened, Councilman Hewitt and Tanya walked through to the Queen and Council of Lode's meeting room, a vast cavern of ice.

From the dripping chandeliers, to the hearth large enough to fit three of Tanya, to the huge table in the shape of a horseshoe, everything was ice. It was like being inside a freezing crystal, the roaring fire and candelabras on the table notwithstanding.

And there, on a raised platform behind the table, were thirteen frozen thrones, identical except for the two in the center. The one in the absolute center was a foot higher than all the others and in it sat the Queen.

The one to her left was empty. Councilman Hewitt's seat—the Queen's left hand.

Tanya gulped. The councilman—*the count*, she thought, suddenly remembering his true rank and the extent of his height over her, which was nearly infinite in scope—dropped her arm and swept into the deepest bow she had ever seen performed by a man; his nose brushed the floor.

"My Queen and Council," he said, in a low, soft voice entirely different from the one he had been using up until now, all the oil wicked away. "Forgive my lateness, but I have received news of the lost artifact of the Aetherical College."

A cacophony of overlapping explanations, recriminations, and questions erupted around the table.

The Queen raised one hand, not very high. The room fell silent as a tomb.

She was so stunning to look at, it made Tanya shudder. It was as if she *were* the Glacier, carved out of enchanted ice, given life.

The Queen didn't speak, but Councilman Hewitt nodded at her as if she had. He reached behind him and drew Tanya forward by the elbow.

"Curtsy," he hissed in her ear as she moved in front of him.

Tanya didn't need to be told twice. Suddenly understanding why she needed to be dressed in beaten silver, holding on to her skirt for dear life, she knelt, stifling a gasp as the cold hit her knee. She bent her torso all the way forward, bending her eyes away from the Council and the Queen until all they would have to see of her was the top of her immaculately curled head.

From above her came Councilman Hewitt's new, muted voice. "Your Majesty, esteemed colleagues, allow me to present this young woman, a loyal citizen of Lode, to the Council and to her Queen. Will you be so indulgent as to allow her to rise?"

Tanya heard nothing, but a finger in her back signaled that the assent had been given, so, slowly, praying to every god she had ever heard of that she wouldn't trip over her train, she rose until she was standing straight.

The councilman allowed for a moment of silence—presumably

so the Council, made up almost entirely of wizened old men, could evaluate her—and then cleared his throat.

"Tanya is a poor but honest orphan of the Port Cities," he said, his voice rich with compassion. "She lost her parents in childhood and has been earning her living respectably ever since, never once falling to the vice or criminal acts so many others of her station have allowed themselves to be driven to. Young Tanya, motivated by nothing more than a desire to be of service to the Queen and Council, accepted a position with one of your own corps commanders, Your Majesty, as a domestic worker. You can imagine this innocent girl's shock and dismay when she witnessed her commander—the very representation of her Queen—upon arrival at Your Majesty's own sponsored College of Aetherical Manipulation, rather than announce himself as a commander of the Queen Corps and request an audience, order a dead-of-night raid on the scholars' vaults."

Here, the councilman paused. Tanya had been expending some effort in staring straight ahead during the councilman's bizarre recitation of what she supposed might be liberally termed her biography, but looked up sharply here, joining in the shocked hush that followed this pronouncement.

The quill was stolen by *Rees*? That made no sense! Not that Rees was above it—he *had* made a deal with the Tomcat, after all. And, yes, with the exception of Darrow, his corps was unusually well-stocked with scoundrels. And they were so very poorly provisioned . . .

But no, it *still* didn't make any sense, Tanya decided. First of all, Councilman Hewitt himself had signed his orders—orders the entire company were very clearly anxious to follow. And secondly—and more importantly—Rees simply lacked the imagination for such a wild gambit. Tanya looked up at the Council, to see if they were buying the tale.

They mostly looked awkward, shifting uncomfortably in their seats, coughing discreetly into napkins. Tanya wanted to look at the Queen, but found that she couldn't quite *sneak* a look at her; it was too disrespectful, somehow.

Apparently satisfied with the reception, however impenetrable Tanya found it, the councilman continued.

"Imagine the situation this poor, pitiable young woman found herself in," he said, crossing in front of her. "How could a commander of the Queen's Corps raid an institution sponsored by the Queen herself? But what could she do; she, an uneducated naïf from the Port Cities, friendless and in his power? The answer, Your Majesty, gentlemen, is nothing. But though uneducated, this young woman is no fool. She watched, Your Majesty. She listened. And when the corps was set upon by thieves in the woods, she had the presence of mind—no, the courage"—he turned and looked at Tanya with such a well-pantomimed reverence that she found it downright alarming— "the courage and the loyalty to her Queen to make her escape with the item stolen by her untrustworthy employer.

"She wandered in the woods for days, hiding, foraging, not knowing to whom she could turn for help, but determined to return the scholars' artifact to you, Your Majesty. Nobody, she knew, would know better how to advise her, alone and betrayed as she was, than her Queen."

There was a dramatic pause, but the effect was somewhat dampened by a stomach-wrenching creak as an icy side door, apparently less used than the grand one through which Tanya and Councilman Hewitt had entered, opened and Sir Lurch attempted to surreptitiously tiptoe his way to the empty chair all the way at the far end of the horseshoe.

Tanya tried to catch Sir Lurch's eyes, but the captain of the guard was either too preoccupied to look at her or was deliberately avoiding her gaze. Or . . . he didn't recognize her. Which was a shame, because as far as Tanya was concerned, this was rather going off the rails—how was her ring of fire and the gold rain going to feature into this story, with her participation characterized as it was? Did they think they could keep such events from the Queen and Council?

*Could* they?

One of the younger councilmen leaned forward.

"I wonder, Hewitt," he said eagerly, "if the stolen artifact is the very same one the dean described in his letter asking for additional funding. If I recall, a delegation from the college was set to demonstrate its powers in front of this Council in a fortnight."

"It would certainly stand to reason," answered Councilman Hewitt smoothly. "This corps commander must have had a spy within the college itself."

One of the crotchety-looking council members, a white-haired man with a pointy nose and a stinking cigar, waved away the smoke in front of his face and snapped his fingers; a crystal ashtray appeared.

"Obviously it is the same artifact," he growled, with a sideways look at his younger colleague. "What else could be worth stealing from that damp old fortress? The pertinent question regards the theft itself. You, girl!"

Tanya's head snapped up. "Yes, sir!"

He resumed possession of his cigar. "Councilman Hewitt claims you are observant. Let us see. First, your commander's name—which, quite honestly, Hewitt, should have been included in your initial recital. We don't require a three-act play. The name, girl."

"Commander Kiernan Rees." She couldn't have resisted the command in the old councilman's voice even if she wanted to.

There was a ripple of noise along the horseshoe, but the old councilman simply smiled.

"Rees," he said, disdain dripping from his voice like butter off toast. "Yes. It would be Rees. Now, how long were you in Commander Rees's employ?"

Tanya squirmed. The true answer was about three days. But somehow that didn't seem quite long enough to match the picture Hewitt had painted . . . ?

Finally, she said, "I came into Commander Rees's employment two weeks ago," she said. This was true.

The councilman accepted the answer at face value. "And, during the tenure of your employment, did any courier deliver a communication to the corps?"

She hesitated. "Not that I saw, sir."

"Did he meet with any of the scholars prior to the theft?"

"I am . . . not aware of any meetings prior to the theft."

"Well, did he have any communications with anyone other than corpsmen prior to the theft?"

"Sir?"

The councilman banged his fist against the table. "Think, girl! You may be a simple maid as Hewitt asserts, but even you must realize that one does not carry out a heist of this level of sensitivity without knowing *what* one is stealing! The letter from the college was sent to us, the Council. I know I didn't tell Rees, so who did?"

"Gentlemen." Councilman Hewitt stepped in front of Tanya. "I posit that this girl, brave and loyal as she is, cannot have specific knowledge as to the theft. She is a domestic. She is not trained in the art of spycraft. What tavern maid would be?"

The old councilman snorted. "All of them, in my experience."

"The fact is, gentlemen," said Hewitt, ignoring the man, and directing his attentions to the younger, more excited-looking members of the Council, "I brought Tanya before you not merely to inform you of the theft, but to present an artifact of great importance to the whole of Lode to her Queen and Council. Tanya." He turned to her. "You may cease the burden of concealing this great artifact. Present the quill to your Queen and Council."

Suddenly feeling a little foolish to be playacting in this little pantomime, Tanya awkwardly removed the quill from her hair.

"Now come forward," he ordered silkily. "And present it to the Queen."

Tanya obeyed, walking with her eyes down toward the center of the horseshoe, until she could just see the Queen's glimmer from under her eyelids. She knelt and held the quill out, nestled in her bare palms.

# Chapter

**T**anya had never known a louder silence. She remembered the first time she had seen the quill, huddled around a box with Jana, how they had gasped, dazzled at the glitter. But these were members of the Council. Surely, they had seen sights far more bewildering than a feather, even *this* feather?

Tanya was still looking down when a cool, firm fingertip found her palm. As the Queen's bare skin traced all the way around the feather, probing the lines in her hand, calluses and all, Tanya became aware that she was shaking.

Still, she didn't dare look up.

The Queen's fingertip disappeared from her palm, an absence Tanya felt as immediately as a torn bandage off a scabbed knee. When it came back down, it hit the feather, pressing down on the spine.

A tremor shivered through Tanya's whole body. The Queen pressed harder and Tanya gasped.

The magic feather erupted, shooting black and white sparks that hit the ceiling, then rained back onto the icy floor in a shower of gold flakes.

The Queen herself gasped and Tanya finally looked up.

The Queen was clasping Tanya's hand in her own, her eyes wide and wondering as gold floated all around them as leisurely and naturally as cherry blossoms falling off a tree in spring.

The Queen wasn't a living flower. She wasn't a snow sculpture, remote and too distant to be anything but beautiful.

She was ageless and nameless, but this was also a flesh-and-blood woman with sharp fingernails and a dimple in her chin.

The last of the gold shattered to the floor and the Queen's gaze fell with it, her eyes meeting Tanya's.

The Queen blinked, but she didn't remove her hand or look away. She stroked the quill all the way down its spine. The quill shivered and turned over, like a dog wanting its belly rubbed.

The crotchety councilman cleared his throat and broke the silence. "Your Majesty? Might I examine that quill?"

It was still gently glittering, emitting a blueish light. The Queen gave it one more stroke and lifted her finger. It flickered quickly through black, purple, and red before settling into its customary shining white and nestling back into Tanya's palm—instead of a dog, now a kitten in need of a nap.

"Of course, my dear duke." Tanya's whole body stiffened at the sound of the Queen's voice. It didn't sound like it came out of a human being. The Queen of Lode had a voice like a harp.

"You may stand, Tanya," said the Queen. Tanya obeyed, stumbling on her ridiculous hem as she did so. The Queen didn't seem to notice. The bland smile on her face didn't move.

The Queen's eyes really were something. They were a swirl of color and ever changing, one minute, black and gray; another, blue and green; the next, gold.

It made them extremely hard to read.

"Would you please bring the quill to the Duke of Xane?"

Tanya had never even heard of the Duke of Xane, but she brought the quill over to the man with the cigar. She knelt in front of him, careful to not bend as low as she had to the Queen.

He plucked the quill out of Tanya's open hands and suddenly the council room dimmed. The quill twisting through the duke's gnarled fingers was just a simple feather quill—soft, clean, and sharpened, but just a feather.

The quill had gone dormant.

The duke frowned, not in displeasure, but confusion. "What happened to it?" he asked. When no one answered, he rapped Tanya on the forehead with it. "Well, girl?"

Tanya looked up. "You're asking me, my lord?"

He sighed. "I'm too tired for deference. Yes, I'm speaking to you. You are the foremost expert in this quill in this room. Why's it gone dark?"

Tanya took a moment to consider her answer. There was much she didn't understand about the quill or how it worked. But there was also a part of her that knew the answer to the duke's question—specifically, the part of her burning blood-red with hidden tattoos.

*Are you ready to be important?* Councilman Hewitt had asked.

She took a breath and stood up straight, or as close as she could get with the gleaming beehive weighing down her scalp. Her bones creaked out of the curtsy, sighing as her left hip instinctively slid out to meet her hand.

It didn't matter if she was *ready* to be important—she *was* important now.

The duke raised his eyebrows slightly as Tanya shed the simpering, simple peasant and the tavern wench peeked out to take a breath of fresh air.

"I'm not a scholar, my lord," she began.

"Actually, it's 'Your Grace.'"

"Right," she said, frowning at her mistake. "Apologies, Your Grace. Clearly, I'm no scholar, and I'm no wizard either. I don't know why the quill does what it does, but I *think* I know why the quill's dark."

"And?"

She paused. "You're not going to like it, Your Grace."

"I don't like most things. Tell me anyway."

"It's dark because you're the one holding it, Your Grace."

Muttering erupted around the horseshoe. She ignored it and went on being important. "Give it back and you'll see," she said.

To her slight surprise, the duke passively complied and, sure enough, the good little quill exploded in a shower of silver sparks, like firecrackers on a holiday.

"Right," said Tanya, growing warm with all the eyes on her. "See, when I hold it, it wakes up. I think it's because I'm the one who's used it the most, so now it's used to me. It . . . likes me." *And its fed on my blood*, she didn't add—that would have been too important, too fast. No need to be impractical.

"Used it?" The Queen's voice thrummed through the ice chamber. "Show us how you use it, Tanya."

Feeling naked without her curtsy, Tanya nodded and looked away from her sovereign as quickly as she could. "May I have a piece of paper, Your Grace?"

Paper was supplied, as well as a chair, and Tanya pulled up to the horseshoe, tucking her feet into the leg joints, as if it were any other chair at any other table. It was the count's sister's bedroom all over again. *A chair is just a chair, even in an ice chamber owned by the Queen,* she told herself, and, licking the tip of the quill, began to write.

She started to request a map of the Capital, but then remembered what she was there for, crossed it out, and instead wrote, *Show me a map of Griffin's Port.*

Her home bloomed over the paper, shining and plain and beautiful. *Salt, stone, coral,* and in the harbor—*everything.* Just everything in Lode.

She ran her fingers over the harbor for a moment and then, almost afraid to look, turned her attention to the Smiling Snake.

She put her thumb and forefinger on the spot. The parchment thrummed under her skin. In a very real way, this *was* the Snake. She drew her fingers out and together; out and together. The image sharpened until she could see the herb garden, gone to hell since Froud's death, the empty stables, the crack in the foundation on the eastern wall, and—*there it is*.

The quill flew over the parchment. The cavern shuddered like it was in a thundercloud and something crashed onto the ice with a splintering crack.

Sir Lurch got up out of his seat and retrieved the item, setting it on the horseshoe in front of the Queen.

It was a heavy slab of broken wood, dirty and weathered, stripped of its lacquer—but the carved serpent was still grinning.

"This is the sign for my tavern in Griffin's Port, Your Majesty," said Tanya, addressing the Queen. "I brought it here, using the quill."

"I don't understand," said the Duke of Xane after a pause. "The quill can move objects great distances?"

"Not quite," said Tanya. "It works like aetherical manipulation. It can move single-source matter. I just moved that piece of oak here—that's why the paint isn't on it anymore. It's probably sitting in little green shavings on the ground. But that's not actually what's so useful about the quill."

"What's that?"

Tanya scanned the parchment and then flipped it around so the councilmen could see. "Look here," she said, pointing out a blue line. "Because I moved the sign, this river has started to overflow."

"Junkoff."

"Right. But if I do this"—Tanya began scrawling with the quill along the edge of the river—"I can redirect the excess water over the falls in Polnya's Port. Problem solved."

"Impressive. But can you move anything more interesting than a meaningless scrap of driftwood?"

Tanya's eyes narrowed. "As I said, Your Grace, the sign for the Smiling Snake is made of oak. But yes, I can move anything, divert anything, increase anything, decrease anything that you name. I'm confident of that."

"*You* can? Don't you mean the quill can?"

She held it out to him. "You're welcome to try again, Your Grace. I can try to show you how. Anyone with a high capacity for organization should be able to manage it."

"The duke has a very high capacity for organization." Tanya stiffened as the Queen's voice unexpectedly filled the room, effortlessly, gently. "So, why does it only work for you, Tanya?"

"I . . . don't *know* that it does, Your Majesty."

The Queen nodded. "Gentlemen, will you pass the quill around and see what you can make of it on your own parchment? Let's settle this."

The quill traveled around the horseshoe. With each man, the quill sputtered against the parchment and, finally, went dark.

Eventually it made its way back to the Queen. It twitched against her palm and was eventually persuaded to emit a faint blue light.

"Well, Tanya," said the Queen. "It does appear to have a marked preference for you. Perhaps you could show *me* how to use it."

"It would . . . it would be my honor, Queen, I mean, Your Grace, or rather, Majesty." Tanya took a breath and willed herself to stop babbling. "It would be my honor and privilege, Your Majesty."

"Excellent. You will join me in my private study for dinner. Sir Lurch, will you please escort Tanya back to her quarters? My dear Hewitt, she has, I assume, been given a suitable set of rooms?"

The Count stepped forward swiftly. "I have installed her in my own sister's chamber, Your Majesty, and sent Violet to attend on her."

"Very well done. Tanya is our guest and is to be honored as one who has performed a great service to the Council and the kingdom. And to me. Sir Lurch?"

Sir Lurch appeared at Tanya's elbow and began to move her toward the exit as steadily as a tide.

"We will be dining just the two of us, Tanya," said the Queen, suddenly putting on a set of rimless spectacles and shuffling a previously unseen stack of papers. "You may tell Violet that there is no need to be dressed for a court dinner. You are to be comfortable."

Tanya stared as the immaculate, impenetrable Queen was transformed by a simple pair of spectacles into an attractive, even beautiful, but thoroughly human and businesslike woman, perhaps not much older than Tanya herself. Tanya didn't even realize that she had been removed from the chamber until a smooth wall of ice slammed shut behind her.

"The Queen always means exactly what she says," Violet said as she pulled dresses out of the armoire by the armload. "And if she wants you to be comfortable, you'll pick the dress that makes *you* comfortable. I'll not do anything to disobey the Queen's command."

Tanya thought this was a bit much. "It wasn't a command," she told Violet. "Really, she was just being polite."

Violet pursed her lips.

Tanya, who could purse her lips with the best of them, matched her glare. "Well, I'll tell you this much, I won't be squeezed into another ridiculous atrocity that you decide to call a gown."

A small, scurrying sound drew Tanya's eye as Jasmine entered with an armful of fresh linen.

"That," said Tanya, surveying the maid, "looks like quite a comfortable dress."

Jasmine and Tanya were built along entirely different lines, Jasmine lithe and narrow, where Tanya was round and bouncing. But luckily—for Tanya anyway—the junior cleaning staff at the Glacier weren't allotted figure-specific tailoring in their uniforms. So, Jasmine's dress—a boxy, brown shift of soft cotton—actually fit Tanya rather well, the fabric straining around her hips, the square neckline falling in a fetching but respectable line.

And perhaps most importantly, the sleeves went all the way past her wrists.

At Sir Lurch's knock, she stood and took a last look in the mirror, pleased at what she saw. Tanya took his arm and allowed him to lead her out of the tower to the Queen's private study.

It took rather a long time. At her sigh at passing the mile mark, Sir Lurch gave Tanya a sympathetic smile. "The Queen," he explained, "requires privacy. None of the courtiers are placed near her apartments."

Eventually, though, he did stop walking. "Here we are," he said.

Tanya looked up, expecting to see another grand door, perhaps also made of the living ice of the council room's or some even more fantastical substance.

Instead she saw a platinum cage reaching all the way up to the ceiling. The bars were in the shape of icicles.

Sir Lurch stepped forward and twisted three of the icicles in a specific pattern: two triple turns, followed by a double turn. The front of the cage slid open and Sir Lurch stepped aside. It took Tanya a second to realize that he was waiting for her to actually enter the cage.

She looked to the ceiling and the floor, but saw nothing but amber and quartz. She really would be entering a cage. Still, she was a tavern maid in the Glacier and the Queen had taken her quill. She had no choice but to do as she was told. So, smothering a gulp, she picked her skirt off the floor and walked inside . . .

. . . And immediately began to sink.

# Chapter

17

"**H**ey!" Tanya grabbed at the icicle bars, but the bottom of the cage was descending too fast, and gravity peeled her fingers from the metal. "Sir Lurch, I formally protest! This is—oh, all the hells that ever was!" Tanya banged her fist against the wall in frustration, instantly regretting it as the fast-moving, rough-hewn stone scraped her knuckles.

Tanya plummeted down a narrow chute of stone, a gray and unremarkable material, especially compared with the splendor of the Glacier overall.

It was dim and cold in the chute. The light at the top shrank to a pinpoint and a flickering white illumination began to rise up around her—similar to the magical, fireless flames Sir Lurch had conjured on their way into the palace, but wilder, moving like amphibian creatures in a stream, lightning-quick and unpredictable.

The cage picked up speed. Tanya had to grasp the back of the cage just to stay upright. And then, with a neat popping sound, the cage stopped. Cautiously, Tanya lifted her head and saw another metal grille, this one carved in the shape of stars.

The grille slid open. Tanya stepped forward, but an explosion of light forced her back down. She threw her arms over her eyes.

"What the—?" Tanya didn't have the wherewithal, the words, to form the end of her question. She looked again and found that, even though the light was bright, brighter than sunshine, it didn't hurt her eyes to look at it.

She stepped forward hesitantly, one foot after the other, into the light. It was like stepping into a world of white. She had vaguely expected it to feel warmth on her skin, but it was cool—not the cool of a breeze, but the chill of broken ice.

Tanya stepped deeper into the bright white and smelled something familiar—briny and smoky. Cheered, she kept walking.

The smell grew stronger and the light dimmer, until suddenly the white floated away like smoke and she was in a round room, standing in front of a modest-size table set with Limn Bay mussels in a bacon and sage broth: a Port Cities specialty.

"I'm so glad you could join me, Tanya."

Tanya whirled around and saw the Queen enter the room through a stone-bricked archway dripping with icicles. At least, she was pretty sure it was the Queen.

The Queen was barefoot with her hair down, dressed in unadorned gray and those glasses from the council room. She wasn't wearing the crown.

She stopped under the arch, smiling slightly. Tanya wondered what she was waiting for, until she suddenly gulped and remembered herself, sweeping into the deepest curtsy she could manage—deeper, actually. The cage, the light, the barefoot ruler of all Lode—they all served to disorient the tavern maid and she tripped on her own feet on her way to the floor, stumbling to her knees.

"All hells," Tanya cursed as her bones collided with the hard, freezing floor, and then immediately bit her lip to keep her from uttering an even worse profanity.

The Queen laughed. She stepped into the room and bent to help Tanya up with a smooth, chilly hand.

"I don't mind informality in this room," she said. "No need to be embarrassed."

Tanya privately disagreed. She allowed the Queen to help her off the floor and then bent her head respectfully, her hands clasped in front of her waist.

She sensed the Queen stiffen in front of her. "I believe I requested that you be comfortable," she said, her voice hard.

Tanya raised her head a fraction of an inch. "I'm quite comfortable, Your Majesty, thank you," she said.

"You're not." The Queen's voice was firm and dismissive. "You're standing as if you're here to serve the dinner rather than eat it."

Despite the cold of the room, Tanya felt heat begin to rise in her face. Still, Tanya answered, her voice measured and polite. "I apologize for displeasing you, Your Majesty."

"Again! I asked for your comfort. You don't look comfortable; you look like a servant."

As the Queen's voice reached disdain, Tanya snapped. "Perhaps I'm more comfortable as a servant," she spat. "Has that occurred to you?"

There was a sharp silence and Tanya contemplated imminent death. For all she knew, yelling at the Queen of Lode was treason. But the Queen laughed again and Tanya dared to look up.

Still giggling, the Queen draped herself across one of the chairs and reached for a silver filigree carafe. She poured a bubbly golden liquid into the two waiting glasses. "Do you know, I suppose it hadn't," she said, eyeing Tanya with interest. "That was quite stupid of me. Arrange your body however you choose, Tanya, but please do sit. Join me in a drink."

Tanya forced her shoulders to unclench and obeyed, sitting across from the Queen.

The Queen handed her a glass. "Here," she said. "We should toast."

Tanya accepted the glass, wondering what she and the Queen of Lode could possibly have in common to toast. But then the Queen surprised her, clinking the glasses together, and saying, "To our quill."

The Queen and the wench locked eyes for a moment. Tanya once again noted the whirring chaos of the Queen's eyes, muted by the spectacles, but not extinguished. She couldn't read them.

Tanya clinked her glass against the Queen's. "To our quill," she said quietly.

The Queen smiled again and lifted the glass to her lips. Tanya did the same and nearly spat out its contents in confused surprise.

"Unusual, isn't it?" asked the Queen, taking another serene sip.

"What is it?" Tanya examined the liquid with professional curiosity. "It doesn't taste like any wine I've ever had."

It also didn't *feel* like any wine she'd ever encountered, and she lived in a tavern in a central port of Lode. She didn't drink much, but she'd tasted every wine that passed through the kingdom, from the sour sparkling wine fermented in the archipelago of islands between Gobel and Mourit, to the sweeter reds pumped in the cisterns of Lode's own arid mountain plains. None of those wines' bubbles expanded upon hitting the tongue or exploded against the back of her teeth, making them tingle and chatter.

The Queen looked at the wine critically. "It's something I've been working on with the court chemist and one of the magic makers—oh no," she said, catching Tanya's glance. "This has nothing to do with aetherical manipulation. It's a little more academic that that. I've been studying with this particular scholar since I was quite young. Tell me, what does it taste like to you?"

Tanya was a little alarmed to hear that the Queen was a dabbler in "academic" magic, whatever that meant. But she was also a barmaid presented with a new alcohol, so she took another sip.

Tanya frowned. "It's odd," she said. "It looks like it's going to taste tart or fruity, because it's so clear, but it doesn't. It tastes . . . gamey. Salty. Maybe a little smoky? More like a whiskey, except with no sharp finish."

The Queen applauded lightly. "Well expressed," she said. "You must know your business very well to give such a clever description."

"What makes a wine taste like that?"

The Queen began ladling mussels into Tanya's bowl, a translucent porcelain specimen. "Why, you do," she said. "It's not exactly wine. I've been calling it a 'cordial.' The clever thing about that cordial is that whatever it tastes like, feels like, even *looks* like, depends on the person imbibing it. It can be quite informative."

Tanya put the glass far away from her and the Queen laughed again. "Aren't you going to ask what it tastes like to me?" she asked.

"No, thank you," answered Tanya. "That seems rather rude."

"I see. You believe me to be rude? It's all right," she added, when Tanya stayed tight lipped and silent. "I imagine my servants told you that I say what I mean. I said I wanted you to approach this meeting of ours in comfort. I may be wrong, but I also imagine speaking freely is the mode in which you find the most comfort."

Tanya folded her arms. If the Queen wanted a freely given opinion, she'd get it. "All right then," she said. "For starters, to be clear, I have nothing against using alcohol to manipulate. But I also think it's the height of, if not hypocrisy, then at least obliviousness, to demand comfort of one's subordinates, trundle them into a cage with no explanation, and, finally, use alcohol-based subterfuge in order to learn trivia of some obscure nature about them within the first five minutes."

Retrieving a mussel from the aromatic broth and neatly cracking it in half, the Queen listened attentively. She nodded when Tanya finished.

"Thank you for that candor, Tanya," she said. "Those are reasonable reactions. I will take them into consideration while conducting such interactions in the future."

As the Queen spoke, Tanya saw the swirling chaos of her eyes slow down, contract, and begin spinning in the opposite direction, as if a mechanical gadget were recalibrating. Was she a Queen or a machine? Tanya didn't have an answer, so she began to eat, and nearly swooned at the taste. Mussels in sage-and-bacon broth was a dish she had made a million times a month, but she never had the time to cook a shellfish stock long enough to get this depth of flavor. It was a humble dish, but the kitchen staff had treated it with respect.

Tanya had secretly hoped for something to criticize. It felt safer to be disappointed in the food in this place.

The Queen wiped her mouth with a linen napkin and pulled a lever next to the hearth.

"In the spirit of eschewing both hypocrisy and obliviousness, allow me to at least explain the cage," said the Queen. "This, as you know, is my private study. I have gone to great lengths to keep it private. Only a few people know the passcode to the entry chamber—the cage—which is the only point of entry into this chamber large enough to fit a person." A bell rang out and a silver door slid open above the fireplace, revealing rounds of steaming hot bread dripping with herbed butter. The Queen lifted the tray to the table. "The other point of entry," she added, "is this dumb-waiter from the kitchen. There is another passcode for opening it from the kitchen side, and it is known only by the head pastry chef, who was my nursery maid and has my complete trust. Of course."

"Of course," muttered Tanya, totally overwhelmed. She reached for a piece of bread and hissed as her finger brushed the white-hot tray. She snuck a suspicious glance at the Queen; she had pulled the tray bare-handed and her hand was as white and steady as before.

The Queen continued. "And once the entry chamber reaches the study, any person will be scanned by the cloud."

"That light—that was a cloud?"

She rolled her eyes and Tanya felt herself relax; it was a gesture she understood. "Well, no, not really," answered the Queen. "That's just what I call it. No, that's another one of my experiments. The light scans whoever enters it and if they're on my list, it dissipates."

"What if they aren't?"

The Queen only smiled and answered a different question, drawing a butter-poached porgy, arranged on a bed of crisp, many-colored tomatoes, from the dumbwaiter. "I like to keep my security measures known only to those who need to know them, which is why Sir Lurch didn't tell you about the cage ahead of time.

"Any other questions?" asked the Queen, pulling out the quill from her sleeve. "Because I have *numerous* questions."

Tanya's eyes widened at the sight of the quill. Its barbs were wilted and drooping as if exhausted, gaps gaping between them as if the feather had been flattened like flowers between pages in a book.

But the quill was still blinding white, and sparkling like a newly polished diamond. Tanya couldn't be sure, but it seemed to have been using a *lot* of magic.

"You got it to work?"

The Queen smiled grimly. "After a fashion," she said. "This quill *should* be a very handy bridge between more traditional, elemental magic and the aetheric strands, but, as you suggested, it seems to only want to work for you. I accessed its power, but I had to use brute force methods, and precision was impossible. Now," she said, opening a drawer and pulling out two leather notebooks, a pot of ink, and a plain pigeon quill. "You made me a very generous offer in my council room, to walk me through the use of this quill."

"Are you sure you wouldn't rather wait until you finish your meal, Your Majesty?" asked Tanya, staring as the Queen simultaneously inked the plain quill and crammed a forkful of tomatoes into her mouth. It somehow didn't seem quite the thing for a Queen to drip sauce all over herself while taking notes on a tavern maid's instructions.

The Queen opened the more worn of the notebooks and frowned. "Why? I should have thought you'd be used to working through meals."

"I am, but . . ."

"No buts," said the Queen, pushing the new notebook toward Tanya. "I work through my meals, too. Teach me."

And so, Tanya did. As an array of dishes made their way to the chamber—chilled corn chowder with spot prawn, a frozen puree of some sharp yellow fruit, a medallion of pan-seared goose liver in a port wine sauce—Tanya stained her fingers, Jasmine's dress, and the fine linen tablecloth with ink as she drew map after map, list after list, and arrow after arrow, to demonstrate the feats the quill could perform.

By the time Tanya finally reached the limit of her knowledge, the fire was low and caramel custard was melting in dainty dishes. There was the detritus of half a dozen demonstrations piled around them.

An entire charred willow branch . . .

A small mountain of white powder lifted straight from the White . . .

A carpet of pink rose petals from the duchess's garden . . .

Tanya had even attempted to pull through the aether some unidentifiable black sludge from the volcano in Bloodstone. It had worked, sort of. A fat raindrop of the stuff had materialized above them, hovered there for a moment, and then slipped to the table with an awful squelch and began crawling toward Tanya with finger-like tendrils. The Queen quite sensibly slammed a goblet over it and shunted it off to the side, to be dealt with later by one of her experts. Tanya didn't like the sound of that particular expert, but the goblet—a heavy iron thing—seemed to be containing the sludge, so she assumed the Queen knew what she was doing.

"And that's basically it," finished Tanya. "If you always keep an up-to-date map, keep it large enough and check it very regularly, theoretically you should be able to perform any feat of aetherical manipulation while also nipping any junkoff in the bud."

The Queen had been furiously scribbling in her notebook throughout Tanya's entire demonstration. She held up a finger and finished drawing some sort of figure. She put her pen down and studied what she had drawn, the room silent and even colder than before as the last of the fire died out.

The Queen slowly pushed her glasses up from where they had drooped to the tip of her nose. She looked up at Tanya.

"Thank you," said the Queen. "That was very informative. Coffee?" Before Tanya could answer, she had already pushed the lever.

"You're welcome," said Tanya, taking a moment to remember that customary response. She felt strangely invigorated—this had been good work! She fiddled with the quill, twirling it between her middle and forefinger.

The coffee arrived and the Queen began fixing a cup with cream and three sugars. To Tanya's surprise, the Queen passed it to her. Tanya accepted it, but raised an eyebrow at her host. There was no one in the Glacier in a position to tell the Queen of Lode how Tanya took her coffee. Lady of Cups, there was no one in *Lode* in a position to tell *anyone* how Tanya took her coffee; no one had ever asked. And yet the Queen, somehow, knew.

The Queen poured herself a cup of coffee, leaving it black. "How extensive was your education, Tanya?"

Tanya blinked. That was not a question she had expected.

"Not very, Your Majesty," she answered. "I went to the village schoolhouse for a month or two when I was about ten, but mostly my guardian trained me to run the tavern."

"And it was your guardian who taught you to read and write, to do basic math."

She nodded. The Queen looked thoughtful and Tanya braced for a series of questions about when her parents died, the man who had raised her, where he was now, etc.

She was wrong. "So, you don't know any other languages?" asked the Queen. "What about history? Economics? Any of the natural sciences?"

Tanya swallowed a too-large gulp of hot coffee. After she had coughed herself clean, she answered, "I've never been anywhere but the Port Cities, but, as to languages, I could probably get by in Moray and Lumen. I've got a little bit of Gobi and Kiley, and I'm actually rather good at Junn. A man who stayed with us for six whole months only spoke Junn. I know at least pleasantries in most of the languages that pass through Griffin's Port, I guess."

The Queen was listening closely—very closely. "That's very good," she said. "Good, that you can pick up languages so well, I mean. That's useful."

"I . . . I suppose so."

"And what about social education? You picked up languages, so I imagine you also know a fair amount about foreign art and culture, pathways to trade, idiosyncratic customs, that sort of thing. Although not politics or economics, I would imagine, and, on the cultural side, nothing above a certain class. Is that accurate?"

"I don't quite know what you mean by politics or economics."

The Queen nodded. "Precisely. I imagine your domestic training has been extensive. Cooking, cleaning, brewing, the whole bit?"

Tanya bristled a little at her life's work being referred to as a "bit," but pride forced her to agree. "Yes. I'm an excellent seamstress, a skilled laundress, I can clean anything, and I'm the best cook in the Port Cities."

The Queen nodded and made another note. Seemingly to herself, she muttered, "Economics, history, politics, higher math, chemistry, physics, diplomacy, and etiquette."

Tanya wanted to snatch the notebook out of her hands. "I'm sorry?"

The Queen shut the notebook and pushed it to the side. "What are your ambitions, Tanya?"

"My ambitions?"

"Yes. You left the tavern in which you were raised in order to serve a corps commander. You must have had some sort of desire for your life that wasn't being fulfilled in Griffin's Port, some sort of goal. What is it?"

Tanya stared for a moment and then doubled over laughing.

The Queen looked slightly nonplussed. "No one ever laughs when I ask them what they want. They bow deeply and beg for it. This is unusual. I can only imagine you're attempting to make some sort of point. What is it?"

Tanya, still giggling, wiped tears out of her eyes. "I didn't leave my tavern voluntarily. Your corps commander—actually, *you*—you forced me out of it. Rees had a writ of requisition."

"That makes no sense. A writ can commandeer, but not permanently evict people from their own property, not with a competent clerk nearby."

"Apparently, as far as you were concerned, it wasn't my property."

The Queen frowned. "But . . . oh. Tell me," said the Queen. "Your guardian. Was he a relative?"

"No. He wasn't."

"And he's dead?"

This was spoken in a neutral voice, shockingly unemotional for a sentence containing the word *dead*. Tanya thought that she should be offended, but instead she was just sad. She nodded.

"I see. I imagine he neglected to leave a writ of leaving?" At Tanya's nod, the Queen clucked her tongue against her teeth in disapproval. "How very annoying of him. To be honest, this happens far more frequently than you would think. There is no civic education in the provincial parts of Lode whatsoever. I really need to do something about it." She looked at Tanya appraisingly. "If you were an orphan, living with a guardian who was not a relative, I can surmise that you have no known family. And, forgive me, but I'd be shocked if you had a fiancé back there; you're not quite mewling or simpering enough. There's nothing waiting for you in Griffin's Port, then?"

Tanya lifted her head to meet the Queen's churning eyes. "There will be once you give me my inn back."

The Queen smiled. "So that is your ambition."

"That's the reason I left Griffin's Port, Your Majesty. I was told that only you and your Council could reverse the writ. You say I've done you a service. All I want as a reward is what is already mine in any way that counts, and is of no use to you at all. I want the deed to the Smiling Snake."

"Why?"

Tanya blinked. "What do you mean?"

The Queen leaned forward. "Why do you want the deed to the Smiling Snake?"

"Because . . . because it's mine. I've earned it."

"Is that all? Wanting what you've earned is something that I can well understand, Tanya. Believe me. But is that the only reason you want it?"

"Isn't that enough?"

The Queen shrugged. "I suppose, for someone of your position, it could be. But, to me, that seems rather plain—rather bare. Sad, honestly. Do you enjoy the work?"

Tanya bristled. "It's an honest day's work, Your Majesty. Do I always thrill to scrubbing dishes and kicking out drunks? Maybe not. But I can take care of myself, my guests, and my inn. I enjoy being able to say that."

The Queen smiled. "I see. You enjoy being useful."

Tanya stood up, ready for this interview to be over. "I do, Your Majesty, and I'm not ashamed of it. I know that no one will ever be able to claim that I haven't earned my place. Not everyone can say that."

"I quite agree with you."

Tanya had already opened her mouth to continue arguing and was left to gape as the Queen went on.

"Class, wealth, connections, knowledge—all that can be conferred or withdrawn," said the Queen, looking wistful and pouring another glass of cordial. "At least it can if you're the Queen. And I am the Queen. To be honest, none of that means any more to me than any other tool. True unique utility though, that's valuable and rare. But I reject your premise."

"My premise?"

"Your underlying assumption that the only suitable outlet for you to be useful is in being a tavern wench of Griffin's Port. Don't misunderstand me; I don't despise tavern wenches. Someone has to do that work, and I daresay there's a great deal to it that I'm not in a position to appreciate. But you're useful in a very different way now. If the charm of the Smiling Snake is in self-reliance, and not in scrubbing a soup pot, then you have other options. Better options. *Bigger* options." The Queen leaned forward. "The world is much larger than one tavern. Why would you limit yourself?"

Tanya sat back down and reached for the cordial. She poured a little and drank it down in one gulp, before asking, "Are you offering me a job, Your Majesty?"

The Queen looked pleased. "You're a smart girl," she said.

The compliment struck a sour chord in Tanya's ear. It was condescending. "The Glacier is no doubt much grander than the Snake, Your Majesty," she said. "But cleaning a kitchen here isn't different than cleaning one in Griffin's Port and at least there I'm my own superior. I don't think it would be 'smart' of me to accept the honor of serving the Glacier in recompense for my inn."

The Queen laughed. "You misunderstand me. I'm not offering you a job as a domestic."

Tanya frowned. "What then?"

The Queen refilled both their glasses. "I'm not sure exactly what to call it. It's not a lady's maid. If you were a man, I'd probably call you a private secretary, so, let's go with that. The job is my private secretary or, if you prefer, 'Private Secretary to the Queen of Lode.'"

"What?"

The Queen looked thoughtful. "Yes, I think that's about right," she said. "In this position, you'd take notes in all Council, diplomatic, military, and advisor meetings. You would keep my priority notebook and my schedule. You would be given full access to this chamber, my records room, and my library. You would appear to be just like any other secretary to nobility."

Tanya stopped internally spinning at the word *appear*. She looked at the Queen, who had apparently been waiting for her to catch her meaning, because she nodded approvingly and continued.

"In addition to the standard secretarial duties," she said, reaching for her glass, "you would have particular responsibility in the management of this quill."

Tanya felt her grip on the quill tighten. "Management?" she asked.

"Yes, the management," said the Queen, reaching for her notebook. "I will, of course, have ultimate authority over its use and I will be providing the overall strategy—prioritization, volume, partnerships—but I will need someone with skill to handle the day-to-day duties. You know what I mean."

"I'm . . . not sure that I do."

"But of course you do! I have it written down right here: You said that as long as a large enough map was kept updated and consistently monitored, I would be able to perform any feat of aetherical manipulation while simultaneously eliminating or otherwise ameliorating any junkoff. I didn't misunderstand you."

"No, but—"

"That wasn't a question." The Queen put down her notebook. "Really, Tanya, you look nonplussed. What is the matter? I've made myself perfectly clear."

"*You* plan to use the quill? Daily?"

The Queen laughed. "Of course I plan to use it. What's the point of it existing, if it's not being used?"

"But isn't it . . . not . . . well . . . isn't it . . . ?"

"Spit it out."

Tanya gulped. "Well, it's not exactly yours, is it? It belongs to the magicians. The ones Rees apparently stole from."

The Queen smiled. "Yes. He did steal it, didn't he? It's clear that an artifact of such great power isn't secure *anywhere* if even an upstanding man like a corps commander on an envoy mission from the Queen herself could be tempted to steal it from such a venerable company as the scholars of the Royal College of Aetherical Manipulation. Except for the Glacier, that is. It's secure in the Glacier under the direct supervision of the Queen."

Something snapped into place in Tanya's brain. She looked at the

Queen and found that the Queen was looking back at her. Waiting to see if she would understand on her own.

Slowly, Tanya said, "You secretly ordered Rees to steal the quill."

The Queen raised her glass in a silent toast to Tanya.

"But why?" asked Tanya. "You didn't *have* to steal the quill. I know for a fact that the college was dying to present it to you themselves. I mean . . ." She stumbled as the Queen raised an eyebrow and Tanya realized that she had deviated from the official story. "I assume they must have been. Didn't Councilman Hewitt say they had written to ask you for permission to present their quill?"

"They weren't asking to present the quill to me," said the Queen quietly. "Think, Tanya. How would that request have been worded? With whom would they have requested an audience?"

"With the Queen and Council. Oh. *Oh.*"

The Queen nodded and pulled her hair back roughly. "The Queen and Council," she said, her voice bitter. "Always the Queen and Council. Do you know how long I've been Queen, Tanya?"

"No."

The Queen nodded. "Do you know my age?" she asked. Tanya shook her head. "Do you know my ideas about trade? The preliminary test results coming out of the research centers I've set up in the shallows behind the Bloodstone tar pits? Whether I need a biological heir? Tell me everything you know about my reign."

It was an order. "I know that the Queen and Council rule Lode," said Tanya honestly. "And I know that you live in the Glacier."

"Exactly. And, by the way, I don't know that you can rightly call what I and the Council have accomplished ruling. We have maintained Lode. We have not moved it forward."

"Why not?"

The Queen smiled, without joy and without pleasure. "Because that was how the Council designed it—many, many years ago. They like Lode how it is. They have taken pains to keep it in stasis. I believe that the people of Lode deserve better. They deserve a true queen. And with the quill, I have everything I need to become that true queen.

"And for that," she continued, looking straight at Tanya. "I need you."

# Chapter

anya shook her head. "I don't believe it," she said.

The Queen's eyes blazed. She got up and paced the room before whipping around to snap at Tanya, "I can't quite believe it either, but here we are!" She took a deep breath and started again. "I don't know why I can't work the quill the same way you can. Don't mistake me, I got it to work. I moved matter from point A to point B. But it wouldn't stand up straight and sparkle for me. It will only do that for you." The Queen's still-firing eyes narrowed. "Why is that, Tanya? I'm very well versed in magic. I have had years—decades—of instruction in every form of magic you've heard of and all the ones you haven't, too. I have no small amount of innate talent. There's no reason the quill shouldn't do for me what it does for a tavern wench. I wonder"—the Queen took a step forward—"whether the scholars, once they get wise, hitch up their robes, and make their way to the Glacier, will find themselves also locked out, as it were? What odds would you give it?"

Tanya stood up. Hidden underneath the plain brown cloth of her borrowed dress, Tanya felt her tattoos begin to *move*, and then to burn. "Thank you for your generous offer, Your Majesty. But I just want my inn back." She quickly folded her arms, just as the fabric around her wrist began to singe.

Luckily the Queen wasn't looking at Tanya's arms, she was looking at the quill. She picked it up. "I like this quill," she said, rolling it around her fingers. "And I believe, under normal circumstances, I could get it to like me. But these are not normal circumstances and I do not have time." She dropped the quill. "I do not accept your refusal. My offer has been altered to a command. From your Queen."

Tanya lifted her head. "If I refuse your command?"

The Queen laughed. "How do you propose to do that?"

Tanya smiled grimly. "You said it yourself: You don't rule alone. There's always the Council. I'm sure many of them would be happy to return the quill to the scholars and the Smiling Snake to me."

The Queen walked back to the table and poured out some cordial. She examined the contents of her glass in the dwindling firelight. "Are you threatening me?" she asked calmly, dipping her finger in. "How interesting."

Then she whipped around and threw the cordial in Tanya's face.

The liquid hit Tanya's face with a bubbling chill and she shrieked in surprise, instinctively throwing her arms up to protect her eyes.

The Queen caught sight of Tanya's sleeves, melting away over her marked arms, and grabbed the girl's wrist. Tanya attempted to yank her arm back, but the Queen's grasp was like an iron vise.

The Queen raised a questioning eyebrow at Tanya, but didn't speak. Instead she pulled Tanya's arm closer with one hand and, with the other, conjured a ball of the same white light that Sir Lurch had struggled to ignite, but which *she* accomplished with a quick and elegant flick of her wrist.

Tanya struggled and started to protest with an indignant, "Your Majesty," but the Queen simply frowned and pulled her closer.

Too close—the quill started spinning in place on the tablecloth as Tanya's exposed flesh came closer. The Queen's lips parted and she dragged herself and Tanya down to their knees, forcing Tanya's arm down on the table.

As it spun faster and faster and closer and closer, the quill's pointed edge grazed Tanya's skin and her tattoos began to glow and writhe, forming into new shapes around the map: from diamonds, stars, and curlicues of wind, it retwisted into icicles, snowflakes, and a crown, curling all the way around her bicep.

"That," declared the Queen, watching closely, "explains a lot, I think. But let's see." The Queen licked her finger and touched the glowing red squiggles growing on Tanya's flesh. Her finger came away with a faint, brilliant red smudge, as if she had dipped her finger in luminescent paint. The Queen put it in her mouth and sucked.

She looked up at Tanya. "You are full of surprises, aren't you? Tanya, bastard tavern wench of Griffin's Port: dabbler in blood magic. Who would have seen that coming?"

The Queen snapped her fingers and the witch-light went off. She released her other hand's grasp on Tanya's hand.

Tanya backed away from the table, her sleeves hanging off her arms in smoking strips of cotton, her tattoos slowing down and dimming to a variation of their previous red, a slightly darker shade, closer to purple, as if the chill blue of the Glacier had infected them.

She searched for an exit, even as she knew there was no way out except the way she had come in, when, suddenly, she found she couldn't move her feet.

Tanya looked down. Her feet had literally frozen over. A layer of permafrost, like what caked the hulls of the ships during snowstorms in Griffin's Port, cemented her to the floor, an ice block extending past her toes and upward toward her knees.

She squirmed, but it was no good. She had seen great merchant galleys stuck in port for a week under thinner ice. A single tavern maid wasn't going to pull herself out if they couldn't.

She looked up at the Queen and saw that she had gone into a slight crouch, both palms out and pointing at Tanya's feet. There was a look of concentration on her face and her fingers were outlined in a shimmering blue light with a slight, sick-looking, yellowish tint.

The same blue-yellow tint of the ice freezing Tanya's feet to the ground.

"Again, Tanya," said the Queen. "I would like to offer you the position of Private Secretary to the Queen of Lode. Do you accept?"

Tanya licked her lips. They weren't dry; she was stalling for time. "What do you need me for that you can't do by yourself?" she asked finally. "You're the Queen."

The Queen smiled. It was a hungry smile. "Tanya, with the quill, I can comprehensively control the flow of natural resources throughout the entirety of Lode. Asking what I need the quill for is a waste of time and imagination. Do better." She lowered her hands and stepped closer. "The question isn't, what *could* we accomplish with this quill? With my authority and strategy; your skill and organization? What *couldn't* we do?"

Tanya flinched. Because she knew the answer.

The answer was nothing. There was nothing they couldn't do. Nothing at all.

The Queen stepped forward again. "Think, Tanya. You were born into about as powerless a position as exists in Lode: a foundling who grew up to be a disinherited and abandoned tavern wench. But you're clever. You're observant. You're a person of obviously untapped talents. It takes talent to master such an unwieldy and experimental tool as that quill as quickly as you have, blood magic or no. Most of my councilmen couldn't have done it and they have the advantage of a first-rate education, whereas you, based on your spelling and penmanship, are just barely on the right side of illiterate. Yet *you're* a useful person."

"What's your point?" broke in Tanya. "I don't need a recitation of my features and failings. Tell me what you're saying."

The Queen's grin widened. "Have you ever looked at the people in power and thought you could do better?" Tanya drew in a quick breath. The Queen saw and advanced. "Have you ever thought that if only *you* controlled things, if only everyone left everything up to you, the world would be much better off? Tell me, Tanya: Don't you know better? Don't you know *best*? Aren't you always *right?*"

Tanya closed her eyes. She felt dizzy and visible; vulnerable. And something else.

The Queen's voice hardened. "Imagine feeling that way and having to suffer the indignity of being called a Queen. Imagine having an army of people to attend to every small wish, but having no true power over anything that matters. Imagine being the Queen of an entire nation, full of riches, and never even being allowed to leave the Glacier!"

Tanya opened her eyes out of sheer surprise. "You've never left the Glacier?" she asked, incredulous.

The Queen stepped back and, for the first time, hesitated. "Of course I've left the Glacier," she said quickly. "I was speaking metaphorically."

The swirl in her eyes sped up. The Queen was hiding something.

She stepped back, retreating into perfect posture. "I will ask you one more time, Tanya," said the Queen. "Will you help me remake the world, in *our* image this time? Will you agree to work with me?"

Tanya forgot that her feet were frozen to floor by some mysterious magic. She forgot that the Queen had lied, and lied again. All of it was washed away in a flood of white-hot desire.

She wanted to say yes.

Even the old Tanya, the one she had been before leaving Griffin's Port, the tavern wench of the Smiling Snake, would have thought the entire setup at the Glacier was shockingly inefficient. There was an inconsistent hierarchy, for one thing. Who was in charge, the Queen or the Council? There was a disorganized staff, for another. Sure, the staff was plentiful and talented, but not on regular shifts, not if Lady Louisa's chamber had been allowed to fall into disarray. No one, it seemed, had the leadership to take control, to pay attention to the details, to create a system that worked and that everyone understood.

Tanya could do better. She knew she was always right. But the Queen was offering her a chance not to organize just a tavern, or even the Glacier; she was offering her the chance to organize the *world*.

She looked at the Queen. "Would I have to listen to anybody other than you?" she asked. "If I say yes, I don't want anyone telling me where to go, what I can't say, who I need to pay attention to, be deferential to. I don't want to have to depend on anyone."

The Queen smiled, a real smile, wide and welcoming. "I believe we understand each other perfectly, Tanya," she said. "If you say yes, you won't even have to be deferential to me. You will have to obey direct orders from me, but I don't anticipate that we will disagree often enough for it to be a frequent necessity. And if anyone, inside the Glacier or outside it, does anything that waylays, involuntarily compels, or even simply displeases you, you will have the power to remove them from your vicinity in the fashion of your choosing."

The Queen leaned forward. "Say yes, Tanya, and you will never have to depend on anyone's good opinion ever again. Stay effective, stay helpful, and you will be beyond the reach of others' whims. Forever."

Tanya felt herself smiling.

"Where do we start?"

# Chapter

19

They started in the dungeons, in the dead of night, standing in front of a shadowy cell. Three amorphous shapes slept in bunks.

The Queen held out her hand. "Give me the torch," she said. "These bars are pure cast iron. Open them for us, please."

Tanya peered through the cell. "What are they even doing here? Why were they arrested?"

The Queen gave her a quick, sidelong look. "After the theft from the Royal College was reported, the Council issued a writ of questioning for Commander Rees's corps. The commander gave up these two as the culprits. The scholar is not under arrest. I just needed to keep him quiet and out of sight. I confess he required some . . . chemical subduing."

Tanya shook her head, clucking her tongue in disapproval, and made a few quick strokes with the feather. The bars vanished and the women stepped inside.

The Queen looked around. "It certainly is dreary in here, isn't it?" She reached into her sleeve and retrieved several smooth white stones. Saying a word in a language Tanya had never heard, the Queen tossed them into the air, where, with a crack, they ignited into cool white witch-light and hung, suspended, in the cell.

"That's better," said the Queen, sitting on a low stool. "Now we can all see each other and converse like civilized people."

The prisoners began to wake up—well, two out of three anyway. Rollo, likely immune to wizard tricks like suspended lights, was still fast asleep. But Greer and Darrow were peasants and had never seen anything like them.

Greer bolted upright and shot his arm out for a weapon he no longer had. He clenched his fingers into a fist and vaulted off the top bunk, landing not six inches from Tanya.

The corpsman paused, confused, fist still at the ready. "Tanya! How did you get here? Did Rees catch you?"

"Um, not quite."

"Tanya," said the Queen pleasantly. "Do me the honor of introducing me to your friend? That one, too." She extended a finger behind her where the witch-light revealed the figure of Darrow, just sitting up.

Darrow's eyes went wide. He joined Greer where he stood, frozen, staring at the Queen.

"This is the Queen," said Tanya flatly. "This is Greer and Darrow. They're corpsmen."

"We mustn't forget the scholar," added the Queen, turning around. "The little lord's fast asleep." She stood up and moved toward Rollo's bunk.

Leaning over, the Queen pushed Rollo's hair off his face.

"Don't—" said Darrow sharply, before going pale and clumsily bowing.

The Queen looked up at him curiously. "I'm not going to hurt him, Mr. Darrow," she said softly. "I know his father, for the Sky's sake. On the contrary, I'm here to reunite him with his college." She took two pale fingers and placed them one on each temple. "Wake up, Lord Rollo," she whispered.

Rollo whimpered a little in his sleep and began to stir. The Queen quickly removed her hands before he could panic and struggle against them—which, judging by the wild look in his eyes, he would have.

"Good evening, Lord Rollo," said the Queen. "Your college is here to take you home."

Rollo struggled to a sitting position. "Where's my quill?" he asked, rubbing his eyes. "Did you get it?"

"The quill is quite safe, Lord Rollo," said the Queen. "See?" She gestured to Tanya, and Rollo's eyes, bleary as they were, narrowed. "It is in my custody now. And my control. Is there anything you require before Sir Lurch conducts you to the rooms set aside by your principal? No? All right." The Queen raised her voice. "Lord Rollo is ready for his escort now."

Greer started giggling from the other side of the cell. Tanya looked at him sharply and he gestured helplessly toward the Queen, trying and failing to smother his hysterical mirth.

Tanya didn't see what was so funny, but the Queen didn't seem insulted. She barely seemed to notice.

Sir Lurch reached the cell. He bowed deeply to the Queen, less deeply to Rollo, and, after a moment's hesitation, threw a quick nod of acknowledgment at Tanya.

Addressing Rollo, Sir Lurch held out an arm. "May I have the honor of escorting my lord to the college's apartments?"

Rollo scowled at the arm, as if the gesture were an insult, but took it glumly when he couldn't get three steps without trembling. Sir Lurch nodded to the Queen and removed Lord Rollo from the cell.

Once the four of them were alone, the Queen moved to Rollo's vacated cot and sat, absently testing the feel of the bed with her hand.

The Queen addressed Greer and Darrow. "Will you oblige me with your full names?"

Darrow stepped forward, bowing so low his nose brushed the frozen ground. "Rafi Darrow, your Majesty," he whispered respectfully. "From the Glassland Meadows."

The Queen nodded, a placid smile on her face. "Your rank, corpsman?"

"Field-commissioned sergeant, Your Majesty."

The Queen lifted her hand and, as if controlled by remote puppetry, Darrow rose, staring at her, transfixed.

Her gaze drifted to Greer, who was not bowing. He was watching the ceremony warily.

"Mr. Greer," said the Queen. "Are you very angry with me?"

He started. His eyes flickered to Tanya; she nodded. If the Queen asked a question, she expected an answer.

Greer turned to the Queen with a stiff bow.

"Your Majesty," he said, his voice loud, but relatively respectful. "My name is Drew Greer. My people are nobody, so it couldn't possibly matter, but they're hunters in Killian Township, if you're curious. I'm just a grunt—no rank, but basic corpsman."

"You *are* angry with me."

Greer looked up at her. "I don't know that," he said, after a moment. "I know that I'm angry to be imprisoned for a theft that I didn't commit. I know that I'm very angry with my commander. I don't know that I have any reason to be angry with *you*."

The Queen seemed pleased with the answer. "I have a proposition for the two of you," she said. "Are you interested?"

Darrow answered softly. "We're sworn to do what you command, Your Majesty." He looked uncomfortable. "Why ask?"

"Because it's clearly going to be something she doesn't want anyone to know about and therefore morally suspect, Darrow," muttered Greer. "You're way, way too nice, but you don't *also* have to be stupid."

The Queen watched the exchange with interest. "I should meet more people," she said, mostly to herself. "It's one thing to understand psychology and the milieu of the low-rank corps recruits from an academic point of view, but it's most illuminating to watch you both.

"Unfortunately," sighed the Queen, pulling out a pearl pocket

225

watch, "I don't currently have the time. I need you both to tell some very minor lies to my Council. I'll tell you what to say. You may add whatever embellishment you prefer—in fact, some low-end color and confusion will likely help sell your testimonies. Do you object to lying to nobility?"

Darrow and Greer looked at each other. Greer shrugged and, with a gulp, Darrow turned back to the Queen and shook his head.

"Excellent. I need you both to make it very clear that Commander Kiernan Rees planned and executed the theft of this quill from the Royal College of Aetherical Manipulation entirely on his own inspiration. I trust neither of you have any particular loyalty to your commander." It wasn't a question. "Any concerns?"

Greer slowly raised his hand. "I have a couple."

"Proceed."

Greer took a deep breath. "You've just given us valuable information. How do we know you won't find a way to eliminate us after we've done what you want?"

The Queen smiled faintly. "You don't know," she admitted. "But don't panic. Yes, I could throw you back in here, or somewhere worse. However, I would be a foolish queen if I were to throw away something useful. And I am not foolish. Are you?" They didn't answer. "I didn't think so. Remain useful and not foolish, and we shan't have a problem. What was your other question?"

Greer jerked his head in Tanya's direction. "What happens to the tavern wench?"

"That," said the Queen firmly, "is now entirely up to her." She stood. "If you gentlemen will excuse us, Tanya and I have a kingdom of resources to marshal and commandeer. Sir Lurch will be back to escort you shortly."

The Queen walked out first. Tanya turned to the corpsmen. "Good night," she offered. Greer opened his mouth and made a gesture as if to grab her arm, but Tanya spun away and hurried to catch up with the Queen.

Once they were out of the cell's sight line, Tanya asked her last question. "How long have you been planning this?"

"A very long time."

"You needed a commander like Rees," said Tanya slowly. "Someone just barely competent enough that he could be advanced through the ranks without objection, but contemptible enough that the Council would be only too delighted to jail him. He's the perfect scapegoat."

"Yes," answered the Queen. "Although, as you've noted, Tanya, the scholars were bringing me the quill. I didn't *need* to steal the quill in order to gain access to it."

Tanya understood. "You knew Rees was crooked," she said. "You knew others would try to steal it from him and you didn't trust him to keep the quill safe. You wanted the quill to cause chaos."

"Only temporarily," said the Queen. "Just enough so that I had a pretext to claim its exclusive use for the throne. The quill will not be causing any more chaos. Greer and Darrow will provide reliable, even sympathetic eyewitness testimony, considering what their commander put them through, and Sir Lurch's men already have Rees in custody. I've had the necessary maneuvers in the works for months."

Back in her study, the Queen snapped her fingers three times and the wall illuminated from within, revealing a complete diagram of the Glacier.

"Your task," said the Queen, stepping to the wall diagram, "is to isolate the council members in their chambers. No one will be able to go in or out unless you or I allow them to. Once you freeze over their chambers, we'll keep them that way until they each sign documents ceding full veto and authorization power to me. For some members, this will be quick. Count Hewitt will need time to adjust, but he'll come around. Others, like the Duke of Xane, may be our guests for some time. There is just one thing I should mention."

Tanya raised her eyebrow. "You think I haven't realized that I can't use normal ice? Just tell me where you got that stuff you froze my feet with and I can get started."

The Queen laughed. "You *are* of use, aren't you? As for where I got that 'stuff,' well"—she put her arms out—"you're standing in it."

It took a moment for it to dawn on Tanya what she meant, and when she finally understood, she felt a tingle of anticipation, of excitement, shiver down her body, and her tattoos begin to pulse. "It's the Glacier itself," said Tanya. "I take ice from the Glacier."

The Queen nodded. "The Glacier is the oldest edifice in Lode, by centuries. No one knows who built it, or how, not even me, and I know more about this ice than anyone living. If you freeze their rooms using Glacier ice, no one will be able to chop their way through. Except for you and me; we alone can reverse the imprisonment. Tanya?"

"Yes?"

"This has to happen *this way*, and it has to happen before sunrise. If we use anything other than Glacier ice, the more retrograde Council members will be broken out by their household guards and they will seize control. You and I will no longer be able to do our work. We will not matter. We will be less real than we have ever been."

Tanya met the Queen's eyes, for once still. "Then I'd better not fail," she said.

The Queen nodded, put on her crown, and exited through the cloud to claim her throne.

Alone, Tanya turned to face the map. The Queen was nothing if not thorough. Every chamber containing a member of the Council was neatly labeled. The Queen had also outlined the structure of the

Glacier itself. All Tanya had to do was move a few chunks of palace foundation around.

"Easy peasy," breathed Tanya. She plugged the quill in and her tattoos began writhing, rearranging—and then stopped, with a visible shudder.

Tanya frowned and brought her forearm closer to her eye. A rough architectural diagram had formed as she'd ordered, but the elemental labeling was stuttering. She could see *gold, mahogany, moonstone* flicker in and out, eventually becoming static—everywhere except for the walls, floors, or foundations.

There, there were no labels at all. Nowhere on her arm did it say *ice.*

Tanya suddenly felt how quiet it was and her heartbeat sped up to a roar. If she couldn't *find* the ice, she couldn't move it, couldn't manipulate it. But how could that be? Ice was just water frozen over. Any child knew that, and she had moved plenty of water. Lady of Cups, she had moved water the very first night she had possessed the quill! And now, when it was so crucial, the quill couldn't even label something as simple as *ice.*

Unless . . .

The Queen had admitted she didn't know exactly what the Glacier ice was. What if the quill didn't know either?

"No, no, no," moaned Tanya, pulling out the quill and sticking it back in, wiping the tattoos clean. "Map the Queen's private study," she ordered. She could physically *see* the ice here, on the walls and hanging from the ceiling in sharp stalactites. The quill *had* to pick it up.

She watched, her heart dropping below her stomach, as a network of three connected chambers populated itself on her arm—blank.

Tanya sank to her knees. She had been bested. If the quill couldn't recognize the Glacier ice, there was nothing more she could do. All the power she had convinced herself she had—it was a lie. She was surrounded by what she needed and couldn't do anything to use it.

She was useless.

The icy floor was chilling her to the bone. Tanya knew she should get up, that sitting there in just a flimsy dress was a good way to give herself pneumonia, but she couldn't bring herself to care.

*Just let me freeze here*, she thought miserably, closing her eyes against the tears stinging them at the corners. *Let the Glacier take me.*

Her eyes snapped open. She looked up, saw the icicles above her. She looked down and saw her incomplete tattoo.

Tanya stood. She reached above her head and plucked the lowest hanging icicle, a sharp, splintery specimen. With the other hand, she unhooked the quill and scratched a twin diamond underneath the first one on her wrist.

She replaced the quill and took a deep breath. "I can do this," she whispered, and, before she could change her mind, plunged the icicle into her arm.

The pain was immense.

Tanya had expected the sting of a puncture and the panicked rush to the head of bloodletting. She had not expected an audible roar of fire to explode behind her temples or her eyes to fill with searing stars.

Tanya felt the whole of the Glacier quake and crack. There was a distant shout and the closer crash of smashed glass—or maybe it was ice. Her tattoos exploded into rivulets of blood and the quill shot straight up, exploding with a black-and-white light.

Gasping with effort and pain, Tanya grabbed it. She had no other surface to write on and no longer felt the cold, so she pulled off her dress and laid it on the floor.

There was no ink, but she did have blood.

Shivering, she drew and wrote and watched as her blood twisted on the rough cloth, forming her arm, her wrist, her fingers, the tines of the feather, its spine, and finally, its sharp point, sticking into a rough diamond on her wrist.

And then, there it was, running through the *blood, bone, muscle—Ice.*

Tanya smiled and stuck the quill back into her arm. The Glacier exploded into existence on her arm, the tattoos red and gold both, and everywhere she saw it: *ice, ice, ice!*

She made a few quick strokes with her fingertip. Now that the quill could recognize the ice, it was as easy as she had anticipated, and within minutes it was done. Tidy caps of impenetrable ice covered twelve doorways, twelve water shafts, and twelve hearths.

Tanya removed the quill and then, more slowly, the icicle. She lifted up the icicle, shining red, and let the quill fall to the floor.

Her arm sewed itself back up with a crunching sound, the sound of ice freezing around wood.

The quill snapped to attention and, careless of gravity, attached itself to her wrist, its feather a light caress against her forearm, the last sensation she was aware of before she collapsed, falling as easily and softly as snow.

Just before she lost consciousness, she managed a single triumphant thought:

*No one else could have done that.*

Her eyes closed before she could see the tattoos turning paler and brighter, until they shone like ice streaked through with blood and then turned to gold.

Part Two

# Chapter

"Tanya!" The Queen's voice echoed up from her study. "Tanya, now!"

It was not quite four A.M. In the months that Tanya had been serving as the Queen's private secretary, she had never been able to break the habit of jerking awake as soon as first light hit her, but it was still full night, and so she twisted among her pillows to lie on her stomach, hoping the voice was a very irritating dream.

There was a sound like chimes and then the very irritating dream was by her bedside, ripping off the blankets.

"Hey!" cried Tanya. "All right, all right. I'm sorry, I thought I was dreaming." She rubbed her bleary eyes and then looked at the Queen. She frowned. "What's wrong? What's happened?"

The Queen, plain and stern in her hooded gray work robe, didn't choose to answer. She simply walked back to the cage and pointedly waited, her arms crossed.

Tanya rose and dipped a quick, habitual curtsy before kicking her feet into her sheepskin slippers. She shivered and grabbed her own robe, made of soft rabbit fur; the fire had banked overnight. Most of the Glacier was kept warm by a networked overlay of magical energy the Queen maintained as easily as breathing—something to do with increasing the speed of the invisible matter of air. But Tanya's tower room was isolated, its only point of egress being the cage that had first taken her to the Queen's study.

It went up higher than even Sir Lurch had been aware of. The Queen had never had a secretary before, so no one had needed to know.

Tanya yawned and passed by her nightstand, holding out her wrist. The quill snapped off the table and into place along her arm, like a well-trained puppy.

She joined the Queen in the cage.

"Lovely of you to join me, Tanya," she said acidly as they descended. "I had no idea having a helper at my call would be so convenient. I use 'call' euphemistically, you understand."

"Yes, Your Majesty."

"Because you quite literally weren't at my call. The phrase isn't 'at my beck and *fetch*,' is it?"

"Yes, I understood, Your Majesty. I apologize." The Queen nodded, but still had her lips pursed, annoyed, and her eyes behind her glasses were red and tired. "Is there, by any luck, coffee already made?"

The cage landed and the Queen gave her a withering look. "I have been working since I left auditions, Tanya," she told her, stepping through the cloud. "You tell me if you think they were enervating enough for me to forgo caffeine."

Tanya's jaw clenched sympathetically. There was definitely coffee. She followed her Queen into the cloud.

That demonstration of beautiful fighting men Tanya had witnessed upon her arrival to the Glacier had been no mere entertainment, but one of several steps in a long, long, *long*—as long as the Queen could manage, really—process of winnowing down the list of suitors for her hand in marriage.

The fights were a long-standing tradition, the performances ranked by deadliness and beauty. There were a few additional trials that were also tradition, but since taking control of the Council, the Queen had invented several steps of her own.

Some, Tanya privately thought, were rather obvious in their ridiculousness—clear delaying tactics. Tanya had never been a third-born son of a king, but she assumed that they had better things to do than compete to arrange the most artful table display. But even more suitors had arrived at the Glacier since the Queen's bloodless coup. And what had come after.

The Queen's private study had transformed into a two-woman war room, but instead of troop positions and artillery stores, the variables being negotiated were grain, water, earth, gas, metal, fiber, stone, and wood. There were two large desks, but the real work took place in two other places.

The first was the map.

It was enormous, seven by seven feet—ten by ten when the extensions were put on. It hung on a bright gold easel contraption that either locked into place upright, or flipped ninety degrees to lie flat, as it was now. It was a colorful, detailed topography of the whole of Lode's territory, sky, sea, and land, overflowing with words and detailing in brick-red ink—Tanya had decided to call what came out of the quill now *ink*, but she wasn't quite sure that was true—alongside tidy check-marked charts, keeping track of any additions or deficits she enacted with the quill. The map took up half the room.

The other half of the room was the Queen's laboratory.

The lab was a glittering cacophony of steel and glass, flame and bubble. A maze of tubes interspersed with bellowing copper pots rose two feet above the mirrored table, the remainder littered with small piles of "experiments."

Those experiments were why the suitors were still coming, though it was clear that the Queen had no intention of picking one of them as a partner. Those experiments were why no one was complaining that the Queen had upset the status quo of centuries when she neutralized the Council.

A mineral compound that prevented infection, a metal alloy that was stronger than steel and lighter than tin, and, most recently, a gaseous solution that, carefully aimed, could knock a battalion unconscious with one puff without affecting any of one's own soldiers—these were the experiments that were making Lode rich. Always in favor of efficiency, the Queen had readily accepted Tanya's blood binding of the quill and left her to the map, while she strategized and dreamt at her shining laboratory.

But that wasn't where the Queen went this morning. After pouring another mug of coffee for herself, she went to stand at the map. "Look at this," she said to Tanya. "I said, *now.*"

Tanya had stopped by the coffeepot as well. "Listen," Tanya said, pouring herself her own cup. "I had to sit through that table-setting contest, too, *and* I had to do it while keeping score—by metrics I *made up.*" She walked across the room and stood next to the Queen. "Now, what's wrong?"

"Look!"

Tanya took another sip of coffee and looked up. "Oh no," she sighed. "Not again."

One of the first acts the Queen had signed into law upon her assuming complete control of the Council established a permitting system for any aetherical manipulation over a certain quantity of matter. Any manipulations that could have a discernable effect on the economy had to be approved ahead of time—fifty clerks had been reassigned to process the requests. Hobbyists and researchers could move a little matter around—the Queen was not shortsighted enough to believe she could enforce a complete ban on the practice.

And, of course, there would *always* be criminals. Sir Lurch had charge of a special corps to investigate and neutralize any operation that grew large enough to pose a threat to her and Tanya's organization of the kingdom. Rollo had stayed on at the Glacier as a consultant. Tanya believed the wizard was overly enjoying the dignity that came with a corpsman uniform—or maybe he just liked wearing pants again.

Theoretically, these precautions should have prevented any errant junkoff from endangering commerce or, more importantly to Tanya, screwing up her calculations.

Theoretically.

"*How?*" asked Tanya. "Didn't Sir Lurch find the last of the gang operating out of the winery?"

"Mmmhmm. Yes, he did."

"Well, he must *not* have. I read the same intelligence reports you do. There's no other unauthorized operation large or skillful enough to cause flooding this intense. Have him check again."

"It's not the gang, Tanya."

"It has to be." The Queen didn't answer. "How do you *know* it's not?"

The Queen sipped out of her mug and pulled a long, thin pearl needle out of her hair, sending the locks tumbling over her shoulders.

"Because I have jailed the entire town of Ruby Ridge as well as anyone found in the surrounding forest, a full thirty-mile radius. They have all been chemically subdued, therefore none could possibly be performing manipulations at this level." She used the hairpin to point at the map. "Look closer at the flooding."

But Tanya couldn't take her eyes off the Queen.

"You jailed an *entire town*? What about the children?"

"I jailed them, too. There *are* talented children, Tanya, I shouldn't have to tell you that."

Tanya felt a lump form in her throat. "You didn't . . . ? You didn't drug the children, did you?"

"Of course I did." The Queen looked up at Tanya and blinked. "How else could I be completely sure that they weren't causing this junkoff? It won't do them any long-term harm. The innocents will be released eventually, not, I imagine, particularly worse for wear.

239

They're not *hurt*, merely sedated. Now, come on Tanya, look at this flood." Tanya didn't move. The Queen snapped her fingers in front of her face. "Tanya. Focus. The flood."

Tanya felt as though she were trapped in a fog. But the Queen snapped her fingers again and the quill was quivering against her skin and she looked.

"There's no labeling," she said slowly. "It's not water."

"No, I don't think it is. But look where it's coming from." The Queen pointed.

"Bloodstone," breathed Tanya. Tanya drew the quill to her fingertips and placed it on the dark, spreading blot. She made some quick strokes, directing a small diamond of the stuff to the quadrant of the map she had designated as their study.

"I'm not sure that's wise," began the Queen, but it was too late.

A large, viscous bubble of writhing black sludge formed above their heads. It hovered there for a few seconds, making a sucking, slithering, whispering sound that turned Tanya's blood to ice.

The bubble burst and the black sludge flew across the room in countless snakes of gunk. The whispering got louder.

Unlike anyone else Tanya had ever met, the Queen was always fast enough. She shoved Tanya to the floor.

"Get under the map and stay there," she ordered, and Tanya scrambled to obey.

The Queen widened her stance and began rolling her wrists, arms, and fingers together in a swift, intricate pattern, generating a chilly white light. She shot her fingers outward, sending the light into the sludge snakes, one by one, but lightning fast. The sludge paused in midair and dropped to the ground as if concussed.

The Queen ran to the table and grabbed as many cups and plates as she could carry. "Tanya, help me," she called. "Trap them with whatever you can find. What I did is going to wear off."

Tanya scrambled out from under the map and the two rushed around until they covered each and every drop of sludge. They stood together by the map, panting, as the sludge began to rattle their prisons.

"Let's get out of here," the Queen said wearily, making her way to the cage. "I'll send word for Rollo to get a containment crew in here. Do you want breakfast?"

Tanya quickly moved to catch up with the Queen, not eager to spend a moment longer trapped in a room with the sludge.

"I could eat," she said as the Queen shut the cage.

The kitchens were always manned, so it didn't take long for them to send fresh almond pastries and more coffee up to Tanya's room. They often ate there. Tanya had yet to see where the Queen slept. She wasn't sure that she did.

"What was that?" Tanya finally asked.

"To what are you referring? The black matter or the light?"

Tanya shrugged. "Both. Either."

The Queen layered her pastry with a thin coating of honey and crammed half of it in her mouth. The Queen did *eat*, anyway—constantly, mechanically, and without any obvious enjoyment.

"Do you remember what you brought through from Bloodstone that first dinner in my study?" asked the Queen. "I trapped it for my scholars to examine later." When Tanya didn't answer immediately, she frowned. "Did you *forget*?"

"That was also the night I provided essential assistance to a coup, while *also* performing an unprecedented act of blood magic, so perhaps I let that *particular* mystery slide, thank you *very* much."

The Queen ignored the rudeness, as was her wont—Tanya had been trying to get a rise out of her for weeks, but she seemed immune to rudeness as long as the perpetrators remained useful.

"Well, it's the same material," the Queen continued. "Obviously. I experimented with various levels of cold and various gasses, and finally came up with something that at least appears to stun it, temporarily. But truly, I . . ."

Tanya leaned forward. The Queen never hesitated. "What is it?" she asked.

The Queen frowned. "That's just it. I don't know what it is. The quill doesn't even seem to know what it is, as you've seen. It seems to only come from Bloodstone and tonight it . . . started *spreading.* Rather rapidly."

"But what's it *doing?*"

"That's the problem! I have no idea. None! But I did some quadrant mapping of the illegal manipulations and junkoff last night, and found something, well . . . rather disturbing."

*More disturbing than drugging children?* Tanya bit down the question. That wasn't her job.

The Queen continued. "There *was* a gang of illegal aetherical manipulators operating out of Ruby Ridge. We weren't wrong about that. But they weren't responsible for all the manipulations we had attributed to them—interrogations have made that clear."

Tanya shivered at the word *interrogations.* "Then who?"

"The gold mine overflow, for example," mused the Queen, not answering the question. "The tunnel through the reefs."

"Your Majesty . . ."

The Queen put down her pastry and looked at Tanya.

"The unauthorized manipulations that have had the most economic impact aren't *manipulations* at all," she said. "It's junkoff. From somewhere else."

Tanya frowned. "But Sir Lurch has monitors nearly everywhere. I mean, except . . . oh no."

The Queen nodded. "The junkoff is being *caused by* the black matter," she said. "*Someone* is manipulating it. And it's coming from Bloodstone."

# Chapter

anya sat back, digesting what the Queen had told her. She wasn't sure *how* to feel, but soon landed on annoyed.

"I don't understand why we can't have monitors in Bloodstone," she blurted out. "Don't get me wrong—you couldn't pay me enough to join that corps. But it is still in Lode and you are the Queen of Lode. Why can't we just do there what we did with Ruby Ridge?"

The Queen raised an eyebrow.

"You mean why can't we just jail and drug children?" she asked archly. "I would have thought your peasant prudery would have prevented you from making such a suggestion."

Tanya flushed. "I don't make policy," she said hotly, crossing her arms. "I'm merely asking questions."

The Queen sighed. "Well, it's very tiresome of you considering that it's a question I've already answered," she said. "Yes, Bloodstone is in Lode. It belongs to me. But it operates under its own rules and I can do nothing to combat that from the Glacier."

"Then why don't you *go* to Bloodstone? Arrest them?"

The Queen chortled. "Tanya, arrest who? Everyone in Bloodstone is a criminal—*everyone*. I simply don't have the manpower and, to be honest, it wouldn't be worth it. Crime is inevitable in any kingdom. Leaving it to freely consolidate in a particular area isn't the *worst* strategic decision the Council ever made." She took another bite of pastry and sip of coffee. "There is also the problem of the Gate."

"What gate?"

The Queen's mouth turned down. "There's wild magic in Bloodstone. It all comes from that damned volcano. I swear, I have brought refugee after refugee here from Bloodstone for interviews and experiments, I have interrogated and chemically analyzed every criminal who has ever been anywhere *near* the place, and I still don't understand a single thing about that volcano—it's maddening, Tanya, and I won't take it anymore! I *won't*, I *refuse!*"

Tanya instinctively leaned away, blown back by the unfamiliar venom in the Queen's voice, the rage in her eyes.

The Queen seemed to catch herself and sat back, training her eyes on the floor. In a moment, she looked back up, her face returned to its normal placid self.

"The Gate," she continued, her voice as even as if the outburst had never happened, "*decides* whom to admit. You must be explicitly invited by someone the Gate has already accepted, or it must sense something about you."

Tanya rolled her eyes. She hated magic. Well, she hated it when *other* people did it. "What must it sense?" she asked warily.

"As I said, I'm not entirely certain. It seems to admit children always—"

"We are *not* sending a child into that place."

"And criminals," the Queen continued. "It admits criminals."

Tanya was taken aback. "Oh," she said, thinking. "Could you . . . I don't know, trick it? Steal my shoe, or something? Or have Sir Lurch do it?"

"Tanya. I'm the Queen. By definition, nothing I do is criminal. And if I order Sir Lurch to do something, then he is merely following my orders, and that is not a crime either. I *have* thought of this before." Suddenly she looked straight at Tanya and her kaleidoscope eyes started to spin.

Tanya hated when they did that.

The Queen blinked and her eyes went flat again. But she was still staring at Tanya, in a way the tavern maid didn't like.

"What?" she asked. "Why are you looking at me like that?"

The Queen smiled. "You're a criminal, Tanya," she said. "You stole a tiara, if I'm not mistaken."

"Hang on, I was *ordered* to do that," Tanya protested.

"Not by me. And *my* word is law, not 'the Tomcat's,' or whatever ridiculous name he goes by. And you *voluntarily* evaded capture by the corps. No one asked you to do that—that was on your own initiative, and with the aid of a stolen item at that!" She looked at Tanya critically. "Add in the blood magic—which, and I'm not sure you're aware of this, is actually illegal—and I think the Gate will let you in."

Tanya stood up and paced the room.

"Say the Gate does let me in," she said, still pacing. "What am I supposed to do then? How am I going to find out where the sludge is coming from, let alone who's controlling it? I'm assuming they don't hand you a map of criminal enterprise upon arrival. That's all supposing that there even *is* someone behind it and it's not some sort of more than usually creepy *natural* phenomena. And say I do, somehow, find out *any* of this—what do I do then? Arrest them? *Me?*"

The Queen shrugged. "I don't see why you couldn't. You'll have the quill with you—of course you will, Tanya. I don't like it, but that quill would be useless to me without you now that you've mucked about with your blood. You could simply wrap the perpetrators in bars of iron and transport them via air to the Glacier. And I won't send you alone. As far as how you'll go about finding out the origin of the black matter . . . you're resourceful, Tanya. You'll figure it out." She started giggling. "Maybe you'll get a job as a tavern wench! Gather gossip over beer pitchers or whatever it is you did for all those years."

Tanya felt as if she had been slapped. "Maybe I'll do that," she retorted. "Maybe I'll decide to wrap whichever corpsmen you send in iron instead of the manipulators, and just stay in Bloodstone." The Queen collapsed backward, overcome with laughter. Tanya had to raise her voice to be overheard. "The Tomcat said there was a decent tavern—maybe if he's still there I can get a recommendation."

The Queen, still chuckling a little, began to compose herself. "Oh, don't be insulted, for the Sky's sake, Tanya," she told her. "You know I think that work was simply *wasted* on you—that's all I found amusing." She sighed contentedly, the last of the laughter leaving her body. She picked up her coffee cup. "You didn't tell me the Tomcat was based in Bloodstone."

Tanya sat back down, dejected. "He's not," she said. "He had particular business there. Something to do with the tiara I stole, actually."

The Queen froze midsip. She spat the coffee back in the mug and set it down.

"The Tomcat's caravan went to Bloodstone when, exactly?"

"Immediately after the heist. They were packing up when I ran away."

The Queen nodded. "Which duchess did you steal it from?"

"I . . . don't know actually," answered Tanya, surprised. "They never said and I never asked. Whichever one lives on the edge of the White."

The Queen stood abruptly. She walked around in a perfect circle, her fists clenched tightly at her side. Then, she picked up her coffee mug, examined it closely, and smashed it, *hard*, against the table, sending daggers of porcelain hurtling across the room.

Tanya deftly ducked. "Your Majesty!" she cried. "Luckily, that's not the first time someone has smashed a mug in my face, but Lady of Cups! *What* are you doing?"

The Queen, in fact, was calmly sitting back down. "I was venting my feelings," she explained. "It's something I need to do on the rare occasion on which I discover that I have made an error."

"You smash something every time you make a mistake?" asked Tanya, dropping to her knees to gather the shards. "How do you have any dishware left?"

"Don't be silly, Tanya, it doesn't always have to be a dish. And, any-way, it's only happened seventeen times—eighteen, including today."

Tanya stopped and gave the Queen a withering look. "You've only made eighteen mistakes. In your life."

The Queen shrugged. "As far as I'm concerned, yes. And my con-cern is the only concern that matters."

Tanya continued her cleaning. "What a luxurious life you do lead," she said dryly.

The Queen was silent for a moment. "I could, you know," she said.

Tanya stood and cast about the room for a dustpan. "Could what?" she asked distractedly.

"I could live a luxurious life." Tanya stopped and looked at the Queen, curious at the tone in her voice—almost wistful.

"I was never supposed to actually *rule*, you know," she said, her eyes whirring. "I was a child for a long time. I was a girl for, I swear, even longer. They didn't think they would have to deal with a woman. That's the point of the suitors, you know; that's always been the point of the suitors, for every Queen of Lode in memory. It was meant to distract me." She looked at Tanya and smiled wanly. "It worked very well for my mother, you see."

"Your mother?" Tanya suddenly realized that she had never con-templated the fact that the Queen must have had parents, and that they were gone.

Just like hers.

"Yes. My mother was never very studious. She was good at wear-ing dresses and waving and sitting imperiously at the head of the council room, and that's all the Council wanted from the Queen. At least that's what I've gathered—I never met her. And she loved the suitor tests. She loved my father, too, I suppose. I'm told he was very handsome and not particularly bright, so they were likely very well matched. They died when I was six months old—boating accident."

"I'm sorry."

The Queen looked up at her, surprised. "Why? I told you I never knew them. Why would it make me sad that they died?"

"It's just what people say, Your Majesty."

The Queen shook her head. "I've never understood that custom," she said. "Why would people apologize for something they didn't do?

"I was never like my mother," she continued after a brief silence. "While I was very little, the Council could do what they liked, especially when they kept me distracted with experts, tutors, books—they thought I was busy enough, engaged enough, that I didn't notice that I wasn't being the Queen. That I wouldn't notice because I was still so little, for so long. They thought I wouldn't figure it out, but I did. And I fixed it. I only forgot one thing." She shook her head, and when she spoke again, her voice was back to normal. "Never mind," she said. "I had a lot on my plate."

Tanya had never been so close to shaking royalty before. "What did you figure out?" she asked. "What did the Council do?"

The Queen didn't bother to look at her, let alone answer the question. Tanya swallowed a sigh. The Queen did that from time to time. The best thing to do was to ask a different question, one she was interested in answering.

Tanya asked, "Why is blood magic illegal?"

That got the Queen's attention. "Blood magic is illegal because it is both unpredictable and irrevocable."

"What do you mean *irrevocable?*"

"I mean, Tanya, that even if the actual magical working is reversed—say, a reanimation or a binding, such as you have managed with the quill—the blood is poisoned. Usually this matters little because the person whose blood was used is dead. That's another reason it's illegal: It's very rare to have blood magic without murder. You are a very unusual case. No one who is both well informed and rational performs blood magic using their own blood. To do so is to expose oneself to enormous risk and not just of blood poisoning— which to be clear, is almost impossible to treat. The manifestations are so different depending on the blood used, that no one has developed any methods to treat it, not even me. And that's only half the danger."

"What's the other half?"

The Queen leaned forward. "Blood magic upsets a balance in the aether. The first people to use aetheric manipulation as we know it today came to it through blood magic. Blood and magic together create a conduit through the aether; all that it takes to access that conduit and follow it back to its source is, again, blood and magic. Have you ever heard the phrase 'Blood calls to blood'?"

Tanya thought she had. "I always thought that had to do with family; some kind of 'loyalty-between-nobility' thing."

The Queen uttered a short laugh. "No. It's referring to blood magic. Skilled practitioners of blood magic—very dangerous people—if they find another blood user's conduit through the aether, can track that power, commandeer it, even, if they're good enough. You're awfully exposed, Tanya."

Tanya stared at her. "And you've let me keep doing it?"

The Queen lifted her eyebrows. "Of course I have! Even if the donor is dead, it is extremely dangerous to reverse blood magic! The energy released is practically impossible to control. Why would I put us in such danger? And why would I risk my reign?" The Queen lifted her hood and headed for the cage.

But Tanya's strategy worked. The Queen's tongue loosened by something that interested her, she answered the earlier question, though Tanya scarcely cared anymore. "One thing the Council did was give various magical artifacts they didn't want lying about the Glacier to random aristocracy as gifts," said the Queen, twisting the bars in the opening combination. "My mother had such a wealth of highly born, unimaginative, and uncurious friends, it was quite easy to pass these artifacts off as mere sentimental trinkets. I have spent many years collecting these items in secret. I missed one."

The cage opened and the Queen stepped in.

"The tiara concentrates and amplifies aetherical energy," she said, the cage sliding shut. "Whatever it is that that volcano does, that tiara is increasing its power by a factor of three hundred, at least. We don't have any time to waste."

The Queen slipped out of sight. Tanya sat down heavily on her bed, sinking deep into the cushioned layers of her mattress.

Whoever had outfitted this room after she blood magicked herself into unconsciousness had done a beautiful job. There was copious light, soft places to sit everywhere you looked, and there were books—Tanya had discovered that she *loved* books, loved learning, and these were particularly lovely books. She brushed the one on her nightstand, a history of Lode bound in velvet and embroidered in gold.

*Kind of like me*, she thought, looking down at her tattoos still shining gold on her skin. They squiggled into new shapes every day as the quill changed the world, but they were always gold now.

Tanya did not want to go to Bloodstone. The Queen had told her that she would never have to do anything she didn't want to ever again—*unless by her command*, Tanya remembered ruefully.

The Queen was always very specific. But the Queen would also never risk an asset, so she must believe Tanya would be safe.

*And she's right*, thought Tanya. *I am impervious to harm now. I can protect myself better than anyone in Lode. So why do I still feel so unsettled?* Bloodstone was just a city—a terrible, terrifying city, but as the Queen said, Tanya had the quill. What else could she possibly need to feel in control?

Suddenly Tanya smiled.

After dressing, she made her way through the cloud and found the Queen at her desk, looking fresh as a snowflake in white and silver, signing a piece of paper for Sir Lurch.

"Tanya," the Queen greeted her without looking up. "Perfect timing. I was just signing reassignment papers for your corps escort."

"Cancel them. I want Greer and Darrow."

The Queen looked up. "Sir Lurch, is that acceptable to you?" she asked.

"Whatever is acceptable to you, Your Majesty, is acceptable to me," he answered slowly. "However, I don't know that Greer or Darrow would be glad to receive such an assign—"

"Then it's settled," interrupted the Queen, smiling. "I'm glad you've given this some thought, Tanya. Is there anything else you require?"

"There is, as a matter of fact."

"And what is that?"

Tanya smiled. "I require a horse."

# Chapter

Tanya was the first to arrive at the departure point, a desolate, deserted field about a league behind the armory. It was the first night the weather decided to turn truly cold. She was dressed in her new traveling coat, a long brown affair trimmed in green tweed that fit snuggly around her torso before flaring out flatteringly to her toes. She clutched the quill tightly in her fist, slightly muffling its glow—the only thing lighting her way.

It was important to get to Bloodstone quickly, the Queen had argued. The sludge had spread even farther in the past twenty-four hours. Tanya had to *fly* herself and her escorts there.

It was important that Tanya and her escorts be allowed to do their work when they got to Bloodstone, Sir Lurch had countered. It was possible that whoever was behind the illegal manipulations had some way of monitoring *them*, too, and it wouldn't do to tip them off with a public light show originating from the Glacier.

This was the compromise Tanya, who didn't want to go anyway, had brokered. She would fly there, but not when anyone was looking and not from the Glacier. She would land in the Tomcat's abandoned camp, more for symmetry's sake than any other reason.

And if her traveling companions didn't *like* it, she thought, turning at the sound of hoofbeats, well, neither did she. It was just the best way.

"Miss me, horse?" she called cheerfully, having decided she absolutely refused to call the mare Gillian.

As the mare came into view, Tanya drew an irritated breath. "Oh no," she said, shaking her head. "I never said I wanted you."

Rollo jumped off Gillian's back and started mumbling in the mare's ear.

Tanya crossed her arms. "I apologize, my lord, but this is a classified mission. You can't be here."

Rollo turned and surveyed Tanya with disdain.

It was almost a shame, Tanya thought. In some ways she and Rollo were quite similar: both organized, both resourceful, both determined, both in possession of a complicated relationship with a horse. In a different world, they might have been friends.

Unfortunately, in this one, after a solid month of stiff curtsies, curt nods, pointed comments, snipping, sniping, and eventually snapping, that potential had evaporated into the aether. In fact, Tanya was almost positive that there wasn't a single human being who annoyed her more and was almost proud to imagine that he would say the same about her.

Rollo left the mare and stood in front of Tanya.

"If you get Gillian injured in any way," he said tightly, "I promise you, there will be consequences."

He exploded in a mass of feathers, disappearing high into the pitch black.

Tanya looked at the mare. "He thinks that frightened me, doesn't he?"

The mare harrumphed grumpily, but trotted up to Tanya quickly enough and flicked her gently in the face with her mane—well, almost gently.

Greer and Darrow came next, both out of uniform for the first time that Tanya had ever seen. Greer was in a gray wool cap, brown pants, brown vest, and a black-and-gray checked shirt. Darrow was in a long, dark green hood that stretched over a silvery tunic of fine woven material and tight black trousers tucked into high black boots.

There was a clumsy darn on Greer's left elbow and a tidy one on Darrow's right shoulder, and Tanya realized with a start that these were the boys' own clothes. This was how they had appeared before Rees recruited them.

Tanya started to greet them, but Greer didn't give her a chance.

"Mistress Tanya," he said, with a tight bow. "Honored to be included in your company."

Tanya took a step back. "What? Mistress who?" She looked at Darrow, who shrugged, glancing at Greer with a strange mix of exasperation and worry.

Greer was watching the path with a rigid, soldierly posture. Darrow sighed and joined him, chucking him on the shoulder—a friendly gesture Greer ignored. Warily, Tanya joined them, standing on Greer's other side. The mare trotted up to stand next to her and the four stood in a straight line, waiting for the Queen.

The Queen didn't have to be there, of course. Tanya could have conjured the wind alone.

But the Queen wanted to watch.

The four of them peered into darkness until suddenly there she was, a witch-light held aloft by Sir Lurch, illuminating her standing in the field, dressed all in black.

She looked at them from a distance and then approached.

Her eyes slid over Greer and Darrow, who bowed in turn. "You have your orders, corpsmen?" she asked.

"Yes, Your Majesty," said Greer, still in a bow.

The Queen nodded absently, not really interested. She stood directly in front of Tanya.

"I want to know where that magic is coming from," she said evenly. "I want to know who is using it and then I want you to stop them. Don't kill them, though—I'll want them back at the Glacier. I have questions."

Tanya tightened her grip on the quill.

"I wasn't planning on killing anyone," she told her Queen. "I don't like the idea of kidnapping anyone much better."

The Queen shrugged. "Your magic is stronger or theirs is," she said. "They'll take you or you'll take them." Tanya heard herself inhale sharply. "But my gamble is quite literally on you, Tanya. I truly hope not to be disappointed."

"I truly hope not to be *taken*, so yeah, me too."

The Queen smiled. "I'll miss you, Tanya," she said. "We understand each other."

Tanya felt a sensation she couldn't quite recall building behind her eyes. "Your Majesty . . . ," she began.

"Let me put something together to keep you upright." The Queen stepped back. She lifted her arms and shot streaks of cold white light out of her fingertips.

The beams weaved in and out and around each other, forming a large, circular filigree cage. Tanya, the mare, and the corpsmen, Darrow dragging a wagon with their trunks behind them, stepped in.

Tanya stuck the quill in her arm, calling *wind*, swirling it faster and faster within the cage until it lifted into the air.

Then they flew.

It wasn't as much fun this time—it was freezing that high up in the air, and Tanya couldn't see anything at all except for the mare's rump directly in front of her face, and exposed by a twitching tail—Tanya suspected by her design. But it *was* much faster this time, and Tanya was glad for the Queen's magic cage. Tanya was nowhere near as disoriented upon landing as she had been last time.

That came in handy when, a moment after Tanya took her first few steps on solid ground, she was impeded by a wiry arm around her neck and knife's point against her ear.

"I don't particularly like it when people fly," came the buoyant rasp in Tanya's ear. "And I *really* don't like it when people steal into my camp in the middle of the night. That's bad luck for you, sister."

Tanya gasped. "Jana?" The arm tightened and the knife pressed harder. "Jana, stop! It's me, it's Tanya!"

"Tanya?" Jana let go long enough for Tanya to whirl around and hold the quill aloft, illuminating her face. Jana stepped back, but she was still in a fighting stance, one knee bent behind the other, her knife arm outstretched. "You look different."

"I do?" Tanya looked down at herself. "I . . . well, I did get some new clothes. And I'm clean. You're not used to seeing me clean."

Greer looked up from where he was puking in the bushes. "Who are you talking to?" he asked, struggling upright. "Tanya, we're not supposed to talk to anyone until Bloodstone."

"Oh, it's 'Tanya' again, is it, corpsman Greer?" she asked witheringly.

"Corpsmen!" Jana did a mind-bendingly quick triple aerial cartwheel, maneuvering around Tanya and landing with a neat roundoff behind Greer, who quickly spun around, fumbling for his own sword. "Oh! It's you," exclaimed Jana, smiling as if seeing an old friend. "Hi, again!" She flipped her dagger around and raised the hilt. "Bye, again!"

"You don't need to do that," Tanya said, stepping in front of Greer.

"She does, actually," said Greer hotly. "Now move out of the way, *Mistress* Tanya, and let me do my job. Darrow!"

Darrow looked up from where he was sitting on the ground, shaking his head back and forth. He sprang up. "Sorry!" he yelled, sticking his finger in his ear. "My ear is clogged! I can barely hear you."

"OK, but you can *see*, can't you? Move!"

Jana cocked her head to the side, looking at Tanya. "These guys are with you?" she asked skeptically, before stiffening and adjusting her posture. "Or are you with them?"

"No, no, they're with me," said Tanya, taking a few steps closer to Jana, who instinctively backed up. "They're with me. No one's going to arrest you, or lay a hand on you, I promise."

"The hell I'm not!"

"Greer, no." Tanya spun to look at him. "Jana is—"

"I don't care who she is to you," cried Greer, going red in the face. "She knocked me *unconscious*."

"Look, she does that to everybody."

"I really do," offered Jana, sheathing her dagger. "I wouldn't take it personally."

"See?" said Tanya. "She's putting away her knife. And besides, what I was *going* to say is that Jana is from Bloodstone."

Greer frowned. "No one's *from* Bloodstone," he said.

"*Jana* is. She grew up there. Right?"

"Well . . ." Jana hesitated, giving Darrow time to finally amble up and offer her a confused bow. "Oh, hey there, cutie. Riley will be sorry to have missed *you*."

"Where is Riley?" asked Tanya, looking around the empty camp. "I thought the Tomcat had deserted this camp, but, well, *you're* here. Where's everyone else?"

Jana shrugged. "Bloodstone, I imagine. If they'd left, the Tomcat would have already sent scouts after me. Not that they would have found me. But I would have found them."

"You ran away from your contract with the Tomcat? Jana! He's going to kill you!"

"You think?" Jana backed up, raised her arms, and went into a handstand. She backflipped onto a boulder, then vaulted high in the air, swinging herself around a tree branch. Her legs wrapped securely around it, she swung upside down, nocked an arrow into her bow, and let it fly—it came so close to Tanya she felt her hair raise with displaced air.

Still swinging upside down, Jana smiled. "He can try," she said. "But I don't think he'll bother. He was planning on setting up shop in Bloodstone permanently; he doesn't need a tracker in there—there are enough scryers to drown one each day and never run out. And from where I'm standing"—at this Jana somersaulted neatly off the tree—"that leaves a job opening out here."

Tanya raised her eyebrows. "You're starting a gang? How's it going?"

"Slowly," she moaned. "I think my standards are too high. I wish I could have convinced Riley to run away with me, but he was scared of getting killed. He's not as good at violence as I am. But then again, I'm a crap burglar." She eyed Tanya and the quill. "What are *you* doing? Are you free?"

Tanya felt her mouth twist in a smile. She was as free as one could get in Lode: emotionally unencumbered and mostly in charge.

Darrow answered instead, "We're on a mission, miss. To Bloodstone."

There was a moment of silence and then Jana dissolved into laughter, collapsing onto the ground.

"I'm not sure I understand what's funny," said Darrow, gently puzzled.

"Nothing," answered Greer caustically. "She's a lunatic."

Jana's laughter got louder, until she eventually got herself together, and speaking through hiccups, answered, "First of all, look at you calling me 'miss.' You are very cute. Second of all, you're telling me that Tanya, after escaping in as spectacular a fashion as I've ever seen just to *avoid* going to Bloodstone, stealing Riley's horse in the process—he is truly pissed about that, by the way, and he's going to steal her back the second he sees her, so watch it—less than half a year later, she comes back here on her way *to* Bloodstone? Why did you bother running away at all?"

It was an excellent question and it made Tanya incredibly angry. She rolled up her sleeves and felt a warm bite of satisfaction when

Jana, Greer, and Darrow all recoiled at the sight of her tattoos, writhing and terrible.

She held out the quill. "Here's what's going to happen," she said, her voice light and cold, a perfect echo of the Queen. "You, Jana, are going to lead us to Bloodstone. Along a path that has not been overtaken by that black stuff, please. When we get there, you are going to be our guide. You are going to listen to what I say and follow my orders. I have the quill. Rank is irrelevant. Are we clear?"

"Yeah, OK," said Jana, with her hands up. "But I'm not gonna let myself get murdered, quill or no quill."

"That's fine. I don't want you to get murdered either. That would be distracting." She turned to the corpsmen. "Any arguments from either of you?" They shook their heads, Greer looking sober and Darrow instinctively standing in front of both him and Jana, as if his sheer width could protect them from the quill.

It couldn't. Tanya lifted her fingers from the quill and it snapped into place against her arm. "Then let's get some sleep. Jana, you're in charge until we get to Bloodstone."

Tanya retreated to her tent as soon as it was erected. Though she had picked her companions herself, she felt a tightness in her chest whenever she had to talk to them.

Tanya didn't know how to account for it. Why should she care that they weren't offering her, what? Friendship? Kinship? She had never felt kinship—nontransactional kinship anyway—in Griffin's Port, and she had thrived. And her relationship with the Queen—that was explicitly transactional and Tanya had never felt more fulfilled.

Outside, it quieted. Tanya pulled out her history of Lode and began reading, the words moving faster for her than they had a month ago, lulling her to sleep.

Something soft hit her in the face and fell in her lap. She looked up and saw Jana holding her tent open, smiling gently.

The other girl's eyes were bright in the darkness. "I'm returning it," she told Tanya. "I washed it and everything."

Tanya picked up her nightdress, feeling the worn fabric, the frayed satin ribbon at the neck, the rip she had mended in the armpit. Jana coughed. "I guess you've got nicer ones now," she said.

Tanya looked down at herself, at the brand-new slip of silver. "It feels nice to sleep in silk," she admitted.

Jana bit her lip and stepped inside, lowering to her knees. She looked behind her, as if to confirm that the tent was closed.

It was.

She crawled toward Tanya until she couldn't get closer and then sat back on her heels. Tanya could smell her, the moss she had been using for a pillow, the honeysuckle she was always chewing, and sensation flickered down her spine.

Tanya suddenly remembered she had felt kinship once—with Jana and Riley, in the Tomcat's camp. They had been friends with her when it didn't help them to be.

At least she thought what she had felt for Jana was kinship.

Jana reached out and put her hand on Tanya's cheek; her hand was cool and scratchy with calluses.

"Thank you for returning my nightdress," Tanya whispered, frozen.

Jana smiled and leaned forward—slowly, slowly, slowly—until Tanya felt her quick breath on her own, suddenly itchy lips, and the thief swerved, kissing her on the cheek.

It was a leisurely kiss, lingering and soft. Jana sat back, then kissed her again, hard and fast on the lips, and scampered out of the tent.

Tanya leaned back on her pillow, poisoned blood thrumming through her veins, her mind racing—*reeling*—and blank. She was sure she wouldn't sleep at all.

Except she did. She slept like a baby, or a princess.

Jana rather uncharacteristically insisted they start immediately after dawn. But by the time the sun was high in the sky, Tanya saw that she had been right. Long before they stopped to water the horses, an unaccountable heat had swelled and the chill winter breeze was too gentle to pierce the thick, gummy air.

Tanya stayed on the mare's back as the horse bent to drink out of the stream. She would have preferred to get down, stretch out the growing ache in her thighs, but the beast wouldn't let her. Every time Tanya tried, she bucked or shuffled.

If the mare was going to be dragged to Bloodstone with a thief for a guide, the girl responsible for that indignity was going to be as uncomfortable as it was possible to make her.

The girl in question stretched her arms above her head anyway and rotated her hips in the saddle. She looked out at the flat, shining river and thought longingly of the fog of her home; the way the rolling of the ocean kept the air always in motion.

Jana came up next to her and handed her up a canteen. "Thirsty?"

Tanya grabbed at the canteen and drained it.

"This doesn't make sense. It's winter! Why is it so hot?" demanded Tanya. "I've had it with nature not making any sense. This is why the quill is so essential—there's no other way to keep things controlled! The Queen is—" Tanya stopped abruptly, but her brain finished the sentence without her.

*The Queen is right.*

"The Queen?" asked Jana curiously. "You don't mean you actually got an audience with the Queen and Council?"

"Of course not," Tanya answered quickly. "Just . . . someone should do something about it. The Queen and Council should."

Jana laughed. "I don't think they could do anything about this heat," she said, refilling her canteen. "It's always hot on this road. It's always been hot on this road and it will always *be* hot on this road." She looked up at Tanya, sobering. "That quill is a good weapon, but it isn't going to protect you from the fact that Bloodstone houses demons."

Tanya shuddered, thrown back into the nightmare landscape that Bloodstone had echoed through her childhood.

# Chapter

23

**T**hey followed the river for the rest of the afternoon. Eventually the pebbly strip of beach metamorphosed into crumbling caverns of rock and boulders that had been tumbled into stepped cliffs, steep enough that Tanya had to dismount and lead the mare with rope.

The rock changed color as well as formation. The brown, white, and black from the forest floor darkened to red and black, some studded with icy chunks of quartz. Everything green fell away as they picked their way down a nearly invisible path—no more trees, no more flowers, no more grass. No more squirrels either, although as the sun sank away Tanya thought she could see bright animal eyes peering out at her from the crevices.

As they descended—her ears popping as they rode—the temperature got more unpredictable, alternating between pockets of an oddly wet cold and breaths of fire. And the smell of brimstone and bad, old magic just kept growing.

The group tightened into a single-file column as what had previously passed for a path narrowed further and further until just before sunset, when Tanya found herself hovering at the edge of a cliff, staring down a stone bridge at least one hundred feet in the air over boiling rapids.

"Um." Tanya looked quickly from side to side, searching desperately for any other route across the chasm. But all she saw were steaming waterfalls.

She heard Greer and Darrow behind her start to shuffle and shift. She didn't blame them.

*She* shouldn't have been scared. She knew that if worst came to worst, she could always fly. But, on the other hand, it wouldn't be smart to *advertise* that—not so close to Bloodstone.

Tanya rode the mare step by painstaking step across that bridge, no more than three feet wide, fear competing with almost tangible wet heat to suffocate her.

Eventually the mare deposited her back on solid ground, and Tanya found that they were at the mouth of a vast cavern. Two tall, wide slabs of granite stretched into the hazy yellow sky at opposing angles. They were joined in the middle by an iron gate, glowing red as iron pokers after being thrust in a fire. The bars of the gate were tall and sharp as spears.

They had reached the Gate of Bloodstone.

Jana approached the Gate, reaching out her hand to touch the iron. Tanya winced, expecting a shriek of pain and a scorched hand.

But that didn't happen. Jana swallowed hard, spit in her hand, and pressed it against the gate.

She quickly let go but her spit stuck, smoking, sputtering, until it erupted in a wreath of flames. Just as quickly as they erupted, the flames went out and a rain of ash fell to the soot-stained rock below.

The gates to Bloodstone soundlessly slid to the side, dissolving into the granite walls, opening the city to them. Jana smiled. Not looking behind her, she strutted through, saying, apparently to the Gate, "They're with me."

Greer and Darrow looked at Tanya, eyes wide. Wordlessly, she gestured after Jana. They both hesitated, and for a moment she wasn't sure they were going to obey. But they eventually exchanged a glance and followed Jana, hands on the knives hidden in their belts. Tanya was the last to go through, half expecting the Gate to slide shut on her, slicing her in half.

The first thing she saw was a canal of boiling, lava-laced . . . well, she supposed it was water, but it wasn't like any water Tanya had ever seen. It was iridescent orange, red, and green, churning like a witch's cauldron and bubbling swiftly down a winding canal.

She raised her eyes and viewed a network of canals crisscrossing the city as far as she could see—which wasn't very far in the steam. All manner of boats went about their business on these waterways, piloted by every manner of human—young, old, huge, tiny, one-legged, male, female—all wearing thick gloves and suspicious expressions.

"Tanya!" She turned and Jana's face appeared out of the steam. "Come on," said the other girl, already having hopped off her horse and bopping around as if she were safe at her own dinner table— which, Tanya supposed, in a way, she was. "You don't want to get lost this close to the Gate of all places. And once we get away from the Pitfire, it becomes a lot less steamy. Easier to see." Jana disappeared into the fog again.

"Pitfire?" Tanya called. She climbed off the mare and handed her reins to Darrow—the mare was too busy looking around with disdain to protest very strongly—and followed the thief. "What's that?"

"Did you notice that none of the boats had oars?"

Rough, singed, red brick appeared under her feet. "Yes, come to think of it," Tanya said, watching her steps. The steam seemed to be lifting. "Some sort of fan propeller? There are a few fishing boats in Griffin's Port that have those now."

"No," said Jana, her face materializing. "The Pitfire"—she pointed to a wide pool of the suspect water near the Gate—"powers the canals. The pilots still have to steer—and stop, which isn't a picnic—but they don't have to row."

"But what is it?"

Jana waggled her eyebrows up and down. "Magic." She grinned and slid across a green, slimy patch of brick into the steam.

Tanya was frustrated. She had asked a sensible question and

received nonsense in return. Wrinkling her nose in distaste—the smell by the Gate was a mixture of ash, sweat, spoiled eggs, and fried lard—she struggled through the steam after Jana.

"There's no need to be glib," Tanya said, carefully stepping over the slime. "This is your hometown after all, it's perfectly reasonable of me to inquire as to some basic . . ." Tanya's voice trailed off as her vision cleared and Bloodstone proper appeared in front of her. "Some basics of infrastructure," she began again, but her heart wasn't in it. "Perfectly reasonable . . ."

Bloodstone hit her first as a mass of color: red streets, yellow skies. At every corner was an open brazier, throwing licks of orange flame into woodsy, wine-soaked air. But mostly the color came from the citizens.

No one wore gray homespun or brown leather. There was wool and leather aplenty, but in bright pinks, violent greens, and unnatural purples. And the people themselves! No two looked alike. She looked left and saw a sunburnt giant of a woman, nearly seven feet tall, broad shouldered and strong, but so skinny that her collarbones looked like they could cut steak. Dressed in flowing blue silk, she was haggling with a bespectacled ball of flesh that eventually rearranged itself into a white-haired man in red-and-green striped coveralls. Tanya stepped forward and saw that neither had a stall—they were simply standing in the middle of road, arguing over the price of a giant lizard with lazy gold eyes being walked on a leash by the fleshy man.

She looked right and gasped before she could stop herself. The spasm of fear passed, leaving Tanya feeling silly—because all she was looking at was a small, upright woman of late middle age, perhaps ten years younger than Froud had been. She was the least conspicuous person on the street, or she should have been. She was clad in a long black dress, plain and unadorned, her hair tucked neatly into a white cap. The only ornament she wore was a twisted brass chain, long enough to reach her waist. A small hourglass hung from its links, filled with some shining black substance. A breeze—sharply cold after so long in the heat—blew down the street and lifted the woman's cap slightly, revealing a solitary green curl.

The woman from Bloodstone that had so terrified Tanya as a child had had green hair.

Suddenly the woman stopped on her path and deliberately turned her head. Tanya tried to follow the woman's gaze, turning her own head, but it didn't lead anywhere except back into the steam.

When Tanya looked back, she found that woman's gaze had locked onto *her*.

Tanya felt a spasm skitter up her spine. The woman was looking at her as if she recognized her—had been expecting her. Tanya didn't like it.

The green-haired woman smiled at Tanya. It wasn't friendly.

Tanya's fear evaporated in the face of simple, familiar, *beautiful* affront.

Tanya may have very well met a woman with green hair from Bloodstone as a child, but not this woman. This woman was a stranger. And strangers had no business staring at visitors to their city and making sinister smiles at them. Even Uncle Tommy had manners!

She folded her arms and approached the green-haired woman.

She was the wielder of the quill. No one could touch her. And manners were manners.

"May I help you, madam?" Tanya asked. "Have we met?"

Still, the woman in black smiled. "Why would you ask that?" she asked. Her voice was pitched low and pleasant, her accent arch and patrician—as aristocratic as any duchess who had ever passed through Griffin's Port.

Tanya rolled her eyes. "My lady will excuse me," Tanya said, her voice sarcastic. "I had assumed that one so *high* as yourself would have a good reason for soliciting my attention."

The woman's eyes dropped down Tanya's body and widened. She gasped.

Tanya was shocked. "Really, madam," she exclaimed. She knew she was a reasonably well-grown girl, but this was beyond the pale. She looked down to make sure her collar hadn't slipped.

It hadn't—but her sleeve had. The quill vibrated, pushing up the cloth and revealing itself, sparkling like black diamonds.

The woman acquisitively clenched her fists. Tanya stepped back, disturbed by the woman's gleaming eyes. A strange buzzing started to gather at her temples as Tanya, panicking, realized she was physically *unable* to look away.

A hand thumping on her shoulder broke the black-clad woman's spell. Tanya gratefully turned to the source and was surprised to see Greer, staring the woman down.

His hand still protectively encircling Tanya's shoulder, he nodded at the woman—a formal, respectful nod. When Tanya turned back, the green-haired woman was gone, already floating up one of the canals in a red raft with literally flaming flags flapping from the navigator's pole, the fire obscuring some device in black thread.

Tanya turned back to Greer. "Was she . . . ?" Tanya struggled to even say the words, as silly as they sounded. "Do you think she was going to curse me?"

"I have no idea," he said. "This place seems kind of fucked, though."

He removed his hand from her shoulder and held it out for her. She accepted it, allowing him to help her across a slippery patch of cobblestone.

"Thank you," she said.

Greer gave her a tight smile in response and suddenly Tanya was grateful, so grateful, for Greer. Not because he had rescued her from the green-haired woman; she was sure she could have done that herself eventually. No, she was grateful for his rude stare, for his suspicion, his reliable cynicism—for *Greer*.

She moved away. People *had* to stop touching her; it was too distracting. Tanya didn't know how normal people got anything done. "Did you see where Darrow and Jana went?"

Greer pointed her through the fog. "They went ahead to the tavern," he said. "Jana was kind of a brat about it, but eventually agreed to take him." He sounded like himself again, Bloodstone apparently having shocked the stiff corpsman from him. "Want me to escort you down the thoroughfare, tavern wench?"

Tanya smiled back at him. "Don't call me wench," she said.

# Chapter

The other green-haired woman, the one who had terrified Tanya as a child, had not been lying about Bloodstone. The place *was* a nightmare.

The twisted buildings oozed with slime, black and sickly white. There was greenery aplenty, but even the loveliest of the growths creeping across the road, or over the rooftops, were poison: itching ivy, hemlock, nightshade; a flowering purple plant, exotic and emitting a thickly sweet odor, made Tanya shudder to even look at. The air was humid except when an icy shudder cut through the moisture like a knife slicing rancid butter.

Firecrackers pounded the sky, as if the city were under siege. Greer bolted them out of the path of no less than three melees—Tanya was no stranger to drunken brawls, but at least the men of Griffin's Port had the basic decency to only pummel each other with fists. These street battlers used brass knuckles, knives, ropes wrapped around an adversary's throat and pulled tight, all in daylight!

There was something else about the place that made Tanya uneasy, something that sank into her like a stone as they approached the large inn on the far side of the thoroughfare.

In the Port Cities, late afternoon in the marketplace, the street was mostly populated by women. Wives, pouty older daughters, cooks—tavern maids—replenishing their pantries, bartering with the traveling traders for the occasional fine silver or silk.

There were no women going about their boring, daily business on the main thoroughfare of Bloodstone.

Tanya frowned as she watched a knife sharpener service a long line of men with swords, nary a housewife's butcher knife in sight. It didn't make sense. There had been women piloting the canal boats. In the outer part of the town, there had been women— outlandishly dressed or unsettlingly formed, like the green-haired woman, but women.

Everything Tanya knew about commerce-based cities (which Bloodstone decidedly was, however unsavory the nature of the commerce) told her that women were making the place tick. So, where were they?

"Greer, Tanya!" Darrow appeared, speaking over a nearby explosion of indeterminate origin. "There you are. Jana said there's only one real inn, so I left Gillian with the stable boy—some people rent rooms in their homes, but that didn't seem safe."

A rat the size of dog ran by, chased by a pale boy with sharp teeth screaming obscenities.

Greer laughed. "No?" he asked. "What gave you that impression?" Tanya couldn't suppress her own giggle.

"Herold the Wild, it can't be my wayward protégée? How utterly delightful!"

Tanya stopped laughing. Bracing herself for a flurry of knives, she took a deep breath and turned.

But there were no knives—no thugs at all. There was just the Tomcat, and his arms were wide open.

"It is you!" Completely ignoring her companions, he advanced and wrapped her in an oppressive hug before anyone could think to object. "Let me look at you." Still holding her arms, he stepped back, swiftly taking in her new cloak, her high-quality boots, her fat traveling trunk—and her armed guards.

Tanya wrenched herself halfway out of his grasp, pushing up the sleeve on her quill arm as she did. Just then a sparkler sailed over their heads, highlighting her tattoos and the quill, glowing black against her skin.

The Tomcat smiled. "You clean up well, don't you, my girl? You make your uncle Tommy very proud."

Greer stepped forward and again placed a hand on Tanya's shoulder. She shrugged him off, not wanting him to make that a habit.

"This is your uncle, Mistress Tanya?" he asked, looking at the gangster suspiciously.

"Not by blood, sadly," sighed the Tomcat theatrically. "But I have a great deal of family feeling for this talented young woman." When neither Greer nor Tanya responded, the Tomcat raised an eyebrow. "Tanya, is something amiss? You don't look happy to see your uncle Tommy."

She wriggled her fingers and the quill slipped into her hand. The Tomcat's eyes widened.

"I wasn't sure you'd be happy to see me," she said slowly. "All things considered."

"Because you turned down a job offer? Honestly, Tanya, what do you take me for?"

"When there are chains involved, you can't call it an 'offer,' *Uncle Tommy*."

"Oh, pish posh," said the Tomcat, waving his hand dismissively. "Water quite thoroughly under the bridge, my dear—or the volcano, as it happens. The tiara ended up being sufficient, for my immediate purposes, and has yielded a very profitable partnership. And now here you are, and I have another chance to woo you. What *are* you doing here?"

Greer stepped up. "Our mistress is here looking for business opportunities," he lied coolly. "Like everyone else in Bloodstone. If you have a proposal for her, you'll have to talk to me. I'm *her* protégée."

The Tomcat's eyes narrowed, drifting from Greer to Darrow and back again.

"What fine specimens of guards you have acquired, Tanya," he said, bowing to Darrow. "I trust they won't object to my buying their mistress dinner? You, sir!" Without waiting for an answer, the Tomcat strode past Greer and addressed Darrow, who was looking rather nonplussed, but *very* well muscled. "If you will take up Tanya's baggage, I will be glad to make your introductions with the tavern's proprietress. It helps to have an introduction with Madame Moreagan. Come!" He grabbed Darrow by the elbow, who looked behind him helplessly, but allowed himself to be taken over the inn's threshold.

Tanya looked up, shielding her eyes from the violent explosions still ripping apart the sky, and took in the device on the marble sign.

*The Witch*, it said, spelled out in shining black script, next to a mother-of-pearl and ebony mortar and pestle.

Tanya felt herself smile.

She took a step back to evaluate. The tavern was apparently the only building in Bloodstone where anyone bothered to do any exterior scrubbing. Tanya could only imagine what the endless steam did to a building; the dwellings she had passed that weren't rotting from the outside in were covered in thick layers of soot from the braziers that lined the streets. But the Witch's alabaster façade looked brand-new.

It was a very large, squat structure—a pleasingly symmetrical rectangle. To its left was the tidy-looking stable, and to the right was a tall fence. Through the slats of the fence she could see a flash of an onion patch and an ancient crab apple tree.

Greer sighed and followed Darrow, pushing the iron door handle.

Tanya followed him in. Immediately, she was hit with a thick, spicy smell, laced with a familiar bitterness that kept her nose twitching, trying to figure it out. She was puzzling over it when Darrow, pointing, said, "The lady behind the bar told us you should take that one," and led her to the table nearest the fire, already set. Tanya lifted up a silver dish cover and realized that she was starving.

She sank into the plush red leather of the chair, too fixated on the meal to even question why she was being given the best seat in any tavern, and fell upon the food.

And the food was not bad at all. The lamb chop was a minute or two overcooked and a little greasy, but the red wine sauce was rich and warming—*better wine than I would have used to make sauce*, Tanya noted. The mashed potatoes were featherlight and buttery, but could use a touch more salt and maybe a pinch of pepper? The greens she found she couldn't criticize at all. The cook on them was fine, but it was the flavor that made them the bright spot of the plate. The charred garlic had more snap and bite than any she'd ever eaten and the leaves and roots themselves were savory and bright, balanced perfectly between acid and earth. She wondered if they came from the fenced-off garden.

She poured herself a glass of cider from the jug someone had placed at her elbow and took a breath. Scolding herself for still caring about tavern management—and realizing that the table had been set for one, Greer, Darrow, and Jana having been served at the bar—she finally took a moment to take in the Witch.

Thirty seconds was all Tanya needed to realize she'd located the women of Bloodstone.

The main room of the Witch was, to an untrained eye, exactly what one might expect of the tavern in a town like Bloodstone. It was cold gray stone dripping with damp, the dim lighting furbished by kerosene-soaked rags burning precariously in high-placed sconces formed out of unceremonious lumps of iron—more like repurposed chains from a prison camp than sconces.

There were two long tables and six matching benches stretching across the room between one wall, where Tanya sat by the fire, and the other, actually a vast bar—and they were chaos. A wrestling match had overturned an entire bench and the pounding from the spectators kept knocking a nearly passed-out fellow headfirst into his stew.

The rest of the room was kept in overpowering shadow. The tables in these corners—for the room really did appear to be almost all corners—were quieter, more subdued, and much, much more frightening.

The bar was the true masterwork. The shelves in the back stretched all the way up to the soaring ceiling, an endless ribbon of narrow ledges, every inch of which was covered with unlabeled bottles of different shapes and sizes—orange, red, blue, purple, green, some even bubbling. The bar itself was gargantuan yet modeled on an elegant curve. It was an impressive sight, made even more impressive when you noticed that the entire apparatus, from the storage to the bar top to the stools, was made entirely of bones.

Not bone scraps or carved bone—*bones*. Fingers, feet, femurs . . . and skulls. Lots and lots of skulls. Not all of them were human, but not all of them were *not* human.

The Witch was all this—every sight, sound, and smell backed up every nightmare Tanya had nursed of Bloodstone as a child. But Tanya was no longer a child and could see behind the facade.

The food had been fresh, well prepared, and conceived with care. All the surfaces were rigorously clean. The bite Tanya had smelled in the air felt familiar for a reason—it was bitter lemon solution, the best solvent Tanya knew for getting water stains out of wood. There was clean linen on her table.

Tanya reached out a hand to graze the stone of the wall, which appeared slimy and damp. She took her fingers away and rubbed them together. She smelled them and smiled.

It wasn't mildew or unchecked condensation. It was beeswax. It was playacting. It was theater.

There were women here. More specifically, there were women like Tanya here.

She leaned back in her chair, sipping icy-cold cider out of the correct glassware, and saw a flash of light at the far end of the bar—the swinging door of the kitchen.

The kitchen was lit with a pure, sanitary light that made Tanya want to go take a bath in it. She caught sight of an older woman in a black dress, counting keys with pursed lips, before she crossed the bar into a small office, shutting the door behind her.

Tanya started to feel truly comfortable for the first time since she had closed what she had thought was her inn to bury Froud. She sighed and poured another glass of cider.

People she recognized from the Tomcat's gang joined the throng at the center table. She leaned back into the shadows, counting on the fact that no one would look for a tavern wench at *this* table. But she eyed them hungrily, smiling as little Lukas looked about ready to faint and even easygoing Riley—*Riley!*—was eyeing his neighbors warily, one hand on the knife hilt sticking out of his belt.

She started to laugh. Even the *chaos* of the room was under complete control. She saw that now. The tables were arranged the way they were in order to separate the ruffians who would eat anywhere from clientele conducting actual business. The mess was centrally located and centrally *limited*—like dirt swept into a pile in the center of the room before being collected by the dustpan. There was no way for anyone who felt like causing *real* trouble to escape consequences: The doors and windows were all a comfortable distance away, and—*yes, there it is*, thought Tanya—a crossbow propped up next to the office door.

Tanya knew better than to ever underestimate a woman who had that many keys. Anyone who wanted to cause real trouble would be dealt with indeed.

"What's so funny?"

Jana was standing over Tanya, pouring herself a glass of cider. She was her normal insouciant self and clearly not frightened by her surroundings. But Tanya looked closer and saw that the thief's shoulders were high and immobile.

"I'm a little homesick, that's all," answered Tanya. "I . . ." She looked at Jana, remembering her face near her own. "I loved my tavern."

Jana made a motion toward an empty armchair at one of the corner tables, but then hesitated, looked toward the bar, and opted to lean against the hearth instead.

"Not surprised," Jana said, wriggling as she struggled to get comfortable against the brick. "This dump will make you wax nostalgic about being trapped in a ditch, let alone a pleasant seaside town."

A sharp, wincingly high screech floated through the window from the street, followed by a crunch like bones under a wagon wheel— which Tanya realized it might very well be.

She shuddered, less out of fear than distaste. "It's not exactly picturesque out there, no," she agreed. "But at least there's a nice tavern."

Jana choked midsip. "A nice tavern?" she asked, still coughing, liquid dribbling out the side of her mouth. "You like the Witch?"

Tanya felt embarrassment creep up on her, almost as if she had betrayed the Queen, betrayed who Tanya was now. "Well, the décor isn't to my taste," she said slowly. "But, I . . ." Tanya hesitated as she saw something simmer behind the other girl's eyes.

"What?" Jana demanded. "You what?"

Tanya found she didn't want to disappoint those eyes, but truth was truth. "This is clearly a well-run inn," she admitted. "The proprietress knows what she's doing."

Jana sputtered unintelligible syllables for a moment, before forming the accusation, "That's insane. You're insane."

Tanya folded her arms, piqued at herself for caring. "Jana. I understand you have issues with Bloodstone. But this is a well-organized, comfortable, and apparently thriving inn. Even if the mashed potatoes needed more salt."

A voice behind her added, "Did you notice that the new girl didn't render all the fat out of that chop?"

# Chapter

**T**anya jumped and the key-holding woman she had seen before emerged from the far side of the hearth, kitty-corner to where Jana was standing, clenched fists at her sides.

"Jana, stop dirtying yourself against that soot and bring over a chair," the woman said. "You look like an ill-trained valet."

Tanya gaped as a muscle twitched in Jana's cheek and she averted her wide eyes away from the woman.

"Oh, Lady of Cups," sighed the woman, stepping forward herself to pull over the vacant chair. She smiled a gracious smile at a solitary occupant of the nearest corner table, an androgynous near-skeleton dressed in red silk, and neatly flipped the chair around with one hand, jamming it toward Jana.

Jana sat.

"That's better," the woman pronounced, but in a tone that spoke less of approval than of relief that spilled wine had been mopped up before it could stain. "And now you should introduce me to your companion."

Jana's face was pale and stony. Tanya decided to save her. She stood, dipping a shallow curtsy. "Tanya, ma'am," she said. "From Griffin's Port."

The woman waved a hand upward. "I appreciate your manners, but Thomas has informed me that you are to be given every deference." She smiled. "I should be curtsying to you."

She didn't curtsy. After a long, awkward moment, Tanya sat back down, feeling somehow bested.

The woman in black smiled even wider, a secret, oddly toothy grin, like a wolf about to pick the scraps off a bone.

She placed her hand on her chest. "I am Madame Moreagan, and I am the proprietress of the Witch." She paused to throw out an arm to block a black-eyed (literally, he had two black eyes, one of which was older than the other and turning green) man from passing behind her and, without turning her head, reached into his front pocket and removed a crystal ashtray.

Madame Moreagan snapped her fingers four times—once, then twice, very close together, and then, after a pause, a fourth time. Men at the central tables jostled to be the first to appear at her side, pick up the bruised thief, and drag him out of the tavern.

She saw Tanya observing this operation and smiled again. "Do not worry, Mistress Tanya," she said. "That was my signal to simply make him sorry, not to take revenge."

Tanya frowned, trying to figure it out. "Those men work for you?" she asked.

"Not exactly. I am rather picky about who I employ. But I make it a point to return favors. I also make it a point to remember when favors are not offered and who declines to perform an office for me. Jana, are you about to eat with your hands?"

Tanya turned and saw that Jana had a finger-full of mashed potatoes halfway to her mouth. She was saved, unexpectedly, by the arrival of the Tomcat.

"Madame Moreagan," said the Tomcat, bowing elegantly "You never seem to age."

"I take great care not to, Thomas," she said, still looking at Jana. "Is this one with you now?"

The Tomcat's face darkened, but his eyes flickered to Tanya and when he spoke his voice was mild. "Jana? Sadly, no, not anymore. It's a pity. She's an excellent tracker."

"Is she?" Madame Moreagan sniffed. "I'm glad to hear she's managed to make herself useful somewhere."

Jana stood. "I'm getting a drink," she announced loudly, and stalked off to the bar, muttering to herself.

"I suppose you have your reasons, Thomas," the older woman said dryly. "Personally, I never got much use out of her."

Tanya watched as the Tomcat followed Jana's progress with a glare before pressing on. "My dear Madame Moreagan, I am coming from our friends the Others, and was hoping you could lend me a maid to draw my bath. I'd like to freshen up and dine like a civilized gentleman."

Madame Moreagan nodded her approval. She moved her right hand and a girl in a white cap stepped forward, dipped a curtsy, and turned toward the staircase in one neat gesture. The Tomcat bowed twice, once to Madame Moreagan and once to Tanya, then followed the maid away.

To Tanya's surprise, Madame Moreagan stayed. She stepped around the table and appropriated Jana's vacated chair.

"Now. What's a serving-class girl from the Port Cities doing occupying a position of honor in the Tomcat's rotating band of crooks?"

Tanya blinked at the older woman's bluntness, the quick change from the unctuous tones she'd used in front of "Thomas," and even in front of Jana.

"I . . ." Tanya hesitated. After all, what was the real answer? "I was on my way to the Capital," she said slowly. "I was set upon by the Tomcat's thieves. They wanted the mare—that is, my horse. They wanted my horse."

"A horse is a reasonable reason to accost an unprotected young woman. But why bother courting you after already abducting you? Other than the obvious reason, that is."

"I beg your pardon," Tanya said. "I am respectable."

Madame Moreagan cocked her head. "As you say. It's hard to imagine another use for you."

That word: *use*. Tanya knew she was being baited, but couldn't let the insult stand. Froud hadn't raised up a useless girl, quill or no quill.

"As it happens," she said, holding her head high, "he wanted to keep me because I am the best cook the Port Cities has seen for a generation. Yes, I did notice the mangled cook on the chop. And you're wasting that wine in the sauce. Not my idea of tavern management."

At that, Madame Moreagan blinked and then, grinning, stood.

"If you're finished with your meal, I'll take you to your room," she said. "I believe I know where you'll be most comfortable."

The brisk steps of Tanya's hostess, to her surprise, led her past the winding staircase and around the corner, stopping at a little wooden door hidden underneath the serpentine railing.

Madame Moreagan lifted her keys and selected the plainest one, made of thin, silver metal. It had been invisible, nestled between an ornate brass one topped with a carved star and a heavy black iron one with four wide prongs. There was something soothing about its simplicity.

The tavern keeper turned it in the lock and the door silently swung open on well-oiled hinges. Tanya slipped through the narrow opening and found herself in what seemed an entirely different building from the Witch.

There was no sign of the ancient stone in the main room. Instead, Tanya found herself in a corridor paneled with slats of fragrant cedar the color of buttered toast. The dim shadows of the dining room clearly had no place in this part of the building. Candles of clean white wax in glass and porcelain sconces were placed at regular intervals, reflecting golden light onto the pearl-colored silk carpeting. Someone had painted dainty roses and violets along the bottom of the wall. As she and Madame Moreagan progressed down the hallway, lemon, lavender and the distinctive smell of fresh laundry filtered into Tanya's nose. She breathed deeply.

Madame Moreagan stopped in front of one of many doorways, all of which were curved and freshly painted white. Using the thin key yet again, she unlocked the copper-plated lock.

Madame Moreagan entered first and crossed the room to a night-stand, lifting a lamp that was the big sister of the sconces in the hallway. She drew a match out of her sleeve and, scratching it to life on a rough-ridged key at her belt, lit the wick. The room bloomed into sight.

Tanya felt the oxygen flowing into her lungs.

The room was constructed, floor and walls, out of lacquered wood the same warm shade as the corridor. There was a round woven mat of pink and yellow braiding in the center of the room. The bed was nestled up against the wall, just the way Tanya had her own at the Snake. But rather than a pile of cloth and quilts, this was a real bed, with a low platform and a tall, squishy-looking mattress, piled high with embroidered pillows.

One spelled out in blue embroidery thread a saying Tanya knew well: *Lady of Cups, Preserve Our Preserves.*

There were no windows, but the center of the angled ceiling had been cut out, the wood replaced with glass. Tanya stepped under it, squinting.

"It's usually too steamy and cloudy to see much through the sky-lights," said Madame Moreagan behind her. "But sometimes you get the stars and you always get the dawn. I hope you'll be comfortable here, Mistress Tanya."

Tanya turned back to her hostess. "Very comfortable, indeed," she answered, careful to keep her voice no more than polite. She had not expected to find her happy place in Bloodstone. "Thank you."

With a nod, Madame Moreagan swiftly padded on silent feet across the room and shut the door behind her.

Tanya, suddenly exhausted, collapsed on the bed and shut her eyes.

When she opened them again, the lantern was still burning, but the lights from the hallway were no longer shining under the door.

The Witch was silent.

Tanya sat up on the edge of her bed and examined the skylight. It was, as Madame Moreagan had warned, too cloudy to see the placement of the moon in the sky, but it was clearly the middle of the night.

Tanya sighed. Even in the Glacier, she had never become accustomed to sleeping through the night, and now here she was, alone and wide awake, with nothing useful to do—nothing at *all* to do, but sit and stare and wait until dawn.

Something pounded on the floor, stopped, then pounded again, harder.

Tanya pulled her feet back up to the bed. Something was pounding on the floor of her room from beneath the floorboards. Tanya was not sure exactly how one was supposed to react in this scenario. Should she hide beneath the pillows? Construct a weapon?

The pounding stopped and there was a loud creak.

The rug lifted a foot off the floor, making it resemble the toy forts the village boys in Griffin's Port made out of boxes and canvas.

And out poured light.

# Chapter

**W**ithout breathing, Tanya stepped carefully toward the rug, rubbing the quill.

She pinched the edge of the rug and, with a silent prayer to the Lady of Cups, threw it back, revealing the trapdoor that had opened in the floor. Golden light illuminated a wooden ladder.

Tanya knelt. The ladder went down about fifteen feet through a tunnel of tightly packed sand and stone. Flickering sconces lit the way, but the tunnel was too long for Tanya to see what was on the other side.

Tanya twiddled the quill between her thumb and forefinger.

She grasped the top rung of the ladder, easing first her left foot and then her right into the hole. The ladder was solid and heavy; it didn't shake.

Tanya climbed faster the lower she went and landed squarely on both feet, feeling the warm sand wriggle between her toes.

The tunnel was narrow, but more than tall enough to walk without crouching; a light breeze found its way into Tanya's hair and tickled her nose with the faint smell of burning rosewood chips.

Tanya kept walking. She didn't know for how long, but she wasn't tired—in fact, she was suddenly hungry, and ready to start her day. She thought she could smell fresh bread and wondered whether she was under the kitchens, but she heard nothing at all, not even her own footsteps.

That is until she turned a sharp corner and the sand path dropped away, depositing her, stumbling, at the mouth of an enormous, noise-filled cavern.

The stone walls jutted out unevenly in places, with one side interrupted by a waterfall tripping merrily into a smoking, bubbling brook. It was warm here. Tanya undid the buttons on her blouse.

Modesty didn't seem a concern. Of the perhaps 150 people milling around the cavern, probably 147 were women.

Tanya had never seen so many women in one place in her life: fat women, thin women, pale women, dark women, tall women, and teeny tiny ones, all of them wide awake and extremely busy.

An array of booths ringed the perimeter: enormous barrels filled with soap that had been rigged to churn laundry; a rosy-cheeked girl with her curls tied up in a knot on the top of her head merrily hacking precise cuts of pork to order off a carcass lying across a clean, steel table; a short woman with formidable breasts holding her hand to a little green-looking waif's forehead, then uncorking a brown glass bottle and measuring a portion into a smaller vial; a middle-aged woman with one white streak swirling across dark hair elbow deep in a clock; and, yes, a bored-looking girl, small and round, minding a bar stocked with cider, sherry, port, and freshly baked, buttered biscuits.

Tanya had stepped into an underground marketplace.

She started to make her way to the food, but Madame Moreagan stepped in front of her, blocking her path.

"Oh no," said the tavern keeper, in a voice that evinced no surprise. "Did the noise from the Night Swap wake you?"

"A trapdoor opened in my room."

Madame Moreagan theatrically put her hands to her cheeks. "Our apologies," she said. "But, actually, you're in luck. It's not every visitor to Bloodstone that finds their way to the Swap."

"This is a swap meet?"

Madame Moreagan began walking, motioning with an imperious hand for Tanya to follow her.

"The Night Swap," said Madame Moreagan, "is the reason why Bloodstone is still standing."

The older woman was no longer dressed in the austere black that fit the main room of the Witch like a broken-in boot. Instead, her form—softer and shorter than it had seemed that evening—was wrapped in a dressing gown of lavender velvet, tied in the front with a gold silk sash and topped with a ruffled collar of the same material. Gone were the heavy pointed boots, replaced with soft blue slippers. The strained black bun was loosened, white streaks falling in waves to her collarbone.

The keys were still hanging around her waist.

Madame Moreagan led her to an alcove where some faded and squashy brown leather chairs had been set up around a tea table. She ordered them hot cocoa and muffins.

Sitting, she said, "As you might imagine, Bloodstone is a rather transient community."

Tanya nodded. "I know all about that," she said. "I grew up in the Port Cities."

Madame Moreagan shook her head. "Forgive me, my dear, but you know nothing about it," she told her. "Sailors and pirates come and go, yes, and innumerable travelers pass through your sweet little dead mermaid gate. But the soldiers and pirates have roots there, responsibilities. And you have the shipbuilders, the merchant docks, the tax collectors, the fisherman." She smiled. "The tavern maids. There is no shortage of people in Griffin's Port who make sure the rips get sewn back together and the mussels are picked through before steaming."

"And Bloodstone doesn't?"

"Bloodstone *didn't*," Madame Moreagan corrected her, lacing her fingers together. "It does now. Because *I* started the Night Swap."

Tanya frowned, suspicious. "Why are you telling me this?"

Madame Moreagan smiled. She leaned forward and plucked a corn muffin from the basket that had been left for them.

"When I arrived in Bloodstone," she said in between nibbles, "the city was nothing but open season for criminals and worse—real monsters. There were dead in the streets. No one took responsibility for burying the bodies. There was alcohol, but almost no food and what there was would make you quite literally sick. No woman was safe. And," added Madame Moreagan, curling her lip in distaste, "there was incompetent magic hanging over everything."

Tanya folded her arms around her waist, concealing the quill. "Magic?" she asked, trying to sound innocent.

Madame Moreagan sighed. "Sort of," she said. "Nothing so organized as a reasonable magical system: herbs, stars, stones—you know the thing. The problem is that, long ago, some wizard or other blasted Bloodstone into existence with a spell—I couldn't even tell you what it was meant to do—and then left. So, this whole dratted volcano has all this . . ." She waved her arms around in front of her and continued, "*Magic* running around. Totally unsupervised, there for any amateur to tap into, and I have already told you the sort of people Bloodstone attracts. And this was before the so-called Aetherical Revolution, so everyone was even more of an amateur than they are now. It was really quite dangerous."

Madame Moreagan's words echoed in Tanya's head, reminding her of something she herself had once thought, and in almost exactly the same words. "What changed?" she asked uneasily.

Madame Moreagan spread her arms wide, as if to encompass the entire Night Swap. "I began speaking to the other women," she said. "It wasn't easy. Some of the women who came here were as bad as the men—truly devious creatures, with no fellow, or rather, *sisterly* feeling. Others were simply useless. But some were simply like myself, in search of a place that could challenge and enhance our natural abilities."

"Which one was Jana?" Tanya hadn't planned on asking that question.

Madame Moreagan's mouth turned downward. "Jana wasn't a woman," she said. "She was a little girl when her father was so incon-venient as to die in my inn."

Tanya remembered the little girl she had been when Froud had taken her into the Smiling Snake and was suddenly furious. "So, she didn't matter?" she asked hotly.

"Of course she mattered. She wasn't a unique case, you know. Many little girls, more than you would imagine, end up stranded at Bloodstone, and most of them aren't taken there by loving, albeit crooked, widowed fathers. They're trained and housed by me, or one of the other women in this room. Most leave when they're old enough to take care of themselves and we wish them well. Some stay and continue to work, with me, or elsewhere. And anyone who's left goes to the Others. And let me tell you, they're all damn lucky to have the protection of the Night Swap. Jana would have been, too, had she accepted it."

"You raised Jana?"

She snorted. "I certainly did not. The girl lived under my roof and rules for less than a year. She refused to settle. She was unin-terested in the work, incapable of avoiding mischief, and quarrel-some. One day, she told me she quit and never came back to her bedroom. Never came back to the Witch at all except as a paying customer. She was all of eleven the last time I had any hand in her."

Tanya absorbed all this. She had at least been suited to the life of an orphan growing up working in a tavern. It fit her like a glove. But what if it hadn't?

She had never thought of herself as lucky before.

Tanya was quiet for a moment. Then she asked a question; not why had Madame Moreagan allowed a child to fend for herself in

Bloodstone, why Jana had left, or whether she ever thought about the little foundling she had almost raised.

Tanya asked, "Who are the Others?"

Madame Moreagan made a face like there wasn't enough sugar in her lemonade. She reclined and inclined her head backward and slightly to the left.

"Do you see those women in the black dresses and white caps?" she asked quietly.

Tanya followed the bend of Madame Moreagan's head and again felt a spasm of fear as she saw the green-haired woman from Bloodstone's thoroughfare bargaining with a broad-featured woman with tangled red hair over the price of a cask of wine. She was attended by three other women, dressed identically and standing still—a splash of cool and dark in so much vibrantly colored commotion.

Tanya felt a tickle at her wrist—the quill waking up and lightly pulsing through her sleeve. She clenched her arms around her waist, willing it not to sparkle.

"I see them," she told Madame Moreagan.

"*They* are the Others," said Madame Moreagan, primly taking a sip of cocoa. "They're the only reason magic users are even slightly under control in Bloodstone. I don't approve of their methods, but I cannot deny that they've been effective."

Tanya frowned. "I don't like the sound of that," she said. "What are their methods?"

Madame Moreagan sighed and put her mug down. "They worship and serve the demon that lives at the core of the Volcano, or, rather, what *was* a volcano before it exploded and formed Bloodstone," she said wearily. "Think of them as particularly unpleasant temple attendants. They do something to hold the aetheric strands in stasis, and since they set up shop in the Volcano, none of those amateurs we were discussing seem able to manipulate matter at *all* within the city gates. The only magic we have in Bloodstone now is the good, old-fashioned, skill-based kind, which, however unsavory the results might sometimes be, are at least predictable."

Tanya stared. "I'm sorry, did you say those women serve a demon?" she asked.

"Yes." Madame Moreagan wrinkled her nose. "Nasty business to involve oneself in if you ask me, but there's no accounting for taste or inclination."

Tanya had disliked how the green-haired woman had looked at her and the quill. She liked it even less now that she knew the quill *should* have gone dormant the moment she crossed the Gate— and that it was her own unwillingness to ignore a slight that had alerted the Others, the preeminent magic users of Bloodstone, to the fact that it *hadn't*. The very same people whom she had been commissioned to investigate now had an advantage because of *her* mistake.

Tanya stood and gave a quick, polite curtsy to Madame Moreagan. "Thank you for the cocoa and hospitality, Madame Moreagan," she said. "It has been extremely interesting and a generous use of your time, for which I have the greatest respect. I'll say good night now. Or good morning. Whatever it is."

"Now, hold on," said Madame Moreagan, bracing her hands on the arms of her chair, as if preparing to battle. "I didn't expend my indeed valuable time for hospitality's sake. A few questions, madam, if you please."

The Other caught sight of Tanya from across the room.

"I really must get back to my room," said Tanya quickly. "It isn't seemly for me to be out unescorted at this time of night."

"You are not unescorted, you are with me. I understand from the Tomcat that you were formerly employed as a tavern maid. Which tavern precisely?"

The Volcano witch said something to her companions and then began making her way toward Tanya and Madame Moreagan. "What?" Tanya asked distractedly.

"Where were you employed prior to, let's call it 'joining,' the Tomcat's gang?"

The quill was beginning to vibrate more insistently. "At the Smiling Snake, in Griffin's Port."

"And what was this employment's duration?"

"Roughly ten years. Look, I really must return to my room."

"No." Madame Moreagan snapped her fingers and two burly women in well-worn leathers strapped with knives appeared out of the shadows. "You may leave when I have conducted my interview. Sit."

The witch stopped her progress across the market when Madame Moreagan's bodyguards appeared. She didn't look scared at all, but she was curious—and cautious, Tanya noticed. She stepped to the side and began to examine some embroidered satin pillows.

Tanya sat down.

She looked at Madame Moreagan. "I have no idea why you would be so curious about me, one might even say rudely nosy," she said crossly. "I'm just an ordinary tavern maid."

Madame Moreagan smiled a little. "Yes dear, I know," she told the girl. "Now describe to me your duties at the Smiling Snake."

Tanya shrugged. "Everything: cooking, cleaning, laundry, seamstress work for guests. I did the brewing and the ordering. I served behind the bar and at tables. I made preserves and tonics and broke up fights. I kept the key to the cashbox."

Madame Moreagan's smile widened. "Perhaps I should have asked what weren't your duties. Quite a paragon I have in front of me."

Tanya shrugged off the compliment, uncomfortable with praise for what had simply been the work of her life. It didn't seem appropriate.

"I didn't do the gardening," she admitted. "I have a brown thumb. Froud managed the herbs and such."

"And Froud is . . . ?"

"He is . . ." Tanya trailed off. She swallowed. "He *was* my guardian and the owner of the Snake. But he's dead."

"I see," said Madame Moreagan. "And who has possession of the Snake now?"

Tanya felt a refreshing spasm of anger flow over her. "It was requisitioned. The day I left Froud at his temple for burial, the Queen's Corps requisitioned it. They then ransacked it and left it standing empty—and locked."

Madame Moreagan nodded, looking thoughtful.

"Look, what is this about?" asked Tanya, leaning forward against the table, energized by the return of anger over losing the Snake. "This is very out of order, to interrogate a paying guest like this."

"But you're not a paying guest."

Tanya blinked. "Well, no, not yet. But I assure you, ma'am, tavern wench or no, I have more than enough money to cover my bill, even for the private room. I *will* be paying."

Madame Moreagan shook her head. "No, dear. You're not staying in one of our guest rooms and you won't be charged for your board."

"Then exactly whose room have I been sleeping in?"

"Your room," answered Madame Moreagan, lifting up her key ring and sliding off a key identical to the one she had used earlier. She pushed it across the table toward Tanya with a well-groomed fingernail. "That key will let you into every room in the building, except for the other girls' rooms, or my office—unless I want you to have access to my office, but let's not get ahead of ourselves, shall we? It's just a simple little enchantment—nothing I needed the white-caps for." She sat back in her chair and pushed her fingers together thoughtfully. "I believe we'll start you in the kitchen.

In time, if you're as good as you claim, I'll need you to take over its management."

Tanya, for the first time in a long time, was speechless.

Finally, she poked the key back across the table with her own, sharp fingernail.

"I'm not looking for employment at the moment," she said icily. "Thanks all the same."

"No? Then what are you looking for?"

Tanya sighed. "I just wanted my inn back," she said wearily.

Madame Moreagan nodded sympathetically. "I understand. But your home is gone, my girl," she said. "Orphan foundlings who grew up as tavern wenches don't win one over on the Queen's Corps. But, Tanya of Griffin's Port, the Witch has a place for a girl like you and *only* for a girl like you. I want you. All your skills, the trades and tricks despised as common—I need them. I won't live forever." Tanya raised her eyebrows and Madame Moreagan smiled widely. "Oh, don't misunderstand, I'll live a good long time, much longer than I should. I have already lived longer than one would think possible—oh yes, dear, the Others do have some useful skills, and I have my own rather storied history. But I am not immortal, and I need sturdy women such as yourself to continue my work. It will not disappear—I won't allow it. And you never know: One day you might call yourself Tanya of Bloodstone."

# Chapter

anya flinched. "I don't think so," she said, through clenched teeth. "Now, please excuse me."

She stepped away from the alcove. The cavern was too crowded to avoid the Other, still hovering at a nearby booth. Tanya gave her as wide a berth as possible, but it wasn't wide enough and the witch slid out a boot of glossy black leather, forcing Tanya to stop in her tracks.

"You are welcome in our Swap, Tanya of Griffin's Port," said the Other, frank possessiveness infusing her well-bred voice. "But our temple is your true destination. Our Lord of Brimstone and the Hush commands it." The Other stepped closer. "You *will* seek us out. This we know. When you are ready, you may alert our servant, the Tomcat"—Tanya looked up sharply—"and he will conduct you to us. We shall see which faction in Bloodstone you'll truly serve. But know this, girl: The Volcano claims you."

For the first time since entering the steaming radius of the collapsed volcano, Tanya felt goose bumps raise the hairs on her arms. She willed the fear to drain away.

She brought up a picture of the Queen, who was probably poring over the map at that very moment, waiting for Tanya to fix their problem. She remembered that fear was irrelevant to her now. She had important work to do.

Tanya lifted her head. "I would be honored to pay my respects to your temple, at your earliest invitation," she said brightly. She curtsied at the witch, then turned and dropped a lower curtsy to Madame Moreagan, who was, after all, her hostess. The older woman was watching the exchange with a puzzled and wary eye. Tanya swallowed a gulp. "I will bid you good morning," she said.

Tanya didn't dare stop to breathe until she had stepped into the tunnel and turned the corner. Then she collapsed backward onto the wall and closed her eyes, breathing deeply and wriggling her toes until they were partially submerged under the tightly packed sand.

She pretended for a moment that she was on the beach at Griffin's Port. It wasn't a resort town, but a working port, so the beaches were narrow and scrubby, littered with ashy driftwood. But the sand was cool in the summer and warm in the winter and the breeze carried a bracing slap of salt.

Tanya breathed.

As she reentered her room under the skylight and the remote glow of dawn, she decided that she had to get out of Madame Moreagan's room. She didn't know precisely how the tavern keeper functioned, but there was magic involved as well as simple brute force. Tanya had a feeling that the longer she stayed in this bed, the quicker she would become one of the Witch's girls.

But first she had to check something.

Tanya sat on her bed and examined the quill. It was still black, but it seemed to be *working*. It was sparkling, responding to her touch; her tattoos hadn't altered.

Tanya tentatively plugged the quill into its diamond, and it slipped in easily, just like always. She slipped it out and cast about the room for something to write on, eventually opening the nightstand drawer, and locating a white damask handkerchief.

"That'll do," she muttered, flattening it out on the top of the dresser. She furrowed her brow. It had been some time since she had conjured something small—something that wouldn't be noticed.

She drew the Witch and its garden. Her eyes widened as the multitude of exotic growths populated itself over the handkerchief.

A few quick strokes later and a sprig of lavender landed on her bed. Tanya sighed, relieved. She stretched out her arm, searching for junkoff, but found no new squigglings—she would keep an eye on it, but the lavender had been small, so maybe there wouldn't be any.

*Small, but effective*, Tanya reminded herself, cheering up that she was not defenseless after all. Whatever the Volcano witches had managed with the aetheric strands around Bloodstone, for whatever reason had no effect on her quill.

She dressed quickly. Violet had packed a trunk's worth of what amounted to her new uniform: plain white linen blouses and matching sets, in various colors, of a structured vest and narrow skirt that flared at her ankles. Tanya chose one in cerulean blue damask, embroidered in dark thread with stars.

Tanya emerged into the main room of the Witch. Other than a few sturdy girls in black, armed with dishcloths and buckets, and a dim lump slumped in the corner by a window, the room was empty.

Tanya made her way to the lump.

"Has anyone been by with a coffeepot yet?" she asked, pulling out a chair, jolting the lump awake. It straightened up very slightly.

"Don't know, do I?" it answered, in a foggy approximation of Riley's voice. "I was sleeping, or trying to."

Tanya rolled her eyes and looked back at the bar. It was empty, but her twitching nose searched out the familiar sweet mud scent she was seeking, and found it sitting discreetly on one of the lower shelves of the serving sideboards.

When she looked back, Riley was upright, staring at her with bright, interested eyes.

"Jana told me you kidnapped her and forced her into Bloodstone," he said wonderingly. "I thought she was lying."

Tanya snorted. "You don't have to pretend to be happy to see me," she told him. "I—"

"But I am," Riley interrupted, a smile breaking out over his face. "I missed both of you."

"Really?"

"Yeah." He smiled again, dimples popping out on his chin and left cheek.

Tanya wanted to look away, save herself a pang. But, as Riley fully woke up and the smile warmed his eyes, she searched her feelings and didn't find one. He had rejected her before she fled, but the memory had no sting.

Her memory instead suddenly flooded with Jana kissing her in the dark.

*Ping, ping, ping* went her stomach.

Shoving that unprofitable sensation down as far as possible, Tanya stood and strode behind the bar. None of the black-clad girls stopped her.

Tanya located two mugs of brown pottery on the bottom shelf of the sideboard and snagged the coffeepot with one hand as she rose.

After she had poured two cups, she looked around for an icebox; there wasn't one—at least not one in the main room.

In no mood to have her coffee in any way other than her preferred way, she left the mugs steaming on woven trivets on the bar and walked into the kitchen of the Witch.

She felt an unexpected surge of temptation.

The Witch had a kitchen four times the size of the Smiling Snake's. The entire right-hand wall gleamed with silver-and-black stove-ranges, neatly fitted to immaculate ovens.

A long worktable of blond wood extended down the center of the room. Tanya lightly ran her fingers over the surface; it was even and rough all at once. It was end grain wood—the best possible cutting surface for preserving the quality of good knives. Tanya had only one small end grain cutting board hanging over the sink in the Snake's kitchen.

A curling wisp of condensation drew Tanya's eyes to a door, constructed from some dull metal. It opened to reveal an icy room with venison, suckling pig, wild boar, pheasant, duck—every exotic meat Tanya had ever wanted at the Snake—hanging from the ceiling; all the fish Tanya could recognize, as well as some she couldn't, and buckets stacked taller than she was of strange creatures enclosed in iridescent shells of pink and purple and gold; enormous yellow squashes, bushels of purple broccoli, and tomatoes in shapes and colors she would have thought impossible—all neatly categorized in their own wooden crates; and all the way in the back, a wall of cheeses, blocks, spheres, and cylinders, clearly labeled and aging into perfection.

This, then, was what Madame Moreagan was offering her. She could have management over this domain.

In a daze, Tanya walked to the dairy section and selected a chilly jug of fresh cream, still frothing at the top.

Riley eyed her with alarm as she crossed the room.

"Who said you could go into the kitchen?" he asked as she set the tray in front of him, absentmindedly arranging it so the handle of his mug faced him.

Tanya sat down. "Tavern wenches can go into any kitchen," she said tartly. "We have magical powers that allow us to push open doors and walk through them."

"All right, sourpuss." He grinned, reaching for the mug. "I was just asking."

Tanya studied the boy in front of her. His clothes were creased, his hair was rumpled, and he stank of a barnyard.

"You're filthy, Riley," she said, fighting the urge to lick her thumb and wipe away a brown streak from his forehead. "What have you been doing with yourself?"

He took a long gulp of coffee. "Guarding the horses," he said. "*Some* of us have to earn our keep with more than a stolen feather."

Tanya drew her eyebrows together. "Do you mean you sleep in the stables?" she asked.

"Wouldn't exactly call it sleeping."

Tanya felt frustration rise in her chest as Riley dripped muck into her meticulously prepared coffee cup. She pulled it out of his reach.

"Honestly, Riley," she said. "No one steals from Madame Moreagan. The Tomcat should have known that she could guarantee the safety of the horses under her roof. We're in Bloodstone, you idiot. We need to stay alert. You should have gotten a room and slept."

"I couldn't have, all right?" he broke in, turning red. "The Tomcat wasn't going to pay for my room and I gave him all my own discretionary funds as a down payment on the mare that, thanks to you, I've now had to steal twice—yeah, that's right, I'm taking her back. Is that understood?"

She knew the mare expected to reunite with Rollo, but Riley didn't have to know that. "Did the mare have a good night?"

Riley brightened a little. "I think she's warming to me," he said. "She let me give her a nice going-over with a hot comb and didn't kick me once."

The door to the tavern banged open and a slim figure dressed in black from the mask over their face to the gloves over their fingertips sauntered in.

Riley sat up straighter, his hand going to his belt. Tanya waited for the feather to prickle against her skin, the way it always did when there was danger. But it didn't, so she stood.

"May I help you?" she asked, her hand automatically finding her hip. "They don't appear to be open for breakfast yet, but I can manage coffee, if you'd like?"

Tanya's voice rang out in the quiet room, startling her with her own authoritativeness. *This is not your tavern,* she told herself sternly. *You pushed the key back across the table.* But Tanya was back in an inn and, somehow, her body wouldn't let herself sit and relax.

She began to seriously consider the possibility that she was constitutionally incapable of not being a servant when the figure spun in a graceful circle and whipped something straight at Tanya's head.

# Chapter

28

hat something turned out to be tiny, but hard and sharp, making Tanya squeal as it bounced off the bridge of her nose and landed on the table.

"Ow!" Tanya held her hand up to her nose. "Did you break my nose?! Am I bleeding? Riley, does my nose looked messed up?"

"No more so than usual," he said absently, focused on the shimmering ballistic in front of him. "What the . . . ?"

Tanya dropped her fingers from her smarting nose and joined him in staring at what the stranger had mysteriously lobbed at them.

It was small and circular, sort of like the balls the boys hit back and forth with racquets in the Port Cities. But it wasn't made of knotted rags or wood. When she looked at it from one angle, it looked like steel, but when she moved her face a little to the left, it looked like glass; one second it appeared to be made of gold, the next it looked like a duck egg.

"Sorry about that," said a muffled voice by the door. Tanya turned, remembering to be angry, when the figure pulled off the mask and yawned. "For some reason, that thing never goes in the direction you aim at."

"Where did you get it?" asked Riley as Jana shook her hair out of a net. "What's it do?"

Jana threw her head down and began finger-combing out the mats in her hair. "Beats me," she said.

Riley dubiously poked it with the point of his knife. "It looks expensive," he said.

"It better be," Jana said, pulling off the black sweater, revealing a camisole in an even darker black, and sauntering up to the table. "It was a bitch to steal. You're bleeding," she said, turning to Tanya.

"I'm aware of that, thank you!" Tanya spat out. She stalked behind the bar to grab two discarded rags from the bar back. She stuffed the smaller into her nose, curling her lip at the smell of used-up soap.

The two thieves sat calmly drinking coffee, Riley out of Tanya's mug and Jana out of Riley's.

Tanya stood over them, mopping up her bloodied front. "Riley dripped mud into that coffee," she commented to Jana. "Or at least it looked like mud, but he slept in the stables, so I wouldn't count on it."

Jana spat the coffee onto the table.

Tanya eyed the mysterious ball. She didn't approve of something that wouldn't stay itself. "Why did you steal it, anyway?" she asked. "If you don't even know what it is?"

Jana shrugged and began to flip her knife open and closed, pretending not to eye the doors behind the bar, the ones leading to the kitchen and to Madame Moreagan's office.

"I needed something to keep me busy," she said. "Saw it in a booth in the market and thought it looked like something I could sell."

Tanya shook her head. "How do you live like that?"

"How do you not?"

Tanya looked down at herself and sighed. "You people are a curse," she complained thickly, her voice muffled with the terry-cloth jammed up her nostrils. "I simply cannot stay clean when I'm with you!"

"Then why'd you come back?" asked Riley, nonchalantly looking into the befouled coffee cup.

The question—delivered with a studied offhandedness—took Tanya aback. She suddenly realized that Jana and Riley assumed she had come to Bloodstone to rejoin the Tomcat's fold, had come back to *them*.

Before she could decide how to answer, the door opened and Darrow, wearing only a thin cotton vest and a shorter version of his tight herder pants, jogged inside. He was breathing hard and Tanya immediately tensed.

"Darrow, what's wrong? Where's Greer?"

Darrow stopped in his tracks, looking flustered. "He's probably still sleeping," he said. "I was just on my morning run."

"Your morning run, huh?" said Jana, climbing up on the table for a better look. She put her chin in her hands and grinned lasciviously. "Tell me, corpsman, did you go by the Pitfire or do you *always* get so nice and sweaty?"

Darrow looked down at himself and modestly crossed his arms, scratching a red spot on his elbow. But Tanya thought she could see him smile.

It was a nice smile. "Darrow, you remember Riley, I assume?" she said. "He's a . . . friend. Riley, Darrow is—Riley, are you *choking?*"

Riley was bright red and coughing out coffee, the misbegotten mug finally thoroughly knocked over.

Jana reached behind her and slapped Riley hard on the back, still grinning up at Darrow. "He's fine," she said, eyes dancing. "Aren't you fine, Riley?"

Riley composed himself, shaking off Jana. Still red, he stood, staring at Darrow.

Darrow smiled at him and stepped forward. "Rafi Darrow," he said, shaking Riley's stiff hand. "We didn't get a chance to meet last time."

Riley's eyes flashed and he wrenched his hand out of Darrow's grasp. "Yeah, well, I didn't want to give you a chance to arrest me," he said hotly. "What's he doing here?" He looked accusingly at Jana. "You didn't tell me *he*—I mean, one of those *corpsmen*—was here." He punched her in the shoulder.

"Hey!" she cried. "It was just a prank, Riley!"

Darrow stepped forward. "I *am* sorry for any offense or worry I caused," he said earnestly, looking Riley in the eyes. "Any action of mine that made you fear for your freedom or safety, I took solely in the pursuit of duty, which was sworn in service to the Queen's Corps. They don't reflect any personal feelings of disrespect for you. Or disapproval. I hope I may earn your trust in that regard."

Riley had gone red again. "Oh," he said, his shoulders slouching uncomfortably. "I mean, if you're here with Tanya, whatever, it's fine now. Just don't get too close, corpsman!"

Darrow turned to Tanya. "Do you need anything from me, miss? If not, I believe I should bathe."

"I think you can just call me Tanya at this point, Darrow," she answered dryly. "Go ahead." Darrow bowed briefly to Riley and Jana, and went up the stairs. "The only thing I need help with right now, I need Madame Moreagan for, unfortunately."

"How may I assist?"

Tanya bit back a curse and turned.

Madame Moreagan—looking identical to how she had looked the day before (and probably the day before that and the day before that)—was standing on the bottom step of the great staircase, one step below Greer, who was somehow looking both sleepy and alarmed.

Madame Moreagan surveyed Tanya, bloody and coffee stained. "I see," she said, her tone full of gravity. "That won't do at all."

"What?" Tanya, having quite forgotten the state of her, looked down. "No, that's not what I need help with."

"Some breakfast, then," said Madame Moreagan smoothly, stepping off the staircase and moving to the table, sweeping up the mess
of stoneware silently, almost invisibly. She snapped a finger and one
of the kitchen girls appeared at her arm to take the bundled mess.
"And some fresh coffee."

"No." Tanya had to execute yet another fast spin to keep up with
Madame Moreagan, who, though she *seemed* to be gliding across the
floor at a leisurely pace, was somehow already behind the bar and
pulling out a fresh tin of coffee from some hidden cabinet. "This has
nothing to do with breakfast, Madame Moreagan."

The Witch seemed to wake up all at once. The door burst open
to let in a mix of dusty, well-dressed travelers and grizzled, imperious
locals, all seeking caffeine and fried meat, while the rest of the Tomcat's company came tumbling sleepily down the stairs, mismatched
armor clattering the whole way.

Suddenly a girl in low-cut pink was installed behind the bar as
if she had never left and girls in brown dresses were carrying bas-
kets of toast to the corner tables. Tanya smiled at the synchronicity,
the swiftness of the response, and then stopped her smile cold in its
tracks when she noticed Madame Moreagan eyeing her hungrily.

Tanya took a deep breath. "Madame Moreagan," she began. "I'm
grateful for your hospitality, for the free room—" Jana snorted. Tanya
shot her a glare. "I'm grateful for the room, but I need a new one. A
*guest* room, that I'll be paying for."

Madame Moreagan pursed her lips, surveying Tanya thoughtfully.
"No," she said finally. "I don't think I have another room for you. If
you want to stay at the Witch, you'll stay as my guest. In *my* room."
She turned and disappeared into her office before Tanya could protest.

Greer, who had waylaid one of the maids to pluck toast out of her
basket, walked up behind her. "Morning," he said finally, mumbling
around a half-full mouth.

Tanya was furious.

Specifically, she was furious at Madame Moreagan. But Madame Moreagan had gone. So instead, she turned to Greer. "The Queen didn't send you with me to wish me good morning," Tanya hissed. "She sent you to protect me and so far, you've abandoned me to the whims of a sinister tavern keeper and had a nice, lazy sleeping in. What kind of job would you say you're doing?"

Greer blinked at her for a moment, before balling up his fists at his side. "The *Queen* didn't send me anywhere," he hissed right back, his eyes flashing with anger. "If I'm not mistaken, I'm here because *you* wanted me here."

Tanya felt a flush rise in her cheeks. "*I* am the private secretary to the Queen of Lode," she retorted. "I am entitled to whatever escort I wish and I don't have to explain myself to anyone, least of all a corpsman with no rank, earned or otherwise. Darrow can talk to me like that; he's a sergeant. You can't."

Greer was also turning red. He drew himself to his full height— not very great, but taller than she was—and stepped closer, so close her nose brushed his chin.

Tanya looked up at him, meeting his cloud-colored eyes.

"What?" she demanded. "What is it you want to say? People are going to start looking soon."

"No one's looking at us, Tanya. This is Bloodstone. We're the least interesting thing in the room."

"I think you had the right idea when you were calling me 'my lady.'"

"You forget: I know you, tavern wench."

Tanya snorted, but felt her cheeks grow hot. "Yes, well, I'm not a tavern wench anymore. Say what you're going to say and then move out of my way. You only think you know me. For every ten of me you've met, I've met a hundred of you."

"No, I know *you*, Tanya. So, what I have to say is this: What are we doing here?"

"You *know* what we're doing here. We're locating the source of the power coming from the Volcano and stopping it."

"That's what we're *supposed* to be doing. That's not what I see."

Tanya laughed at this, suddenly feeling giddy with the adrenaline of the fight. "No? What *do* you see?"

"I see a lonely girl who's happy to see her friends. *Including* me."

Tanya stopped laughing. "Look again, corpsman. Riley!" The thief looked up. "Find the Tomcat and tell him I want to see the Others."

Riley went pale. "Are you sure?"

"Yes. Now, please." Tanya shoved past Greer, stopping to whisper in his ear: "You are resources, not friends. I don't have friends. You don't know me, corpsman."

# Chapter

The next morning, Tanya rode the golden mare down the main thoroughfare of Bloodstone at the head of the Tomcat's pack.

The mare had apparently had another pleasant, restful night, because she plodded down the rough cobblestones of Bloodstone at an even, almost sleepy pace, giving Tanya plenty of inconvenient time to brood.

Despite riding on the warm back of the mare, in the strong sunshine and the steam, she shivered.

She could feel Jana riding behind her. The girl thief had been sitting with Riley and the rest of the Tomcat's men at breakfast and she could think of no rational reason to send her away. Jana seemed to want to stay near Tanya—it was frightening. Not that Tanya was frightened of *Jana*. It was her *want* that frightened her—her affectionate smiles, and every touch, and the way Tanya had actually wanted her there, too, if she was being honest.

She could also feel Greer next to her, only a couple paces behind, his eyes boring into the back of her neck like he knew what was in her head. It made her want to scream—*Tanya* didn't even know what was in her head. How could a corpsman whom she'd only spoken to a handful of times in her entire life?

Tanya was so engrossed in her own swirling thoughts that she didn't notice that they had arrived at their destination until the Tomcat reached out to grab the reins from her hands, pulling the mare up short.

"It would be prudent to watch your horse's step here," he said. "The footing gets a bit unreliable."

There was a cracking sound and the mare reared back as a chunk of the ground three feet across splintered from the rest of the marble walkway and simply fell away, leaving a gaping chasm in its wake.

Tanya nudged the mare forward a few steps and peered down. She quickly put her arm under her nose as the rotten, stinging smell of sulfur floated up, an almost visible miasma of corruption that made the moist air shimmer.

Tanya squinted, wanting to see deeper into the crater. She nudged the mare again and, after the equine equivalent of sigh, the mare complied, carefully and slowly stepping her way to the newborn crater's edge.

Tanya gasped.

She had expected to see fire. They were in a collapsed volcano, after all, and the heat was a tangible, living thing clawing at her pores. A raging river of fire would have been alarming certainly, but logical.

Underneath Bloodstone, however, there was nothing so simple as fire.

It was an endlessly deep pool of the black sludge. It shone as it writhed and weaved under the rock, more like a snake than a river. It looked like tar or like oil, but tar and oil were sluggish substances. This black *thing* was quicksilver, darting back in and out of crevices, pooling in that niche and spiraling in this one. It emitted a violent sucking noise, as if it were devouring some unseen prey with the force of a tornado.

As she craned her neck over the mare's ears, she couldn't help feeling like the black sludge was *alive*—like it was talking to her.

It made shapes; told stories. Tanya saw a lantern, swinging in the wind of a dock; a boy, painfully handsome in profile; a key, ornate and flaking away with rust.

A woman's hand coalesced and reached out of the swamp, grasping at Tanya.

Tanya let out a shriek and the mare stumbled backward, neighing in protest. They got clear of the chasm and began to pant, both covered in sweat, the moisture from the mare's flank soaking into Tanya's skirt. Shivering, Tanya wondered if the mare had seen what she had, or something else entirely.

The Tomcat and his small entourage had sidestepped the crater, cutting across the cracked earth until they picked up the marble pathway again. He was at the end of the path, looking at her with a studied blankness on his face.

The walkway was bright white, tracing a meandering path up to a narrow opening in the side of the Volcano itself, on the eastern side of where the mountain had originally split, spewing out the lava that had formed Bloodstone.

It was dark past that opening. Tanya couldn't see where it led.

The mare tossed her golden head and trotted up the path, her feet making a neat, clattering sound, waking Tanya back up to herself.

Horse hooves, the quill on her arm, the rustle of her skirt: These things were real, not shadowy shapes in black slime, conjuring pictures out of Tanya's own head.

Tanya pushed the damp hair off her brow. She could manage this.

The opening into the Volcano was uneven, cut straight from the rock, and so slender that the company would have to enter single file, but it was enormously tall, tapering to a narrow point at the top, some thirty or forty feet above Tanya's head, crowned with a single, enormous, black diamond.

The doorway had no knocker or lock. Tanya gulped. Anyone who doesn't lock their door either has nothing worth stealing or knows that they have nothing to fear from an intruder.

If Madame Moreagan was to be believed, this was a temple of demon worshippers, and so she was inclined to believe the latter.

"Let's just get this over with," Tanya whispered to the mare. She dismounted and they followed the Tomcat, squeezing through the gap into the darkness of the Volcano.

For the first few minutes the darkness was absolute, thick and claustrophobic—as was the silence. But slowly a rustling—a *whispering*—shivered into Tanya's awareness. She twisted her head behind her, trying to locate the source of the sound, but everywhere was black as pitch . . . until it wasn't.

Like the whispering, the light started slowly, just a thin line of crimson in the corner of her eyes. Then, all at once, the mare stumbled as the rock path fell off into a round antechamber filled with muddy, red light. It sealed up behind them.

Tanya knew immediately what the antechamber reminded her of and felt her usually iron stomach turn a wobbly somersault.

The curved walls were pink and glistening, divided into channels, and dripping with viscera in yellow, brown, and the unmistakable rust of blood.

It was as if they were standing inside the butchered chest cavity of some giant beast.

Except this beast wasn't *dead* and butchered—it was *breathing*. The walls were pulsating and strung throughout with a grotesque lattice of veins, pumping the black sludge.

The quill began to vibrate and cast out a bright white light, illuminating and making transparent the white cotton of her blouse.

The sludge halted and the whispering sound stopped. Then the sludge was moving faster than before and the whispering intensified to the roar of a sea being ravaged by a hurricane.

The band of thieves instinctively tightened into a knot behind Jana, who, double-outlaw though she may have been, was still their strongest fighter. After a shared uneasy glance, Darrow and Greer joined them, and Tanya followed, pulling out her quill and craning her neck upward, scouting for danger. But there was nothing to fight, just this enormous organ and the sludge. There was also no escape—no doors, no passageways.

With a sucking sound, a gash opened up between two channels and a young girl walked out.

Tanya joined several of the men in shrieking.

The girl was unperturbed. She appeared undernourished and unnaturally pale—as if she hadn't been under the sun in months. She was also completely bald. But she stood straight as a steel rod and reacted to ten armed men and one Jana baring her teeth with nothing more than a polite smile.

"You are expected," she said, addressing Tanya. "This way, please."

She turned and led them through the rift, which was narrower than the tunnel had been. The back of Tanya's hand brushed against the wall and came away sticky, smelling of iron and entrails.

The girl led them into a room that was the older sister of the ante-chamber. It was made of the same organic material, was the same round shape, and was strung through with the same sludge.

But if the first chamber was a private altar, this room was a massive temple, the walls climbing one hundred feet high to form a grand, pointed dome. The veining of the sludge was arranged in a pattern of unsettling esoteric symbols that Tanya didn't want to learn to read, but somehow couldn't stop staring at.

A long table of bone grew straight out of a heightened ridge on the squishy floor. Behind it was a row of seats made of the same living bone, more like thrones than chairs. They were carved with the same symbols as the walls and had high, pointed backs crowned with jewels. The thrones grew larger and more opulent toward the middle of the table, trading moonstone and mother-of-pearl for sapphires, rubies, and finally, at the very center, another black diamond.

The women in the thrones at first glance appeared identical. A sustained glance showed the differences—wildly differing in tones, a mole, a crooked nose, a rosebud mouth. But they *seemed* the same. They all sat with iron spines and folded arms, and were dressed in plain black dresses and white caps covering their hair.

Their eyelashes and eyebrows were green.

Their bald guide quickly joined a ring of girls forming a half circle behind the high table, all of them as shorn as she and clad in black, a simpler cut than the women in their thrones. The girls were all thin and sun-starved, but alarmedly calm and poised.

The sludge moved along the walls, curling lovingly into the spaces between the novices. A glow rose in the girls' hollow cheeks as it passed by and Tanya felt her eyes drawn to its circuitous, voluptuous path, following the sludge as it formed a spiral, first spinning left, then right. It felt like it was taunting her.

*It's just mud*, she told herself firmly, willing herself unsuccessfully to look away. *It's not doing anything, it's not alive!*

But, a quieter, more honest voice whispered: *That's not true.*

The woman in the center throne cleared her throat and Tanya ripped her attention away from the sludge.

The woman was on the older side, and had retained a sharp beauty, with smooth skin the color of rosewood and wide cheekbones.

"Be welcome to the Volcano of Bloodstone," she said in a voice like whiskey spiked with molasses. "You may step forward to pay your respects to the Lord of the Lava and the Steam."

Stepping forward slowly, not wanting to lose her footing on the viscera of the floor, she finally reached the dais and curtsied.

"I believe you wished to see me, madam?" asked Tanya, aware that she was only barely succeeding at keeping her voice even and determined to ignore that fact. She raised her eyes.

The Other sat back in her chair. "When the Tomcat first arrived at our temple to place his petition before our Lord of Licking Flame, we were not very inclined to listen. He wished to commandeer our lord's power for access to the secret landscapes and hidden realms that are within his grasp. However, we are not in the habit of distracting our Lord of Burning and Smoke with tawdry proposals to contract his power for the commercial enrichment of others. Particularly not"—here her voice hardened—"when a petty thief attempts this sacred access by bribing the Lord of Bloodstone, He Who Controls the Flame and the Spit, with some forgotten trinket of one his servants."

Here the priestess lifted her hand. At this signal, one of the handmaidens turned to the pulsating wall and thrust her arms inside. After some turning, twisting, squelching, and squashing, her hands returned to the light, bloody but firmly grasped around the tiara.

Holding it carefully, she carried it to the dais and placed it in front of the head priestess. The priestess picked it up, lightly and casually, holding it out toward Tanya.

"You stole this, did you not?"

Tanya put her hand on her wrist, feeling the quill, the power that was backing her. She disengaged from her curtsy and stood up straight. The Other raised an eyebrow.

"Yes," said Tanya defiantly. "I stole it."

The Other looked merely amused. She turned the tiara around in her hand. "This tiara has a very long history of being stolen," she told Tanya. "It was stolen from me, many years ago, along with much else. But what that *man* behind you could never begin to understand is that I never missed it. I found all the riches I needed and more in service to the Lord of Bloodstone."

Tanya snuck a look at the Tomcat, who was looking deferential, but glowing in his gold-buttoned waistcoat and mirror-shiny boots.

She flexed her quill arm. "The affront of the Lord of Soot and

Sludge must not mean very much if you reward disrespect with access," she said tartly.

The Other smiled faintly. "Soot and sludge," she repeated. "Yes, that is part of him." She leaned forward. "Would you like to examine his 'sludge,' as you call it?"

Tanya had to swallow her bile. In truth, she wanted to run as far away from it as possible, but her mission was to gain information about the magic emanating from the Volcano.

*Your magic is stronger or theirs is,* the Queen's voice echoed in her head. *They'll take you or you'll take them.*

The Queen had taught her to trust her own power above all else. The Queen was waiting. Tanya would not be taken.

"If it pleases you, Madam," she answered, keeping her voice as neutral as she could.

The high priestess nodded to the Other next to her, the one from the thoroughfare and the Night Swap, who smiled rather nastily. She rose, walked to the wall, and reached in her pocket for an ornately carved, iridescent white scoop.

Tanya watched as the Other held the edge of the scoop to one of the wall veins and *extracted* the sludge in its chamber. Turning to Tanya, the Other walked slowly to her.

"Open your hands," she ordered Tanya in a low, soft voice.

Tanya wrinkled her nose but held out cupped palms. Smiling wider, the priestess poured the contents of the scoop into Tanya's hands.

She felt her fingertips go numb the second the first drop fell. By the time the fourth and fifth fell, though, they were on fire, a white-hot, invisible fire that spread up her arms, over her shoulders, across her chest.

Tanya shrieked and felt the quill shriek with her, filling her whole body with its convulsive vibrations, her tattoos shuddering across her skin, shuddering in pain. Still yelling, still in agony, she wrenched her hands apart and tried to drop the sludge on the floor, but it wouldn't move—it stuck to her and spread.

"Will you listen to our Lord Demon, Tanya? Will you let him in?"

Tanya fell to her knees with exertion and pain, feeling rather than hearing the swift footfalls that brought Greer and Darrow to her side as the roaring sound of the sludge reverberated overwhelmingly through her ears.

"Get it off!" she shouted over the din as the sludge crept over her chin and began to spread across her face. "Get it off me, now!"

Through her panic, she saw the high priestess and saw that she had changed position. Instead of leaning back and idly twisting the tiara around her wrist, she was leaning forward with both hands flat on the table, the tiara high on her head. Her eyes were closed and she was whispering in tandem with the whispering of the sludge.

The dais next to her was empty. The Others and their novices were coiling themselves into a spiral, sinuously moving as one organism, like a serpent—or like the sludge itself, now racing through the veins in the walls as if escaping a fire.

As they coiled, they began to hum and emit a violent orange-and-black glow.

"Stop it," cried Tanya as the sludge crept up her face. "I will listen to the demon of the Volcano. I will listen!"

The head priestess opened her eyes and removed the tiara. The other Volcano witches stopped their interweaving. The veins in the walls slowed their pumping. The sludge on her face retreated, vaulting off her skin like a live thing.

The head priestess spoke into the hushed silence that followed:

"Tanya of Griffin's Port, meet the Demon of Bloodstone."

# Chapter 30

Tanya struggled for breath. "The sludge . . . *is* the demon?" she asked, still rooted to the floor, while Greer awkwardly patted her shoulder.

Darrow had his eyes closed and was whispering prayers to his own god. As she got to her feet, she saw that Riley also had his eyes closed and was making the violently clenching and unclenching fist that she knew was the method of prayer to Herold, patron god of criminals.

The Others were calmly rearranging themselves into their original formation, unfazed by the unholy display.

"The Volcano is the body of our sacred demon," said the high priestess, looking upward with ardent affection. "We are inside our Lord of Boiling and Whispers as we speak. The black matter is his lifeforce, his will—his *blood*. It is a living manifestation of his influence."

Tanya looked at the tiara, horrified. "And you can control it using that," she said, her voice a whisper. "You're using the magnification powers of the tiara to expand and direct his influence across Lode."

"What was that?" asked the priestess, her voice sharp.

Tanya didn't even bother to dissemble. She looked the priestess in the eye.

"Let's not waste time," she said flatly, and rolled up her sleeve. She lifted the quill, which looked as though it had been shocked, each spine standing on edge.

"If you can do that with the tiara, what do you need with this?" asked Tanya. "Why am I here?"

The priestess's eyes went wide and she stared at the quill with something that was like hatred, but not quite—or at least not only.

The Other looked away from the shimmering lights of the quill and held out her hand. "I will examine it."

Tanya stuck out her chin. "If I refuse?"

The silence was deafening. Even the hum of breathing from the sludge and veins stopped.

"Why would you refuse?" asked the Other after a moment. "In fact, who are *you* to refuse? Is it yours?"

The feathers leaned backward over Tanya's wrist in what was almost a caress, and she smiled. "Try to take it from me and find out," she taunted. "Higher authorities than you have made that mistake."

Some of the Tomcat's men behind her smothered shocked laughter, but the Other didn't. Instead, she stood up and stepped off the dais, walking around the long table until she had passed her second-in-command and was standing in front of Tanya.

She was no taller than Tanya nor was she an otherwise imposing figure. But she did radiate a certain solidity that Tanya couldn't remember ever encountering, as if the woman were one of many rolling hills. The seaside girl in Tanya was discomfited.

"It allows you to wield it," said the woman, carefully eyeing the quill, but keeping her hands to herself. "Sometimes power finds us. Other times, we have to find power. Neither way is better than the other. Tell me, are you free?"

"I'm free enough."

The Other turned to look at the women and girls behind her, a faint smile on her lips. "All who serve the Volcano are free," she said softly. "What was that, boy?" she asked, turning suddenly to Riley.

Riley blanched. "I didn't say anything," he said quickly.

"Yes, you did," she said, coming to stand in front of him. "You didn't think anyone could hear you, but I did. Say it again."

Riley visibly swallowed, but bravely lifted his eyes to meet hers. "I said that it didn't look like your little girls were even free to leave this cave," he said defiantly, and then tensed up, as if bracing for a blow.

The Other stepped even closer to Riley, forcing him to arch his back and bend away from her.

She looked at him a long moment and then abruptly turned away to move once again toward Tanya.

"There is freedom in sacrifice," she said. "In service to a power greater than oneself. I wouldn't expect a street rat pickpocket to understand."

Riley blushed scarlet and again balled his hands into fists.

The Other ignored him, focusing on Tanya, on the quill in her hand.

"But a girl who had charge of a fishing village inn before she was twelve," she said softly, circling Tanya like a vulture lazily riding a breeze. "A girl who knows what a true skill learned means for the soul; a girl who refuses to accede to a stranger's request, no matter that stranger's power; a girl who has learned to use such a powerful object, who has been chosen as its favorite, its wielder—I might expect that girl to understand the freedom involved in serving the Volcano."

Tanya gripped the quill tighter and the vibrations from its fibers shot through her nerve endings into her bloodstream, a strong coursing of power that was either pain of the highest order or immeasurable pleasure; she couldn't tell.

"You know nothing about me," she answered the priestess coldly. "You can recite the facts of my life all you want. You're right—I understand what it means to be of use. I *am* of use, *without* the assistance of a demon that has chosen to lord itself over a city of corruption and chaos. You can't tempt me with the glory of being *of service*. I am nothing if not that."

The priestess still circled and Tanya felt her next words on the back of her neck as much as she heard them.

"You truly believe the Queen, pathetic and ensorcelled, trapped with her youth and beauty in that iceberg, represents a higher power than we do? You poor, poor child. You have been greatly deceived."

"What do you know about the Queen?" Tanya sneered at the priestess's back as she moved to regain her throne.

The priestess snorted as she sat. "I know a great deal more about that deluded, stunted, power-mad child than you do, Tanya of Griffin's Port," she said. "I know more about her than *she* does. I know that she thought commissioning some pitiful little fools of magicians to manufacture your little toy would be enough to seize control of this kingdom. It will not be allowed.

"Don't misunderstand me, young Tanya," she continued, leaning forward. "I understand how powerful that quill is. And you and your developing skills have already been very useful to us."

"Useful to *you*? I beg your pardon. I don't serve demons."

"Just as you don't steal, and would never imprison, or allow innocents to suffer. Our lord can see inside you, Tanya; you cannot hide. I know what you have decided to call victory in your failed quest for your tavern, and it is a lie. Ask yourself this: When did the demon begin his spread? Was it before you unlocked the power of that quill with your blood magic, or was it after?" She leaned in. "We could *feel* it when you flew. We followed you through the aether. Blood calls to blood and *we* are blood magicians, too."

There was a profound silence in the chamber. Tanya felt Greer and Darrow fall back. She turned and saw them huddled together, far away from her. She looked to Jana and Riley—their eyes were trained on the ground, anywhere but on *her*.

"I think I would like to leave now," said Tanya, snapping the quill against her wrist, seeing no need to hide her powers any longer. "This has been unforgettable, thank you very much for the nightmares, which way to the exit, please?"

"Out the way you came," the priestess said pleasantly, pointing to the now-solid wall they had walked through. "I'm sure you can find your way through, with the help of all your *friends* here. Just remember, Tanya: We know why you're here. And we've already won."

Jana had to eventually hack their way out with a pickaxe from Riley's pack, tearing a gash through the wall with a moist ripping sound. The Others placidly watched from their dais.

Their wreck of a procession was quiet as they filed out of the temple, breaking free into the corrupted, but cooler, clearer air of Bloodstone. The mare immediately galloped away and across the bridge, giving the chasm a wide berth, whinnying in extremis the whole way.

"Horse!" called Tanya, hurrying after her, but the mare was too fast. "Damn it! Riley, do you think she'll find her way back to the stables? Riley?"

Riley wasn't moving. His own horse had been too wide to make it through the temple's archway and had been left tied to a scrubby tree just outside. The rest of the Tomcat's men, and the man himself, hurried down the path, but Riley stayed, his face buried in his horse's neck, breathing in and out slowly, eyes closed.

Tanya was shoved, hard, from behind. "Hey!" She turned. "Stop it, Jana!"

Jana pushed her on the shoulders again, sending her stumbling backward. "What was that all about?" she shouted. "What was all that about the Queen? What could the Volcano witches want from you? Who *are* you?"

Tanya pushed her back. "I didn't know a thing about those witches until I got here," she yelled back. "You're *from* Bloodstone! Who are you?"

"Do you know what you've done?" Jana was shouting, her voice matching the roar of the nearby falls, the whispering of the sludge.

Sticky wind blew her hair back and it stuck against the sweat on her brow. "You can use that quill because you've bound it with *blood?*"

Tanya felt panic surge in her chest. "I could always use the quill," she told her. "I can use it *better* because I bound it with my blood. It's a *good* thing, Jana, I'm going to be able to fix *everything*, everything wrong with Lode! Everything wrong with the *world!*"

Jana laughed, a nasty, mirthless laugh. "Well thank you, Your Highness, for the great honor of you getting so much power over the rest of us. That's just what we needed, more *oversight.*" Jana's breath caught in her throat in what was almost a whimper.

"I *trusted* you," Jana whispered. "I *wanted* to trust you. Do you know how long it's been . . . ?" Jana broke off and shook her head. She wiped her eyes with the back of her hand, balled up both fists, and charged Tanya.

Acting on instinct, Tanya put up her hands in defense and found them crushed to her side as Jana caught her up in her arms and kissed her hard on the mouth.

The kiss was fierce at first, angry and sharp. Tanya tasted salt and kissed her back.

They broke apart, their eyes flashing, Jana's still angry, Tanya's still defiant.

Jana shoved Tanya again, and then wordlessly went to join Riley by his horse.

Tanya put her face in her hands, her temples aching. She dragged her fingers over her eyes, recoiling when she saw that they came away blackened, her skin stained with sludge.

And there was Darrow at her elbow, holding a clean handkerchief.

"What are you doing?" she asked sharply. Darrow only shrugged, his eyes gentle. The gentleness in them hurt. "Where's Greer?"

He pointed. Tanya turned and saw Greer standing alone at the edge of the chasm.

Suddenly Greer screamed—a wordless, angry, pained cry that just went on and on, past the point when Riley and Jana had disappeared back down the path, and it was just the three of them again.

And then he screamed some more.

Tanya, Darrow, and Greer made their way back to the Witch on foot. Tanya stumbled briefly to the stable and found the mare, submitting meekly to a determined currying by Riley.

She softly called out for them both, but either they didn't hear her or they chose not to.

Tanya crashed through the door of the Witch, pulling notice from no one but the yellow-dress girl behind the bar. Madame Moreagan was nowhere to be seen, but the girl's jaw clenched sympathetically as she passed a slender tin key across the bar, and Tanya knew the proprietress had not changed her room.

After she had changed into a crisp new uniform, this one a rich brown color embroidered with solemn burgundy butterflies, Tanya surveyed the pretty white door leading away from the maid's corridor into the main room of the Witch. She didn't want to leave it. She liked it there. It was clean, it was straightforward, it was peaceful; it was an oasis of mundane, rigidly clean housekeeping, bathed in bright light. Tanya understood this place and, more than that, she understood how she fit into it.

At the Witch, she could be safe from the Volcano, she could be safe from *everyone*. She could be as in charge as she had ever been at the Snake; Madame Moreagan had practically promised it. And wasn't that all she had ever wanted?

She lifted her arm and looked at the quill, firmly implanted on her gold-strung skin. She stroked it and it nuzzled her back. The quill turned over on her arm and nestled in deeper, like a kitten going to sleep. Tanya took a deep breath and reentered the main room of the Witch.

She found Greer sitting alone at the bar, staring into an untouched glass of pale amber beer.

Tentatively she asked, "May I join you?"

Greer wordlessly pulled out the stool next to him and Tanya sat. The yellow-dress girl stepped forward.

"What can I get you, Miss Tanya?" she asked.

Tanya didn't bother asking how she knew her name. "A cup of tea, please. Whichever kind you like best." The tavern wench dimpled prettily and reached for a kettle.

"How are you feeling?" Tanya asked Greer.

Greer's only answer was to laugh.

"Thank you," said Tanya as the tavern maid set down her tea. She looked back at Greer, no longer feeling quite so solicitous.

"I don't know what could possibly be construed as funny," she commented.

Greer looked at her, and then looked back at his still-full glass.

"I have three older brothers, one younger brother, and one younger sister," he said finally. "They're all really similar. They're all like my dad and his little brothers. And all of their kids."

"You said they were hunters, right? In Killian Township."

"I said that. And it's sort of true. I mean they *are* hunters, all of them, my sister, too, and they pay taxes to the collector in Killian Township. But they don't really live there."

"Where do they live?"

Greer finally picked up his beer and drank half of it in one gulp. "They live in the woods," he said. "The Greer Family Compound. They don't like outsiders. They don't like traditions that aren't their own. They have a lot of traditions." Greer's voice was distant as he talked about his family—as if they were strangers. "There are a couple of other families with compounds in the woods around Killian Township," he said. "There's a community, a culture. Maybe I was being unfair."

"You didn't want to be a hunter?"

He shrugged. "I didn't mind the hunting part. And even if I had, I could have wildcrafted like my mom instead—that means foraging, for mushrooms, roots, herbs, that kind of thing. Usually the girls learned that side of things, but it wasn't unheard of for sons to follow that path. It wasn't about the work." He paused and then sighed wearily. "I just hated it there. I hated it so much."

Tanya shrugged. "So, you left. Makes sense to me."

He laughed again. "I did more than leave, Tanya," he explained. "People don't leave the compounds. I left my family. If I went back, they wouldn't shun me. They'd be hospitable enough. But I wouldn't be their son or their brother anymore. Leaving isn't just leaving with my people. I had never quite believed that, but I knew it was true when I'd been in Killian Township a month and no one came after me. They could have. I might have even gone back with them. But they didn't. Why pretend I belonged there when I clearly didn't?"

Tanya digested this. It was hard for her to imagine having *people*; to understand what it would mean to leave them. "That's when you joined the corps?" she asked.

"Not right away," he said with a rueful grin. "I've had some 'adventures,' I guess you could call them, but they were never as much fun as they seemed in books. I was on a merchant caravan for a while. I liked meeting new people, but I didn't like the buying and selling, and I didn't like the people who did like it. I could never make them laugh. I like making people laugh.

"I tried mining in the copper veins, but there's too much darkness and nobody talks—can't blame them, it isn't safe to get distracted, but still. I didn't fit in. There were a few other places. I tried being a hand on a dairy farm, an apple orchard—a tavern. That's where I was when Rees blew in one night with an empty commission sheet. I brought him his beer. I kept making him laugh. He found out I knew how to shoot, how to use a knife, how to live in the woods, and that I liked to travel. I was about to get fired from the tavern anyway—the tavern keeper thought my mouth was too smart—so I was easy to recruit. Now *you* look like you're about to laugh."

Tanya tried to wipe the mirth from her face, but failed. "I'm sorry, Greer," she said. "You've given me a history in which you don't like *anyone*, including your own people. But you were charmed by *Rees?*"

"It wasn't about him. We moved from town to town, and everywhere we went he picked up someone who was . . . kind of like me. Unhappy sons, bored apprentices, loners." He shrugged. "I fit in. I didn't like them all, but I belonged. And then, somehow, we also picked up Darrow."

"Where is Darrow? Is he OK?"

"I don't know. He cried when we got back to the room. It's a loss for him, too. In some ways, it's harder."

Tanya was puzzled. "What'd you lose?"

He looked up sharply. "I knew it was sketchy when we broke into the college, but at least we still had a commander and a mission. We had papers from the Queen and Council. And the *service* is what matters to Darrow. His sworn duty. It didn't matter what he was being ordered to do, just that he was doing it with integrity. But then you came along and we lost everything. Our entire corps. I can't speak for Darrow, but that time in jail . . . I thought that was it. And that maybe jail was where I belonged. Then the Queen said I could be useful to her, so I gave it a shot. But today in that volcano . . . that demon whispered to me about the Queen, Tanya. I knew she had drugged children before, but today I *saw* her . . . I know what it showed me was true. I can't go back to being a good little soldier to a madwoman, Tanya. I'm . . ." He looked at her. "I might as well have stayed on my compound, shooting deer with my stoic father and humorless brothers. But I can't even do that now."

# Chapter

**T**anya listened. She took a sip of her tea.

She looked across the room to where Jana and Riley were cowering silently. She looked back at Greer, drowning his sorrows.

She may not know what to do about the Queen or the Others, but she knew how to fix *this*.

She smacked Greer sharply across the face.

"*Ow*," he cried, rubbing his face. "*Why* would you do that?"

"Snap out of it, Drew Greer," she told him. "You are not a sad, lonely boy wandering around the woods with his bland brothers. You made what sounds like a smart decision and you left. You've had adventures instead. Stupid, corrupt, possibly sanity-threatening adventures, sure, but who cares? Why shouldn't that be good enough for now? You want friends? Look." She caught sight of Darrow coming down the stairs and pointed. "There comes your friend. He's a little sad today, fine, but he's generally a pretty cheerful soul. Want to belong, make people laugh? Make him laugh. Make him happy. But mostly, just stop *whining*, please, for the Lady's sake. Look," she said, pointing to the center table. "There's Riley and Jana. Riley's a thief, but he's smart and dedicated. And I think," Tanya exclaimed, the truth finally dawning on her, "that he might be able to make Darrow smile again."

Greer turned to look. "That guy? The morose weirdo who broke into a castle and spent the last hour crying on a horse's shoulder? *He's* going to cheer Darrow up?"

Tanya raised an eyebrow. "Who was it who screamed for half an hour after we left that temple? Was it Riley? Because I'm pretty sure it wasn't." She pushed him off his stool, shoving him toward the table. "I'm in charge and I say you go. Miss," she said, turning to the bar and hailing down the girl in yellow. "Do you have any rooms left? One of the private ones, with its own bathtub?"

The girl bit her lip. "I'm sorry, Miss Tanya, but I'm not sure I'm able to rent you a room," she said. "Madame Moreagan—"

Tanya cut her off. "It's not for me," she said, pointing behind her. "You see that boy over there, the skinny one? He's been sleeping in your stables. I want to pay for his room. I'd like it to be the nicest one you have available. Here." She opened the purse sown into her pocket, pulling out a handful of gold coins. "I'll pay in advance. Do you have one of the good rooms free?"

The girl smiled. "We have the red room," she said. "I know it sounds ghastly, but it's just called the red room because of the curtains and the bedspread. It gets the best morning light in the inn and has an extra-squishy bed."

Tanya pushed the coins toward her. "Perfect. What's your name?"

"Lorna, miss."

"I'm not miss, I'm just Tanya. Lorna, a round for us two and those four people. And the key."

Lorna nodded and piled a stack of glasses and a pitcher of cider on tray. With a wink at Tanya, she added a round of soda bread, mouthing, "On the house." She pulled a miniature version of Madame Moreagan's key ring out of her pocket and extracted a single brass key.

Tanya took it. Balancing the tray against her hip with her other hand, she moved through the bar, dodging a spilling beer to her left, a sliver of broken whiskey glass to her right, to where Riley and Jana sat huddled over their drinks.

They looked wan and anxious. Tanya smiled wide and set the tray down in front of them.

"Anyone for a free round?" she chirped, before beckoning to Darrow. "There's room over here, corpsman. Yes, right here. I always take care of the men of the Queen's Corps." Tanya hip-knocked one of the Tomcat's men farther down the bench, to make room next to Riley. With a nervous glance at the thief, Darrow sat. "Good. Is there anything else I can get for you?"

"What are you doing?" The question was asked by Jana and Greer at the same time. The two looked at each other warily.

Tanya, not sure how to answer, didn't. Instead, she reached behind her and grabbed Greer by the elbow, depositing him on the bench next to Jana. "Riley," she said, leaning toward him. "Here is the key to your new room. For the Lady's sake, order a bath."

Greer couldn't quite suppress a chuckle and even Darrow smiled. Jana didn't break her moody glower, but Tanya thought that, out the corner of her eye, she saw her mouth twitch.

Riley just looked at her blankly. "I don't have a room," he said, pushing away the key. "I told you."

Tanya stood up straight, hand on her hip. "And I told *you* that this was your *new* room," she retorted. "Meaning you didn't have it before and now you do. Stop it," she said, holding up her hand to block his protest. "It's not a present, it's payment. I owe you for the horse."

There was a crash and a shout. Tanya heard voices raise behind her, the squeak of a chair being dragged across the floor, a sliver of metal against leather. Her hands started moving automatically, efficiently dispersing the glasses from the tray.

Riley turned the key around in his fingers. Darrow watched him closely.

"You should accept it," said the corpsman quietly. "You acted with honor in the Volcano. The money comes from *your* ruler. You deserve it."

Riley glanced at Darrow, a glimmer of a smile on his lips. He took the glass of beer from Tanya's outstretched hand and held it up to her.

Tanya nodded at him while the scuffle behind her got louder, the onlookers' screams sharper. Greer jumped at the noise as the grapplers tumbled into the table next to them, sending it lurching to the side.

On reflex, Tanya reached out to steady Greer's glass. She winked at him.

Then she grabbed the empty tray with both hands, spun around, and smacked both combatants on the head.

It couldn't have hurt much, but it was enough for them both to look up woozily and briefly disengage. Tanya pulled them apart by the ears.

"Enough! Look at you two! You haven't had more than a drink apiece yet," she scolded, counting the empties in front of their abandoned seats, "and here you are already disturbing the other patrons' dinners. There's no excuse for sloppiness this early in the night, and if you don't behave, I'll have you thrown out. Then where will you go? Don't smirk at me, my man." She put her face right up against the one who was guffawing. "I can and will do it."

The man blinked and cast a quick glance toward the bar. Tanya followed his gaze. Madame Moreagan was standing outside her office with her arms folded, watching. She shrugged, a curious smile on her face.

Tanya shoved him down. "Sit," she ordered. "If you're good, I might bring you a free whiskey. And, you." She pulled the other fighter up by his shirt-front. "You go to the bar and tell that nice Lorna that I say to serve you as long as you act like a gentleman and not a second longer." She shoved him forward and straightened the collar of his rival. "I'm glad we understand one another."

Both men looked at each other, then back at Tanya. She signaled to Lorna that they needed another drink for the fighter, and both men, seeing that she kept her promise of a free round, meekly obeyed.

Tanya sighed and sat down, squeezing in between Jana and Greer.

"Why'd you do that?"

Tanya turned to face Jana. She was staring into her glass, looking more dejected still than Tanya had ever seen her.

Tanya frowned. "Because it was bothering me and I could," she answered.

Jana listened to the answer, swirling her beer around. Finally, she asked, "How do you live like that?"

Tanya felt her shoulders release. "How do you not?" she answered. Jana looked up then and finally smiled—a smaller smile than usual, but a smile.

Jana stood. She stretched. She yawned. She ruffled Riley's hair.

"I'm going to find some trouble," she announced. "You"—she smacked Tanya lightly on the back of the head—"don't try to stop me."

"Never." Their eyes met. Tanya felt a tug, a desire. She felt an impassible gulf widen between them. She smiled at Jana. Jana smiled back, dipped her hand into the pocket of a passing drunk, lifted out a watch, and slipped into the crowd.

"I had almost forgotten where you came from."

Tanya turned to Greer. He looked flushed. "You're good at that," he said.

"I'm good at a lot of things," Tanya commented. "Breaking up bar fights is just one of them."

Greer smiled then, a warm, genuine smile unlike any Tanya had ever seen him wear. It was like the sun coming out after a hailstorm.

That night, Tanya did what she had done almost every night of her life: She played hostess at a tavern.

The Tomcat's men, giddy from the horrors of the Volcano, eventually fell in around Riley, clambering over and across the central table. One of them started singing, and the others joined in. They sang love ballads, raunchy story-songs, and, when they found out that Tanya was from Griffin's Port, a sweet dirge about a mermaid, doomed to become foam after falling in love with the land.

Jana eventually returned, several gold coins richer and armed with a set of obsidian dice. She set up shop by the fire, taking the locals of Bloodstone for all they had. There were a few scrapes and blows to the face from that direction, but Tanya kept an eye out and it was never anything Jana couldn't handle.

Across the Witch, there were lovers' quarrels, debts of honor contested, jokes so funny boys peed themselves, one hysterical girl sob/yelling in the corner to weary friends, two older gentlemen trying to seal a deal for goods best left unspecified, and then there was Tanya, flitting from table to table, greeting newcomers, bringing drinks, taking orders, slipping the tips behind the bar for the other girls, smoothing ruffled feathers, applauding performances—being the tavern wench that she was, however much had happened to make her forget it.

But it was different now. She wasn't doing it alone.

At first, she barely noticed. Greer took a tray overloaded with beer and meat pies off the bar and shuttled it to the back, held high and steady over his head, and she shrugged—he *had* just told her that he once worked in a tavern. It *was* a heavy tray; he was probably just being gentlemanly.

But then he signaled her from across the room for backup, making a face at a patron that she found she knew how to read—a too-drunk man from Tomcat's camp needed cajoling to bed. Once she had rubbed his back and pushed him up the stairs, there Greer was again, waiting to give her a stack of empties.

The next time she turned around, Greer was hanging over the dignified dealmakers, both wizened and stern. Tanya saw one of them laugh. Greer clapped him on the back as he moved on, a rag over his shoulder.

She and Greer ran the tavern together that night. She hadn't asked him and she never would have thought to. But there he was—competent and reliable.

When the Witch finally calmed down, she sat by the abandoned hearth, the fire burning low. Jana was gone, the Lady knew where. Darrow and Riley had both gone off to bed hours ago. There was just Greer, wiping down the table.

"Why did you do this tonight?" she asked.

He kept scrubbing, his eyes on his task. "Why did you?"

"I'm not sure," she admitted. "I knew how to. I don't know how to do . . . other things."

"I think you can probably do whatever you want to do."

Tanya smiled ruefully. "I have the quill and the trust of the Queen. But I don't know what to report to her. I don't know how to stop the Others."

"Maybe you don't know what to do because you don't want what the Queen wants," he said.

Tanya raised an eyebrow. "You're skating very close to treasonous speech there, corpsman."

He smiled briefly. "I just follow orders. I leave the strategy to my intellectual betters. I'd leave it to you if you wanted."

The fire went out. It was dark in the Witch. Dark and empty.

Tanya shivered. "I should go to bed," she said. But she didn't move.

Greer looked at her. He sat, bringing his eyes level with Tanya's. They were pale enough that Tanya's own eyes adjusted quickly to see them. They were almost all she could see.

"When I said you could do anything," he began.

"Greer. Stop." A rush of distinctly pleasurable fear swept through Tanya.

"No, let me say this." He put his hand on the table, very close to hers, but not touching. "When I said you could do anything you wanted, I didn't mean because you had the quill or because of the Queen. You don't need either. You, Tanya of Griffin's Port, are equal to anything without them."

Tanya let out a breath, but it came out a sob. Greer looked at her sharply and lifted his hand from the table, bringing it to her face.

He picked up a piece of her hair and pushed it behind her ear. He leaned closer, his unevenly cut bangs brushing against her forehead.

"Only if you say I can," he told her.

Her heart beating fast, Tanya gulped and nodded. At the bottom of her vision, she saw him bite his lip and move closer, then his lips closed on top of hers.

She breathed and he moved away.

"I'm sorry—" he started to mumble, but was cut off as she cupped his chin with both hands and kissed him back.

It didn't feel like it did when Jana had kissed her and her heart beat wildly, pings vibrating all over her body. But that, she thought, kissing Greer, softly, exploratively, was because Jana was Jana and Greer was Greer.

"*If* I'm not interrupting . . ."

At that icy voice, Tanya and Greer broke up, sweaty and awkward. Tanya accidentally dragged her fingernails across his neck and he jumped backward, toppling a nearby chair.

Madame Moreagan watched them fumble, her arms crossed. "May I have a moment of your time, Miss Tanya? I believe your bodyguard can clean up the rest of this mess without you." She turned and went into her office, pointedly leaving the door open a fraction of an inch.

Tanya stood. "I should . . ."

"Yes," said Greer, jumping to his feet and grabbing up the rag. He began to furiously scrub the already clean table. "I'm fine here."

"Uh, OK." Greer was looking anywhere but at her. She could relate—she wasn't sure she wanted to meet his eyes just then either. She didn't know what she'd find there, what she wanted to find, what he would find in *her* eyes . . . She didn't know anything.

There had been no reason for her to kiss Greer. She had never kissed anyone before; she'd only *been* kissed.

She turned, straightening her hair, her skirt, whatever else she could think to straighten.

*Thank the Lady of Cups for Madame Moreagan,* she thought. She needed to have an interaction with absolutely no emotional content whatsoever. She set her face to neutral and strode into the office, closing the door behind her.

She stifled a curse. Madame Moreagan's office looked uncannily like Froud's. There was a flower on the heavy wooden desk, a single pink rose in a simple crystal vase, and a bunch of dried lavender hung in the corner, perfuming the space with a clean, womanly smell. But everything else was the same: the same dark wood and tall lanterns, the same locked boxes and overstuffed bookshelves. It was the same size, the same shape.

It was, in fact, what Tanya had always imagined the office at the Snake would be once it was hers.

Madame Moreagan caught her looking. "Does everything meet with your approval?" she asked archly.

Tanya forced herself to look the tavern keeper in the eye, but it didn't help. If this office was what she had always imagined would be hers, then what was its owner? Her future? Her true self? "How may I help you?" she managed.

Madame Moreagan sat back in her chair. "You had led me to

believe you weren't interested in joining our little operation here at the Witch," she replied. "What changed?"

"Nothing's changed," answered Tanya uneasily.

The older woman cocked her head to the side. "People who attempt to commandeer my tavern have previously found themselves on the wrong side of a crossbow—the lucky ones, that is. I think, however, that you knew that. And yet you did it anyway. Why?"

Tanya didn't answer. Madame Moreagan smiled. "That's all right. It was more of a rhetorical question. Something for *you* to ponder. Perhaps while you read your letter."

"Letter? From who?"

"I'm not sure. I didn't read it."

"How polite of you."

"Nothing of the sort," corrected Madame Moreagan. "If messages are delivered to my tavern, I feel no compunction of any kind about reading them, regardless of the addressee; if the Witch is implicated, in even the smallest way, then it is my business."

Tanya frowned. "Then why . . . ?"

"I didn't *choose* not to read it," answered Madame Moreagan, reaching into her sleeve and pulling out a slim rectangle. "I wasn't *able* to read it. That interests me."

She handed it over to Tanya, who recoiled from the cold—a sharp, spiky, *familiar* cold.

It was a rather fine envelope that looked to be made of cream-colored vellum. But it was thoroughly encased in a shining layer of silvery ice.

"I tried melting it," commented Madame Moreagan. "Obviously. I even used a little magic powder that will usually set *anything* on fire. But it was quite impervious to my efforts."

Tanya turned it over in her hands. Her name, "Tanya of Griffin's Port," was fuzzily visible through the ice, but there were no other directions. There was, however, a thin line of sterling silver running through the top edge. Madame Moreagan watched as Tanya ran her finger across it.

"I saw that," noted the tavern keeper. "I suppose the only way to open that letter is to somehow remove the silver, to create an opening for the envelope to fall out." There was a pause. "Do you have a way to do that, Tanya?"

Tanya was luckily too cold to flush and hastily jammed the letter into her pocket.

"Thank you, Madame Moreagan. For my letter, and," she added, "for not shooting me with a crossbow."

"Do you know why I didn't?" she asked. Tanya shrugged. "Don't shrug at me like Jana. You know why. I didn't stop you because you were doing an exemplary job. And don't you shake your head at me! The Witch isn't easy. I don't imagine Griffin's Port smiled at a tavern wench hitting customers over the head with a tray, but it was exactly what was needed here. You saw that." The sun began peeking through the window. Madame Moreagan opened a folder on her desk and started looking through papers, checking off list items with a fountain pen.

"You have a talent for this, Tanya," she said, her eyes on her work. "It's not just the result of training and experience. Even if you choose not to stay at the Witch, you might consider what it means to turn your back on a talent." Madame Moreagan looked up. "I'm busy now. You may go."

# Chapter

**T**anya walked into back into the main room of the Witch. Greer was gone.

It was that liminal moment in a tavern, when light illuminates the empty floor and anticipatory hush prevails. Tanya stood in front of the bar, taking in the orderly row of bottles on their shelves. She might almost be back at the Smiling Snake, about to start another long day.

There had been no time to think back then.

Tanya hummed a melody she remembered from the woman who'd left her on the docks as she walked back to her room.

Sitting on the bed, she drew out the Queen's letter and, using her blouse as paper, removed the silver seal, and opened the letter from the Queen.

*Dear Tanya,*

*You might be wondering how I got a letter to you so quickly. I certainly hope you are—you're no use to me at all if you've stopped questioning things that don't make sense, simply because "magic."*

*It is magic in a way, but nothing that required any great power, merely careful preparations and the initiative to take advantage of my own prison.*

*For several years now, I have been using my Winter Underground to systematically tunnel throughout Lode. I have constructed a complex network of ice tubes across* my kingdom, installing waypoints, manned by loyal corpsmen, at strategic points. With such a network complete, sending missives through these tunnels requires nothing more complicated that speeding up the crystallization of ice through the careful and specific energizing of atoms. I am aware that this is beyond your understanding. I am also aware of how diminishing you find the experience of ignorance—in this case, set your mind at ease. It is beyond the comprehension of anyone who is not me.

You may have noticed that I have a particular facility with ice. It is not a mere aesthetic preference. It is because, one hundred and nineteen years ago now, the Council inexorably stitched me—body and essence—into the Glacier.

Partially, it was to preserve me. You worked in kitchens, so you must know: Nothing keeps meat fresh like freezing it. I told you I was a child for a long time. I was not speaking figuratively.

They wished to keep me a child and they wished to keep me paralyzed—or frozen, if you wish to be whimsical about it. I like to think they thought themselves very clever to be actualizing such infantile metaphors. Regardless of their intentions, I cannot leave the Glacier. I can go as far as the field you departed from, and even then, I can stay no longer than twenty-two minutes or I freeze solid. I do not thaw until I have been back in the Glacier for at least forty-three days, and I am weak for several months after. As you may imagine, I spent years experimenting with my limitations. They have proven quite immutable to date.

They made a mistake, however. The Glacier may be in me, but I am just as much in it. I adapted. I learned. I made do. And I prevailed.

You should now be wondering why I am telling you this. Why would I make myself vulnerable by sharing such a secret with anyone, even my private secretary? If you are as smart as I hope, you will have guessed: It is because I need something from you.

I created the Royal College of Aetherical Manipulation for a very specific purpose. I directed their research in such a way that bent it to my intentions, which were of course to seize my throne from those who would take it from me, in the past, present, and future. To ensure that outcome, I needed tools to control all the magical industry in Lode, and hopefully, someday, even farther. My investments led to young Lord Rollo's pet project: the quill. It was a brilliant piece of engineering, and I have no doubts that I would have wielded it quite effectively.

But then something quite unexpected happened. A tavern wench fed it with her blood.

The quill was not designed for blood magic. It was actually quite modest in scope before you commandeered it. No trained magician would have been so foolish as to risk even accidental blood magic. I certainly wouldn't have. But what's done was done and suddenly you, and only you, Tanya, could literally move mountains. You could raise tidal waves. I don't believe you've even begun to imagine what you could do if you tried. You can fly, Tanya.

It may not have been bad policy to allow crime to consolidate in one area of the country. Unfortunately,

*the council members who imprisoned me in the Glacier
did not have good government in mind when they gave
complete control over that volcano to those women,
the Others. Yes, I'm sure you've met them by now. I'll
elaborate in a moment. But first, understand this:*

*That demon and his worshippers are squatters. They
have no claim on Bloodstone. They were given dominion
over that volcano in a pact with "my" Council, in
exchange for chaining me to the Glacier and to youth—
to powerlessness.*

*In other words, their only authority is my captivity. I
intend to break both.*

*The black matter has continued to expand, spreading
from village to village. It has begun whispering to the
people it finds. You remember the sample we brought
through? It spoke to me last night. It never did that
before. The Others are getting bolder.*

*I do not like what the black matter said.*

*I no longer care about the nature of the black matter
or the Volcano. I have a servant with the power to
simply remove it and I am, as is my obligation as Queen,
pressing my advantage.*

*My new order is this: Destroy Bloodstone. I cannot
do it myself, and it is a waste of a place, populated by
the worst of Lode. It is living treachery. Destroy the
place and all inside: The black matter may have spoken
to them all. None can be trusted. Destroy Bloodstone,
remove yourself and the quill from danger, and I will do
the rest.*

*You have seen what we can accomplish in just our
short time together, Tanya. Imagine if I wasn't confined*

to the Glacier. Imagine if you and I could sail around the world, reshaping it to become orderly, equitable, enlightened, organized!

Destroy Bloodstone. I enclose a list of explosive compounds. Use as many as you wish, or if you have a better idea, I defer to your judgment.

My deference is an honor, Tanya. Do not disappoint your queen.

Sincerely,

*Her Royal Majesty, the Queen of Lode*

**This message will self-destruct upon reading.**

The letter froze in Tanya's hands and then shattered into a million, unreadable pieces.

# Chapter

Through the skylight, Bloodstone dimmed from morning to afternoon, and finally to sunset, and Tanya was still staring at the pieces of the letter.

Tears stinging the corners of her eyes, Tanya tried hard to feel nothing. To believe in nothing but her own abilities to rewrite the world and do a better job of it than those in power had done. The Queen believed that she could do this, and she was asking something of Tanya—not asking, presenting it as *necessary*. The Queen had never been wrong before. They had that in common.

When Tanya was small, Froud had given her what she needed: a way to be important and thus, a way to be safe. He had given her a tavern. Ever since then, she hadn't relied on anyone else for anything.

But Froud was dead. Her tavern was standing empty. Now there was just the Queen. And the Queen *wanted* her to rule.

But she would have to crush people first.

A sharp knock sounded above her head. Tanya looked up and, scraping ice off her lap, jumped to her feet.

Jana was splayed across the skylight, knocking to come in.

"Hang on!" called Tanya through the glass. She upturned a laundry hamper she found in the wardrobe and clambered on top.

She put her hand on the glass. There were no latches to lift or locks to pick. Jana moved her hand so that it was covering her own and Tanya met her eyes. She removed her hand and the quill slid into her fingers.

A minute later, the glass vanished and Jana tumbled through the skylight into Tanya's arms. Together they toppled sideways off the hamper and landed, limbs tangled together, on the floor.

"Are you sure you don't want to join my gang?" asked Jana, propping herself up on her elbows to peer upward. "Because I don't think anyone's ever *broken into* the Witch—at least not anyone who's lived to tell about it."

"I guess you'd better be careful then."

Jana grinned and reached out a hand. Tanya took it and they pulled each other to their feet. "Don't you worry about me," Jana told her. "Whatever else happens to me, I know one thing: I'm gonna *live*."

Jana's hand, still clasped between Tanya's own, suddenly felt cold. "You don't know that, Jana. You can't know that." Tanya let go of her hands and took a step back. "You obviously have something you want to say to me. You went through enough effort."

"Tanya!" Jana closed the gap between them and picked up her hands again. "No one's seen you all day."

"And you were worried?" Tanya snapped. "I thought I had disgusted you with my blood magic and you wanted nothing to do with me."

Jana took another step closer, their faces close enough to feel each other breathe in and out. "That's not quite how I remember it," she said softly.

Tanya looked away and Jana finally dropped her hands. When she spoke again, her voice was hard and light—brittle. "Darrow said it's true. You work for the Queen. More than work for her, he made it seem like."

Tanya looked at her sharply. "It's not like that. I'm her private secretary."

"Oh?" Jana turned and began to pace the room, flicking her knife in and out of its sheath. *She just needs her hands to look busy,* Tanya realized. *She's nervous.*

*She should be.*

"How did the Queen of Lode come to make a tavern wench her private secretary?" she asked, her fingers still rapping her knife. "That sounds like a real job—the kind nobles from fancy families go to fancy schools to fight each other for."

Tanya didn't know whether she wanted to laugh or cry. "The Queen doesn't care about money or family. She only cares about whether you're useful to her. She's pure that way." Tanya watched her pace. "Did you come here to ask about the Queen?"

Jana stood in front of the bed and looked at the hole in the ceiling. "Is she nice? The Queen, I mean. Do you like her?"

Tanya looked at the killer in front of her. "The Queen would like *you*," she said. Jana turned slightly. "You're unusual and unusually talented. The Queen likes that.

"The Queen loves Lode. The Queen is not frightened of power. She feels it's her obligation to use all the power she has, all the time, and to always be growing her power. She's ruthless and relentless. I think she may be a little insane.

"I like her very much."

Jana didn't move. Tanya stepped toward her and touched her on the shoulder. At that touch, Jana whirled around, her knife out.

"Hey," said Tanya, putting her hands up. "You don't have to do that. I don't want to hurt you. Jana? Oh . . ." Jana looked up finally and Tanya could see that she was crying. "Jana . . . it's not like that with the Queen . . ."

"You think I'm *jealous* of the Queen?" Jana shoved her. "I don't get jealous, Tanya. If I want something, I take it. That's why I'm here."

Tanya raised an eyebrow. "First, please don't make a habit of shoving me. I don't enjoy it. Second, if you think I'm as easily kidnapped as I once was, I have very bad news for you."

Jana grabbed her face so quickly Tanya gasped. "I don't want to kidnap you, stupid girl," she hissed. "I want you to stop doing whatever it is you're here to do and let me take you far away from Bloodstone and that volcano. I want to *save* you."

Tanya grabbed her face right back. "I. Don't. Need. *Anyone*. To. Save. Me," she whispered fiercely. "Do you understand that? I don't need anyone and I don't need you."

Jana lifted her chin. "You can't stop me from saving you," she said. "I'm too strong."

Tanya kissed her then, *hard*, crushing her mouth against hers. Jana, the athlete, went limp and Tanya pressed her against the door.

When Tanya broke away, both girls were breathing hard, and explosions were going off behind her eyes.

"You're not going to make me leave you here," Jana breathed, pressing her forehead against Tanya's. "You heard the Volcano witches, right? That black gunk is coming for *you*, Tanya. Blood calls to blood."

Tanya froze. She let go of Jana's face.

"Say that again," she said slowly.

Jana screwed up her face in confusion. "Blood calls to blood? Why are you *smiling*?"

Grinning, Tanya threw open the door. "Because I was right. I *don't* need any of you," she told Jana. "Not even the Queen. I can fix this myself."

Jana scrambled after her. "You can't do *everything* alone," she yelled. "You can't be dumb enough to think that."

"Oh yes I can," Tanya retorted. "I always have, haven't I?"

"And how has that worked out for you?" asked Jana, her arms out in appeal. "Are you where you want to be?"

The Witch rocked on its eaves, pitching Jana and Tanya down the corridor, a rolling roar from below groaning through every corner, roiling the footing. There was a shocked silence throughout the building and then shouting and then the rumbling ceased.

Jana and Tanya shot each other a glance before pushing their way into the tavern.

Carefully organized chaos was the Witch's natural state, but nothing about the scene Tanya saw looked planned. Spilled stew splashed over the bar, dripping onto the floor, tables were askew or overturned, glasses smashed, and the well-prepared maids were nowhere to be found. Patrons were rubbing knocked skulls and bruised elbows, exclaiming loudly.

And there, in the very back of the room, along where the southern and western walls met, Tanya saw a pool of black sludge condensing, expanding, and finally, inexorably, trickling down to the floor.

Tanya set her mind grimly. It was either do what needed to be done, or blow up the Witch.

She bolted from Jana, shoving her way through the throng. She needed to get out of the Witch, get somewhere she could plan.

It was full night in Bloodstone and the sky was lit up with colorful fireworks—signals or maybe warnings of what may have felt like an ordinary earthquake to ordinary people. Tanya knew better.

She made her way to the stable—the one building with no lights in the window. The one where just maybe she could work in peace.

She conjured a small ball of flame to light her way and slid open the stable door. Once she had closed it securely behind her, a sharp kick on her back sent her to her knees, setting the stable floor alight.

"Hey!" she cried, quickly conjuring water to douse the flames. Rubbing her sore back, she turned and faced her attacker from the floor. "Was that completely necessary?"

A sneering humph and flick of a tail was her only answer.

Tanya stood up, her hand still on her back. "People literally die from being kicked by a horse, you know," she addressed the mare.

The mare rolled her eyes and stamped one foot hard enough to send straw flying six feet in all directions. Tanya rolled her eyes back. "Fine. Maybe," she admitted, advancing to the mare, "I deserved a tiny kick—just a *tiny* one, mind you—for taking you to that volcano. But we're even now, you hear?" The mare simply turned her head, presenting her backside.

Tanya laughed. "Very elegant," she said. "Are you sure your Rollo's a lord?" She pulled out a little notebook—one of many she'd had sewn into all her skirts—and palmed the quill.

She wrote: *Map me the Volcano of Bloodstone, including the current location of the temple room. Keep updating if it moves.*

The lines began to squiggle and churn. As Tanya waited, she addressed the horse again. "Honestly, horse, I don't know what you see in Rollo." The mare whirled and bopped her hand hard, her eyes flashing furiously. "Fine, he made a very good feather, but that's really *it*."

Before the mare could answer, Tanya was hit from behind by something small, sharp, fast, and strong enough to knock her to the ground, sending the mare scampering.

While Tanya lay on her back, the small object exploded into a full-grown person and ground Tanya's face into stable floor.

"You are such an *amateur*," hissed an enraged, reedy, familiar voice.

"Rollo!" Tanya struggled, pinned beneath his moderate weight. "Get off me!" He grasped at her arm, painfully pinching her skin, trying to peel off the quill. "That's not going to work—stop it!"

She wrenched one arm free and elbowed him in the ribs. He yelped and toppled off her. Snapping her fingers, she scrambled to her feet, the quill in her outstretched fingers by the time she was fully upright.

But Rollo had moved as fast as she had and the two stood off, both in a fighting stance—her with her quill and him with his wand, both of them with their rage.

"What do you think you're doing?" she seethed. "You work for the Queen, Rollo! You can't attack her secretary just because she stole your *toy!*"

"It's not a toy!" yelled Rollo. "And as for your precious *Queen*— you know what, don't move." He drew a few quick figures in the air with his wand and suddenly Tanya, who had started to run for the door, felt newly formed ropes of straw wriggle up from the stable floor and wrap themselves around her ankles, knocking her to the ground. "Some of us don't need to steal other people's work in order to use aetheric manipulation."

Tanya stuck the quill in her wrist and knocked him over with wind. "And some of us wouldn't try to stop someone who uses their *hands* to perform aetherical manipulation by knocking out their feet," she yelled at him, still struggling to sit upright. "What *about* the Queen?"

Rollo scrambled back up, his eyes blazing. The mare whinnied softly, soothingly, but Rollo was too angry to hear her.

"The Queen, your accomplice in being a bloody *dabbler*, has begun plans to raze any villages she's decided are contaminated by the sludge. Already, she's destroyed the three villages closest to Bloodstone. She's *burning* them to the ground. There have been no warnings, no evacuation orders. The sludge has been talking to her. She's convinced that if a town is contaminated, the townsfolk will be, too. She's starting a *war* against her own people!"

"Yeah, I'm aware of this, Rollo!" shouted Tanya, struggling to free her feet.

Rollo's grip tightened on his wand. "You were? How could you . . . how *dare* you—?"

"I didn't know that she'd already started," said Tanya, fumbling with the straw, trying to think of a material that would cut them off of her. "But I am on top of it, Rollo, if you would just get out of my *way* . . ."

An enormous cracking sound filled the air and it was if the world turned sideways. The ground rumbled, sending Tanya sliding across the stable floor and crashing into Rollo. An explosion rocked the air and the screaming sounds of Bloodstone at night reached a fever pitch.

Tanya looked furiously at Rollo. "Untie me," she ordered. Wordlessly, he sliced through the air with his wand and the ropes unraveled at her feet. She grappled upright, her footing slipping with the plunging ground and, with her arms spread out for balance, made her way outside.

The fog of Bloodstone was illuminated with a sickly red light, the night air looking as though it was filled with atomized blood. Sharp bolts of acid-green light shuddered across the sky.

Somebody screamed and a deep crack split the main thoroughfare in two. A groaning, then a whispering, filled the air, and the two halves of Bloodstone bulged, peaked, and slid, forming a million more tiny cracks. Thick black sludge poured out.

Tanya looked toward the Volcano and saw a single funnel of the stuff pouring straight into the air from the peak of the temple.

She turned furiously to Rollo and saw that he was looking just as furiously at her.

"Now look what you've done!" she shouted at him. "The longer I wait to fix this, the more there will be to fix! You arrogant, spoiled boy—you've wasted my time!"

"I've wasted *your* time?" he cried back. "I spent years studying aetheric manipulation and how to channel it and you've done nothing but pervert my work. And now, when faced with a new threat, when we need new tools the *most*, the best chance we have is useless because of an ignorant, meddling little nothing of a *wench*." He grabbed her wrist. "Give me my quill back and let *me* fix it."

"Hey!" someone shouted. Tanya whirled and saw Jana standing next to Riley and Darrow, eyes blazing. "I shot you once, kitten, and I'll do it again if you don't let go of her before I finish this sentence."

"What did I say, Jana?" Tanya wrenched her own wrist away. "I don't need your protection. Certainly not from *him*." Another explosion sent the ground quaking and Tanya made her way toward the trio. "Darrow, I *order* you to get me somewhere quiet."

"That . . . might be difficult, miss."

"Difficult?" Riley laughed and it was then that Tanya noticed he and Darrow were holding hands. "Look around, Tanya. Bloodstone's never quiet, but I've never seen anything like this."

"Get me a table, at least. I need to *work*."

"What kind of work?" She turned to see the newcomer. Greer's hair was wild and his eyes drawn, as if he'd been rudely awakened. Which, Tanya thought, was likely.

But recently awakened or not, he was looking at Tanya with alert eyes.

"What kind of work do you need to do *now*, Tanya? In all *this*?" he asked, gesturing around the chaos. "What can't wait?"

*He knows*, Tanya thought with a sudden stab of panic, and then forced the pangs down. She was under orders from the Queen to stop the sludge, using whatever method she deemed fit. This was her *job*.

She met his eyes stubbornly. He gulped.

"What?" asked Rollo warily. "What's she going to do?" He looked at Tanya, saw her set jaw. "No," he said. "Not even you would be so reckless."

"It's not reckless," Tanya insisted. "I did it with the Glacier ice, I can do it with this."

"It's not even *remotely* the same thing," shouted Rollo. "You have no idea what the ripple effect could be."

"I don't have to!" she shouted back, waving the quill. "This *does.*"

"OK." Jana stepped in between them and with a single, fluid movement unstrapped two knives, one in each hand. "Someone tells me what you're talking about now, or I start doing what I do best."

Rollo started laughing, a hysterical, mad laughter. "This tavern wench is going to perform the most complex blood magic bonding I've ever heard of with a substance she can't even identify."

"What? No. Tanya, you can't—"

"Yes, I *can.* You said it yourself, Jana. Blood calls to blood. I did it with the Glacier ice. If I can siphon some of the sludge into the quill, it will become known to it, and with the authority of, yes, my *blood,* I'll be able to manipulate it. I'll be able to stop it."

Darrow shook his head. "You can't know that, Tanya," he said quietly.

"I know that if I don't, the Queen will *act,*" Tanya told him. "You think that's less risky?"

"No, but . . ."

"No, nothing, Darrow. You've sworn to serve the Queen and she has ordered you to obey me. Now get me somewhere I can do what needs to be done."

Darrow swallowed. Finally, he answered: "No."

"Excuse me?"

"No, miss. I won't help you do this." As he spoke, Riley's hand crept up his back, cradling around his shoulder. "It's too dangerous."

Tanya sneered. "You mean you don't think I can do it. Fine. I'll do it alone."

Jana stood in front of her, barring her way. "All respect to the corpsman, but screw 'won't help you.' I won't *let* you. You're going to get yourself killed."

"Same." The voice came from behind her and then Greer pushed past her to stand next to Jana; the two shared a glance and closed ranks, standing shoulder to shoulder. "I won't let you do something so risky. I *can't*."

Tanya stepped forward and looked from one to the other. "You won't, huh?" She looked past them to Riley and Darrow. "You two won't either, I guess?" They clasped hands and nodded.

Tanya nodded back. "I respect that decision," she said, stepping back. She put the quill back in her wrist and closed her eyes. She muttered under her breath, ordering the aether.

"What is she doing?" asked Rollo suspiciously. "You, girl thief, stop her—"

Before he could finish the sentence, Tanya had conjured a tiny poof of the knockout gas the Queen had formulated just a few days before. The pink cloud hovered briefly, then dropped directly onto the faces of Riley, Darrow, Greer, and Jana.

They fell, just four more bodies in the road of Bloodstone.

She turned to Rollo. "You going to stop me, too?"

"No." Rollo had taken a few steps back. "Go to all the hells, if you like. I'll stay conscious, thank you."

Tanya looked at her notebook—the sludge wasn't registering. There was no label for *demon*.

"Fine," she said, remembering that she had had to plug directly into the Glacier for that ice to register. "But I'm taking your horse."

# Chapter

34

The mare cooperated up to a point. But by the time they finally made their way through the overflowing Pitfire, across the ravaged rocky ground, and past the chasm of demon blood—now a raging ocean with waves thirty feet high—and reached the temple gates, she lost her patience.

Tanya jumped off Gillian's back to avoid being thrown. The wind, hot and sticky, whipped her hair into her eyes, and she had to shout over both the roar and the whispers, now grown to a cacophony of taunts.

Tanya put her hands on her hips. "You're going to lose your nerve *now*? I thought you were magic!"

The horse turned away, facing back to Bloodstone, toward Rollo. Away from Tanya.

*Abandoned child*, whispered the sludge. *Meaningless girl.*

*No one.*

"That's fine." Tanya raised her voice even higher, needing to drown out *no one*. "I just needed you to get me here fast." She shoved past the mare and stood at the mouth of the temple. "Go back to your little magician and run far, far away with him—the Queen won't be kind to traitors. I don't need any help from here."

Tanya heard a scrap of whinny behind her, but was determined not to look back.

She entered the temple.

The sludge had flooded the walkway. It squealed under Tanya's boots as she walked and crawled up her ankles until it found skin. Then it wrapped itself around her and squeezed.

Tanya heard herself scream, an involuntary cry of pain she couldn't feel ripping through her throat because she was numb from the neck up, on fire from the chest down. Then the invisible, infernal fire shot through her skull and she fell, carried swiftly down the passage by the current of sludge.

She grasped at the fleshy walls, but couldn't get a grip. Clutching the quill, she jammed it into her arm and, out loud, screamed, "Ice!"

Ice exploded into existence, freezing the wall in front of her. Losing no time, Tanya threw out her fist and punched. She stuck, the sludge rolling by without her.

"Ha!" shouted Tanya. She wrenched her foot up and away, kicking through ice over and over, sending frozen chunks of bloodstained cartilage flying, until she had managed to carve a rough hole.

*Nuisance*, whispered the sludge. *Useless*.

"Shut *up*." Tanya, nerves exploding with pain and exertion, grabbed at the hole with both hands and hurled herself inside.

"Yes," she whispered, her cheek against the pulsating veins of the Volcano. She unplugged the quill from her arm and stabbed the point into the sludge wrapped around her leg, piercing her skin.

"Take it," she whispered weakly. The quill obeyed, sucking the sludge up with a gurgle, the pain in her leg beginning to pulse in a matching rhythm.

As soon as it was done, and the pain had receded, Tanya allowed herself a smile. The sludge was in the quill. All that was left to do now was take control of the situation.

She had done it.

She pulled herself off her stomach and sat up, leaning her head back, getting viscera in her hair. She breathed, collecting herself, giving her nerve endings a moment to recover. She could afford that now.

Against all odds, Tanya was about to win. But the people who set the odds had always been wrong about what she was capable of.

*When I turned up at Griffin's Port, the fishwives said I'd never survive,* she thought. *I did. When Froud died, Rees said I'd never make it through the Marsh Woods alone. I did.* Now Rees was in chains and *she* was private secretary to the Queen of Lode.

She picked up the quill and looked at it. "No one thought I could be the one to use you," she told the quill. "I was too common and you were too high above me. Look at us now." She twirled it around. "The thing is, everyone else is a fool. Blood magic is 'too dangerous' for me? I'm just *fine*. This *sludge*"—she sneered down at the river—"tried to hurt me, but I'm fine. If I listened to anyone else's opinions about what I could or could not do, I'd probably be dead by now. If I believed in *anyone* else, this whole dratted volcano would already be up in smoke. This started with just you and me. Let's end it."

The quill was shaking in her fingers, a ripple of black moving through its spines, but it didn't concern her. By now Tanya knew that no matter what the quill was doing, as long as she stayed practical, didn't panic, and no one got in her way, she, alone, could do anything.

She plugged the quill back into her arm and everything went red.

Tanya was floating through a sea of warm, wet blood. She wasn't breathing, but she didn't need to. Her heart was beating just fine without oxygen.

She revolved in place, feeling her pulse tap insistently on the side of her neck, pumping *something* through her veins. But if she wasn't breathing, how could the blood move? She raised her right hand, but all she saw was the quill, stained red.

She raised her left hand and saw the veins in her wrist were engorged and pulsating.

They were black.

Tanya screamed and the red rushed into her mouth, filling her head with a roar of whispers.

∞

When Tanya came to, she was lying on something hard and hot. She opened her eyes and found herself on the bone table in the altar room of the Volcano witches. The thrones were empty.

Behind her, the priestesses chanted joyously. Tanya didn't know the language, but the vowels were long and languid, the consonants hushed and slippery. She tried to sit, but found that she couldn't, that she was being kept prone by some invisible pressure.

She managed to flop over to face the chanting and was confronted by the sight of her arm. She gasped.

The quill was still stuck in her arm, its portal no longer a diamond, but a flame. And it wasn't a tattoo anymore—*never had been*, Tanya suddenly realized—but an open wound, oozing black sludge.

All the way up her arm, it was the same, the terrain of Bloodstone wrought in swirls of black. She looked down and saw that she had been stripped to her shift, revealing a map of Lode all the way down her body, carved into her skin in shining, black demon's blood.

The wounds were moving—changing, exploding, rearranging, the way they did when she performed aetherical manipulation. She looked at her wrist: The quill, black now, was vibrating, her own fingers twitching and maneuvering, without her telling them to.

"Welcome, sister."

Wearing the tiara, the head priestess stood above her, her underlings dancing in circles behind her, laughing, hands joined, steps light, as if the whispering of the sludge were the jolliest music.

"I'm not your sister," said Tanya, struggling to move.

The priestess reached down to touch her forehead and showed Tanya her fingertip: It was dripping with sludge. "You are now."

Tanya began to cry. "What did you do to me?"

"I? Why, I did nothing, Tanya! I believe you were the one who invited Our Lord of the Pulse and the Secret into your blood. And what *useful* blood it is."

Tanya winced. "The Queen will hurt you for this," she promised.

"We are dealing with the Queen," said the priestess. "And when I say 'we' I mean *you*. That's what made your blood so delicious to Our Demon of the Heat and the Buried. You are blood-bound to the landscape you've twisted and to the Glacier ice you've stolen. And the Glacier is bound to the Queen. She can order all the villages burnt to a crisp that she likes; Our Lord of Ash and Char *delights* in it. But she is trapped and therefore powerless. We will soon overtake her. It is already happening." The priestess leaned forward. "Would you like to see?"

When Tanya didn't answer, the priestess removed the tiara and settled it on Tanya's head.

Her vision was immediately flooded with town after town on fire, of ships exploding, of troops marching—and of sludge slowly, inexorably encroaching on it all.

Tanya watched in anguish as sludge climbed trees, suffocating birds, turning greenery black. And behind it all, she saw the quill in her arm, moving the sludge with *her* blood.

"No more," she begged. "Take it away."

"As you wish." The tiara lifted and Tanya could see where she was again.

"What will you do with me now?" asked Tanya.

The priestess looked surprised. "We'll use you, of course. Isn't that what you always wanted? To be useful? To know that only *you* are capable of something important? All we're doing is what you asked for, what you've been chasing since the moment you cut yourself open for power.

"It was inevitable," said the priestess, leaning in again, so that she and Tanya were eye to eye. "From the moment your incapable mother left you on that beach to fend for yourself, you were destined to seek power over others. Blood magic is the ultimate act of self-isolation. It creates power out of self alone, for the self alone. It will always call to those who reject common, tawdry, *human* love. You were destined to serve the demon." She smiled then, a cruel smile. "Perhaps that's why your mother left you. So that you could *serve*."

Tanya turned her head. The high priestess, cackling, resumed her place with her sisters. The chanting grew more intense, more purposeful. Tanya felt the new grooves in her skin shift again, and then, and only then, she began to weep.

She had been wrong. And her friends had been right.

Each time Greer tried to help her, Jana tried to protect her, Riley to teach her, it wasn't because they thought she wasn't capable. Darrow hadn't disobeyed her order because he wanted to undermine her power. They had acted the way they had because they *cared* for her. They argued with her, because they *respected* her.

They questioned her because they knew her and loved her anyway.

Tanya wept, because that possibility had never occurred to her.

Her first memories were of strangers looking at her as a useless speck, as *nothing*. Then she grew older, grew capable, but nothing changed. Anyone that looked at her diminished her, if they even noticed her. She was just a tavern wench, after all.

Tanya wept because she had *listened* to those strangers. Other people did nothing but diminish her, and so she had concluded that other people were incapable of anything *but* diminishing her.

*Not everyone*, she remembered, unable to lift her hand to wipe the tears dripping down her nose. Froud hadn't. *Froud didn't see nothing when he saw me*, she thought. But as soon as he had taught her what he knew, he began to fade away in front of her eyes. As she grew capable, he grew weak.

She'd learned that all she could be was what she could do alone.

*Froud getting weak wasn't your fault*, Tanya thought. *He was old and you took good care of him when he needed it.*

*But this—the impending destruction of Lode, your friends in danger of drowning in demon blood—this is your fault.*

Tanya sniffed, sucking the tears up her nose. Crying had never helped her before and it wouldn't help her now.

But she knew someone who could.

Tanya shut her eyes and located her heartbeat. She listened closely. She matched her breathing to the rhythm. This demon was nothing to her and it was time to kick him out. She was no one's apron to be scrawled on.

Tanya was the most capable person she knew. She *would* fix her mistake.

The night went on, long and slow. The priestesses did their work and Tanya, their canvas, did hers. She started small. Just her big toe; she concentrated hard and, in concert with her next heartbeat, she bent it forward.

It obeyed. Tanya, ignored on the altar, smiled.

She moved up from there; a rolled ankle, a flexed calf, a clenched pelvis, a contracted stomach. It took time, but eventually, she shut her eyes, said a quick prayer to the Lady of Cups, patron goddess of barmaids, and shut her hand into a fist.

She reached out with her mind and found the quill.

She didn't try to manipulate any aether. She didn't have any element in mind that she wanted to conjure or make disappear. Instead, she concentrated every ounce of her will into moving the quill.

It slid ever so slightly. She smiled, waited for an hour, and did it again.

Infinitesimally small bit by infinitesimally small bit, she pulled the quill out of her wrist.

Just before it was about to fall into her waiting hand, Tanya stopped. Held it in place. She didn't know if the Volcano witches would notice or not and she was done taking unnecessary risks.

*It was a very inefficient way to have lived*, Tanya scolded herself. *Truly, you should have known better.*

And, anyway, she had a better idea.

"Excuse me," she called out. "I have a complaint!"

The chanting stopped and she heard steps behind her. "You will not interrupt the ritual," came the soft voice of the second-in-command.

Tanya rolled her head to face her, careful to keep the rest of her body motionless.

"I assume you eat?" she asked.

The question seemed to take the priestess aback. "What?"

"*Eat,*" said Tanya. "You know: Cook plant or animal matter and put it in your mouth. Chew and swallow and therefore not die. No? Any of you? Well, I do. It's rather important to me, actually."

The second-in-command raised a green eyebrow. "We eat in our own way in our own time, little magician," said the witch. "You will learn."

"Oh, I have no doubt. But if you eat, you must also eliminate waste." The priestess wrinkled her nose. "I agree, ma'am. It is not a topic for polite conversation, but unless you want a puddle all over your altar table, I suggest you buck up and brave it. I've been here some hours, you know."

The priestess looked behind her to where her superior was sitting cross-legged in the dead center of the chamber, the tiara on her head, a blissed-out expression on her face. She flicked her hand out dismissively, not even bothering to open her eyes.

Tanya felt two novices move behind her and two more came to stand in front of her. Together, they lifted her up and carried her to the wall. One put her palm out and a fissure opened.

The novices moved languidly, luxuriantly. Tanya smiled to herself. No one else ever moved fast enough.

The quill slid into her fingers. The high priestess's eyes sprang open, but before she could cry out a warning it was already done. Tanya twisted out of the novices' grasp, hurtling herself out of their arms into the fissure.

She found Ironhearth with her mind's eye, pulled out *steel*, and then propelled it in front of her, closing off the fissure.

She had escaped. She had also effectively locked herself in a hole inside the Volcano. But that didn't matter right now.

She pulled off her shift and laid it flat. She could hear pounding on the other side of the steel, shouting, the whisper of the sludge slithering across her body.

She licked the quill and placed it against the shift. "Map Bloodstone," she whispered. "Put *Rollo* in the center."

Bloodstone bloomed across the cotton. She scanned her map and there he was, just inside the Gate—he was leaving.

She frowned and moved the Pitfire, blocking his exit.

She watched as the little circle labeled *Lord Magus Rollo of Vermillon's Pass* stumbled backward. "Not yet, magician," she said. And then, grimacing, she stuck the quill back into her arm. She drew it back out, dripping black sludge.

Tanya put the quill against the Gate. "Now listen to me for once, my *lord*."

She wrote:

*I was wrong. You were right. About to do something unpredictable. Be ready to fix my junkoff. You'll know when.*

Tanya sat back on her heels. The words soaked into the shift. Rollo didn't move. She waited and still he didn't move.

He was with her.

Tanya picked up the quill and began to weep.

She thought of the Queen and the Lode they could have made, an imaginary, beautiful, unfree utopia; she thought of the Queen herself, whom she had believed in, who was beyond restraint, and whom she was betraying.

She thought of Riley and Darrow holding hands. She thought of Jana's hands on her hips, of Greer's lips on hers. She might never see any of them again. She might never see anyone again.

She was putting her trust in *Rollo*.

She put the shift back on. She sniffled and wiped her eyes. She kissed the quill—it quivered and she hesitated. But she thought of Griffin's Port, imagined it covered in black sludge, and did what needed to be done to save them all.

Tanya snapped the quill in half.

**T**anya floated in a dim fog shot through with pockets of silvery light. She spun, suspended, watching particles of light shimmer in the moonlight.

She floated downward and the fog cleared enough for her to see weathered wooden planks, iron poles, large white boulders washed smooth by the tide. She fell closer and saw the Geode Sea at sunset, misty, green-gray, and raucous.

The docks at Griffin's Port.

There was a woman walking down the beach, away from the docks. She was tall and broad shouldered, her dusty auburn hair streaming loose and long, behind her. She was barefoot, her ankles wrapped in bangles.

Tanya still floated above the rocks.

"I'm still here!" she shouted silently, the words leaving her mouth in silent bubbles. "Mom, stop! I'm not behind you! *Stoooopppppppppppp!*"

Tanya plummeted and hit the rocks below with a sickening crunch.

*Crunch. Crunch. Pop. Bang. Bang. BANG.*

Tanya's eyes flew open, but they met nothing but darkness. She tried to move, but struggled, pinned down by heavy, calcified chunks of what used to be the body of a demon.

She coughed and choked on ash. Coughed again.

The banging paused. "*Tanya??* Tanya, tell us where you are!"

Tanya reached out an arm and banged on the steel plate, which was now partially crushed and bent around her body. "I'm here," she called out, her voice rough and garbled. "Behind the steel!"

Frantic footsteps approached and something dented the steel from the outside.

"Move out of my way," said an impatient voice. Rollo. He muttered a few unintelligible words and the steel disappeared, wiped out of existence as if it had never been, revealing Rollo, Jana, Greer, Darrow, and Riley, staring down at her as if she were risen from the dead.

Which she supposed, in a way, she was.

Jana leapt forward and rolled the biggest rock off of her hips. Darrow crouched next to her and swept away the smaller ones as she worked, clearing the way for Tanya to sit up.

He offered her his hand, and Tanya went to grab for it, before Rollo yanked him back. "Don't touch her," he told him. "Not with your bare hands."

"What? Why?" asked Tanya, before finally looking down on herself. She gasped.

The wounds on her skin had closed, but they had not vanished. Instead of open, liquid pools, the map of Lode was written out across her skin in brand-new, thick veins of dark black. If she looked closely, she could see her faint, ordinary, pale blue veins behind them, but only if she looked closely.

Tanya touched her wrist with an experimental fingertip, following a new vein. She looked up at Rollo. "What happened?"

He swept off his cloak and threw it to her. While she wrapped it around herself, he pulled out kidskin gloves.

"When you broke the quill, the sludge exploded off the ground, shooting through the sky," he said, pulling her up with both hands. "Shooting back to this volcano."

"Where are the witches?" she asked.

"We don't know," answered Riley. "Not exactly."

Tanya was finally standing. She looked around the altar room; it was wrecked, still, and silent. No whispers. The thrones had dissolved into piles of shapeless bone and obsidian, almost as if they had melted.

Where the altar table had been was a crater. She stepped forward and peered down. There was no bottom that she could see, but there, impossibly far away, she thought she could see a glimmer of red fire.

"You think they somehow escaped down there?"

Riley shrugged and wiped his sweaty, soot-stained forehead. Now that she looked, Tanya could see that they were all disheveled, filthy, worn out—as if they had been through battle.

"The Tomcat always said there were secret passageways to hidden realms," he told her. "That's why he wanted an alliance with the Others to begin with. Maybe that's one of the passageways. Either way, they're not here. Neither is that black stuff."

Tanya held out her arm. "Are you sure about that?" she asked. No one answered.

Tanya dropped her arm. "I need to touch somebody," she said.

"That," began Rollo, "is an incredibly reckless idea—" But before he could finish, Jana grabbed her hand.

Nothing happened.

Greer started laughing. "You were worried about nothing, Rollo," he said, smacking the smaller boy across the shoulders. He turned back to Tanya and Jana. "He was going on and on about how breaking a blood-magic bond always has consequences for the magician. I tried to tell him you were a tavern wench, not a magician, but he can't take a joke. . . ." His smile faded as he looked at them.

"What?" Tanya turned to Jana and gasped, dropping her hand like it was on fire.

Jana was pale, wide eyed, and quietly weeping. As soon as Tanya let go of her hand, she fell to her knees. She breathed, her face down.

They waited. When she looked up again, she was calm, but her eyes were filled with anguish.

"It whispered to me," she told Tanya. "When I touched you, it went inside me and it said . . . it said horrible things."

"What did?" asked Greer, his voice hollow. Tanya looked at him and saw his eyes were wide.

Jana looked at Greer, too, and swallowed. "Tanya's blood," she answered. "There's a demon in there now."

"Well, get it out!" cried Riley, cutting through the shocked silence. He turned to Rollo. "You're a wizard. I've seen what you can do. Tanya, you have no idea. When you broke the quill, Blood-stone started coming *apart*. Literally, splitting into pieces, fire everywhere—*he* filled in the gaps, knitted the place back together. He can fix you!" He turned back to Rollo. "Right?"

"No." They all looked at Tanya. She shook her head. "He can't. The Queen told me herself. Blood magic has unpredictable side effects. Breaking a blood-magic bond has even worse ones. And they're irreversible."

Darrow swallowed. "You can . . . never touch anyone again? Ever?"

Tanya shook her head. But Rollo cleared his throat.

"There's quite a lot we don't understand about blood magic," he told them imperiously. "It's not a respectable area of study and thus most respectable magicians have studied it very little. *But*—"

"But?" interrupted Jana from her knees. "You can get that thing out?"

"*No*." Rollo sighed and crossed his arms. "Unless I'm very much mistaken, that demon is inside Tanya permanently. But that doesn't follow that it always has to be in charge. There may be ways of . . . controlling it, that she could learn. With time."

They absorbed his words until, finally, Tanya smiled. "All it takes is a little discipline," she said, almost to herself. "A little common sense and organization."

"What, Tanya?" asked Greer, offering her his—sleeved—arm, as Jana got to her feet. "What did you say?"

Tanya looked at him, still smiling. "Don't worry about it," she said. "Get me out of this hole."

As soon as the volcano—Tanya didn't feel the need to capitalize it in her head anymore—imploded, Madame Moreagan had seized control. The older tavern keeper's preparation and quick thinking was the only thing that had kept Bloodstone, rocked by earthquakes and buried under hardening lava and debris, from being looted, burnt down, and abandoned in the chaos.

Instead, three weeks after the collapse, Bloodstone was as bustling as ever. And, of course, there were still knife fights in the streets, smugglers under bridges, and muggings in alleyways. It wouldn't have been Bloodstone without them. But there were also organized crews rebuilding the Pitfire canal system, with only the occasional black eye or shouting match. A disgraced shipwright's assistant that Madame Moreagan had found somewhere was teaching them how to build fan propellers for the boats, now that infernal energy from the volcano wouldn't keep them going on their own.

And the Gate still stood. If the Queen knew that anyone could come through now, she hadn't shown her hand. If the Queen's prison of ice had melted away with the Others, she hadn't used her freedom to come charging after Tanya.

Not yet, anyway.

"Are you sure you won't come with me?"

Tanya was in the stables of the Witch, watching as Jana tied a saddlebag to a new horse, a pretty, spirited gray mare Riley had stolen.

Jana was facing away from her. Tanya was aware that Jana had been avoiding her eyes for days. She understood. Jana didn't want Tanya to see the fear in them. Tanya was grateful.

"I'm sure," said Tanya, with a genuine pang of regret. "I'm no rogue. I'd just slow you down."

Jana put her head against the horse for a moment. Tanya heard her exhale.

When Jana had asked Tanya to go with her, she had wanted to. She wanted to see Jana move, laugh, even fight, every day if she could. But Jana was Jana, and Tanya was Tanya. If Tanya left with her, she'd be living Jana's life, not her own. If Jana stayed—well, Tanya hadn't even asked.

She didn't want to hurt her.

In a flash, Jana had closed the distance between them and had Tanya's face in her hands.

"Jana!" Tanya tried to move away, but her grip was too strong. "It's not safe."

Jana laughed. "It's never safe," she said, urgently pressing her forehead against Tanya's. "It was never safe, for anyone, ever." She shut her eyes, gulped, and carefully, slowly, put her lips on Tanya's.

Tanya kept her eyes open and her hands to herself, but kissed her back.

Jana let go and Tanya felt tears build in the corners of her eyes. No matter whom she loved from now on, they would always have to let go too soon.

"I'm coming back for you someday, tavern wench," Jana promised. She jumped on the horse. "I'll kidnap you if I have to."

Tanya looked up at her and smiled. "I know," she told her. "I look forward to you trying." Jana grinned back, reined up her horse, and was gone.

Tanya walked out of the stable to find Rollo on Gillian, impatiently looking at his pocket watch.

"That took you a full fifteen minutes," he announced. "I don't see what you could possibly be doing that would necessitate prolonging our stay in this literal sinkhole."

Tanya patted the nose of her new horse, a young chocolate-colored colt with skinny legs, and climbed on. "You didn't have to wait, *Lord* Rollo."

He sniffed. "I did it out of respect to Gillian's misplaced affection for you. Don't be flattered."

"Never." Tanya took one last look around at the city of her nightmares and nodded at Rollo. "Now, let's get out of here."

Their destination was six miles away, a small hamlet on the eastern edge of the Marsh Woods adjacent to the vast, calm Mirrorglass Bay. It was a freshwater bay. The name of the town was Freshwater. There was fly-fishing, mussel beds fat with pearls, mushroom bogs—a million things the ocean-bred Tanya knew nothing about.

Or there had been all that before the Queen had burnt most of it down.

Most people had left, but some had stayed. Most buildings had been razed, but some were still standing.

One that was still standing was what had been the Freshwater tavern before its owner, a crotchety old woman, fled to her niece's farm the second the sludge had shown up.

Tanya liked that its previous owner had been smart enough to cut and run. And she *really* liked the local scuttlebutt that the woman had decided to make it a permanent retirement, and that abandonment of over four weeks meant that, by law, it was hers to claim.

Tanya and Rollo rode through Freshwater's gate. It was shaped like a bullfrog; you entered through its mouth. The tavern wasn't so well situated as the Snake had been, so they had to ride a little, slowing down to accommodate the children running down the road, and the young men who had been conscripted as temporary bricklayers.

Tanya had no doubt that the Queen would come for her one day. But it wouldn't be today and it wouldn't be tomorrow. It would be when the Queen was good and ready; when she had a foolproof plan that would make her punishment more *useful* than simple revenge.

The Queen could be patient. And that gave Tanya time.

They finally arrived at their destination.

The tavern was still standing, but really only technically. It wasn't livable yet. But its poor location meant that, except for in a few places, the base structure, made of golden-brown brick, was still fundamentally intact.

The roof, formerly and still occasionally tiled with brass-bound terra-cotta, was a different story.

But Darrow was working on that.

Tanya hopped off her horse. "Do you need anything, Darrow?" she called up. "Want to take a break, let me fix you some lunch?"

Darrow smiled and waved. "What?" he called. "I can't hear you!"

It was rather loud just there—some little girls were splashing in the pond nearby, trying to catch a turtle.

Tanya put her hands around her mouth. "I said," she began, "do you want me to fix—"

"He's fine," said Greer, strolling up next to her. He had his throwing knives collected in one hand. "One of the girls from the dairy brought him something. *She's* going to be disappointed, but he's fine."

Tanya shaded her eyes against the sun reflecting brightly off the water. "You're still going to do this, huh?" she asked.

Greer nodded at Rollo. "He says there are things at the college the Queen shouldn't get," he said. "He needs help to make sure she doesn't. I saw him knit a city back together with a stick. I believe him."

Tanya turned. Rollo was still on Gillian, stiff and formal—though Gillian *was* trying to buck him off, as gently as one *could* buck.

"He's certainly very determined," Tanya said dryly. "It's a pity the great masters of the Royal College turned out to be nothing but well-educated mercenaries. But you got through once before, right? Even if the Queen has upped their security—which I'm sure she has; if she's paying their bills, she wants their work safe—I think you'll get through. He's an irritating little twit, but the boy can do *some* impressive things."

Greer smothered a smile. "Hey, why isn't Riley coming with us?" he asked suddenly. "Isn't he supposed to be some great thief?"

"The best, I think."

"So, what then? Trying to impress his upstanding new boyfriend with legality?"

Tanya shrugged. "Maybe he wants to try something new." She smiled at Greer. "I'd have thought you, of all people, would understand that."

Greer smiled back. "You know I'm only going because I owe Rollo, don't you?"

"What could you possibly owe Rollo?"

Greer bit his lip. "You," he said simply. "If he'd left, we'd never have known where you went. We'd have never been able to get you out of that volcano without him. We'd have drowned in sludge first."

Tanya concentrated hard as Greer's hand reached for hers. She was working on listening to the demon in her veins, tracking it, maybe one day controlling it.

Greer winced as they touched, but didn't let go. "As soon as I'm done, I'm coming right back to you," he said. "To this." He looked around the jolly, busy, laughing village, and then back at Tanya. "I'm coming right home."

Tanya lifted his hand, kissed it lightly, and released him. She smothered the pang at seeing the pain creases in his forehead smooth out as soon as she let him go, at his instinctive step back.

*He's coming back*, she soothed herself. *He's going to stay.*

For now, it was enough that someone was going to stay.

"You'd better," she told him. "I have plans for this village and I can't run the place alone.

"Speaking of," she said, suddenly remembering all the myriad things on her ever-growing to-do list. "Do you know where Riley *is*? He was supposed to be working on something for me."

Greer pointed past the frame. "He's set up a little shed behind the main house," he said. "Try there."

It was almost too cute to be called a shed. It was more like a somewhat manlier gingerbread cottage from her book of fairy stories. Tanya thought back to Riley's deft understanding of architectural diagrams and shook her head—it was amazing the talents some people wasted when they didn't have the space to develop them.

Riley himself was nowhere to be found. There was a note scrawled on the door—misspelled and clumsily written. But he would get better at that.

*Went to help blacksmith rejoin bellows. Be back soon. No one touch ANYTHING.*

Tanya touched the door, pushing it open.

And there it was sitting on a dusty workbench. A block of wood, cut in the shape of a starburst.

She walked over and picked it up, getting wet yellow paint on her fingers. But it was almost done. She had wanted it painted, not carved, so that she could grow into it. She wasn't sure what it should say yet. Madame Moreagan had been right: She belonged in a tavern.

But she didn't *just* want to run a tavern; she was more ambitious than that now. She knew she wanted a library; she wanted to keep learning. She wanted to find new things. And she wanted to be useful.

So, for right now, it said:

## The Quill
### FOOD * ROOMS * BOOKS * EPHEMERA

She brushed it with her fingers and smiled.
She was home.

### The End

# Acknowledgments

The only thing I ever really wanted to do was tell stories. I'm therefore deeply grateful to continue to be allowed to do this.

My heartfelt thanks have to begin with my brilliant and intuitive editor Maggie Lehrman, at Amulet Books, for her belief in this story and my ability to tell it. I'm extremely grateful to the designer Hana Anouk Nakamura for her gorgeous work and to the incomparable Will Staehle for this incredible cover design.

Additionally, I want to acknowledge, with great appreciation, the hard and invaluable work of Marie Oishi, Shasta Clinch, Regina Castillo, Emily Daluga, Hallie Patterson, Jenny Choy, and the entire production team at Abrams.

My agent, Ali McDonald, has been a stalwart source of support, comfort, and counsel—thank you, girl. And thank you to her erudite assistant Ella Russell for all her help and insight.

I am very lucky to have the friendship and help of talented friends/ writers, and want to particularly acknowledge Justin Brenneman, Allie Schwartz, Anna Hecker, Lindsay Champion, and Amber Lynn Natusch for their excellent notes, Kendall Kulper for her hospitality, and Derek Milman, Kit Frick, Anica Mrose Rissi, Katie Henry, Sarah Nicole Smetana, and Erin Callahan for vital conversations along the way. I also want to acknowledge here the entire Electric Eighteens community, for their unflagging support, good humor, and the real friendships I've found there—thank you for all the much-needed hugs, in person and virtual.

Finally, I always have to thank Sophie Kaplan—who also gave me stellar notes but is mostly just a great sister. Thank you Brooke Gladstone (Mom), Fred Kaplan (Dad), and Ruth Pollock (Grandma) for all the love, support, and encouragement I could ever need.